# THE HAXTON REVIEW

JOSHUA KNAPP

The Maldon Press is an imprint of Redoubt Press, LLC



ISBN 979-8-9938908-2-1 (Ebook)
ISBN 979-8-9938908-1-4 (Softcover)

Library of Congress Control Number: 2026935320

The Maldon Press
P.O. Box 508
Blowing Rock, NC 28605
www.vaubanbooks.com

# THE HAXTON REVIEW

# 1

It is Sunday afternoon and I am in Highcliffe Cemetery again, counting the mosques. I take my time with it. I sit on a cushion of ivy on the edge of a plinth belonging to an angel with half a wing missing and eat my sandwich while I divide Coxthorpe into squares and then move from east to west, counting green domes and stubby minarets and high arched windows that glow golden in the autumn sun.

I count seventeen today, which is fewer than I usually get. My highest ever count is twenty-two, my lowest is fifteen (although I think the twenty-two may have accidentally included a Gurdwara). None of these numbers is accurate of course. Coxthorpe has an earlier generation of mosques that are converted shops or non-conformist chapels or even terraced houses. These were bought by the pennies of the first Muslim immigrants to arrive in the city, and obviously they are invisible from Highcliffe. I don't know how many mosques there are now, but there is no denying that the minarets and domes make an impressive spectacle. As I count them today it fascinates me all over again that a desert God should have come to squat on my hometown, nestling among the moors and the mills. I wonder if he's used to the blustery wet of the place yet, and the cracked cobbles, and the grotty pubs, and the undeniable sadness of it all. I can't help thinking that he's roughing it a bit in Coxthorpe after the oases, souks, and sun-baked towns of his homeland. Let's face it, Coxthorpe is a graceless and charmless city, although it is never mean or cruel. There is a sort of weary love about the place. I hope the squatting God appreciates that. I hope that some portion of it has sunk into the bricks and mortar of his seventeen, or twenty-two, or however many it is, mosques, just as the mosques have sunk into the city itself.

I came off a night shift this morning, so I'm exhausted. I actually snooze for a few minutes on my angel's plinth and wake up with saliva in my beard. I wipe myself, brush the crumbs off my jacket, and dump my sandwich wrapper in the bin, then slip out of the cemetery's north gate and walk down the hill into town.

# 2

THE DAY AFTER your last night shift is always a bit of a pain. If you get too much sleep you won't get off that night, if you get too little you'll be like a zombie and ruin a day off. I had set the alarm for half eleven this morning which had given me four hours, which is about right. When I woke up, I had a cigarette and a beer in the yard, which is my normal breakfast after nights, and decided to go into town. Given everything that followed from the decision, it is irritating that I can't remember now why I made it. I didn't need anything from the shops and Coxthorpe town centre on a Sunday afternoon is a pretty depressing prospect. Perhaps the early taste of beer had convinced me to spend the day boozing, and getting drunk in town felt less desperate than getting drunk at home, with just my phone for company. Perhaps I needed a plan of some sort to structure the day. Perhaps I just didn't want to be on my own. Anyway, whatever the reason, as I stubbed out my breakfast cigarette I decided to go into town. I even made a sandwich for the trip.

. . .

The morning beer and the lack of sleep and the early Autumn sunshine give everything a pleasant, dreamy feel as I drift past the charity shops, tanning salons and payday loan places that line the road down from Highcliffe. Now that I am here, I am glad that I have come. It's good to know that I have nothing much to do and no work for three days.

I have no plans to go up to Haxton until I get to the town centre and come across the Dawah stall. I swear that's true. I am not by nature a busy body. I am aware, of course, that there is trouble up in Haxton, and I know that it's something to do with whites and Muslims falling out about some kind of parade, but there is often trouble between whites and Muslims in Coxthorpe, and until now the Haxton situation has felt pretty distant and unimportant. But all that changes because of what happens at the Dawah stall.

It is where it always is in front of the chip shop in Victoria Square. There are three Muslim lads in robes standing behind it, dishing out literature to whoever might be interested. I know them a bit. I have chatted with them a few times and gone home with glossy leaflets about *The Quran and Modern Science*, or *Jesus (PBUH): Prophet of Islam*, or *The Life of Muhammad (PBUH)*, or *Europe: The Land of the Muslims.* They are friendly, reasonable men, unfailingly polite as they explain their faith to the stubborn Coxthorpe heathen. Today as well as the usual glossy leaflets, there is a pile of rougher flyers, on their stall headed *What's Going on at Haxton?* One of the Muslim lads spots me taking a flyer and comes over.

'We haven't seen you for a while.'

'It's my shifts. I sometimes work weekends.'

'Of course. What is it you do again?'

'Warehouse. I manage a team.'

'Hard for the family. To work shifts.'

'It would be if I had a family. But I haven't, so it's just hard for me.'

The man raises his eyebrows fractionally and then nods at the flyer.

'Have you heard about Haxton then?'

'Yeah, a bit. It's been on and off the news for ages, hasn't it? When's it meant to be happening?'

'Four weeks' time.'

'Really? I assumed it was sooner. It gets talked about a lot at work.'

'What do the people at work say about it?'

'Depends if they're Muslims or not.'

The man laughs.

'I suppose it would. But, actually, everyone should be concerned about what's happening, not just Muslims.'

'Why's that then?'

'Look, the issue isn't the parade itself. As far as I'm concerned, it's about where they chose to have it. They could go to another area and have their parade, no problem.'

'I suppose the people organising it would say that they want to have it in their own neighbourhood.'

'Yes, but why now? It hasn't happened since 1914. So why do they reinvent it now, all of a sudden? And why in a Muslim area?'

Which is a reasonable question. I shrug.

'It's provocative. It's insulting.'

'I guess so. I'll read the leaflet.'

'Good. We need sensible people.' The man takes the leaflet from me and scribbles a phone number on it, then hands it back. 'If you want to talk about it, please call me. Or look at our website, it's on the leaflet. There's a group called Respect Haxton. We've got the council and the police to have a look at it all again, and we're organising a protest. Not just for Muslims, it's for the whole community.'

'A protest sounds a bit provocative.'

The man laughs again. He is actually quite a nice, intelligent bloke. Sometimes he can just about take the piss out of himself. He is my favourite of the Coxthorpe Dawah team.

'Just read the leaflet. Hear our side. That's all we ask.'

'I will. I promise.'

'Thank you.'

The man nods respectfully and moves away. I leave the Dawah stall and walk across Victoria Square, then climb up Briggate to the Bumble Bee, my favourite pub in Coxthorpe town centre. The Bumble Bee still has a proper taproom, snug and lounge, and the doors between the rooms have stained-glass windows depicting wildflowers, bees and sheaves of corn. There is a grate in each room and, best of all, the whole place is lit with gas lamps. Every day, as the light fades, the landlord brings round a pole with a taper stuck in the end and touches it to each lamp in turn, making each ignite with a soft whoosh. I love the gentle light from the gas lamps, especially in winter, in the whispering, dusky time immediately after the lamps are lit. The Bumble Bee feels peaceful and kind and self-contained then, detached from the darkening town, floating in its own pool of flickering, milky light. I love that very much indeed. I love it more than I am able to describe it. Today, of course, the grates are black and cold, and the lamps are dead. I buy a pint and a packet of pork scratchings, and settle down with my leaflet in the chilly gloom of the snug. It is Sunday lunchtime and the barman and I are the only people in the place. The Bumble Bee is right on the edge of the city centre next to Luck Lane, a Muslim area. I don't know how it keeps going really. It is almost always deserted and it's rather grubby as well as beautiful. Stuffing is leaking from the upholstered bench I am sitting on.

I suppose it's only a matter of time for the Bumble Bee.

Anyway, this is what the leaflet says:

### *What's Going on at Haxton?*

*Haxton is a diverse, multi-cultural community. The people who live here are proud of our area and proud of the relationships that have been built between the different religious and ethnic groups that make Haxton their home. Living here is about having respect for your brother or sister no matter what their faith or the colour of their skin. People in Haxton don't believe that our diversity is a weakness, we see it as a strength. As a united community we have recently dealt with the drug taking and immorality in Albert Park, the traffic problem on Cutler Street which was a danger to our kids and various other local issues. In Haxton we know that we can achieve more by working together than we ever can alone.*

*It is sad that a very small group of people who are not originally from Haxton have chosen to cause trouble here. The plan to restore the Rush Bearing festival did not originally come from established Haxton folk, but from people who have recently moved to the area and who seem intent on making mischief and stirring up conflict in their new home. There is nothing wrong with celebrating where you live or having fun of course - people in Haxton like a party as much as anyone else! But the proposed Rush Bearing festival contains elements that will exclude and marginalise one part of the Haxton community. Specifically, the crusader knight figure who is planned to accompany the Rush Bearing procession is an insult to Haxton's Muslims. Everyone who has studied history knows that the Crusades were a time of butchery and humiliation of Muslim people. Everyone who watches the news knows that the Crusaders' bloody legacy lies over Muslim lands to this day, in illegal wars and occupations.*

*After the slaughter in Christchurch and countless other violent attacks on Muslims, the whole world understands that it is criminally dangerous to indulge terror speech or terror symbols that demonise Islam, especially in Muslim areas. Therefore, the Rush Bearing procession must not be allowed to pass, at least in its present form. Respect Haxton calls on people of goodwill from all faiths, in Coxthorpe and beyond, to stand with the people of Haxton as we resist islamophobia and racism. We call on Coxthorpe Council and the West Yorkshire Police Service to respect and enforce the wishes of our community. We call on the organisers of the Rush Bearing festival to re-route their parade and remove from it all symbols of domination and terror. There is still time to put a stop to this dangerous nonsense.*

*We are angry. We are peaceful. We are diverse. We are united.*
*Respect Haxton.*
*www.respecthaxton.co.uk*

A long time ago, I spent a few years being taught about the Bible and one of the main techniques I learnt was a thing called source criticism. This means looking at a chunk of Biblical text and trying to work out which earlier texts had been used to put the finished thing together. Applying the principles of source criticism to the *Respect Haxton* leaflet, it seems clear that at least two, possibly three, different voices are present in its composition. Most obviously there is the voice of contemporary (white) liberalism. The liberal voice is present in 'diversity is our strength', in the emphasis on 'respect', in 'achieving more by working together than alone', and in the awful tagline: 'We are angry. We are peaceful. We are diverse. We are united.' You can sense the liberal good intentions oozing from the leaflet, and also the barely concealed anxiety that those intentions are the soggy sponge that the liberal contributor has bought to Haxton's impending knife fight.

The other voice in the leaflet belongs, inevitably, to the Muslims. It is present in the reference to the 'immorality' in Albert Park that was tackled by the community (a handful of prostitutes were using the bottle bank at the park's edge to entertain their clients - they were seen off by patrols organised by the local mosques who took pictures of the women and their clients and posted them online), and in the mention of 'illegal wars and occupations' in Muslim lands, the latter presumably being a reference to Israel. Less obvious evidence of the leaflet's Islamic voice is the use of the terms 'brother and sister' to refer to Haxton residents, rather than the more obvious 'neighbour'. Brother and sister suggest a religious outlook, which in Haxton can only mean Islamic. And there is also the absence of any mention in the short list of Haxton's recent difficulties of one particular problem, which represented a much more serious 'danger to kids' than a few cars driving too fast down Cutler Street. This problem was the most significant local issue to confront Haxton (and Coxthorpe) in recent years. The silence about it in a leaflet describing the area's community relations is significant, to say the least.

Finally, the leaflet's flat insistence that the Rush Bearing parade 'must not be allowed to pass' might imply a third, more left wing, influence in the text. The infinitive 'to pass' dimly echoes the *¡No Pasarán!* of the Spanish International Brigades, and the other great anti-fascist struggles of the thirties and forties. The left-wing voice is weaker than the other two, but I don't think I am mistaken in thinking that it is present.

Not many people would manage to identify the authorial tensions in the *Respect Haxton* leaflet, except perhaps from spotting the obvious contradiction in identifying Haxton as both a 'diverse, multi-cultural community' and a 'Muslim area'. It feels good to use the critical part of my brain again, even on something so trivial, and I am rather pleased with myself as I nod off over my nearly empty beer glass. (I have fallen asleep in pubs all over West Yorkshire after night shifts, sometimes being woken by bar staff when they finally get fed up with seeing me slumped over their tables. The problem is getting worse as I get older.)

When I wake up, I re-read the *Respect Haxton* leaflet and admit to myself that the Rush Bearing issue has got to me, just little a bit. My curiosity is piqued. I don't have a dog in this particular fight. I live on the other side of town, in a white area. But, still, it might be diverting to witness the Haxton dogs snarling at each other. And, let's face it, I am time rich today. In fact, I am time rich every day when I am not working, which is another way of saying that I am bored most of the time. That may be why I came into town, because

I was bored and because town always holds out the prospect of being a just a little bit less boring than home. And today, town has delivered. Whatever else it may be: pathetic, sad, unpleasant, the Haxton situation doesn't seem boring. It doesn't seem boring at all.

I take my empty glass back to the bar, where the bar man is busy texting. He looks up as I approach.

'Another one?'

'No thanks. I've got to be somewhere.'

'Fair enough,' the barman says. 'Have fun.'

'Thanks. I think probably I will.'

The barman grunts and goes back to his phone. He doesn't bother to wash my glass.

# 3

I PUT *LANTYRN Royd, Haxton* into maps on my phone and stroll back into town, crossing Victoria Square and heading west up Kirkgate, past the university, and then onto the Leeds Road. Haxton is just over a mile from the town centre and, as I approach, the streets increasingly reflect the Islamic community that makes the area its home. There are Halal butchers, Muslim clothes shops and book shops, a couple of Islamic undertakers and, of course, mosques. By the time Leeds Road becomes Gordon Street, which is Haxton's high street and main shopping area, I have become an ethnic minority of one. The pavement is full of old blokes in flowing robes and cardigans, women in various degrees of Islamic dress, young men hanging round takeaway shops, and mischievous kids scampering about and laughing. One or two people glances at me as I pass, but no one insults me or challenges me and, as far as I am aware, no one passes comment about my presence. Haxton's Muslims seem somewhat guarded, but they are not explicitly hostile. At first glance, they do not present as a community under siege from bloodthirsty neo-crusaders.

Following my phone, I walk for five minutes up Gordon Street before turning left onto East Croft and then right onto Lantyrn

Royd. Here the shops change. There is a tanning salon, a Tesco's Express, a couple of bookies, a fish and chip shop and a pub called The White Horse. Halfway down East Croft is a gothic church: St Peters, of the Anglican Diocese of Ripon. A sign outside the Church provides the times of services, which are called 'Masses' at St Peters. Next to the sign about service times there is another which says: *Carpenter from Nazareth Seeks Joiners*, which makes me want to do a massive shit on the church doorstep.

Although I have never been here before, I know a little bit about Lantyrn Royd. The name refers to the area immediately surrounding the road as well as to the road itself, and it is well known in Coxthorpe as the white enclave within Haxton. It came to prominence briefly during the town's riots of ten years ago when the pub and one of the bookies were damaged by rioters. The little community was one of several areas on the periphery of Coxthorpe that were abandoned by the overstretched police and fire-service during those five terrible nights, but the Lantyrn Royd locals distinguished themselves by fighting off the rioters and containing the fire that followed a petrol bomb attack on The White Horse. The area came to prominence again, even more tragically, a couple of years ago when a number of girls from the enclave were abused by Coxthorpe's grooming gang. On that occasion it was a local mosque that suffered a (mercifully ineffectual) arson attack. It is safe to assume that Lantyrn Royd and Haxton are not quite the shining models of community relations that the Respect Haxton leaflet implies.

Lantyrn Royd, the road, is perhaps 400 yards long, ending in a high steel fence which my phone tells me belongs to St Peter's Primary School. Four roads run across it: Clip Lane, Kibden Street, Wrack Street and one at the end called simply 'Friendly'. From my position on the corner of East Croft, each of these streets runs uphill on the right to Gordon Street and downhill on the left to a road that is unnamed on my phone. The unnamed road has a windowless redbrick wall on its far side, higher even than the school fence. This belongs to Haxton's largest Mosque (the name of which I can't remember although I counted its impressive green dome earlier on). The parts of the streets running down to the mosque are cobbled, while the parts running up to Gordon Street are tarmacked normally. Each is narrow and lined with identical black stone terraced houses whose doors open directly onto the pavement. The narrowness of the streets together with the school fence and the Mosque wall give the area a dark, claustrophobic feel. Lantyrn Royd is a southerner's Hovis caricature of the English north, but without the rosy charm. It is not an area that you would happen upon accidentally and nor, to be honest, would you want to. For a moment I consider turning round and going back into town.

I don't turn round. Instead, I pocket my phone and turn left down Clip Lane and then right onto the nameless road at the bottom, where I walk parallel to the mosque wall. There are no houses and no pavements here, the road seems to function only as an access point for the narrow alleys that run along the backs of the four residential streets. These have bins on them, as well as a handful of cats ambling in the shadows and a couple of tatty St George's Crosses hanging limply from gate posts. On my left, the mosque wall is marked by fading graffiti: *Fuck Isis*, *Muhammad is a Pedo* (sic), and, rather plaintively, *England*.

I turn right again at the end of the nameless street and walk up Friendly. Then I turn right again and stroll down Lantyrn Royd towards The White Horse. The pub has a trestle table outside where a dozen or so people are gathered, drinking and chatting. Above the table, fixed to the pub wall, is a board with a blown-up picture of the front page of Friday's Coxthorpe Argus, pinned to it. The paper bears the headline: *Council to Reconsider Haxton Parade Route*. As I approach the table, a stout middle-aged woman at the centre of the group nods at me:

'What are you doing here, love?'

The woman isn't exactly unfriendly, but she is guarded. The rest of the group are suddenly silent.

'I've just come to see what all the fuss is about. About the Rush Bearing thing.'

'Are you a journalist?'

'No. I live at Wheeldon.'

'Dun't mean you in't a journalist.'

'But I'm not. I work in a warehouse.'

More silence from the group as the woman looks me up and down.

'What've you heard about us then?'

'Just a bit of gossip and what I've seen on the telly. And I got a leaflet in town. From the Muslim stall in Victoria Square.'

I fish the leaflet out of my pocket and show it to the woman. She glances at it.

'Yeah, we've seen this. It's bullshit.'

'Why's that?'

The woman moves to one side so that I can see the stuff on the table. There are a couple of clipboards with petitions fixed to them, some biros, and a large street map of the area pinned to a board. The map has a thick blue line on it, beginning at St Peter's Church and extending up East Croft to Gordon Street. Here the line turns left and runs along Gordon Street as far as Friendly where it swings left again. It goes left a third time on Lantyrn Royd and then again onto East Croft from where it runs back to the church. A printed sign at the top of the map reads *Rush Bearing Route*.

'So that's the route of the procession, right?' the woman says.

'Yes.'

'You can see it won't take twenty minutes altogether. And we'll only be in their area for about ten. Less than that probably. It's nothing really, is it? They just want to make bother.' She sniffs. 'Well, some of them do anyway.'

A man in his mid-forties with sleeve tattoos on his beefy arms and a Help for Heroes bracelet on his wrist drops his cigarette and stamps on it. He nods at my leaflet.

'Can I have a look at that, fella?'

'Of course.'

The man takes the leaflet and his eyes flicker over it.

'People in Haxton like a party,' he muttered. 'Fucking hell. It in't like we're having a massive piss up in their streets is it? We could have gone much further with it.'

'What do you mean?'

'The old procession went right through Haxton centre and up to the park. There were stalls and stuff back then. So we've asked for fuck all, really.'

'Yeah,' the woman says. 'And we got it approved by the council. The committee did, all officially, din't we Dave?'

'Yeah, yeah,' says a thinner man, who is cradling pint of lager. 'We did it all official, like. It took a while, but we did it. We're legit. Or at least we were.'

'Right, so it's not like we've done owt wrong. But now they want us re-routed or banned. And for no good reason, neither.'

The woman is staring at me, unblinking.

'Yah, I get all that. But I think...I think...'

'What do you think, love?'

'I think it's the crusader thing that upsets them.'

The woman rolls her eyes.

'It's just a kid in a suit of armour, for Pete's sake. That's all it is. It were part of the procession, back when it were a regular thing. We're just doing what they did before. We want to do it properly, don't we, or else what's the point?'

'Well yes, I can see that. But I suppose they would say that a crusader is quite offensive to Muslims, even if it is just a kid dressed up.'

The man with the tattoos hands the leaflet back to me.

'Bollocks. It in't about that at all. It's just them reminding us who runs Haxton. That's all it is.'

'What do you mean?'

'They want us to be invisible, don't they, or else disappear. They din't shift us with the riots or their fucking rapists, so now they're trying owt else they can think of.' The man picks up a half-full pint of lager from the table and drains it. He wipes his mouth with the back of his hand. 'They in't bothered about some kid dressed up like a bleeding knight. They aren't offended by shit like that, believe me. They pretend they are so that everyone feels fucking sorry for them, but they in't. It in't about that.'

'Who's 'us'?'

The man glares at me.

'What do you mean?'

'Who's the 'us' that they want to be invisible.'

'Us. English people. White people.'

'Oh.'

'Careful Jason,' the woman says quickly. 'Careful about all that.' She turns back to me. 'Listen love, we have to listen to their call to prayer every day, and we don't make a big fuss about that do we? Perhaps that offends some of us, but we don't say owt do we? And that's every single day.'

'I guess so. But I suppose they would say that it's a Muslim area, so you've got to put up with things like that.'

The group murmur angrily and the tattooed man snorts and goes back into the pub.

When he's gone, the woman says quietly,

'But it in't just a Muslim area, though, is it love? We live here too. And we just want our little procession. Just one day of the year. It in't too much to ask is it?'

I really, honestly don't know the answer to that question. I don't know what rules govern disagreements about contested symbols and communities' conflicting rights and freedoms. I'm not sure if anyone knows much about those rules, to be honest, or if they even exist. I have a horrible feeling that those sorts of conflicts might finally be about power and nothing else. But it doesn't seem like the time for a debate.

'I don't suppose it is too much to ask really. And I didn't realise the crusader thing was part of it all originally. I don't know much about it, to be honest.'

'Well it were part of it,' the woman says firmly. 'We can tell you all about it if you're interested.'

'I suppose I am interested.'

'Right, well Dave's our committee chairman.'

The thin man shrugs and grins.

'I can't tell you a right lot about the history, to be honest. I'm more about the buffet and the parking. The logistics side of things.'

'Or else Roger's inside.' The woman jerks her head towards the pub. 'He can explain it all better than we can.'

'Who's he?'

'He's the one who knows all the history, and that. He's researched it all. We just want to do it how they used to do it, love. That's all. We dun't want to cause a fuss.'

'That seems fair enough.'

'So are you gonna sign our petition then, or what? We're gonna give it to the council before they have their meeting about shifting us.'

I've come to Haxton to satisfy my curiosity and kill time, not to sign petitions, but it would take a braver man than me to refuse. I take one of the biros and read the petition statement:

*The people of The Lantyrn Royd area of Haxton must be allowed to celebrate the Rush Bearing festival on the agreed route in the traditional way. We do not wish to offend our Muslim neighbours but English people have rights too. Coxthorpe Council must not cancel or re-route the Rush Bearing.*

I sign my name and add my email.

'There,' I say, handing back the biro. 'I hope you keep your Rush Bearing.'

'Thanks love,' the woman says. 'We're gonna fight like hell for it. If you've got time for a pint there's more stuff inside, with Roger.'

'I'm not in a hurry.'

'Well go and get yourself a drink then.' The woman winks. 'And you can get me one an all. It's thirsty work, is all this campaigning. I'll have a G&T.'

The woman is a distinct Coxthorpe type. Hard as nails, gossipy, cheeky, divorced probably, and still a bit sexy in the right circumstances on a Saturday night. She'll be an absolute bitch if her family or friends are crossed, but generous to a fault and loyal, and definitely the sort of person you'd want on your side in a fight. And she is standing up for something that she cares about with her petition, which must be commendable even if she can't quite articulate what the thing is. In fact, it is rather moving that she can't quite articulate it. I am glad, suddenly, that I've signed up.

'Bloody hell. I only just got here.'

'I know love, and now you're buying drinks for a mucky old woman. It's your lucky day in't it?'

The group snigger and I hurry into the pub. It turns out to be typical of the boozers serving the poor white communities that circle Coxthorpe town centre. There is a single gloomy room with a low stage at one end and a big television screen at the other. There are perhaps thirty people inside: elderly men in jackets and ties, straight-backed and unmoving in front of pints of lager, younger men and women in Coxthorpe Cobras Rugby League tops, and a few kids playing Connect Four noisily in the corner. The White Horse is full of tasteless tattoos, suspicion, and a rough kind of intimacy. It smells of sweat and stale beer, and the carpet is sticky. I order a pint and a double gin and tonic at the bar. As I am paying someone taps me on the shoulder.

'You din't really have to buy me a drink love. They're all tekking the piss out of me outside.'

The woman looks almost shy. I hand her the gin.

'I don't mind. You've been doing all the work. You deserve a drink.'

'Thanks, love. I'm Brenda.'

'I'm Adam.'

'Nice to meet you, Adam. Come and have a chat with Roger.'

Two tables have been pushed together opposite the bar and a number of grainy black and white photos depicting old Rush Bearing processions have been pinned to the wall above. The tables have a cross of St George fixed to the front and are covered with more photographs of old Haxton, together with a stack of booklets. There is a man in his late sixties sitting next to the table. He is dressed in a brown corduroy jacket and has a full beard and thick glasses. He is sipping a glass of red wine and chatting to the tattooed man from outside. Brenda leads me over.

'Roger this is Adam. He's just signed the petition and he's interested in the Rush Bearing. The history side of it and the crusader and all that.'

Roger extends his hand.

'Good to meet you sir. Thank you for your support.'

The man's accent is Yorkshire, but polished Yorkshire. He isn't from Coxthorpe. I would stake my life on it.

'Good to meet you too.'

'What is it that you were interested in specifically?'

'All of it, I suppose. Nothing specific. I didn't know anything about it until it all kicked off.'

The man sips his wine, and winces.

'Are you ok?'

He grins, displaying yellowing teeth.

'It's the chateaux Haxton. It's rather unforgiving.'

I laugh.

'You're probably better off with the lager. Although it's not much better.' I nod at the photos on the wall. 'These are pictures of the original Rush Bearing are they?'

'Well not the original, original. They are the Rush Bearing in its Victorian iteration. But, honestly, I wouldn't bother with them too much. The quality is pretty dreadful. They're just to get people interested.

'Ok, so tell me about it then.'

'It's tragic that you have to ask me that, especially as that you seem reasonably educated.'

'I'm not sure about that.'

'Oh, don't be coy. I've known you half a minute and it's already obviously that you have some sense of the world beyond Coxthorpe, which counts as educated round here. It's sad that even our best people have so little sense of their own history.'

The tattooed man nods and looks me up and down.

'They're the worst,' he mutters before turning and heading to the bar. I watch him go.

'I don't know what I've done to upset him.'

Roger chuckles.

'I doubt you've done anything. Jason's angry, like everyone else. But he doesn't quite know what to do with his anger yet. That's part of the problem, I'm afraid.' He sips his wine again and winces. 'There's a fight on here, Adam. History has come calling at

Haxton. People need education. They need to know what they're talking about.'

Roger belongs in *The White Horse* even less than I do. Socially he is as alien to the place as the old blokes in cardigans and robes up on Gordon Street. And yet here he is, perfectly comfortable, chatting to angry Jason and flirty Brenda and the rest of them, just as relaxed as if he was in the queue at Waitrose. And he seems to be accepted by The White Horse crowd. He even seems to be deferred to. My curiosity is piqued again. I sit down.

'Go on then, educate me. Tell me about the Rush Bearing.'

# 4

ROGER TURNS OUT to be an enthusiast for local history and folklore in the same way that some men are enthusiasts for steam trains or rare breeds of ferret. He is the sort of bloke who founds associations, runs websites, or publishes scrappy journals from their dining room. When he talks about the Rush Bearing, his voice slows and deepens, and he speaks in beautifully sculpted, near perfect paragraphs. At one point he puts his wine down to use his fingers as bullet points, and I can almost hear the PowerPoint clicker as each digit snaps to attention. I would put money on him having been a teacher at some point in his career, although we do not speak about work or family or anything at all, apart from the subject of the hour. When I leave The White Horse forty minutes later, I have a pamphlet in my pocket entitled *Haxton's Rush Bearing: An Ancient Tradition* (by Roger Wrigglesworth) and a fairly thorough understanding of the history of the thing. I say goodbye to Brenda, who is back at her table sipping gin, and make my way slowly through the city centre and home. As I walk, I consider what I have just learnt.

. . .

The Rush Bearing began in the Middle Ages when Haxton was the biggest settlement in the valley and Coxthorpe was a hamlet surrounded by a few outlying farms. Each year, in late September, fresh rushes were bought from outside the village and carried in procession to St Peter's church. The cart carrying the rushes was ridden by the Rush Maiden, an unmarried woman from the parish who apparently functioned a bit like a May Queen. The cart was decorated with corn dollies and rough representations of St Peter, the church's patronal saint, made of blackthorn and willow. Historians apparently regard these as surviving expressions of older pagan gods who lingered in the fields and moors around the village, beyond the sway of the parish priest. The old year's rushes (which must have absolutely stunk after twelve months' service) were swept out of the church and the new ones were spread on the floor of the nave. The Parish's statues of St Peter and the Virgin Mary were then paraded around to appreciate the nice pong, before being taken out through the churchyard and up to the lychgate. Here the Rush Maiden was crowned with a garland of flowers before everyone traipsed over to Goose Common (latterly Albert Park) to get pissed and have a dance. Roger implied that the explicitly Christian aspect of the Rush Bearing festival was waived somewhat during the latter part of the day. The old gods of the fields re-asserted themselves, apparently, away from the dark shadow of St Peters with its rules and saints and virgins.

As Roger explained it, that was more or less it for the Medieval iteration of the Rush Bearing festival. Following the ceremony, the good people of Haxton could attend church without getting the feet caked in mud and shit, at least for a few weeks.

The Rush Bearing was abolished after the civil war, when Cromwell's puritan regime went to war against corn dollies, and dancing, and the old gods. Haxton's celebration was just one of a number of similar festivals that suffered the same fate during the commonwealth, and for some reason very few were re-established at the restoration. In 1862, however, the festival enjoyed an unexpected resurrection. By then Coxthorpe had become an important centre of the wool trade and Haxton had turned into an industrial suburb for the city's mill workers, with a few of their bosses occupying substantial houses on the north side of Albert Park. A local industrialist named Sir Thomas Sedgwick was an enthusiast for Arts and Crafts stuff and for the English folk movement. He was also a proud son of Haxton, a High Tory and a committed churchman of the Anglo-Catholic type. He had provided most of the money for the new St Peter's Church, the original Norman building having crumbled into near dereliction by the mid nineteenth century.

A folk tradition such as the Rush Bearing, involving a church procession, rural crafts and medieval revelry was too tempting a prospect for Sir Thomas to resist and he duly revived the thing, lavishly funding the celebrations from his own pocket and granting his workers time off to prepare for the festival. The revived Rush Bearing came with Sir Thomas's personal stamp, however. The procession now began at the church, where the rush cart received a solemn Latin Benediction from the parish priest. A token bunch of rushes was then placed ceremoniously on the altar, before the cart was taken in procession to Albert Park, led by two candle bearers and a crucifer. The Rush Maiden was perched on top of the cart as in the medieval festival, but she was now accompanied by an honour guard of four figures whom Sir Thomas judged representative of Haxton history. These were: a shepherd representing the wool trade, a monk representing the Cistercian Abbey that had once stood at Weskmear on the east side of Coxthorpe, a Cavalier representing Coxthorpe's civil war history as a Royalist stronghold, and a crusader representing William de'Curzon, a knight from what is now Coxthorpe who had joined the Third Crusade and died at the Battle of Arsuf. The procession was met at Albert Park by an Ox Roast and Morris dancing, the latter involving Sir Thomas himself as master of the Haxton Footers Dance Side. There was ale and games throughout the afternoon, until six o'clock when the revels ended and Haxton's half-pissed citizenry returned to St Peter's for a special Rush Bearing Evensong presided over by no less a figure than the Bishop of Wakefield.

The Rush Bearing lapsed in 1914, when Haxton people presumably didn't feel that they had much to celebrate, and it was never revived after the First World War. Roger suggested that the celebration's joyful innocence was a poor fit for the shocked and cynical years following the armistice. This may well be true, but it occurred to me that the revived festival, rooted as it was in the romantic whim of one of Haxton's biggest mill owners, may have become less attractive to local people as Coxthorpe's labour movement developed. I doubt many people in inter-war Haxton had ever seen a rush, and by then the city's workers had different parades to march in and new crusades to fight.

. . .

I pick up fish and chips and a bottle of wine on the way home and eat my tea straight out of the paper in the kitchen with a tumbler of wine to wash it down. When I have finished, I refill my glass and go out into the yard for a smoke. There two things occur to me. The first is that despite Brenda's desire to revive the Rush Bearing authentically, to 'do it properly' as she put it, the Haxton residents are organising a revival of a revival of the original celebration. More than that, the original festival borrowed pagan components that preceded the Rush Bearing's ostensible Christian theme. The proposed procession might contain elements of authentic tradition, therefore, but it is a tradition with obscure and borrowed roots that has been reimagined at least twice. The question of the Rush Bearing's authenticity is more complex than Brenda might suppose.

My second thought concerns the tension surrounding the proposed route of the Rush Bearing procession. For someone of my age who is even vaguely interested in current affairs (who has *a sense of the world beyond Coxthorpe* as Roger put it) the routing issue is reminiscent of Orange Order walks in the North of Ireland. The right of the Orangemen to march through Catholic areas in their sashes and bowler hats had continued to be source of tension long after the Good Friday Agreement had ended the IRA's armed campaign. And, as with the Rush Bearing, the tensions primarily concerned the power of symbols, and the conflicting freedoms of competing communities. The comparison goes further. I used to have a priest friend from Derry/Londonderry, who suggested that the source of the troubles in the province was to do with the different communities' feelings of encirclement. Catholics in the North of Ireland felt encircled, my friend suggested, by the larger Protestant community in the province. The Protestants in turn felt encircled by the larger Catholic community on the island of Ireland taken as a whole and fretted that *Home Rule means Rome Rule*. The Catholic people of Ireland themselves felt encircled by the much stronger Protestant power to the East, while the mainland Brits felt encircled by the great Catholic powers of the continent. I accept that this is a very simplistic analysis of the Irish troubles, but I don't think it's completely without truth. And it seems loosely applicable to the situation at Haxton. The white-English community in Haxton certainly feels encircled and threatened by the Muslim community that surrounds them, while the Muslim community, at least as it is represented in the *Respect Haxton* leaflet, feels encircled and threatened by the broader British society which it believes views them with suspicion. Both of Haxton's communities are minorities in different ways, and both display the anxieties and defensiveness that come with minority status. The fact that Muslim anxiety about their minority situation is broadly acceptable in polite society, while white-English anxiety is not, doesn't alter the fact.

. . .

I put my cigarette out and go back inside. I do my teeth and take the remainder of the bottle of wine up to bed. There, inevitably, I play on my phone, and I end up chatting to Jaqueline, a 56-year-old divorcee from British Columbia, until about four-thirty. By then I have finished the wine and made a considerable dent in a bottle of Bombay Sapphire gin.

By the time I finally curl up to go to sleep, I am pissed and miserable, and the edges of the curtains are turning grey with the light of a new day. I doze rather than properly sleep, and I have muddled dreams starring Jaqueline from British Columbia. At one point she is perched on top of the Haxton Rush Cart with her breasts exposed to the West Yorkshire elements. An honour guard of crusaders stands around her with linked shields and drawn swords, while local imams lob stones.

As I said, the Haxton issue has got to me, just a bit.

# 5

I GET UP at midday on Monday and catch the train to Hebden Bridge. There I walk over the moors for five hours, amongst the rocks and heather, without seeing a soul, and then get the train back to Coxthorpe and have four pints in The Bumble Bee. The walking and the beer are to try and make sure that I sleep well that night. When I get home, I smoke and watch telly for a couple of hours before putting myself to bed at half eleven. God knows when I finally get to sleep, but I doubt that it is before two. It could be worse, I suppose. I wake up at ten feeling tired, but I make myself get up anyway.

After breakfast, I check my phone and discover that Jaqueline has WhatsApped me three times. The first two messages are routine 'how are you doing' stuff but in the third Jaqueline writes that she hopes I didn't think badly of her following the previous night's silliness. She has an autistic son, apparently, who requires constant care, meaning that her adventures online are her only 'outlet'.

(Was it Thoreau who said that thing about the mass of men leading lives of quiet desperation? I think it was Thoreau. It doesn't really matter who it was. The point is, I don't want to know that sort of detail about Jaqueline. I don't want to know how unhappy she is. And I definitely don't want to know about her autistic son. I know that's awful, but I don't.)

I message Jaqueline back saying that I don't think any the worse of her after Sunday, and that it had been fun. But, I add, it probably isn't a great idea to stay in touch, mostly because of the distance issue. Jaqueline must have been waiting for me to text because she messages back immediately: 'Tell the truth. Are U married?'. I answer that I'm not, but I still don't think it's a good idea for us to carry on messaging. 'Could we just be friends, without anything naughty?' Jaqueline replies. I answer that this probably isn't sensible. 'Ok then,' comes the final message, 'please delete my pics.' I answer that I will.

Which is a lie. I will hang onto Jaqueline's pictures for a few weeks as an aid to masturbation, until I get bored of them. Then I will delete them and immediately further delete them from the recently deleted folder on my phone. I will not show them to anyone else in the meantime. Obviously I don't feel good about the way I have treated Jaqueline, but what exactly was she was expecting? After all, the Atlantic is very big and very expensive to fly across. Did Jaqueline from British Colombia really think that a couple of pictures of her tits and one spectacular one of her vagina would bring me zooming over the ocean to give her difficult life the happy ending she craves? Of course she thought that. On Sunday night, I worked very hard to give her precisely that impression.

I block Jaqueline after the last message, but I feel shitty about it. I feel especially bad about her son.

. . .

The rest of the day is taken up with shopping, ironing and the little bit of housework that I bother with: chucking bleach down the toilet, scrubbing the bath and wiping down the kitchen surfaces. Then at about 4 o'clock, just as I have stretched a pair of jeans across the ironing board and am opening my second bottle of beer, my phone rings. It is my brother Ben, which is extraordinary. He is my only family apart from mum and we haven't spoken since Easter.

'Bloody hell. What do you want?'

'Charming as ever Adam.'

'Sorry. I'm just a bit surprised.'

'Why are you surprised? I am your brother. Brothers are supposed to speak to each other occasionally.'

'Ben, you haven't called me for over six months.'

'Which means you haven't called me for six months either.'

'True, I suppose.'

Ben exhales audibly, as Atlas would if he ever got the chance to put the universe down for a minute or two and a have a cup of tea and a hobnob.

'It's just so hectic down here, with work and the kids and everything. It's absolutely bloody constant. You really wouldn't believe.'

I sip my beer and take a deep breath. In three short sentences my brother has manged a hattrick of implied insults. He has reminded me that he has kids while I do not. He has suggested that his job is much more demanding than mine, in a way that I can't even understand: 'you really wouldn't believe'. And he has also alluded to the fact that, unlike me, he has managed to escape the dull streets of Coxthorpe and set up shop in the affluent and bustling south: 'It so hectic *down here*'. I am pretty sure that he doesn't do it on purpose, and I am probably slightly over sensitive, but it grates all the same. Ben and I don't really get on.

Having said all that, I don't want a row. When we row, I almost always lose.

'Is Miriam all right?'

'Yeah thanks. She's fine. She sends her love.'

'How are Josh and George?'

The phone is silent.

'Ben? Are you still there?'

'Yes, I'm here. George is fucking chaotic, as ever. He's just lost another saxophone.'

'Another one!'

'Yes. On the tube this time. He had gone busking in town with a friend. My guess is that they had been smoking something. Or drinking. Or doing pills or whatever it is they do. Apparently he just forgot about the fucking thing.'

'Has he admitted to the drugs?'

'Of course not. He's not going to, is he?'

'I suppose not. Have you contacted lost property?'

'Yep. Utterly bloody pointless. Nothing reported. Nothing handed in.'

'Oh dear. Must be expensive to replace.'

'About seven hundred quid, but it's insured of course. It's not really the money, though. It's the bloody attitude, with George. He just shrugged when we tried to talk to him about the sax. Literally shrugged. And he's the same about just about everything else: relaxed to the point of absolutely not giving a shit. About anything.'

'He always seems pretty laid back.'

'He's bloody horizontal. He has his GCSEs this year and I can honestly say that I haven't heard him express a single thought about them or about what he might do with himself when they're over, apart from spending the summer getting stoned at festivals. It's fucking embarrassing, apart from anything else.'

I silently toast my chaotic nephew. One younger sibling honouring another.

'I suppose he'll snap out of it all eventually,' I say when I've swallowed my beer. 'Most of us do, don't we? When life finally hits. How's Josh?'

'A lot less fucking trouble.'

'What's he up to?'

'Well, he's off back to college the week after next. He seems happy enough. He spent most of the summer working at Centre Parks on their high ropes thing, then he did a couple of weeks work experience on the paper.'

Ben sounds proud and happy. So much so that for a moment I almost like him.

'Blimey. How did the time on the paper go?'

'I was pleased with him actually. Really pleased. He took it seriously, and I think he genuinely impressed people. He got a couple of pieces in The Weekend about student politics and wokeness and so on, which made it all worthwhile as far as he was concerned. He's been very cool about it all, but he's obviously thrilled.'

The college is Jesus College, Cambridge, where Josh is about to start his second year. The paper is *The Globe*, where my brother is a columnist and where Josh will presumably work one day, hopefully not cranking out the same pompous, self-righteous wank as his father. Josh is friendly and sweet, and there's no denying that he's very bright indeed, but he's also just the teensiest weeniest bit boring.

'Fucking hell, that's impressive. I wish you'd let me know he'd had something in the paper. I would have bought a copy.'

'You mean you don't buy it anyway?'

'Tend to read it on my phone these days.'

Ben exhales again. Louder this time. Exasperated.

'If you want decent journalism, you're going to have to take some responsibility for it, you know, Adam. Or else you'll lose it.'

'I suppose you're right. I do feel like a bit of a freeloader, sometimes.'

'You probably should, to be honest.'

'But there's so much in the paper that I can't stand these days. The shit about trans men in Brighton sorting out the Feng Shui for their birthing pools and posh women columnists from Putney lecturing blokes from Barnsley for being insufficiently diverse. It leaves a bad taste.'

'And the taste would be worse if you actually paid for the thoughts of the columnists from Putney?'

'I think it would a bit. Yeah. I think I'd feel like I was enabling them.'

Ben is quiet again while he works out whether or not he wants a row. Apparently he doesn't want one today either.

'It was actually work that I was ringing about.'

'Really? How come?'

'How much do you know about the thing in Haxton?'

I knew that Ben calling about Haxton from the moment I saw his name on my phone. There is no other reason that he would ring. I switch the iron off and take my beer through to the sitting room. I lie on the sofa and stare at the ceiling.

'It's funny you should say that.'

'Why's that?'

'I went up there on Sunday to see what was going on.'

'Excellent. Excellent. I knew it. You just can't help yourself from fluttering around that sort of thing, can you? Even now?'

'I don't know what the hell that's supposed to mean. I don't flutter anywhere.'

'Oh God, don't get cross. I honestly didn't mean it in a bad way. I like it that you're still into stuff like that. I assume it keeps your mind engaged. And, anyway, I need your help.'

'How come?'

'I've got to write something about Haxton for Sunday's paper. It's meant to be *my hometown in flames* sort of thing. And there was some suggestion that I should go up and have a look round. But if you've already visited I might just be able to swerve it.'

(Which is a shame because by swerving Haxton, Ben is also swerving mum who would love a visit from him. She only sees him for a week at Christmas and another in the summer, and she misses him dreadfully. But I let that pass. I am excited about being drafted as *The Globe's* Haxton correspondent.)

'Ok. Well, I'm happy to tell you what I know. For what it's worth.'

'Great. Great, Adam. Thanks. Your reward will be fucking enormous in heaven. Now tell me everything. And take as long as you want, I've got all afternoon.'

So, I tell him everything. I begin with the Dawah Stall in Victoria Square and the chat I had with the Muslim bloke, and I read the *Respect Haxton* leaflet out to Ben. Then I outline my theory about the different voices involved in the leaflet's composition before describing my stroll up to Haxton.

'Have you ever been there, Ben?'

'Of course not. Why would I have been?'

'No reason, I suppose.'

I describe the geography of The Lantyrn Royd area and talk about walking around the block before meeting Brenda and the crowd of locals outside The White Horse. Finally, I describe my introduction to Roger.

'He seemed pleasant enough. Although he clearly wasn't a Haxton local. He was actually drinking red wine, which...'

'Hang on. What did you say the bloke's name was?'

'Roger?'

'Roger what?'

'Wrigglesworth.'

Ben whistled through his teeth.

'Fucking hell. That's a bit of a result.'

'What do you mean? What's a result? Who is he?'

I hear Ben tapping at a keyboard and then he says slowly:

'Roger Wrigglesworth is a prominent member of the *Civitas Seminar*. He's originally from Leeds but I'm looking at the *Civitas Seminar* website, and it says he's been living in London for the last six years. I'm not sure if that's true though. Some people I know tell me he's been out in Belgium recently working with loony Flemish right wingers. Catholics apparently, for what it's worth. Anyway, he moved to Haxton in early August with his daughter and son in law, who may also be *Civitas* members. It doesn't mention it on his *Civitas* bio, but it seems likely that they moved up there specifically to set up a little cell of activists.'

'Ben, stop. I don't know what you're talking about. I've never heard of *Civitas Seminar*. Who are they?'

'Sorry. Sorry. I'm not surprised you haven't heard of them. Not many people have. Hang on a sec.' Some more tapping. 'Yes, here we are. The tagline on their website describes them as *A Patriotic Think Tank and Education Resource*, which might just about be true if you're looking for education about eugenics, or holocaust denial, or the spread of Sharia courts in Burnley, or Jewish control of the pornography industry.'

'Fucking hell. Really?'

'It's grim isn't it? They're a nasty bunch of cunts but they're not your street level Nazi thug. They see themselves as intellectuals. They publish books and a journal, and run very posh, very select seminars. The sort of thing that attracts creepy bachelor teachers from minor public schools and the odd fucked up Tory peer.'

While Ben has been talking, I have gone back into the kitchen and have been fishing around in the pile of unopened post and half-read magazines that builds up between the fruit bowl and the mug tree. After a bit of searching, I unearth the Rush Bearing pamphlet that Roger gave me. At the bottom of the back page it says: *Published by the Civitas Seminar.*

'Bloody hell,' I say. 'You're right.'

'What about?'

'Roger gave me a booklet thing, *Haxton's Rush Bearing: An Ancient Tradition*. They were dishing them out in the pub. And it's published by the Civitas Seminar people.'

'That could be useful. Can you send it to me?'

'I suppose so. Was he ever a teacher by the way?

'Wrigglesworth?'

'Yes.'

'He was a politics lecturer at Richmond University for eight years in the nineties and early noughties. Apparently he's published some academic stuff about Flemish Nationalism and the EU. He's obviously not thick, which is what makes him so bloody scary. What did the pair of you talk about?'

I describe my conversation with Roger Wrigglesworth as far as I can remember it and outline the history of the Rush Bearing as Roger explained it to me. When I finish, I hear some more tapping on a keyboard.

'That is brilliant Adam,' he murmurs after a moment. 'You are an absolute star. I've got plenty there. I don't think there's any need for me to come up at all.'

'You're welcome.'

Ben is quiet for a moment. And then:

'Are you ok, by the way?'

'Yeah. I'm fine.'

'Great. Well, look, you must come down. I know we keep saying it, but you must. We're talking about drinks or something for Miriam's fiftieth next month. If you're around...'

He tails off. The settled convention, unless we are fighting, is that we end our phone calls by pretending to share a common intention to meet up soon.

'Yeah. That would be great. It will be a little bit dependent on shifts, obviously.'

'Yeah course, the shifts. Bloody hell. I always forget about that. I don't know how you cope to be honest. Look, I'll email you the dates. And, if you're free...'

'Of course.'

'Great, well hope to see you soon, then.'

'Yep. Hope so. See you.'

'Yeah and don't forget to send that booklet.'

'I won't.'

The line goes dead. I put my phone down and finish my beer. Then I go back to the kitchen and put the ironing board away and get another beer from the fridge. I smoke a cigarette in the yard and then go back to the sofa. I go online and end up chatting to Patricia aged 59 from Gibbon, Minnesota. Over a period of a few hours, Patricia and I become firm friends and, as friends will, she ends up sending me some engaging videos of her masturbating with a lilac-coloured vibrator.

I go to bed at half past eleven, which is much too late given that I have work tomorrow. Nevertheless, as I fall asleep there is a little smile playing around my lips which has nothing whatsoever to do with Patricia from Minnesota (sorry Patricia, your videos were impressive, but the brutal truth is that I forgot about you almost as soon as I had cum). No, the smile is because my arrogant and patronising pig of an older brother has asked for my thoughts concerning the situation at Haxton and then has appeared to take them seriously enough to make them the basis of his forthcoming column.

It's complicated between Ben and me.

# 6

I AM ON days - half six in the morning to half six in the evening - on Wednesday, Thursday, Friday and Saturday, and so I do nothing except work, eat, sleep and mess around a bit on the internet. I spend some time on the *Civitas Seminar* website which turns out to be just as awful as Ben implied. Even so, I can't help feeling slightly thrilled, as I skim through articles about *Jewish Ethnic Activism and Neo-Conservatism 1990-2010* or *The Heart of Darkness: Hip Hop and the Caucasian Cult of the Other* that I have stumbled on a real example of a *Civitas Seminar* person, apparently engaged in genuine fascist stuff just down the road. On Thursday, I nip out from work at lunchtime and post Ben the Rush Bearing pamphlet with a note referencing a couple of articles on the website by Roger Wrigglesworth, in case he has missed them.

We lose three Polish lads unexpectedly on Thursday lunchtime when better paying jobs come up in Wakefield, and so I have to work on the warehouse floor for a couple of hours on Friday and Saturday to take up the slack. As a result, my admin gets behind and I end up hanging around for an hour or so on both days after my shift has ended, to get up to date.

By the time I get home at quarter past eight on Saturday evening I can hardly keep my eyes open. I have a quick shower to revive me before nipping round to the off-licence for a bottle of wine. I order a curry and lie on my sofa with my laptop balanced on my tum, eating and drinking while I watch a film about *Civitas Seminar* on OyTube. The video is produced by an anti-fascist group called *Resistance Media* and is structured around an undercover exposé of the Seminar, starring a *Resistance Media* mole. There is quite a lot of shaky film footage, first as the mole meets a couple of *Civitas Seminar* people in a pub to discuss his application to join, and then when he attends a conference about *Jewish Evolutionary Strategy and the Frankfurt School*, held in the back room of a private drinking club in Covent Garden. To my mind, the undercover stuff detracts a little from the film's content. I can't help thinking, as I watch yet another grainy shot of a fascist crotch taken from the mole's hidden camera, that, if you wanted to know what *Civitas Seminar* believed, it would have been simpler to spend five minutes on the organisation's website or even give them a ring? As far as I can tell, the people filmed in the pub, and the speakers at the conference say nothing out of synch with the *Civitas Seminar's* party line. For instance: *Civitas Seminar* believe that there is something called 'racial differences' to do with intelligence and temperament, and they want white people to constitute a 'permanent and controlling supermajority' in the UK. So says their website and so says the brummy bloke in the pub who chats to the mole over pints of lager. Also, while *Civitas Seminar* do not believe that there is a unified Jewish conspiracy to control the world, they do think that elements of Jewish evolutionary strategy (whatever that is) are opposed to the interests of the gentile host societies in which diaspora Jews find themselves. That is the line in the 'Jewish Question' section of the website, and it is echoed by the speaker at the Covent Garden meeting. Finally, *Civitas Seminar* do not deny the holocaust, but they claim to place it in its historical context, both in relation to other holocausts (the Armenians, the Ukrainians) and in relation to the centuries-long fraught relationship between

Jews and Gentiles of eastern Europe, where they suggest there were faults on both sides. The website is clear about this, and it is the line that the brummy bloke doggedly sticks to when the *Resistance Media* mole tries to get him talking about faked crematoria, skin lampshades and the water table at Auschwitz (I think that might count as entrapment, incidentally.) The views of the *Civitas Seminar* people are vile, but they are apparently no different in private than in public. Also, if you can separate the *Civitas Seminar* members from their beliefs, they do not seem to be particularly awful. In fact, they seem to be fairly intelligent and polite, which makes it all the more shocking when they say such dreadful things. If anything, the *Resistance Media* people are more objectionable than the *Civitas Seminar* members, at least superficially. The breathless manner with which *Resistance Media* conducts their infiltration grates after a while, particularly the endless James Bond 'Q' style shots of them fixing secret cameras into their shirt buttons. Their unshakeable conviction about the absolute rightness of their cause is also a bit irritating. It affords the *Resistance Media* team license to do some fairly unpleasant things, notably doorstepping an elderly *Civitas Seminar* member after dark and then intentionally revealing his address. The unstated assumption throughout is that the *Resistance Media's* ends always justify their means, because the views of *Civitas Seminar* members are so utterly beyond the pale. The program's presenters never bother to critique the views of the *Civitas Seminar* people, it being taken for granted that they are self-evidently evil. This pisses me off a bit as well. Unquestioning believers always irritate me, especially when they refuse to acknowledge that that is what they are.

Throughout the video, I have a lingering sense of disconnection between what I am watching and the situation in Lantyrn Royd. There is obviously a link of sorts, through Roger Wrigglesworth (who appears briefly in the background at the Covent Garden meeting) and because the Rush Bearing dispute relates tangentially to the sorts of issues that the *Civitas Seminar* claims to be interested in. But the disconnect remains. The conspiracies and certainties, and the overwhelming self-importance of both the *Civic Seminar* and *Resistance Media* people seem a million miles from Brenda and her tatty petition.

When the documentary is over, I go onto the chat sites and get talking to Cindy from Miami. After half an hour we move to Google Hangouts and then to Skype. Unfortunately, Patricia from Minnesota pops up on WhatsApp while we are skyping, which makes my phone bleep and distracts me. I silence my phone and manage to keep the Skype chat and the WhatsApp conversation going in tandem for over half an hour which requires more than my usual level of dexterity (and is pretty impressive after a bottle of wine and a couple of glasses of gin). Finally, I let Cindy from Miami watch me masturbate. Then I say goodnight to both Cindi and a rather suspicious Patricia and fall asleep. It is sometime after three.

. . .

I get up at half ten on Sunday morning and, because I can't face a beer, I have a fag and a coffee for breakfast in the yard. Then I stroll to the corner shop and buy *The Globe*. Ben hasn't texted or emailed to confirm that 'our' article is in the paper today, but I wouldn't expect him to. I am still excited to see what he has written. I take the paper to a café across the road from the shop and order another coffee while I track the piece down in the huge doorstep of paper that makes up *The Globe's* Sunday edition. After five minutes, I find it in the *Comment Tree* section. It is the paper's *Trunk Read*, extending over a whole double page of broadsheet. There are *Branch* articles on the subsequent pages dealing with related issues such as the growth of the far right and Islamophobic hate crime, and there is an invitation below the piece for readers to join the discussion on

*The Globe's Seeds and Shoots* online forum (and Ben wonders why I don't buy the fucking paper). In the centre of the text of Ben's article there is a large picture of a middle-aged man standing outside The White Horse. He has a pint in one hand and a bulky e-cig in the other, he is shaven headed and heavily tattooed, and there is a cloud of vapour drifting above him. The man looks ignorant and angry, the embodiment of the frustrated, disempowered, dangerous white.

I read the piece very slowly, sometimes stopping and re-reading a passage two or even three times. As I read, my excitement curdles into disappointment. The piece is typical of Ben, which means that it is smug and self-serving, and delivered in the arse-clenching, faux-matey style of one who believes themselves to be speaking common sense truths to power. I don't know how I ever managed to believe that it might be otherwise.

## *The Road to Nowhere*

*The Lantyrn Royd area of Haxton is not the sort of place you are likely to stumble on by accident. Its main street is a dead end, it has a handful of struggling shops and one rough-arse pub, and it is tucked away in a claustrophobic corner of Haxton, a suburb of the city of Coxthorpe in West Yorkshire. Haxton is not the sort of place you are likely to stumble on either. It has a few more shops than Lantyrn Royd, as well as a few more streets, a grotty park and a handful of mosques. The recent headlines should not mislead us: Lantyrn Royd is not a very significant place. It is very easily overlooked within Haxton, just as Haxton is easily overlooked within Coxthorpe, just as Coxthorpe is easily overlooked within a nation whose political class still finds it difficult to recognise the cultural distinctives of communities between Watford and the Scottish border.*

*Full disclosure: I am not one of those people who find it easy to overlook Coxthorpe, because it is my home. Or rather, it was my home. I don't live there anymore. Like thousands of other northerners, I have made the trek south in search of work. But Coxthorpe survives in me nonetheless: in my flat vowels, in the pale blue tinge to my skin, and in my settled conviction that lunch is really dinner and dinner is really tea. That harsh economic realities should have dragged lots of people like me out of the north of England is one thing, to drag the north of England out of us is quite another, and it turns out to be much more difficult. We northern exiles find it very hard indeed to forget either our roots or our short vowels. And most of the time I think this is a very good thing.*

*It is a slow news day when Coxthorpe catches the interest of the southern media class, but my hometown has bucked the trend over the last couple of weeks. The source of Coxthorpe's sudden newsworthiness is the Rush Bearing procession which the locals in Lantyrn Royd have scheduled for the last weekend in October.*

*Taken at face value, the proposed procession seems rather sweet. The Rush Bearing has its roots in a medieval tradition of dumping fresh rushes in the parish church sometime in Autumn so that Haxton folk could pray without getting stinky knees. As with so much else that was fun and festive, Cromwell put an end to the Rush Bearing during the commonwealth, but it was revived in the nineteenth century by Thomas Sedgewick, a pious Coxthorpe industrialist, and it persevered until the great war. Crucially, Sedgewick tweaked the medieval celebrations, adding figures of local significance: a monk, a weaver, a cavalier and a crusader knight, to the original procession. It is the crusader character that is causing all the bother in Haxton and making the headlines. In an area such as Haxton, crusaders are provocative to say the very least.*

*What follows is delicate, but it needs saying. The current problems in Haxton are not fundamentally rooted in economics, or education, or in social opportunity but in ethnicity and religion. In Coxthorpe University's Salad Bowl Survey of 2017, 86% of the Brits in Haxton were recorded as of Pakistani Muslim heritage, while the Brits of the Lantyrn Royd area of the suburb came in at 100% white English. Ultimately, of course, these statistics should not matter. One day they will not matter. But, regrettably, in Haxton and in former mill towns across the North of England, they still matter very much indeed. The immediate cause of the tension in Haxton is the area's Muslim majority taking exception to a crusader knight being paraded through their streets by the white minority. Fair enough. Stamford Hill's Jews would not welcome a festive SS figure trotting through their streets. African Americans in Montgomery would not appreciate a fun KKK character strolling through their neighbourhoods as part of an Alabama Heritage Day. Members of historically oppressed communities have the right to live in peace without the ancient symbols of their oppression being shoved in their faces. Haxton's Muslims are one such community. They have a valid point in resisting the Rush Bearing in its present form, and reasonable people from Coxthorpe and beyond will support them.*

*So far, so obvious to anyone who isn't a far-right nutjob. The interesting question in the Lantyrn Royd/Haxton drama is why the community of Lantyrn Royd has chosen to revive the Rush Bearing now. The answer to that question comes in two halves. The more depressing half is that Lantyrn Royd's locals have been influenced by a bunch of deeply unpleasant outsiders from an organisation called the Civitas Seminar. The Home Office sponsored Anti-Fascist group 'Face Up to Hate' list the Civitas Seminar in the academic section of their Hate Directory. And if you can be bothered you can Google them. They are fascists who are too fat or too old for street fighting and so spend their time writing tedious, pseudo-intellectual nonsense about Heidegger and Wagner as a thin camouflage for their hatred of black and brown people. It pains me that a small number of Civitas Seminar goons should have moved to my hometown and taken it upon themselves to stir up trouble there, but this is what seems to have happened. It is likely that the original impetus for the revived Rush Bearing has come from members of the group. And, irritatingly, the publicity that the Rush Bearing has attracted means that their activity has already been a success, in their terms.*

*The more interesting half of the answer to the question of why the Rush Bearing has been revived now, is to do with the white community of Lantyrn Royd. It is these people (my people, I suppose) who are the true centre of the Rush Bearing story, not a bunch of flabby, pseudo-academic Nazis.*

*The Lantyrn Royd whites have been demonised as racist loonies in the mainstream media and lionised as the last British patriots on a few crappy, far right Twitter accounts. Neither view does justice to them or to their situation, however. Coxthorpe people are more complicated than that. It may be helpful to consider them through the political model proposed by David Goodhart. In his book,* The Road to Somewhere, *Goodhart argues that the old categories of left and right have broken down as effective tools for analysing political affiliation. He replaces them with Somewheres: people who feel a strong affiliation to a particular place, who worry about fast social change and who lack the educational resources to benefit from the opportunities of hyper-globalisation; and Anywheres: people who are less concerned about belonging to a particular place (or even to a particular country), who thrive in fast-changing communities, and who are well placed in terms of their education and social capital to benefit from a globalising world. Anywheres are Remainers, Somewheres are Brexiteers. Anywheres are outraged when Nigel Farage says that hearing no English spoken in a train carriage makes him feel uncomfortable, while Somewheres find his comments perfectly reasonable. Anywheres didn't care that Jeremy Corbyn wouldn't sing the National Anthem a few years ago. Somewheres were irritated at the image of the leader of the Labour Party (their party until recently) refusing to ask the God he doesn't believe in to save the queen he doesn't approve of. Anywheres view the unironic display of the St George's Cross with suspicion. Somewheres definitely do not and may hang the flag from their homes during the World Cup. When they do this, of course, Anywheres are likely to take the piss out of their flag-shagging.*

*You get the picture. By Goodhart's categorisation, Lantyrn Royd's Rush Bearers are classic Somewheres. Globalisation has not added opportunity to their corner of West Yorkshire, instead it has led to ever greater levels of immigration and to the accelerated transformation of their communities. Add to this a set of profoundly difficult economic circumstances, also the consequence of globalisation, and there is small wonder that the people of The Lantyrn Royd enclave cling tenaciously to their inherited sense of their place in the world and to their imagined histories. When I go home, I travel to a very different country from the vibrant and more-or-less tolerant one that I know in London. There is a defensiveness in the air in Coxthorpe amongst the people I grew up with, and beneath that defensiveness there is resentment, and beneath that resentment there is fear.*

*But there is a difficulty with Goodhart's analysis. In constructing his model, he draws too sentimental a picture of Somewhereness, a picture that offers little help to real Somewhere people as they grapple with a relentlessly fast-paced modernity. I don't blame Goodhart for this. The man used to edit a philosophy magazine, he is an old Etonian and the son of a Tory MP. He's a bright bloke, but he can hardly be expected to understand how it feels to grow up in Coxthorpe or somewhere like it. If we are going to take the Rush Bearers of Lantyrn Royd seriously, however, and to offer them a way out of the literal dead end of their community, we must begin by refusing to romanticise their Somewhereness and their enacted Englishness. I know (and I mean that I really know) what 'Englishness' looks like in Coxthorpe. It is always performed in opposition to the alien and threatening other who walks among the 'English' on the cobbled streets of the town. 'Englishness' as a cultural category is no more substantive than is 'Englishness' as an ethnic category in Coxthorpe - a town that was already a hotchpotch of proletarianized former dalesmen, German and Jewish wool merchants, and 19th Century immigrant Irish labourers, before the newer waves of immigration commenced in the 1950s. Coxthorpe's Englishness is always performative, a fantasy fuelled by fear, a faux crusader's blind sword swipe at an irreducibly complex and threatening world.*

*Please pay attention, this is as important as anything I have ever written in this newspaper or any other. The white people of my hometown deserve better than to be relegated to a charming Somewhere status which locks them into unhealthy and defensive relationships with their ethnic minority neighbours, with a fast-globalising world, and with modernity itself. In Coxthorpe, the Somewhereness that David Goodhart celebrates, very quickly becomes No-whereness. It leaves my mates ignored and off the map in terms of economic opportunity, life chances and political power.*

*But if they must not be trapped as Goodhart's somewhere people, nor should the Haxton Rush Bearers aspire to be his anywhere people: cheerfully rootless cosmopolitans who belong everywhere because they truly belong nowhere at all.*

*To have roots is a good thing and (I would say this wouldn't I?) to have roots in Coxthorpe is a very good thing indeed. So here is a suggestion that doesn't come from social science textbooks or glossy philosophy magazines, but from my own lived experience as an occasionally unhappy northern exile in London. Could we imagine the Haxton Rush Bearers as belonging to a third category: the From-Somewheres? Like a Somewhere, a From-Somewhere knows where they come from, and they are proud of it. They may or may not still live in their birthplace but if they have left it, it has definitely not left them. They continue to draw strength from the social networks of their places of origin and also from new networks in the communities they have ended up in. From-Somewheres know that place and belonging are important, and they value institutions, from churches to working men's clubs to football teams, which foster these qualities. They have regional accents; they are not citizens of the world and nor do they aspire to be. However, like Anywheres, From-Somewheres are curious about the world beyond their own immediate streets and are equipped to explore and flourish in a fast-paced and complex modernity. The internet enables them to be at home even when they are hundreds or thousands of miles away, and also to be hundreds or thousands of miles away when they are at home. More importantly From-Somewheres know that national, regional and local identities are necessarily diverse, contested and evolving. They know that to love a place does not mean wishing to see it frozen in amber, and that 'belonging' and 'identity' are categories that need to be mixed with a dash of irony if they are not to manifest destructively.*

*I have a photo above my desk of Coxthorpe Cobras celebrating our victory in the Rugby League Premiership two years ago, and I am looking at it now, as I type. The Cobras fans in the picture are dancing in the fountain in Victoria Square with pints in their hands and broad grins on the faces while the cops watch and giggle in the background. Fans and the police alike are different colours and the turbans of a few of them mark them out as Sikhs. It is indisputable, however, that everyone in the picture - fans, police, Asian-British, white-British - are proud Coxthorpe people sharing a glorious moment in the changing, wonderful, fascinating and occasionally tragic story of their town. Better than anything else, perhaps, that picture encapsulates what a From-Somewhere identity might look like.*

*The proposed Haxton Rush Bearing is another moment in Coxthorpe's story. The immediate task for people who wish the town well is to make sure that the crusader figure is removed from the pageant, or that the pageant is re-routed, or both. For this year, that may be the best that we can manage. The more important and more difficult task, however, is to help Haxton's whites to construct a positive understanding of themselves and of their proposed procession: one which does not place them in endless opposition to their neighbours, one which does not instinctively refuse change, one which feels like a launchpad rather than a limit.*

*A final thought: for various complicated reasons, I don't get back to Coxthorpe as often as I should. But, God knows, I would go back in a flash for a re-imagined Rush Bearing procession that included bhangra dancers, Indian sweets, and lassis dished out at the local mosque. Because I still love my hometown, despite the miles and the years of absence, I have to cling to the hope that such a celebration is possible.*

While I am reading, I forget about my coffee completely and now it is cold. I gulp it down quickly and get up to leave. When I reach the door the girl behind the counter calls me back.

'Hey, you've left your paper.'

I turn round.

'It's alright. I've finished with it. You can chuck it away.'

'Is it today's?'

'Yeah.'

'Well then, I'll keep it for the customers.'

I shrug and pull the door open. Then I turn round again.

'I wouldn't do that. It's got nothing to do with up here.'

'What do you mean?'

'It's all London stuff. It's nothing to do with us.'

'Oh. I didn't realise. I've never read it before.'

'I wouldn't bother starting.'

She picks up *The Globe* and stares at it.

'It looks right serious.'

'It isn't. It thinks it is, but it isn't. It's absolutely crap, honestly.'

Suddenly the café girl grins.

'I'll use it to pick up dog shit in the yard.'

# 7

On Sundays, when I'm not working or half asleep because I'm coming off a night shift, I go round to mum's for lunch. That's been the arrangement since dad died six years ago, although mum and I have never discussed it or formalised it. It's just a thing that we do. I tell myself that I go round to mum's to keep her company, and that's true. But it's also true that my Sunday lunches with mum are the only regular time in the week when I talk properly to someone who isn't either a colleague at work or a woman online. So I'm not just being a good Samaritan, going round to mum's. I think it does my soul a bit of good as well. And it gets me a decent meal.

To take advantage of the autumn sunshine, I walk to mum's rather than drive. Her house is just over three miles away from mine, at the northern edge of Coxthorpe where the streets give way with disconcerting abruptness to the moors. Her neighbourhood, the neighbourhood I grew up in, retains something of a village feel. There are a couple of traditional pubs, a post office/general store, a prominent church, a little bit of a village green, and almost everyone is white. Today, when I knock on the door and let myself in, the house smells of roast lamb and radio three is playing quietly. As I push the door shut, I feel myself become calm in a way that

I never quite manage to do anywhere else, even in my own house. The muscles in my shoulders and neck relax perceptibly. I lean back against the door, close my eyes and exhale. This little semi is deeply engrained with the ordinary, comforting, sustaining stuff of my past. It has a converted loft where I used to smoke rollups with Ben. It has an Aga in the kitchen where mum has baked the chocolate cake I love for as long as I can remember. It has a woodburning stove in the lounge, where I used to lie on my tummy and watch Blue Peter. And, best of all, from the kitchen you can see the moorland gently shrugging its shoulders to mark the beginning of Weskdale, which is the loveliest view in all of England (and the Lake District can go and fuck itself). This semi may be my mum's house, but it is also my home. It always has been, and I can't conceive of it ever being anything else.

'Is that you Adam?'

'No, It's the Coxthorpe rapist.'

'I'm in the dining room.'

I go through to the dining room and find mum sitting at the table with a gin and tonic. She has *The Globe* spread out in front of her. As ever, she looks peaceful. Mum is good at being a widow. She is without obvious self-pity. Dad's death has left a bruise somewhere inside her and occasionally circumstances serve to strike the spot so that the pain is visible, but mostly she is quiet and calm. She is still able to take pleasure in simple, sensible things like a drink and a nice lunch. When I walk in, she looks up.

'Do you want a drink?'

'Why not?'

'Gin and tonic?'

'Yes please.'

'I don't know why I bother asking.'

'Because secretly you hope that one day I'll say no and save you thousands on gin.'

Mum rolls her eyes and gets up. She kisses me lightly on the cheek and then goes to the sideboard and pours me a generous gin and tonic. She hands it to me, and we sit down opposite each other. She nods at the paper, which is open at Ben's piece.

'Have you read it?'

'I have actually.'

'What do you think?'

'Well....'

'Go on.'

'I think...I think he's probably tried his best to tell the truth.'

Mum raises an eyebrow.

'That sounds rather like faint praise Adam.'

'I suppose it does.'

Mum giggles and we both sip our drinks. It's posh gin. Rhubarb. Mum has made it strong.

'But I think you're right,' she says after a moment. 'Actually, I think that's quite perceptive. I think he has worked quite hard to tell the truth. According to his own lights, of course.'

'Exactly. According to his own lights.'

'He said you'd helped with it. He was very grateful.'

'That's nice. I was pleased to help at the time. Not so much now that I've read it.'

Mum frowns.

'It means a lot to him to write about Coxthorpe, you know.'

'Yes.'

'It really does.'

'I know. He's told me that too in the past. The voice of the voiceless and all that.'

Mum peers at me over the top of her specs and then sips her drink again.

'What do you really think of it, Adam?'

'Honestly?'

'Yes.'

'I think Ben finds it very difficult to write about anything without defaulting to write about himself.'

'Go on.'

'I think the stuff about him being a sad, exiled son of the north is self-important wank. I think it clutters some of the things he is trying to say. Not that I agree with those things anyway.'

Her eyes skim across the article.

'Hmm. Yes, I suppose so. In...In a way. But he isn't actually lying about any of that is he? He does miss the north.'

'He's not quite lying, no. But the bit about him going south in search of work gets pretty close. He left Coxthorpe to go to Cambridge for God's sake.'

'Yes. That's slightly overstated. I'll give you that.'

'It's more than overstated, mum. It makes him sound like some Irish famine-victim getting on a coffin ship to America.' I sip my drink again. 'It's fucking weird.'

'Yes. I suppose it is. Just a little.'

'And what he writes about people up here isn't quite right either. It doesn't fit them properly. The *from-somewhere* stuff. I suspect he made that up without really thinking about it. I think he probably just liked the sound of the phrase. I'm not even sure he read the whole of...'

I stop speaking. Mum's eyes are flicking more quickly over the article, and her lips are moving silently. Mum and I are close. We have lunch together most weeks. We go to the cinema or the theatre once a month. We speak on the phone. We get a bit pissed together on gin. Mum loves me and worries about me. Even more than dad, she worked hard to get me set up with a job and a place to live after London, when everything fell apart. In a sense our relationship is closer than hers and Ben's could ever be. But still, she loves Ben with an intense and helpless pride than she could never feel for me. She loves him because of his job on *The Globe*, because of his wife and kids, because of his six-bedroom house in Victoria Park, because of the MPs and media people she has met there. Mum is a bright woman, she knows that her devotion to Ben is unrequited and undignified and a just a little bit pathetic, but she cannot help herself. When she reads what Ben writes, or when she gathers some new scrap of information about his career or about the lives of Miriam or the kids, she glows. And then she secretly regrets that Ben doesn't quite have my kindness or my commitment. Because then he would be perfect and there would be no need for me at all.

All of this is completely unspoken of course. But that doesn't stop it being true.

After a couple of minutes mum pulls her specs off and lays them down on the table with a sharp click.

'No,' she says. 'I think he has been honest, fundamentally. He hasn't told any lies, and he is genuinely sad that he had to leave Coxthorpe, but that's just the nature of his job. He's tried to make it personal, that's all.'

'So do you think he's right about the knight?'

'What knight?'

I can't stop myself from laughing.

'That's exactly what I'm getting at, mum. That's the whole bloody point of the dispute at Coxthorpe and you've missed it because it's lost in Ben-waffle.'

'I hadn't missed it at all.'

I drain my glass.

'So, what do you think? Should the crusader be banned from the Rush Bearing procession? Or should it be re-routed?'

Mum nods her head quickly.

'Of course it should be banned, if it gives offence. As Ben says, it's like a man in a Nazi costume parading through Golders Green or somewhere. It's not acceptable. It's offensive.'

She finishes her drink and stands up. 'Anyway, I must do the carrots.'

Mum walks through to the kitchen and starts chopping. I go to the sideboard and pour myself a second gin and tonic.

'There is another point of view about that,' I call.

The chopping stops and mum appears in the doorway with a knife in her hand.

'About what? The crusader thing?'

'Yes.'

'I don't see how there can be.'

'Well, the people in Lantyrn Royd would say that there is no intention to cause offence, which wouldn't be true of the hypothetical SS guy in Golders Green. And they would also say that the crusader is an integral part of an authentic tradition that they're trying to revive.'

Mum shrugs.

'Well, if that's their point of view, one of the Haxton people should write about it.'

'But that's a bit difficult without a platform isn't it? Ben's in a position to get his voice heard but the people at Lantyrn Royd aren't quite so lucky. And their procession's meant to happen in three weeks' time.'

She shrugs again, unhappily. Mum doesn't like the idea that Ben's isn't on the side of the little guy.

'I'm not sure that's true, Adam, with the internet and so on. Blogs and whatnot. Citizen journalism. Ben says that pretty much anyone can be a journalist these days.'

With that she goes back into the kitchen and starts chopping again. After a moment she calls out:

'I put anchovies on the lamb, I hope that's alright.'

'You know I love your lamb mum.'

'I know. I love you too. Now make me another drink.'

I make mum a Gin and Tonic, but my mind, as I splosh a good measure of pinkish spirit into the glass and chuck in a slice of lemon, is elsewhere. *Pretty much anyone can be a journalist these days.* I am excited, suddenly. My hands are shaking as I add the tonic. When I have finished making mum's drink, I drain my own and then make another, and down half of it on one go. Then I take both drinks and stare out of the window at the first soft fold of Weskdale. *Pretty much anyone can be a journalist these days.* Three wispy clouds are scudding across the sky.

*Pretty much anyone can be a journalist these days*, says mum channelling Ben. Between my mum saying the words and me turning from the window and wandering into the deliciously savoury fug of the kitchen, *The Haxton Review* is born.

*Pretty much anyone can be a journalist these days.* Well, Ben, let's see just how true that is, shall we?

. . .

To be honest, it's not quite as dramatic as that. *The Haxton Review* has a bit of pre-history. The idea of making some OyTube content about the Rush Bearing standoff has been floating around at the back of my mind since my first visit to Haxton. In fact, something like it has been in my thoughts for a lot longer. I have wondered for years if I could write a blog or a Substack about community relations and religion in Coxthorpe (provisionally entitled *The View From Highcliffe Cemetery*), and sometimes, in my fantasy, the idea has turned into a full blown OyTube channel. To that end, I have read and annotated dozens of books of cultural commentary and have spent time daydreaming about producing material that is cynical about multi-culturalism, from a Coxthorpe perspective, while still being sensible and compassionate. I imagine something which applies 'the western tradition' - Aristotle, Aquinas, Locke etc - to questions about Halal school meals and parking around mosques. In my imagination, my stuff is simultaneously down-and-dirty local and properly philosophical (and therefore both more authentic and more intellectually vigorous than anything my brother has ever written). Above all, my imagined content is detached and ironic, and very clever. That has been the plan. But, of course, it's much easier to daydream about being a blogger or a OyTuber than it is actually to get off your backside and write or film something, and I am naturally pretty lazy. So, up to now, my daydreams about a stimulating alternative-media career have remained just that, daydreams.

But the visit to Haxton had got me thinking about it again. After all, the Rush Bearing situation is a news story of national significance about exactly the sort of thing I am interested in, and it's happening right on my doorstep. If I am ever going to start commenting, now would obviously be the time to do it. I wonder, in retrospect, if I didn't make my first trip to Haxton with this in mind. Perhaps I was ambitious as well as bored, that afternoon in The Bumble Bee. Having said that, I'm quite certain that my fundamental laziness, combined with my work and wanking commitments, would still have stopped me doing anything if Ben's piece hadn't annoyed me as much as it did. And, even then, I'm not sure that I would have got started if mum hadn't reminded me about Ben's smug comment about citizen journalism (smug because not everyone can be a journalist, as Ben knows very well).

So, it's mum, quoting Ben, who finally gets *The Haxton Review* off the ground. *Pretty much anyone can be a journalist these days.* It goes without saying that I am grateful to neither of them.

. . .

I settle on *The Haxton Review* as my OyTube name straight after Sunday lunch, as I am walking into town to buy my camera. The name pops into my head uninvited and it immediately appeals to me because of its simplicity and seriousness, and because it is so obviously local. Giving my channel a name makes it feel exciting and real, despite the fact that as yet I have no content, no viewers and no idea how one actually launches oneself on OyTube. I decide to design a proper logo and get some little business cards done when the opportunity presents itself.

The excited feeling deepens when I choose my camera. The smart little bit of tech feels solid and professional when the shop assistant allows me to try it out, and I feel newly committed as I handle it, like Che Guevarra when he finally packs in medicine and picks up a gun. Because I know that my enthusiasm will fade if I don't get going immediately, I buy the camera and then head straight back up the Leeds Road to Haxton.

This time as I walk into The White Horse, I'm not just a curious visitor, I'm an alt-media journalist (which is not something that everyone can be). I am *The Haxton Review.* I am out to right wrongs in my hometown, and fuck off my brother, and acquire a kind of cynical glory along the way.

# 8

'BUT YOU IN'T even from Haxton, love,' says Brenda when I explain what I am up to, 'What do you wanna make a video about us lot for?'

'Because I think what you're doing is fascinating, and it deserves to be heard fairly. I don't agree with everything you're saying, but I think it's important. And people should know about it.'

'But we're doing that ourselves, in't we? With our petition and that?'

'I'm not sure you are though. At least you're not reaching a very significant number of people.' I sip my drink for courage. 'You haven't got a website for instance, have you? But the other side has got a really professional one.'

'Well no, not yet we han't, but we din't think it were gonna be a problem until the council...'

'Look, I don't doubt that you're doing your best, and I'm sure you'll get better at it as you go along. But the fact remains that you have the national media against you, and a very professional organisation on the other side. And your view of things isn't being heard to anywhere near the same degree as the opposition. Basically, you've got a table with a petition on it, and that's outside your own pub.'

There is a muted chorus of grumbles around the table. Brenda is sitting with angry Jason and a middle-aged couple who I don't know. She called me over as soon as I had bought a drink, and I set about explaining my idea straightaway. My brother's article is open on the table in front of us, as it has been since I arrived. So far it is uncommented on.

'So, what would you actually do in these videos?' Jason asks.

'I'd just ask a few of you some questions and film your answers, then chip in a few thoughts of my own. I don't suppose it would be very dramatic and there's no guarantee many people would even see it, but it would be one more way to get your point across. And I do know a few people who know people. And they'd make sure my videos got passed round a bit.'

'But you dun't even live here,' Brenda says again.

'I know I don't. But I live in Coxthorpe, and I care about the place. And that means I have an investment in what you're doing even if I'm not directly involved.'

Jason manages to drink a third of his pint and snort at the same time.

'Coming from Coxthorpe dun't mean owt.' He flicks the corner of *The Globe*. 'The arsehole what wrote this says he's from round here and it din't stop him writing bullshit.'

'I promise I won't be like him.'

'How do we know that you won't?'

'Because *The Globe* is a liberal London paper. It's bound to be unsympathetic to people like you. It can't stand people like you. But look, in a sense anyone can be a journalist these days, and I....'

I stop speaking. The four of them are staring at me. Apart from Jason they don't seem particularly hostile. Just guarded. I drink some more beer and take a deep breath.

'And look, this is going to sound weird, but the other reason I won't be like the guy who wrote the article is because he's my brother and he's awful. Him writing this rubbish is infuriating and it's another reason why I want to tell your story truthfully.'

For a moment no one speaks and then the middle-aged man says slowly:

'What, your brother wrote this?'

'Yeah.'

'He works for *The Globe*?'

'Yeah.'

'It's dogshit.'

'I know it is. I just said it was.'

Jason drinks the remainder of his pint. He sits back in his seat and folds his beefy arms.

'Fucking hell,' he says. 'I should've known.'

'Known what?' I say.

'That you were a prick. A treacherous prick.'

'I'm really not.'

'Yes you fucking are.'

There is a delicate cough. I swing round and there is Roger with a glass of wine in his hand, standing behind my chair. I hadn't heard him approach and I have no idea how long he's been there.

'Is that quite fair, Jason?' he says quietly.

'What do you mean?'

'Well. It's quite a serious thing to accuse someone of treason. Are we certain that Adam deserves that, purely on the basis of his brother's article? The Jewish God might visit the sins of the father upon the son, but it's never felt very fair to me.'

'Have you read it?' Jason growls.

'Of course I have. It's leftist nonsense. It treats Lantyrn Royd folk like idiots, frankly. It's offensive. But we knew *The Globe* would produce something like this eventually, and it seems unreasonable to judge Adam on the basis of his brother's work.'

'He's right, Jay,' says Brenda. 'It in't Adam's fault, his brother's a prick is it?'

Jason frowns but says nothing. After a moment, Roger pats him on the shoulder.

'In a situation like this it's difficult to work out quite who your enemies are, isn't it? Why don't you buy us all some drinks while I have a word with Adam?'

Jason shrugs and slides out from behind the table to go to the bar. Roger smiles at me.

'I wonder if we could have a quick chat? I heard most of what you were talking about. But it might be helpful to clarify a few things.'

'Of course.'

I get up and follow Roger to the corner of the pub next to the fruit machines. I am aware of Brenda's eyes following us, anxiously, as we go. The poor woman flirted with me when I first visited The White Horse, and she let me buy her a drink. She's nice. She likes me. In a different context I would be very happy to chat with her online. But now she is worried that I am on the other side of the curious little fight she has got herself into. She isn't sure whether to trust me anymore. It all depends on Roger, apparently.

Roger turns to face me.

'I don't think you're going to be on Jason's Christmas Card list,' he says quietly.

'I am sure you're right.'

'And it's really your brother who wrote *The Globe* piece?'

'I am afraid it is.'

'Did you help him?'

'A bit. I was flattered he asked for help, to be honest. But I honestly didn't know what he'd write. And that's not why I came up here last week. I came on my own account.'

'Hmm.'

Roger sips his wine and winces. His eyes are bloodshot, and there is the smell of old wine as well as new wine about him. Roger likes his drink, I realise, even when it's horrible.

'And now you want to put something on OyTube about us?'

'Yes.'

'Because you care about the situation here or because you want to irritate your brother?'

'A bit of both.'

He laughs and drinks his wine again.

'Bloody hell, it doesn't get any better. Look, if you have spoken to your brother about what's happening here, you will probably know a bit about me. About my politics.'

'Yes, obviously.'

'And you're appalled of course.'

'Yes.'

'We might talk about that one day.'

'I'm not sure there's very much to talk about.'

'You could put me in a video.'

'I could, I suppose. But I'd like to speak to some locals first.'

Roger raises an eyebrow.

'And I don't count as a local?'

'We both know that you don't. Not really.'

'I suppose you're right. I'm not quite a Coxthorpe man. That's partly why I haven't put anything online myself yet. I'm not local and I'm also rather well known in certain circles for my politics. I'm easy to dismiss.'

'I'm sure that's true.'

'And I'm not sure that most of the genuine locals would create quite the right impression if they were to try and do something on their own.'

'Yes. I can see that.'

'People in our movement are either angry people or else they're fringe people, sensitive people. The canaries in the coal mine.' He sips his wine again. 'But you're a clean skin aren't you? And articulate. And authentically Coxthorpe.'

'Yes I am. I'm all three.'

'Ideal really.'

'So will you let me do some OyTube stuff then?'

'I can't really stop you, can I?'

I make myself meet his eye.

'No, but you can tell everyone not to co-operate with me, which would make things much more difficult. The papers have made it clear that people round here are pretty tight lipped. And it's obvious that you're highly regarded.'

Roger finishes his wine and places the glass on the table next to us with a sharp click.

'You're genuinely sympathetic to us, aren't you? How interesting.'

'I am certainly sympathetic. But that's not the same thing as agreeing with you entirely.'

'Of course it isn't. You're far too respectable to agree with us entirely, certainly too respectable to agree with me. Ok, make your films. Send them to that brother of yours and see if he can get us some exposure. It can't hurt. Let's see how you get on.'

'Thank you.'

'Oh, don't bother thanking me. To be honest I doubt you'll get anywhere. OyTube channels come and go all the time, especially ones connected with my kind of politics. But as you said, we need as much exposure as we can get. Thanks to our friends at Respect Haxton, the council and the police are meeting next week to review the situation. If we can have some sympathetic publicity before that happens, it would certainly be a plus.' Roger stuffs his hands in his pockets and stares at the sticky carpet. 'But look, you should know what you are involving yourself in. To step into my politics, even with only the slightest degree of sympathy, is to place yourself in very choppy waters. If people look at your videos in any numbers you'll be lied to, and lied about, and used by just about everybody.

They will try and buy you and, if that doesn't work, bad things will happen to you. You do understand that don't you?'

'I think so.'

'You don't. No one ever does when they get involved. But you'll learn soon enough. Anyway, how do you propose to start?'

'I want to begin by talking to a few people in here. I thought I could interview Brenda, if she agrees. She makes a good poster girl for The Lantyrn Royd Brits, I think.'

Roger looks up again and laughs.

'I quite agree. And I'm sure that she'll be only too happy to be your star. I think she may have taken a bit of a shine to you, to be honest.'

'I find that hard to believe.'

'Don't be so bloody modest. And I might even be able to get Jason to help out, if you're interested. I have a bit of influence with him, I think, and he might be good as an example of authentically outraged northern male.'

'I'd settle for you persuading him not to kill me.'

'Oh, I certainly can't promise that but perhaps he'll agree to be in a video. Come on, I'll see what I can do.'

. . .

Roger really is the nicest fascist you could ever hope to meet. I follow him back to the table and start setting up my camera.

# 9

*SHAKY-CAM FOOTAGE of the proposed route of the Rush Bearing (Up East Croft from St Peters Church, left onto Gordon Street, left onto Friendly, left onto Lantyrn Royd and back to St Peters). Women in head scarves and Burkas and men in shalwar chemises peer at the camera while the filmmaker travels along Gordon Street. East Croft, Lantyrn Royd and Friendly are markedly quieter. A woman sits on her doorstep and smokes at the top of Friendly, and three drinkers are outside The White Horse. The footage is speeded up. While it runs, The English Civil War by the Clash plays.*

When Johnny comes marching home again hurrah, tala
He's coming by bus or underground hurrah, tala
A woman's eye will shed a tear
To see his face so beaten in fear
It's just around the corner in the English civil war

It was still at the stage of clubs and fists hurrah, tala
When that well-known face got beaten to bits hurrah, tala
Your face was blue in the light of the screen
As we watched the speech of an animal scream
The new party army was marching right over our heads

*The music and the street scene fade. A white screen appears bearing the legend: 'Haxton Review: Somewhere Called England' in black print in a grungy typewriter front. The screen flickers in the style of an old-fashioned newsreel and then fades. It is replaced by a shot of woman in late middle age sitting in a pub. There is the noise of pub chatter in the background.*

NARRATOR: Now then Brenda, thanks for talking to the Haxton Review. Do you mind telling everyone your full name, where you're from and where we are now please?

BRENDA: My name is Brenda Lewthwaite. I'm from Lantyrn Royd. Which is in Haxton, on the east side of Coxthorpe. And we're sitting in The White Horse pub, about ten minutes' walk from my house.

NARRATOR: And you're a regular here?

BRENDA: Yeah. Well yeah, cos it's the only pub round here really. Unless you want to walk halfway into town.

NARRATOR: So, would you say that The White Horse is fairly central to the community in Lantyrn Royd?

BRENDA: Yeah. I suppose so. I dunno if you'd exactly call us a community, like. But there's not much else here is there?

*The camera pans around the pub. There are approximately thirty people drinking and chatting. The pub's patrons are of all ages and there are roughly equal numbers of men and women. Tattoos and Coxthorpe Cobras Rugby League tops are very much in evidence. There is a table of children playing cards in the corner, apparently unattended.*

NARRATOR: I guess not. And forgive me for being a bit blunt, but I notice that everyone here is white.

BRENDA: (Apparently shocked to be asked such a silly question.) Well yeah, obviously. It's all Muslims round here apart from us, in't it? In the rest of Haxton, I mean. And they don't drink do they? Or they in't supposed to.

NARRATOR: But that wouldn't stop them coming here necessarily would it? They could have a coke or something.

BRENDA: Yeah but they don't, do they?

NARRATOR: Apparently not. And where we are Brenda, we're only, what, seven or eight minutes' walk from the large Muslim community in Haxton aren't we?

VOICE OFF: Fucking surrounded.

*There is the sound of laughter. Brenda reaches out of shot and appears to slap someone's leg.*

BRENDA: Behave Jason. Yeah, I suppose we're about eight minutes from them. It depends how quick you walk dun't it?

NARRATOR: Right and do you have any social contact with the Muslim community at all?

BRENDA: Nope. We sometimes go to their shops like, but nothing social, no.

NARRATOR: Why is that?

*Brenda shrugs and glances around, apparently for inspiration.*

BRENDA: I dunno. I mean, where would we go to meet them for starters? There in't really anywhere, is there? We dun't really have much in common with them I suppose.

*Brenda sips her drink.*

BRENDA: Oh God, does that sound awful?

NARRATOR: I don't think it sounds awful. It might seem a bit sad to some people, but not awful. If that's how things are round here, then it's how things are. You're just being honest.

VOICE OFF: It's just what they're like. They in't interested in having owt to do with us. Anyway, I dunno why you're asking all these questions. You're from round here, yourself. You know what they're like.

*The shot zooms out to reveal a man in his mid-forties and a woman in her late fifties sitting on either side of Brenda. Both have a pint of lager on the table in front of them.*

NARRATOR: Thanks Jason. You're right, I do know what it's like to live in Coxthorpe, but not Lantyrn Royd of course. Anyway, do you want to introduce yourself? And you as well Mary?

JASON: I'm Jason. I grew up here and I still live on Friendly. I work in town.

NARRATOR: Thanks Jason. What is it that you do?

JASON: I...I shouldn't really say. There's a social media policy at work. They're funny about this sort of thing.

NARRATOR: Fair enough. I don't want you to get yourself in trouble. And you Mary?

MARY: I'm Mary (Mary giggles). I'm...I'm...Shit, I've forgotten what I were going to say.

BRENDA: Just tell him yer name and where you live, you daft cow.

MARY: Oh yeah (more giggles). Well, I'm Mary and I live at the bottom of Kibden Street.

NARRATOR: Thanks Mary. Now then Jason, do you want to explain what's been happening here recently and why Lantyrn Royd has made the papers?

JASON: Yeah, ok. No bother. What it is, is we've organised a Rush Bearing procession, a sort of tradition thing that we've got going again. It's all arranged, and we've got permission from council and all that. But for no good reason, our neighbours up the road are wanting to ban it. And now all woke people from out of town, the media and that, have turned up to make bother. And they've...

BRENDA: You'd better explain what a Rush Bearing is, Jay. No one's gonna know what it is from outside are they?

JASON: Oh yeah. Right. So the Rush Bearing's like a procession or a May Queen thing. Something like that. It were originally about putting clean rushes on the floor of the church. But really it were just a fun thing for the community, back in the day, in medieval times and Victorian times and whatever. And we just wanted to get it going again but...

MARY: But the Muslim community' has objected to it, cos we've got a knight in it.

BRENDA: Not a real knight.

MARY: Obviously not a real bleeding knight Brenda. Where would we get a real knight from? It's the twent-first bloody century!

BRENDA: Yeah. But I mean it's not even a real pretend knight, with a horse and armour and that. It's just Mick's youngest with a saucepan on his head. That's what I meant.

*Mary collapses into giggles again. Brenda shakes her head and drinks some more of her gin.*

NARRATOR: Ok. Ok. So, what we've got going on is a traditional procession that you're trying to revive in Lantyrn Royd, and one part of that involves a knight. And even though it's not a real knight, or even a real pretend knight, it's this knight that has caused the problem with the Muslim community. Is that correct?

JASON: Yeah. Pretty much. It's pretty much common knowledge mate.

NARRATOR: Yeah, I understand that. I just want to be clear. Can I ask who decided to revive the procession? Who came up with the idea originally?

*Brenda, Jason and Mary look at each other nervously and, apparently, at someone off camera. Brenda and Mary both sip their drinks.*

JASON: I don't see what that's got to do with owt.

NARRATOR: Well, some of the papers have reported that the idea came from people who weren't really local. Who might have come here to cause trouble.

BRENDA: No one on our side's after starting trouble, love. It doesn't really matter whose idea it was to begin with. The thing is, we all got on board with it, din't we? That's the main thing.

NARRATOR: OK. I'll leave that for now. Tell me about the bad knight. Why is it that the Muslim community are objecting to him?

MARY: (giggling) No one has a bad night in Lantyrn Royd, love.

BRENDA: (giggling) That's what you should call your video, Adam: 'Bad Knight in Lantyrn Royd.'

NARRATOR: That's not a bad idea, actually. Maybe I will. But for now, tell me why the Muslim community object.

JASON: It's because the knight's meant to be a crusader, and they say they don't like that because obviously the crusaders invaded Muslim countries back in the day, so it pisses them off.

MARY: But we don't give a shit about all that. We in't trying to say anything about the crusades or history or whatever. We in't trying to offend anyone. We just want to have our parade, like they used to have it.

JASON: And it's debateable whether they really care about the crusader thing anyway.

NARRATOR: What makes you say that?

JASON: Well, for one thing, right, Muslims invaded Europe, din't they, Spain and Vienna and whatnot, so it wan't just us who was doing the invading. But no one ever says owt about that. (Jason appears to glance at the person off camera again, apparently reassured he carries on). Also, round here they just want a way to stop us celebrating anything that's properly English. They want us gone from round here, really. That's their real agenda. They in't bothered about some kid dressed up as a knight. Getting it banned, or getting us re-routed, is just a way to show us who's boss.

NARRATOR: How do you know that they want you gone from round here?

JASON: You don't have to live in Lantyrn Royd long to know it. Believe me.

NARRATOR: Hmm. Ok. Last question. I was interested in what you said about the Muslim community objecting to you celebrating anything properly English, Jason. I know that you've all seen the article in today's *Globe* about the situation here. The journalist is from Coxthorpe and he talks about the white people round here who he grew up with.

JASON: Prick. He said we were like Nazis marching through a Jewish area or summat. Sorry, no offence like.

NARRATOR: None taken, and, for what it's worth, I agree that the Nazi thing is ridiculous. But the interesting bit for me is what he says about Coxthorpe people when they try to do Englishness. (The sound of a newspaper being opened, off camera). Hang on...So, he says that in Coxthorpe Englishness is always performed in opposition to the alien and threatening other who walks among the 'English' on the cobbled streets of the town. And then later he says that Coxthorpe's Englishness is always a fantasy fuelled by fear, a faux crusader's blind sword swipe at an irreducibly complex and threatening world. Just now, you said that the Rush Bearing was about celebrating something properly English, Jason, so I wonder what you've got to say about that.'

JASON: What I've got to say is that I dun't know what the fuck he's talking about. He's one of them that han't got much sensible to say, so he hides it by using long words that no one's gonna understand who han't been to Eton and Oxford and all that. And also...

NARRATOR: (Interrupting) Hang on Jason. I suppose that may be partly true. But to be fair to the journalist, I think he's trying to say that being English doesn't actually mean very much. That white people in Coxthorpe just make up what Englishness means as a way of keeping themselves separate from the immigrant communities here, so that basically Englishness just means not being brown skinned. And I also think he's saying that being English round here is a way of giving yourself a kind of comfort blanket because the world is complicated and frightening, and the communities in Coxthorpe have changed quickly and dramatically, and to announce that you're English somehow gives you a degree of protection from all that, at least in your head.

BRENDA: What, so he's saying that there in't really such a thing as English?

NARRATOR: Yes. More or less.

BRENDA: And that we're just pretending?

NARRATOR: I think so, yes. Sort of. Perhaps imagining would be a better word.

*The picture vanishes and immediately reappears in tight focus on Brenda's face. She swallows the last of her gin.*

BRENDA: Right, well what I've got to say about that is this. I'm proud of being from Lantyrn Royd, ok, just like I'm proud of being from Coxthorpe and from Yorkshire. And there's nothing wrong with being proud of all them things, or of being proud of them all at the same time. They don't...they don't....Shit, what's the word I'm looking for?

NARRATOR: Conflict?

BRENDA: That's right, yeah. They don't conflict. They're like circles, one inside each other. But above all of them, I'm proud of being English. And you can't tell me that being English in't real, just like you can't tell me that being from Lantyrn Royd or Coxthorpe in't real. Mebbe you can't point to Englishness like you can point to that pint and say 'that's what Englishness is', but that dun't mean it in't a real thing.

NARRATOR: So, what is it then?

BRENDA: Listen love, it's how we speak and think, in't it? It's the telly we all watched when we were kids, and the dales, and the beach at Brid, and fish and chips. And...and Duran Duran and the Beatles and Take That. And I suppose it's Shakespeare and all that stuff as well, if that's what you're into. D'you understand?

NARRATOR: I think so. Sort of. But those things aren't fixed are they, Brenda, they change. And other English people would have listed different things.

BRENDA Yeah, course. I in't saying that being English is exactly the same now as it were, say, two hundred years ago, because obviously it in't. It's changed, just like everything changes. But just because something changes dun't mean that it in't real, and that it in't worth looking after. And just cos different people list different things in what being English means, that dun't mean it in't real either.

NARRATOR: Ok. I think I'm with you. Now can you explain what that has to do with the Rush Bearing and the knight?

BRENDA: (Sighing) I can try, love. That bloody knight is summat and nowt, in't it? It's just a kid dressed up. That's literally all it is. If it weren't already part of the Rush Bearing procession, no one here would have thought 'what this thing needs is a knight'. Course, we wouldn't, we'd just have got on with it. But we decided to do this Rush Bearing thing because we wanted to have a party, and because we wanted to hang onto a bit of our history, here in Haxton, and perhaps because we wanted to remind everyone that we were still here. That English people were still here. It wan't anything to do with giving offence or pissing people off or whatever. But then, after we got everything approved, people started making a fuss about it and then the knight started to matter, din't it? It started to matter a lot. Because we shouldn't have to let other people say what we can do or not do when we want to celebrate being English on our own bloody streets. So...so we in't just defending some kid dressed up in a saucepan anymore, we're defending something else. And...And if that journalist...

NARRATOR: Ok, but...

BRENDA: No, hang on a sec, love. One last thing. If that journalist fella wants to say that being proud of being English is a way of giving yourself a bit of comfort, well maybe he's right. But there nothing wrong with that, because there's damn all else round here to comfort you, most of the time. And also, just because being English is comforting, that dun't make Englishness a lie.

*(Brenda sips at her glass and realises that it's empty. She grins and then removes her glasses and wipes her eyes. A soft round of applause is audible in the background.)*

NARRATOR: Last question.

BRENDA: (replacing her glasses) You said that before.

NARRATOR: But this time I mean it. I promise.

BRENDA: Go on then.

NARRATOR: Does this "being English", also mean having a white skin, Brenda?

*Brenda opens her mouth to answer and then closes it again. She swallows twice. Once more, her eyes flicker to someone out of shot.*

VOICE OFF: Perhaps we had better leave it there.

*The tight shot of Brenda's face fades while Mary's voice is heard: 'What did you say Duran Duran for? You hated Duran Duran...' The picture is replaced by a still image of the outside of The White Horse pub. This is replaced, in turn, with a still of St Peter's Church and then of more shots of the immediate area of Lantyrn Royd and Haxton. These turn into shots of Coxthorpe and then of West Yorkshire, and then of England. Within the montage there are pictures of Coxthorpe cloth mills and the town hall, then of the dales, the downs, of farms, and railway lines. The angel of the north appears briefly, as does Hadrian's Wall, the Liver Building in Liverpool, Whitby Abbey, a rave in a field, a picket line outside a colliery, and what appears to be a Cornish fishing village. Big Ben, Horse Guards, the white cliffs also come and go. The impression is of the viewer travelling outwards in concentric circles, away from the drinkers in The White Horse. While the montage plays, the narrator speaks:*

NARRATOR: We will all have our own opinion about how Brenda's summary of English identity - the dales, the beach at Bridlington, fish and chips, Duran Duran, and Shakespeare if that's what you're into - stacks up against other people's efforts to define Englishness. Orwell famously listed gentleness, hypocrisy, thoughtlessness, reverence for law and the hatred of uniforms, along with suet puddings and misty skies as the key characteristics of England. Enoch Powell, in his second most famous speech, spoke about the English language as constitutive of national identity: 'the tongue made for telling the truth in, tuned already to the songs that haunt the hearer like the sadness of spring'. While John Major described Britain (rather than England) as the land of 'warm beer, invincible green suburbs, dog lovers, pools fillers, and old maids bicycling to communion through the morning mist'.

People inevitably have different ideas about what makes a country itself, and those ideas will change over time (not many old maids cycle to communion in Lantyrn Royd, nor are there many green suburbs nearby, invincible or not). But, as Brenda pointed out, just because a thing changes and just because it is complex and multi-faceted, doesn't necessarily make it untrue or unreal.

What began as a local dispute in Lantyrn Royd about a little boy dressed up as a knight has become a test case for ideas and conflicts that feel much too big for the narrow streets on which they are being played out. The locals seem to have become clear, however, once their parade was threatened, that the Rush Bearing was somehow their Alamo, to be defended to the last ditch for the sake of an Englishness which they believe is under grave threat in the dispute. A lot of serious and uncomfortable questions emerge from the fierce little drama that has ensued, but the most pressing is whether the Englishness that the Lantyrn Royd residents feel they are defending is actually a real thing. And by extension, whether any nation is actually a real thing.

*The Globe* journalist seems pretty clear that they are not. Englishness in Coxthorpe, he says, 'is always a fantasy fuelled by fear, a faux crusader's blind sword swipe at an irreducibly complex and threatening world.' Maybe. But if that's the case, then nations as they actually exist are nothing more than administrative units, and places to do business. People from all corners of the world are radically interchangeable and national borders are nothing but a hindrance to the free flow of global humanity. By this account, Englishness is ultimately meaningless, it's just the panicked reaction of poor people and stupid people to a world that they cannot begin to control or understand. Leaving aside for a moment the question of whether the *Globe* journalist would say the same thing about other national groups (The French? The Irish? The Israelis? The Palestinians?) it must be said that it isn't immediately obvious that he is correct.

What if the man from *The Globe* is wrong? What if there is such a thing as England and such a thing Englishness? What if England is a real but complex reality to do with language, landscape, culture and people, and the impact that each has had on the others over the centuries? There would be religion in the mix of Englishness as well, of course, because culture always leans on cult. It would be Christianity mostly, both Protestant and Catholic, but it would be tinged with the paganism and the faerie that have never quite vanished from the darker places of English minds and English land. And there would also be settled modes of living together in the mix of Englishness, enshrined in common law and in what remains of custom and courtesy. This England, if it exists, would be a place that all of us, from the greatest to the least, could call our home. And the English, if they exist, would consent to be governed together here, because they would know that somehow they belong together, that they are tied together by shared responsibilities to the past and to the future, as well as by bonds of affectionate recognition which they do not share in quite the same way with a Frenchman or a Tibetan. This England, if it exists, would be the jealous guardian of local and regional differences within its bounds (Brenda's concentric circles of belonging) against the relentlessly homogenising forces of globalisation and modernity. Finally, this England, if it exists, would be worthy of love. And perhaps that's the most important thing of all, because love is more compelling and more worthwhile than any of the other issues in the Rush Bearing debate. And, although no one speaks about it, there is a funny sort of love present among the drinkers in The White Horse, as well as the more obvious anger and fear. It may be expressed rather perversely but it is there none the less. Love for each other and for their shared home and also for their country.

A lot has been written recently about the rise of populism. Amongst the best of the recent works is National Populism: The Revolt Against Liberal Democracy by Roger Eatwell and Matthew Goodwin. In the first chapter of the book, the authors outline the Four Ds which they believe facilitate the emergence of populist movements. These are: Distrust of politicians and institutions; Destruction of a national group's historic identity, Deprivation as a result of rising inequalities in income and wealth; and De-alignment, the weakening of the bonds between people and traditional political parties. Each of these Ds is evidenced among the Rush Bearers of Lantyrn Royd, so it should be no surprise that they express nationalist and populist sentiments as they struggle to get to grips with the peculiar situation they have found themselves in. But suppose that these four painful Ds, and the tensions they bring, are not just sociological phenomena. Suppose that they are also a route to rediscovering something worthwhile and precious that has almost been lost. Suppose they are a route to rediscovering nation, belonging and home as real and vital parts of human experience. Suppose that Eatwell's and Goodwin's four Ds are the rough road back to somewhere called England.

*The sequence of still shots ends with a picture of a tiny chapel covered in snow, with an old grey slab of a gravestone in front of it. The picture fades and is replaced by a shot of the inside of The White Horse. People are laughing and drinking. Brenda can be seen carrying a tray of drinks back from the bar. The sound of the pub is muted, and the narrator speaks over the top of it.*

NARRATOR: When I asked Brenda if her version of Englishness involved being white, she hesitated and looked to her friends for inspiration and then was unable to answer. The question is important, however, as well as painful and delicate. Perhaps we have to say that while Englishness is not defined by ethnicity and descent, it is not completely unrelated to it either. On the one hand, we must avoid a bleak, biologically determined, racial nationalism, on the other we must avoid the magic dirt theory, that people become English simply by arriving on our soil, with the intention to stay. To say that anyone becomes English by virtue of getting here is to undermine the bonds of mutual commitment and reciprocal belonging that come from shared history and membership of the same descent group. A significant degree of what we might call 'demographic continuity' is important, despite what liberal politicians of left and right may like to believe. And the idea that England is a nation of immigrants is either so obviously true as to be pointless (every nation is a nation of immigrants in the sense that the natives arrived there at some point), or else it is a lie.

The analogy of a family may help. Families are mostly biologically determined. They are the people I share blood with, the people I am given to and who are given to me by nature itself. But we know that people join families through means other than blood. Aunts and uncles get co-opted, children get adopted, people marry in, and these people become full members of the family concerned. It is not always easy to join a family, of course, particularly if the person joining is beyond infancy. There will be work to be done on both sides if things are to go well. But the point is, it is possible for an outsider to join a biological family, and it is good that some people should. Perhaps, by extension, we can say the same thing about the non-white people who live in Haxton and elsewhere in England. We are glad that they are here and they are welcome to join in. They make life a bit more interesting, and they might help to save us from a certain type of staleness. But incorporating people from overseas into Englishness takes effort. Not everything about a mixed society is positive, and it is foolish and dangerous to pretend that it is. Just as we must do the work involved in welcoming new English people, so newcomers (even second and third generation 'newcomers') must do the work involved in joining us. And in Haxton, right now, that work begins by swallowing a bit of historical pride and letting a little boy walk down a shopping street with a saucepan on his head.

*The pub scene vanishes to be replaced with a white screen bearing the legend: 'Haxton Review: Somewhere Called England' in black print in a grungy typewriter front. The screen flickers in the style of an old-fashioned newsreel and then fades. As it does so 'The English Civil War' by the Clash plays softly:*

A woman's eye will shed a tear
To see his face so beaten in fear
It's just around the corner in the English civil war

# 10

THERE ARE THREE rather surprising things about the first ever video released by *The Haxton Review* OyTube channel. The first is how utterly I fail to maintain the ironic, detached tone that I had been aiming for. I never make a conscious decision to come down so firmly on the side of the Lantyrn Royd Rush Bearers. I know that my sympathies are roughly in their direction, of course, and I don't mind that showing through a bit. After all, I had signed their petition. But that was all I had intended. What I ended up with was rather different from the cool commentary I had been aiming for.

I put my partisanship down to the fact that I was among The Lantyrn Royd lot when I actually put the video together and so their situation and perspective are bound to rub off on me. Also, I have my brother on my mind as I write the script, and I think that affects me a bit as well. How could it not, given that he had inspired me to start the channel in the first place? It's the absolute bullet-proof certainty of the modern liberal that gets on my nerves, together with their unshakeable conviction that they represent the uniquely virtuous position in any debate. The liberal's opponents are not just incorrect, they are also, always, utterly morally bankrupt. Add to this, the fact that people like my brother are paid so handsomely for crapping their liberal virtue all over much less well-off people like the Rush Bearers, and it becomes almost impossible to retain any objectivity or distance when one engages with them. Anyway, for whatever reason, my emotions and my words run away with me in the video, and I end up articulating a worldview that I don't know that I possess until I find myself expressing it (and I am still not sure that I do possess it, at least not entirely). The effect is simultaneously disconcerting and liberating. When I last thought seriously about my political convictions, I was still Labour, albeit by the skin of my teeth. That was just before the 2017 election. I have obviously moved quite a lot since then, partly, I suppose, because of the stuff I have been reading. But Labour's drift into emoting, intolerant wokeness also has some responsibility. First of all, the drift baffled me, then it amused me and then, when I finally realised that it was deadly serious, it terrified and angered me in equal measure. I know all the stuff about Labour always having been an uneasy alliance between the traditional working class and middle-class intellectuals, the miners and the Fabians, but it seems to me that the pendulum has swung much too far towards the middle-class intellectuals recently, just as they were turning absolutely bonkers. I didn't vote in 2020. I was grumpy and aloof all through that winter election, a little bit of crumbling cement in the red wall. In 2024, through gritted teeth, I went with Reform.

Having said all that I must admit that when I watch my finished video for the first time, with Jason breathing cigarette smoke down my neck, I feel a twinge of guilt when I think about the decent Asian people I have worked with who would be hurt and furious with what I have said. The stuff about descent groups, and the family analogy feel particularly uncomfortable. I make a conscious effort to bury the guilt as deeply as I can, however. For one thing, Jason would tell me to fuck off if I mention it. For another, it seems to me that things have reached a crisis point in Lantyrn Royd. If you are going to place yourself deliberately into that crisis, as I have done by making the video, you have to be prepared to let your thinking harden and develop rather quickly, and to that end you have to be willing to toughen up, just a little, against certain kinds of superficial sentiment. I am aware of just how awful that sounds. I really am. But what's going on in Lantyrn Royd is complex, and subject to multiple manipulations. What is needed, I am afraid, is a bit of scepticism concerning one's most immediate, and probably learnt, emotional responses.

Another thing: it only occurs to me right at the end of putting the video together that I have spoken exclusively about England, rather than Britain or the UK. I have even mentioned England in the title. I will have to think about Scotland, Wales and Northern Ireland later on, if my channel keeps going.

. . .

The second surprise about the video is Jason. It's not much of an exaggeration, I think, to say that he has loathed me almost from the moment we first spoke outside The White Horse. He dislikes me for being middle class and an outsider, and for questioning, however mildly, the absolute rightness of the Rush Bearers' cause. His loathing deepens when I announce that I want to make a video about the situation in Lantyrn Royd and then deepens immeasurably further when he learns that my brother has written the offending article in *The Globe*. I am a 'treacherous prick' as he tells me to my face, and a 'cunt' as he describes me five minutes later at the bar, when he thinks I can't hear him.

I still haven't fathomed the precise nature of Roger's hold over the locals in The White Horse. But it's impressive, whatever it is. After our chat, he drifts around the pub having a word with a few people while I fiddle with my camera, and then tells me that, if

I still want them, I have my volunteers: Brenda, Mary and - as promised - Jason himself. It's obvious from Jason's contributions to the video that he and I are still not on the best of terms. But what you don't see in the film is that he helps me set the camera up before we start filming and then gives me advice about what shots might work as we go along. It is his idea to start with the tight focus on Brenda, then pull back to interview all three of them, and then to focus on Brenda again for the last bit.

The advice is delivered in an irritated and condescending tone, but it is helpful, nonetheless. That is strange enough considering our relationship, but there is stranger to come. When I have finished filming and am chatting to Brenda over a pint, Jason approaches me again.

'Do you know owt about editing and that, then?'

'What?'

He nods at the camera, now back in its shopping bag on the table.

'Do you know owt about editing films?'

'Nothing at all. I only bought the camera a couple of hours ago.'

He rolls his eyes.

'How are you gonna make yer video then?'

'I dunno. I was going to write some stuff of my own and then just choose a backdrop and bung it all together. I was going to look online if I got stuck.'

'You han't thought this through, have you?'

'Not really, no. It was a bit spur of the moment, to be honest.'

Jason drains his pint.

'Because of your brother's article?'

'Yeah partly.'

'That's why Roger said that we could trust you.'

That comes as a bit of a surprise.

'What, you can trust me because my brother's a reasonably well-known journalist who has written a lot of nonsense about you all?'

'No. Because you hate him. Even if it turns out that you dun't like us very much, you hate yer brother more, Roger says. So we can probably rely on you not to fuck us over.'

'Well that's not quite true, but I'm not going to contradict Roger. I wouldn't dare. Anyway, he persuaded you all to help me, so I owe him that.'

Jason smiles, and for the first time I sense the tiniest bit of warmth in the man.

'He's a clever fella. He's got us to think different about ourselves. He's got us to take a bit of pride.'

'Well, that's got to be worthwhile.'

He smiles again and looks away. He shakes his head and taps his empty pint glass on the table, twice.

'If you want, I can help you out some more with yer video.'

'How come?'

'Because it's what I do?'

'What do you mean? It's what you do for your work?'

'No, course not for work. In me spare time. I'm a OyTuber.'

'I had no idea.'

'Why would you? I only met you last week, and today I called you a prick. We in't exactly friends, are we?'

'No, we're not. Of course we're not. So why do you want to help me?'

He hands his empty glass to a passing barmaid and stares at his trainers.

'Because if yer gonna be making films about us, I dun't want them to look shite. Even if no one's gonna see them. Now, if you want me to help you, you'll have to come with me now. I in't gonna stay up late. I'm on days tomorrow.'

And so I say my goodbyes and gulp my drink and then, without any clear idea of how it has happened, I find myself trotting after Jason as he strolls out of the pub and turns left. He walks quickly down Lantyrn Royd, without speaking, before turning left again onto the cobbled part of Friendly. His house is on the right-hand side, about halfway between Lantyrn Royd and the nameless road which runs parallel to the Mosque.

Following Jason to his home, I feel *inside* Lantyrn Royd for the first time, instead of viewing it from the outside, as a sightseer. The feeling is not entirely comfortable. I realise with new clarity just how cramped the little enclave is. Lantyrn Royd is tiny and isolated, and the blank wall at the end of Friendly dominates the place, sightless and unforgiving. Also, it is only when Jason is fumbling for his key that it occurs to me that I have not yet seen sunshine on the streets of Lantyrn Royd. The area is cold as well as small.

'Come in then,' Jason grunts when he has the door open. I follow him into the sitting room, beyond which I can see the kitchen and, beyond that, the loo. The house is identical to all the others in Lantyrn Royd, and most of the houses in Coxthorpe. Upstairs there will be two bedrooms and out the back there will be a small yard shared with the neighbours. The yard will have bins and cat shit in it.

The sitting room is interesting, however. I was expecting the usual coal-effect electric fire, a huge telly bristling with Sky or gaming stuff, and a couple of tasteless off-the-peg prints on the walls. Instead, there is a wood burning stove, sooty and battered with use, and a scuffed hearth. On either side of the stove there are alcoves which are stuffed with bookshelves, from ceiling to floor. There is a tatty green sofa against the back wall and cheaply framed photos of birds and wildflowers on the walls. Most interesting of all, there is a wooden table pushed against the wall opposite the front door which is stacked with more books and expensive-looking computer equipment, including a high-quality microphone on a boom device which is fixed to the wall. There are two wooden chairs pushed under the table.

'This is where I make me stuff,' Jason grunts. 'Sit down. I'll get a us cup of tea.'

'Thanks. White please. No sugar.'

He disappears into the kitchen while I perch on one of the chairs and study the books stacked on the table. There is one called 'Northern English Mosses' and another called 'Photographing British Flowers'. There is also a stack of journals from an organisation called 'The West Yorkshire Red Kite Society.' I am flicking through these when Jason re-appears with two cups of tea.

'Thanks.'

'I see you found me books then.'

'You can't miss them, can you?' I nod at the shelves. 'Are all those natural history as well?'

'Most of them. The bottom shelf by the window is politics, what I've got into since it all kicked off. But, yeah, the rest's me nature stuff.'

'Is your OyTube thing about politics or natural history?'

'Natural history. I don't know enough about politics yet, do I? I'm the Coxthorpe Dalesman on OyTube.'

'Oh.'

'It's all about the seasons and flora and fauna, and all that.'

'Oh.'

'Don't suppose you've ever heard of me?'

'No. Should I have done?'

Jason shrugs and sips his tea. He still isn't exactly friendly, but he's enjoyed surprising me with his interest in natural history. My surprise is a small rebuke to the snobby assumptions of middle-class people everywhere.

'I've got 25,000 subscribers.'

'Really? I am afraid I had no idea.'

'Why would you, I suppose, if yer not into natural history?'

'I'm afraid that I'm not. Not really.' I sip my tea. 'I mean, I go out walking quite a bit, and I like looking at trees and birds and flowers and stuff, but I can't actually name them. Or very few of them.'

Jason sits down next to me and taps his computer keypad. Under the desk something whirs into life.

'Give us yer camera.'

I do as he asks, and he takes a lead from a tray next to his monitor and plugs it into the camera's back. He plugs the other end of the cable into his computer.

'You should know a bit about natural history, you know. If you come from Coxthorpe, you should.'

'Why's that then?

Still without looking at me, he says:

'Because the town's pretty shitty really, in't it? We pretend it in't, but it is. With all the vape shops and charity shops and nail places and the mosques and all that. But you've only got to look up from anywhere, more or less, and you can see the moors up against the sky. And then you just have to close yer eyes and you can see it all in yer head: the rocks, and the harebells, and the birds and everything.' He sniffs and lights a cigarette. 'And that stuff's better if you know a bit about it, in't it? If you know what some of them things are called. It shows some respect.'

'I hadn't thought of it like that. Not in terms of respect.'

'The moors are the best thing about Coxthorpe. They're ours aren't they? They belong to all of us. We should respect them.'

'I suppose so.'

'We should. And another thing...'

'What's that?'

Jason inhales and taps quickly at his keypad. Brenda's face appears, frozen, on the screen.

'You don't get any Asians up on the moors, neither. Or hardly any.'

'For fuck's sake, Jason.'

'It's true. It in't their land is it? Not really. So, they dun't care for it like we do. They dun't belong to it. They're all dreaming of the mountains in Kashmir, or whatever, not the moors round Coxthorpe.'

'I don't know what Asians dream of Jason. I've never asked them.'

That night, Jason, the Blood-and-Soil Dalesman, helps me to edit my interviews and put together the background shots of The White Horse. I come back the next evening, having written my script, and we record it over the montage of English landmarks. We also film the opening sequence with the flickering title page and the tour of the Rush Bearing Route. The Clash is my idea, but it is Jason who downloads the track and makes it fade in and out as necessary. On the second night, without asking, Jason produces a digital picture of a Highcliffe angel, set against a background of the moors to be the channel's 'cover'. It has 'The Haxton Review' in the moorland sky, in the same newsprint font that he uses for the video title. The picture is simplistic, almost cartoonish, and to begin with I don't know what to make of it. I don't dare tell Jason that (he seems prouder of it than of any of the rest of his work) and, over time, the angel weaves its way into the Haxton Review in my imagination. I grow to love it, in all its shiny oddness. It fits what I want to do perfectly, and I cannot imagine the Haxton Review without it.

At no point over the two nights is Jason more than civil to me. And, apart from our brief conversation about natural history, we discuss nothing but the video. It is fascinating to watch him work. He hunches over the keypad, cursing under his breath, then swings back in his chair, inhales on his cigarette, and peers at his handiwork. When he is doing the angel he grabs books from his shelves and studies pictures of moorland, then lays them face down on the floor, so that there is soon a small lake of upturned books around his chair. Jason is a OyTube craftsman and a perfectionist. Cups of tea go cold at his elbow. Cigarettes burn themselves out in the saucer that serves as his ashtray. And, despite his occasional moaning references to his shifts the next day, he appears to lose all track of time while he is working.

'That's it,' he mutters finally, at twenty past eleven on the second night, when we have watched the finished video through from beginning to end. 'That'll have to do.'

'Thanks Jason.'

'Don't mention it. It's interesting to do summat a bit different.' He leans back in his chair and stretches. The muscles of his forearms ripple beneath the tattoos. 'I'll put it on a stick for you with them pictures, and then you'll have to fuck off. I'm on days again tomorrow. You can upload it yerself.'

'Fair enough.'

'Have you remembered what I said about setting up yer channel?'

'I think so.'

'Good.'

He leans forward and slides a memory stick into his computer.

. . .

The third surprise about the video is that it goes a little bit viral.

# 11

I WALK THE two and a half miles back to my house with my right hand in my trouser pocket, wrapped around the memory stick that Jason has given me. When I get in, I plug the stick into my laptop and watch the video again, and then I create a google account in the name of the Haxton Review. I sign into OyTube using the new account and follow the link to *your channel.* I upload the picture of the Highcliffe angel to be the cover, and then I add a thumbnail shot of the angel's face to serve as its sidebar illustration. After this, I follow the link to *upload new video* and copy *The Haxton Review: Somewhere Called England* from the memory stick. Then I log out of OyTube and log straight back in again. I search for *The Haxton Review* and watch my video yet again, this time direct from OyTube. It looks different now that I know that it is publicly available. I am proud of the work that Jason and I have done, but also nervous. I find myself playing compulsively with my penis in my trouser pocket as I watch, as I used to do at school before an exam or a fight. When it is finished, I log out of OyTube again and then log back in and search for *The Haxton Review.* I am delighted that my video now has one recorded viewer. I send the link to my brother with a covering email:

*Hi Ben,*

*I read (and mostly enjoyed) your piece about Haxton and the Rush Bearing. It inspired me to have a go at a bit of citizen journalism of my own. I have attached the results. I intend to make a few more videos as the mood takes me so I would appreciate any feedback - please be gentle with me! Also, I would be grateful if you could pass the link along to anyone who might be interested.*

*I hope Miriam and the kids are all ok, and that no more saxophones have been abandoned on the tube. Please give them all my love.*

*And do give mum a ring if you get a second. I know that you are incredibly busy, but she really misses you.*

*Cheers,*

*Adam*

Next, I send the video link to Jason with a covering email:

*Hi Jason,*

*I managed to follow your instructions and get my channel set up and the video uploaded. Thanks very much indeed for your help over the last couple of nights. My video would be a lot less interesting and a lot less professional if you had not been holding my hand!*

*I have no idea how many people will watch my stuff (I doubt I am going to be a match for the Coxthorpe Dalesman), but if only a couple of people see it and think about the situation at Haxton in a more balanced way, I will be happy.*

*On that note, I am going to try and make a few more videos, so any help in the future would be very much appreciated. In the meantime, please send the link to any of the Rush Bearing crowd who you think might be interested.*

*Thanks again.*

*Adam*

Finally, I dig out the leaflet I got from the Dawah stall and go to the Respect Haxton website. There is a comments box on the site, and I upload a link to the video with the comment: *Another kind of respect...*

Then I log off OyTube and go on my phone, on the chat sites. I feel curiously exhilarated, as if I deserve a reward. After twenty minutes browsing I meet Tracie, 51, from Minnesota. We instant message on the site for a while and then move to WhatsApp. After half an hour we voice call and then, ten minutes later, we video call. Tracie turns out to be almost emaciated with leathery skin and deep lines in her cheeks. She is lying in what looks like a hospital bed. There is some kind of medical machine on her left and equipment for a drip.

'I am presently in a care facility,' she says, uncomfortably. 'Because of my legs.'

'Fair enough. What's wrong with your legs?'

'My knees are shot. What do you do?'

'I make videos.'

'Cool. Do you enjoy it?'

'Mostly I do, yes.'

'Cool. Wanna jack off for me?'

'I can do.' (I am already pulling my trousers down) 'Are you going to do anything for me?'

'If you want,' says Tracie. 'Let's have a show and tell.'

So, Tracie and I masturbate at each other until we both come and then we chat for a couple of minutes about the weather and Donald Trump before I end the call. I block her straightaway and finally turn my light off just after two.

. . .

The next day is Tuesday, and I am back on nights. I aim to stay in bed until at least half ten to get myself ready for the shift, but I wake up at quarter to eight feeling excited, without immediately knowing why. After a couple of seconds, I remember my video and grab my laptop from the floor next to my bed. I sign into OyTube again and find that my video has had 171 views and has gathered 73 comments. I also have email.

From Ben:

*Hi Adam,*

*Thanks for sending me this. I think that I enjoyed watching it. It is certainly very well put together and it is beyond dispute that you have a way with words. Also, I don't think anyone in either the mainstream media or the alternative media has managed to talk to the Rush Bearers directly yet, so you have managed to get a scoop on your very first outing. Congratulations!*

*I have to say that I don't think that you've been completely fair to what I was trying to say in my piece, although you haven't completely misrepresented me either. We can talk about all that another time. And I will certainly think about people I could send the video to.*

*But look, Adam, do be careful writing about this sort of thing. I have no idea to what extent you actually believe the stuff you say, and to what extent you are just trying to make a bit of a splash. The stuff about white people being like an extended family is somewhat hair-curling! Please may I state the obvious:*

1. *Once you post something online it is there forever. This is as true for you and your critique of the Haxton situation as it is for blokes who send dickpics to strangers. You aren't on facebook or any social media, so maybe that point hasn't quite sunk in yet. But you really should bear it in mind.*
2. *One of the advantages of being a professional, rather than a citizen, journalist is that you have someone to check your work before it's published to make sure you aren't writing anything libellous or dangerous or just plain silly. I am not ashamed to admit that I have been saved from myself countless times by subs. You don't have that safety net Adam (at least I assume you don't) so you will have to edit yourself. If you are going to make more videos (and I hope you do – you clearly have a talent for it) why not have cooling off period before you post something, so that you*

*can come back to it with fresh eyes and see if what you have written or recorded is actually what you want to say?*

*Please take these comments in the spirit in which they are written. I have been in the media game for a long time, so I know some of the pitfalls. I just want you to be careful.*

*And you're right of course, I must ring mum.*

*Cheers,*

*Ben*

And from Jason:

*It looks good. I will send it to everyone. And this is more important than The Dalesman. Of course I will help again. Its all good. Text me.*

I reply straightaway to Jason:

*Cheers Jason. People seem to be watching it, so that's good news. I will text as soon as I get my thoughts together for the next one.*

I don't reply to Ben.

The comments beneath the video are fairly evenly divided between people who broadly agree with my analysis of the situation in Haxton and who think the Rush Bearing procession should proceed on its proposed route with the knight, and people who definitely don't agree with me and who think that the procession should either be scrapped entirely or else be re-routed, or else proceed in penitential mode without the offending crusader.

The people who agree with me range from out-and-out racists, through Daily Mail 'political-correctness-gone-mad' types, to a few commenters who try and follow my argument and develop it. One of the best of these, someone called starky86, suggests that language may serve as better metaphor than family through which to consider English identity. Their comment ends:

*No one says that the English language doesn't exist just because it contains different accents and dialects, or because it has changed over time. The English language is a real linguistic thing despite being diverse and complicated and evolving. In the same way Englishness is a real cultural thing despite being varied and fluid. English people should be proud of both their language and their culture and should defend both. And this way of thinking about being English doesn't have the unfortunate biological connotations of the family image you use. So, it isn't even potentially racist. Just a thought. Thanks Haxton Review for your work.*

The thanks at the end of Starky86's comment are not untypical of the comments I receive from supporters of the video. I am surprised, and rather touched, at how many people thank me for putting the video together and how many encourage me to make more of them. There seems to be a real appetite for the kind of thing I have produced. Having said that, I'm not sure that I completely agree with Starky86's comment. I'm not sure that language is a better controlling metaphor than family through which to consider nationhood. I get it that the family image is clumsy and potentially slightly offensive, but I think that I believe that there is *something* slightly biological about Englishness (although 'biological' isn't quite the right word). In other words, I think that I believe that Englishness is tied to ethnicity and descent to some extent, although not exclusively so. I am still struggling with the question, partly because it is too sensitive for me to think about clearly.

Among the video-approvers there is a substantial group of commenters who are obviously Rush Bearers, or at least Haxton people and locals at The White Horse. These people leave misspelled comments taking the piss out of Brenda, Jason and (particularly) Mary. They are generally not overtly political beyond insisting that the Rush Bearing parade must go ahead. Their loathing for the people who want to stop the Rush Bearing is visceral and often obscene. They wish me and the contributors to the video 'respect' and 'peace'.

The opponents of the Rush Bearing are also fairly varied. The mildest accuse me of short-sightedness and of unwittingly giving publicity to fascists (the poor duped citizens of Haxton are also 'fascist enablers' apparently). The more extreme accuse me of actually being a fascist and advise me to make no more videos 'for my own good'. *No Platform. No Debate.* is a comment that comes up more than once and gathers a few likes. A few comments, apparently from Muslims, ask me how much I understand about Islam and Islamic history, particularly the crusades. These commenters swing between the language of the aggrieved and oppressed believer, and standard lefty riffs about celebrating difference. Their tone moves from passive aggressive to plain aggressive. A typical example: *Muslims should not have to experience humiliation and fear in their own homes. We've already been bombed and invaded; we don't need this shit as well. You aren't helping the situation brother, and you don't get to define what English is. Just leave it alone.*

One opponent of the Rush Bearing surprises me and piques my interest particularly. The commenter, belladonna3, takes me to task over my challenge to 'the *Globe* Journalist' concerning whether they would say that French, Irish, Israeli, or Palestinian national identity is confected and meaningless, in the same way that they seem to believe English identity is. I had meant to suggest that a certain sort of English left-winger will cheerfully deconstruct Englishness but would not dream of doing the same to any other national identity. If one is not prepared to say that there is no such thing as 'Frenchness' or 'Irishness', I was suggesting, then neither should one say that there is no such thing as Englishness.

Belladonna3's point is that Englishness is unique, or very nearly unique, in that it actually is made up. Other countries really, truly exist, his/her argument goes, and therefore have legitimate identities, but England (specifically England, not Britain) is a relatively recent invention imposed onto an archipelago of distinct communities. The real heart of Englishness, in belladonna3's judgement, is not common culture, language, history or whatever, but the dark imperial drive to dominate and conquer. And, as belladonna3 puts it, 'that's not an identity, that's a pathology, plain and simple.'

Finally, there are a number of opponents of the Rush Bearing who explicitly threaten me with violence and two who tell me that they are going to rape my mum while I watch.

There is something absolutely fascinating about reading peoples' responses to my video. The extent to which I have already lost control of the discussion is weirdly compelling, as well as unsettling. That morning, it feels that citizen journalism is a real thing; that the internet really is a force for good, for broadening discussion and education. I feel that I am genuinely engaged in a serious debate about a topic of national importance, even if some of the people I am engaging with are mum-rapists. I answer as many of the comments as I can and then respond to the commenters' responses to my answers so that I soon have three or four conversations on the go at once. I lose track of time completely and forget to eat or wash. I only leave my bedroom to go for a piss or else to dash into my study and grab a book that I need to illustrate a point.

I take a short break at half two to unblock Tracie and message her. She messages me straight back. We go back and forth for a bit and then she sends me a picture of her vagina, and I call her and let her watch as I masturbate. When I'm done, she blows me a kiss and ends the call immediately (which is a refreshing change), and I block her again and go straight back to my video comments. I wipe the semen on the corner of my pillowcase, which is something I haven't done since I was a kid.

At four o'clock I finally realise that I am hungry and so I go downstairs to make a cheese sandwich and a coffee. I have a fag out of the back door and then take the sandwich and the coffee back to bed, without even bothering with a plate. I'm still working at my comments at ten past five when my phone rings. It's Ben.

'Didn't you get my email?' he demands without bothering to say hello.

'Yeah.'

'You didn't answer it.'

'I couldn't think of anything to say.'

'I wasn't trying to be a dick; I just want you to be careful.'

'Yeah I know. You said that.'

'I know how these things can play out. And how long they can last. It's just about being sensible.'

'Yeah. I think you said that too. Thanks for the advice.'

He sighs and then goes on more softly.

'Did you really mean what you said, Adam?'

'About the knight?'

'No. Of course not about the fucking knight. About England being a family of fucking white people.'

'That's not quite what I said.'

'That's how people will hear it.'

'Well, I didn't exactly plan to say it, not quite in those terms, but...but, yes, I meant what I said. In the context of Lantyrn Royd, it makes sense to say it. And if people choose to misinterpret it, that's their problem.'

'It could be my problem as well, actually.'

'What do you mean?'

He sighs again and I hear him sip something. I'm guessing whisky.

'Look I wasn't actually planning to show anyone the video, despite saying that I would. I didn't think it would actually do you any good to have it punted around a national newspaper office.'

'Oh. Ok.'

'But in the end, I showed it to Matt Laurence, to get his take on it. And I only showed it to him because he met you once and liked you.'

'I'm afraid I don't remember him.'

'At our place. Short, fat guy. Alcoholic. You talked about the pope.'

'I'd need more to go on.'

'Blackheads on his nose.'

'Still need more.'

'For fuck's sake. It doesn't matter. The point is Matt showed it to someone who showed it to someone who showed it to someone and eventually, it ended up with Tanya Faulk.'

'Oh.'

'Do you know who she is?'

'Yeah. I think so. She's the media woman, isn't she?'

'Yes she is. Well sort of. Not serious media stuff. She does the Snitcher column. It's shit-stirring really.'

'Oh dear.'

'"Oh dear" doesn't really cover it, Adam. I'm afraid she's going to write about you, in relation to me of course. She wouldn't bother with you if it wasn't for me. But it's too tempting for her to ignore. And she won't be particularly kind.'

'Even though you work for the same paper?'

'Doesn't make a blind bit of difference. In fact, from her point of view, it makes it more fun.' He pauses and sips again. 'Listen, is the video still up?'

'Yes of course it is.'

'It might make things easier...for both of us, if you took it down.'

'I'm not going to do that.'

'It might make everything less embarrassing.'

'I'm not embarrassed, Ben.'

Another sigh. When he speaks again, he is almost whispering.

'Of course you're fucking not. You're producing racist OyTube stuff that directly attacks your brother and you're not the slightest bit fucking embarrassed are you?'

'I am afraid not.'

'You're fucking delighted, aren't you?'

'Are you pissed Ben?'

'Of course I'm fucking pissed. I'm pissed, and I'm pissed off, and I'm worried.'

The phone goes dead.

It's too late, by then, to make any food for my shift so I have a quick wash and do my teeth then drive to work, calling at the newsagents to pick up a pasty, a sandwich, and a packet of crisps on the way. I am not needed on the warehouse floor tonight, so I spend the shift alone in the office, checking delivery notes and invoices while keeping an eye on my phone to check my video's stats. By quarter to midnight, it has gathered 313 views and 217 comments. Just as I am putting my phone down, Ben texts.

*Here's the link to the Snitcher piece on the website. It will be in the paper tomorrow. Congratulations.*

I follow the link to the *Globe's* website. There is picture of Tanya Falk at the top looking knowing, and next to it the headline: *The Snitcher: Trouble at Mill.* The article (if you can even call it that) is quite short:

*My goodness me, but those Coxthorpe boys love a good scrap. I can only put it down to something in the water up there - coal dust and whippet piss, I imagine, but what do I know? As pretty much everyone is now aware, in the greatest northern WTF moment since the Dominic Cooper character suggested that his teacher suck his cock in The History Boys, a number of Coxthorpe perma-twats have arranged to parade a crusader in full Muslim-skewering rig through the streets of Haxton, the town's Islamic area. Inevitably, rough stuff has ensued but, as far as the Snitcher is aware, the crusading locals have so far stuck to their guns, or to their broadswords. Accents (amongst other things) are a bit thick in Coxthorpe, and the Snitcher suspects that the issue may be at root one of translation. The expression 'Have you considered that your crusader knight with his raiment drenched in the blood of innocent*

*Muslims and Jews might be a little insensitive' no doubt lands on Coxthorpe ears as 'Fuck you gammon bastards, what you need is a jolly good replacing and a burka for your mum.' If only we knew someone who could affect the necessary work of interpretation between English and Coxthorpe-speak, to calm the situation down.*

*Actually, the Snitcher does know someone, or rather two people. Step forward the brothers Monkton. Ben Monkton is one of The Globe's very own and a proud son of Coxthorpe, who is much exercised by the weird crap his neighbours are getting up to with their medieval costumery and their racism. Did I just write 'neighbours'? Please excuse the slip of the laptop. Obviously Ben doesn't live in Coxthorpe anymore (they don't do organic oak-smoked pesto in Aldi up there – can you imagine?) but that hasn't stopped him losing his shit over events and penning a lengthy piece in last Sunday's paper about what's going on. Ben, in case you were wondering, is anti-knight but also pro the people who are pro the knight. It's a tricky line to walk but our Ben walks it with style (and, it must be said, a few killer neologisms).*

*Thrillingly, at least as far as this fangirl is concerned, Ben's piece has not gone unanswered. There is a second Monkton on the scene, one Adam Monkton who we are given to understand is the younger brother of the crusading (but in a good way) Ben. Adam is the hip alt-media answer to big brother's boring mainstream. He has a OyTube channel, winningly entitled The Haxton Review. It's early days for little Adam, so far he only has one video posted in which he spends most of his time reviewing not Haxton, but big brother's article. And – be still my beating heart - Adam turns out to be pro-knight and consequently anti-Ben.*

*The pacifying work of translation is, one assumes, on hold as new media dukes it out with old and patriot faces off with liberal. It's brother against brother, dear reader. How dreadful (and, let's face it, also how cool) is that. The mason-dixie line runs right between the organic crumpets and the granola on the Monkton breakfast table. But then, as we know, those Coxthorpe boys do love a good scrap.*

I read the piece through a couple of times. I try a bit to feel offended, but I can't manage it. I am much too thrilled to see my name in the website article and to know that it will be in the real newspaper tomorrow. I text Ben:

*Thanks for the link. It doesn't seem too bad really. She takes the piss slightly, but it could have been a lot worse.*

Ben answers immediately.

*She hasn't mentioned much about what you actually said because she doesn't want to humiliate you. I was the target.*

I reply.

*I am sorry that it's caused you bother. I still don't think it's too bad.*

Ben answers:

*You don't understand, Adam.*

I leave it there and try to get on with some bits and pieces of work. Every twenty minutes I stop to re-read the article and re-watch my video, and all the time I keep an eye on my number of views. The Snitcher obviously has a significant following. By the time I go home at seven o'clock there are 957 views. By the time I wake up just after midday, there are 14, 622.

# 12

THE TROUBLE WITH running a OyTube channel, I realise gradually over the following days, is that you have to keep making videos. And the trouble with that is that it's not always obvious what to make them about. It honestly hadn't occurred to me that this might be a problem, but it is. I said a lot of what I wanted to say about the Rush Bearing in my first outing and I am stumped about what to say next. I still have a lot of thoughts about what's going on at Haxton, of course, but I can't for the life of me think of a theme for the next video. I can't think of a 'hook'. I could go back to The White Horse and do some more interviewing, but it feels defeatist and boring to repeat myself. I could also do a simple voice-over commentary with some local pictures, but that also feels boring and a bit of a cop out. A number of people leave comments beneath my first video suggesting that I speak to some Muslims from Respect Haxton in my next one, to give my channel some balance, but I rule this out as well. For one thing, I suspect I have burnt my boats with Respect Haxton by coming down so firmly on the side of the Rush Bearers. For another, I realise that I am completely uninterested in what local Muslims and leftwingers might have to say. It is the white people of Lantyrn Royd who fascinate me. As far as possible, they are the ones I want to keep my focus on.

On Tuesday night a Muslim taxi driver gets beaten up in the town centre and his attackers apparently reference the Rush Bearing situation as they put the boot in. On Wednesday two white lads get battered with baseball bats on the Leeds Road, between Haxton and the town centre. One of them loses an eye and again the Rush Bearing gets mentioned. I consider doing a video about rising tensions in Coxthorpe, but in the end decide against it. Things are certainly getting more fraught, but once you've said that, what do you say next? There's no point in simply reporting local news on my channel. That would just make me an amateur version of the Coxthorpe Argus, which I definitely don't want to be. I want to do something more considered.

On Thursday, the Respect Haxton website announces that there is going to be a 'day of action and solidarity' including a march from Coxthorpe town centre to Haxton, a week on Saturday. That will certainly be worth filming and commenting on, but it is over a week away and I need some material now.

. . .

In the end the subject matter for my next video finds me. I work Tuesday, Wednesday and Thursday nights and set the alarm for eleven on Friday morning, my plan being to head up to Haxton after lunch and have a sniff around to see if I come across some inspiration. I have not long been up on Friday, and I am still in the yard smoking my morning fag when my phone rings.

'Hello.'

'Hi,' says a friendly woman's voice. 'Is that Adam Monkton?'

'Yes it is.'

'The gentleman behind the Haxton Review on OyTube?'

I had not been expecting that.

'Who is this please? Where did you get my number from?'

'Oh gosh, sorry Mr Monkton. I didn't mean to startle you. My name is Lavinia Shaw. I am the priest in charge at St Peter's Haxton. And I'm afraid that I can't remember who it was who gave me your number. Someone in The White Horse. I hope I haven't done the wrong thing by tracking you down.'

'No. I mean, you probably haven't. I suppose it depends on what you want.'

The Rev Lavinia Shaw giggles while I sip my beer.

'Yes I suppose it does. Well, it's pretty simple. I would like to have a chat.'

'What do you want to chat about?'

Another giggle.

'Gosh, where to start? Look, roughly speaking, the situation is this. The Churches in Haxton have been struggling to come up with a response to the Rush Bearing business from the beginning, and up to now we've had sod all luck.'

'When you say the Churches, do you mean...'

'All of us in the area. Baptists, Catholics, Methodists, Quakers. Although the lion's share has fallen on St Peters, because of where we are. We're right in the heart of things, on East Croft, as you know. And we're the church of the rushes, so that makes us involved whether we like it or not.' She coughs. 'Also, interfaith work is sort of my specialism. It's why I ended up in Coxthorpe in the first place.'

'Right.'

'You don't sound very enthusiastic.'

'To be honest, I'm still trying to work out why you've called me.'

'Ok. So, we've finally managed to sort out a meeting here at St Peters which will bring together people from both sides, with some local church folk who want to try and mediate.'

'Bloody hell, how did you manage that?'

'With great difficulty. By talking to people over and over again. By doing our best to be reassuring. By being honest. I know some people in the Muslim community. And so does my colleague Fr Shaw at The Immaculate Conception. And I also know a fair few of the Rush Bearing lot, of course. And...and...well, I think we are trusted to be honest actors.'

(In passing: I hate the way that the Rev Lavinia Shaw refers to Haxton's Catholic priest as her colleague. As if the priesthood is just another job, like working in a warehouse. As if she is actually a priest at all. For a moment I am tempted to tell her to go and fuck herself, but I don't. I am much too polite and much too excited.)

'I suppose you would be.'

'Yes, but it's been a dreadful struggle to get people together. We've been trying to organise a meeting for weeks and we only got the final confirmations half an hour ago. The distrust here is deep, as you know. And it's getting deeper.'

'And when is this meeting going to be?'

'This evening at seven o'clock. At the church hall.'

'Shit. That's sudden.'

'Yes it is. But it's only two weeks until the procession is meant to be taking place, so time isn't on our side. Also, the council and the police were supposed to be talking about the situation this week, so if there's any sort of announcement, that's probably going to make things even worse.'

'I guess so, if something got decided.'

'Yes. Although, I've no idea whether they even met. There's been nothing announced.'

'Yeah, I haven't heard anything.'

'I know, it is rather odd. Anyway, there's also this counter-demo next Saturday which has the potential to cause all sorts of problems. And I'm sure you've seen, people are already getting hurt.'

'Yes, I've seen the paper.'

'It's dreadful. It's absolutely dreadful. So, the sooner we can get folk talking, the better.'

'I can't disagree with any of that. But I'm still not sure what this has to do with me.'

She giggles yet again. Rev Lavinia has quite a posh giggle.

'Sorry, I'm waffling, aren't I? Look, there isn't going to be any media at the meeting this evening. We're hoping that people might be able to talk more honestly and listen more carefully if they're not being watched.'

'I suppose that makes sense. Although I imagine that you'll have The Argus and the local telly outside.'

'I'm sure we will and that's fine. Just not in the actual meeting. But I was wondering if you wanted to come and have a word with me beforehand, for your channel.'

I have been rolling another cigarette while we have been talking. Now, as I light it, I notice that my hands are shaking, ever so slightly.

'I would love to talk to you. But why would you want to speak to me? Did you see my video?'

'Yes. Yes, I did.' She pauses and then goes on in a more considered, vicar kind of voice. 'Look, it would be fair to say that you and I are not quite on the same page about the Rush Bearing. But it was apparent from your video that you were at least trying to deal with things fairly and thoughtfully.'

'Thanks.'

'Don't mention it.' She pauses for a moment and then says quietly, 'I have to say that I couldn't stomach your image about the white English functioning as a family. I just couldn't. But...'

'You're not the first person to say that,' I say quickly. 'I was just trying to say that the English are a real thing. And, therefore, by extension, a thing that others could join. That's all. I probably didn't make it as clear as I could have done.'

'I think you probably didn't. To be honest, I had the feeling that perhaps you had ended up saying something you didn't quite mean. But I don't suppose that's really any of my business. Now

I wouldn't countenance speaking publicly to someone like Roger Wrigglesworth because he's a genuine fascist and a trouble causer, and I don't trust him as far as I can throw him. But I don't think you're quite the same as him.'

'I certainly don't have the same view of things as Roger. I don't know him particularly well to be fair, but I know him well enough to know that.'

'Thank goodness for that. But you have over 10,000 subscribers to your OyTube channel after making only one video, and I assume that will include a lot of Lantyrn Royd folk and their supporters.'

'I guess so.'

'I'm sure it will. So, talking to you would be a good way of getting in touch with people who won't be at the meeting tonight. It's a bit risky, I suppose, from my point of view, but it will be worth it if I manage to reassure some of our folk.'

'OK. But if I do make a video about you, you appreciate that it will contain more than a straight interview. I will add my own commentary.'

'Yes, I understand that. I told you; I watched your first one. But I still trust you to be fair.'

I stub my cigarette out and toss it in the bin and then drain the last of my beer.

'I would be delighted to talk to you, Lavinia. What time were you thinking about?'

'Super. Absolutely super. How about half five, before the meeting? And would it be ok for you to come to the vicarage?'

'That would be great. I've got a friend who helps with recording and editing and so on. He's from Lantyrn Royd. Is it alright if he comes as well?'

'Of course. No problem at all. See you at five thirty.'

'Yes, see you then.'

. . .

As soon as I have finished speaking to Rev Lavinia, I text Jason:

*Hi Jason, it's Adam. Are you around this evening? I have an idea for my next video.*

He replies a couple of minutes later:

*Yeah not working today or tomorrow so all good for tonight. Is it gonna be about the meeting at the church?*

I answer:

*Sort of (when did you hear about that by the way?) I am going to interview the vicar beforehand in the vicarage. Can you get there for half five?*

He replies:

*Brenda text about meeting. No problem to meet you. But not been funny, that vicar isnt exactly one of us. Does Roger know your seeing her?*

I answer:

*The fact that she isn't quite one of you is what will make it interesting. And no, Roger doesn't know. It's none of his business. See you at half five.*

He replies:

*K*

And that's that.

When I have finished texting Jason, I have another WhatsApp session with Tracie, who seems to be pretty much permanently available, and then check the views and comments from my video. There are now 22,000 of the former and 800 of the latter, and I have completely lost control of the conversation threads. I watch the video yet again (I know it off by heart by now) and for the first time it occurs to me that, despite the smart editing, there is nothing particularly electrifying about the content. I think that I make some reasonable points but, with the benefit of distance, it is clear that I haven't said anything remarkable. So why has it proved so popular? I think for four reasons:

1. The main thing is obviously the exposure it received in Tanya Falk's Snitcher column. I would probably only have received a couple of hundred views without it. People talk about the mainstream media and the alternative media as if they are completely separate and siloed. But of course, they aren't. For one thing there is no clear dividing line between the two: the biggest alternative media outlets are pretty mainstream in their style and approach, and most mainstream media organisations have an alt-media-type thing going on somewhere. Also, loads of alt media stuff is basically just commentary on mainstream sources and, conversely, if the mainstream media pick up on an alt media piece, it inevitably takes off. The relationship between the two is complex and I haven't quite worked it out, but I have certainly benefited from it thanks to Tanya Faulk.
2. The fact that I spoke to real Rush Bearers in The White Horse, their centre of operations. As Ben said, this was a scoop at the time and as far as I am aware, it still is. The White Horse Royd lot are tight lipped with journalists. I got lucky. Mostly, I think, because I turned up at the right moment and because Brenda and Roger happen to like me.
3. The fact that I sent the link to both Respect Haxton and to The Lantyrn Royd community, via Jason. This has led to people on opposite sides of the Rush Bearing debate rowing like mad in the comments, and as far as I can tell this has led in turn to the link being forwarded all over the place.
4. The basic format of the video: interview followed by voice over commentary seems to work quite well. As I said, it's not electrifying (although Brenda's description of Englishness still feels pretty moving) but it manages to be rooted in the actual situation in Lantyrn Royd while reaching out to broader themes.

It is neither too narrow nor too general and vague. And it's not obviously nasty, either.

Whatever the cause of the video's popularity, I have been incredibly fortunate that it has had the reception that it has, and I am determined not to squander my good start. With that in mind, I spend the afternoon planning my questions for Rev Lavinia.

. . .

I decide to walk, rather than drive, to Lantyrn Royd for the interview. I generally avoid driving through town if I can help it and this evening I want to get a sense of the mood in Haxton. As I stroll through the town centre, I reflect on my emotional response to the Rev Lavinia Shaw. I was immensely, disproportionately angry when she referred to the Catholic priest as her colleague, and, if I am honest, I know why. The simple fact is that I can't stand women clergy, and that includes the Rev Lavinia, even though she seems like a decent person, and she is doing me a big favour in granting me an interview. The feeling is grotty and uncomfortable, so I choose not to think about it very much, although I remember clearly when I first became aware of it. There was a long weekend four years ago when I was walking in Norfolk. I was doing about fifteen miles each day, staying in nice pubs and catching up on my reading during the long boozy evenings. On the Sunday afternoon I found myself in a village with one of those East Anglian brick and flint churches, in time for evening communion. (It was south of Cromer somewhere. I can't remember the name of the village, although I can still picture it perfectly). I wouldn't normally consider attending a CofE service, but it was the end of a lovely spring day, the hedgerows were white with blossom, the sky was wide and blue and glorious, and I was feeling sentimental and content and a bit pissed on the excellent local beer. So, I slipped into the church and sat at the back under a war memorial commemorating the sons of the parish lost to the Boar War. I remember breathing the ancient stony smell and feeling the calm, establishment silence sink into my bones while I waited with six other people for the service to begin. And then, when it finally started, there was a woman vicar leading the bloody thing. I hadn't anticipated that at all. It just hadn't occurred to me as a possibility, probably because I was half drunk and because everything else had felt so traditional and lovely. It was impossible to leave without it being obvious and awkward, so I sat through the service with clenched teeth and a feeling like the nausea that comes with a whisky hangover churning in my stomach. The woman was, I suppose, in her early forties. She was slim and dark and not unattractive. And she was bright. She quoted Augustine in Latin in her sermon, as well as mentioning the importance of caring for the poor and outcast. She wasn't in the least pompous or self-aggrandising. In short, she seemed to be a decent vicar. But, even so, I couldn't bear to watch as she consecrated the elements and distributed communion. And when the service was over, I practically ran out of the church to avoid shaking her hand. I had never seen a woman cleric in action before and I still struggle to describe the perfect wrongness of it: it was misplaced and utterly charmless, like watching a squid play football or a sheep drive a bus. When I had escaped, I went straight back to the village pub where I was staying and got more drunk on that delicious beer. And in my room later, I pulled my rosary out of my rucksack and contemplated saying a decade or two. If I was so supernaturally revolted by the spectacle of a woman on the altar, I reasoned, there must be some truth in the Church's teaching that women could never be ordained. And if there was truth in *that* teaching, then, logically, there must be truth in all the rest of it as well. It was a strange sort of twitch upon the thread, half pissed and raging with barely articulate misogyny, but it was a twitch nonetheless and everyone knows that the Holy Ghost works in mysterious ways.

I didn't say the rosary that night. I was too drunk, and, in the end, I just couldn't be bothered. But ever since then I have known that I hate women clergy. Not for considered theological reasons (although I have those as well), but emotionally and viscerally.

And now I am off to interview Rev Lavinia Shaw - lady vicar of St Peter's Haxton and a specialist in interfaith work - for The Haxton Review OyTube Channel. It should be fascinating.

. . .

On my way up to Haxton, I walk past the kebab place where the two white lads were beaten up on Wednesday. There are a few bunches of flowers tied to the lamppost outside and a white woman in her early twenties is taking a selfie next to the makeshift memorial.

'Neither of them have died, have they?' I ask when she has finished taking her picture. She looks at me suspiciously.

'Not that I know of.'

'Oh, I see. I was just wondering because of the flowers.'

'They still got beat up, din't they? One of them lost an eye.'

'Yes I know they did. Did you know them?'

'No. Why?'

'The pictures.'

She shrugs.

'Just for Insta.'

'I see.'

The woman peers at her phone for a minute and then takes another couple of selfies. While she does so, two Asian lads stroll out of the takeaway, light cigarettes, and stare at her.

'What the fuck are you looking at?' the woman asks when she notices them.

'Fuck knows,' one of the Asian lads answers. They both laugh. The woman puts her phone in her pocket and edges towards me, away from the Asians.

'You should go home,' says the other lad quietly, 'before you get hurt too.'

'None of your business where I go,' the woman says. And then she grabs my arm and leads me down the street towards Haxton. The Asian lads jeer.

'Dun't look back,' the woman mumbles as we pick up speed. 'I just want you until the corner, then I'll be ok.' She glances at me. 'Where are you off to anyway?'

'I'm going to Lantyrn Royd.'

'All the way down there. Just walking?'

'Yeah.'

'Be careful.'

'Do you really think it's dangerous, at a quarter to five?'

We walk on in silence for another minute and then stop at the corner. The woman pulls out her phone again and checks her pictures.

'Yeah. It's dangerous at the moment,' she says without looking up.

'Because of the Rush Bearing?'

'The procession thing. Yeah, cos of that.'

'What do you think about all that?'

'I dun't think the Muslims have got any right to tell us what to do.' She puts her phone away and smiles. 'Thanks for walking with me. I'll be fine from here. It's white at the end of the street, so they won't follow me down here.'

'Are you involved in it?'

'In what?'

'In the Rush Bearing?'

'No. Why do you think that?'

'Because you said 'us'. That Asians didn't have any right to tell us what to do.'

She shrugs.

'I meant us. White people. English people. Us.'

'Oh, I see.'

The woman smiles again and walks off slowly down the street. I turn to go and then turn back and call after her:

'What do you think is going to happen with the procession and everything?'

She turns round and grins, then flicks her hair out of her eyes:

'It' obvious int'it. There's gonna be a big fuckin fight.'

. . .

I walk on up the Leeds Road and into Haxton. The pavements are just as busy as they were when I first walked up here, but the atmosphere has changed. People glance at me suspiciously as I walk past, and mothers half pull their kids out of my way. A young man spits on the ground a few feet in front of me and another walks deliberately shoulder-to-shoulder with his friend, so that I have to dip into the gutter to pass them. I keep my eyes on the pavement, and I am glad when I turn left onto East Croft.

Jason is waiting outside St Peter's gate. He is smoking and he has a Tesco bag at his feet.

'Have you just walked up through Haxton?' he demands as I approach.

'Yes. It's only a couple of miles from my house. I could do with the exercise.'

'Don't be a dick. It's fuckin dangerous.'

'Do you really think so? It's half five for goodness' sake. All the trouble's been after dark.'

Jason chucks his cigarette away and steps on it.

'Yeah so far. But that'll change. They've been driving down Lantyrn Royd and chucking things about.'

'Who have?'

'Asians.'

'What have they been throwing about?'

'Couple of fireworks and a bottle of piss so far, but that'll change too.'

'Really? Has anyone told the police?'

'Yeah course.'

'What did they do?'

'Fuck all.' Jason jerks his head at the church. 'When did you get in touch with the vicar then?'

'I didn't. she got in touch with me. This morning.'

'Are you just gonna interview her?'

'Yeah, to begin with. Then add a few of my own ideas later on. Like last time.'

'Right.'

'Jason?'

'What?'

'I don't really know how to put this.'

'Put it anyway you like.'

'Ok. Here goes. What did Roger say about us meeting the vicar, when you told him?'

Jason looks down and scratches his head. Then he stares straight at me and grins. He has the grace to look slightly embarrassed.

'He said it couldn't hurt. He reckoned you might be a good match for a lefty vicar.'

'Well, that's flattering I suppose. He asked you to help me with all this, didn't he? Right from the start? To keep an eye on me?'

He looks down again, then looks up and shrugs.

'Yeah. Yeah. Pretty much.'

'Bloody hell Jason, I honestly thought you were doing me a favour.'

'I was. I am.'

'And you do know that Roger is basically a fascist, don't you? A real fascist I mean. Not just a fascist in the sense that it is used as a term of abuse. Whatever good you may think he's doing here, he's doing it because of his fascism. That's what drives him.'

'I dunno if he'd say he were actually a fascist.'

'Well, he is. And I'm not. You know that too, don't you?'

'Yeah I know that. Roger says you're probably just an old-fashioned Tory, although you probably dun't want to admit it to yerself.'

'Is that what he says?'

'Yeah and yer what he calls a cucked patriot, an all. He's good at sussing out peoples' politics, is Roger.'

'What on earth is a cucked patriot?'

Jason shrugs and grins again.

'I in't sure really. It's like you want to look after your country, but yer too scared to say that you dun't want any more Asians to come over here. Basically, it means you han't got any bollocks.'

'Fucking hell. Does he talk about me a lot?'

'No. Dun't flatter yerself. You in't that important.'

'I'm important enough for Roger to assign me my own personal spy, apparently.'

'Fuck off, I in't a spy.'

'Well, you're something pretty close. But listen, if I'm an old-fashioned Tory, I'm also old-fashioned Labour, so perhaps Roger's not quite as sharp as you think. I don't know if there's a name for people like me really.'

'I can think of a couple.'

'I bet you can, 007. Anyway, at least we're being honest now. You can tell Roger whatever you like, by the way. You always could, I've got no secrets and...and look, I'm still grateful for the help no matter what your agenda might have been. I hope...well, I hope we can keep going together.'

'Thanks. I want to keep doing it.'

Awkwardly, I stretch out my hand. Jason takes it and we shake. His hand feels like warm wood wrapped in sandpaper.

'Good. Thank you. What's in the bag, by the way?'

'A light and a mic.'

'A what?'

'A light and a microphone for the video. I wan't happy with the sound or the lighting last time.'

'Seemed alright to me.'

'That's cos you dun't know what yer doing.'

'Fair enough. You're the expert. Now listen, do you need to check in with Roger or can we make a start.'

'Fuck off.'

I smile at Jason and he smiles back.

'Just thought I'd ask. Let's get going then.'

We skirt the church on an overgrown footpath of cracked concrete, then walk across the small graveyard to the vicarage. It is made of the same black stone as the church and is about the same age. There is an ancient brass bell mounted next to the front door. I press it while Jason shuffles about and glances nervously around the graveyard as if he is expecting an army of Seljuk Turks to charge over the church wall. After a minute the door opens. A plump middle-aged woman with short grey hair and specs stands in the doorway. She is in full clericals and is holding a mug of tea.

'Ah,' she says. 'Hello. I assume that you are Adam?'

'Yes, and you're Reverend Lavinia?'

'I am. Thanks so much for coming. And this is your colleague?'

'Yes, this is Jason.'

'Right. Well come in both of you. I'm guessing neither of you would say no to a cup of tea before we get started?'

We all shake hands and then the Rev Lavinia leads us down the hall and into a large kitchen. There is the smell of real coffee and freshly baked bread, the latter coming from two loafs in baking tins on top of a substantial Aga. A couple of postcards of icons are stuck to the front of the fridge and a few of bits of abstract art decorate the walls. *The Globe* and *The Church Times* are laid out on a wooden table in the centre of the room next to a copy of the Mayor of Casterbridge. It is odd to see such a middle class, educated room in Lantyrn Royd, and for a moment I experience a mild sense of dislocation. Also, I realise, without quite knowing how, that Lavinia lives here by herself and that means that she is probably lonely. She doesn't need an Aga that big, and for a moment the sight of it is dreadfully sad. Without intending it, I feel a pang of concern for Rev Lavinia, even if she is a woman priest.

When Jason and I have cups of tea and Lavinia has a mug of coffee, she leads us back out of the kitchen and along a corridor to her study. It overlooks a large and rather unkempt garden which runs back from the house for about twenty meters before turning right towards Gordon Street. There is a desk and two easy chairs in the room and the whole of one wall is lined with books.

'I thought we could do it in here,' Lavinia says. 'I suppose it's a bit of a cliché, but I thought about having the books as a backdrop.'

'Will this work?' I ask Jason. He peers around for a moment and then pulls a light and microphone and a small tripod out of his bag and places them on the desk.

'Should be fine. If you could just shift that chair to the left so that it's out of the shadow, please Reverend.'

Lavinia shuffles the chair over and sits down. I pull out my camera and give it to Jason who fiddles with it, running a cable from it to the microphone. After a couple of minutes, he puts the camera down and then mounts the light on the tripod and switches it on. Bright light streams across the room. Jason adjusts the beam and then picks up the camera again and peers through it. He nods at me.

'We're good.'

Rev Lavinia has been watching Jason's arrangements silently, peering at him over the top of her specs and occasionally sipping her coffee. Something that I cannot quite describe about the quality of her attention indicates that she is an extremely intelligent woman. And for a moment that unnerves me. Now she glances from Jason to me and back again, and smiles.

'Right. Well, I'm ready if you are,' she says.

'Of course. Great. Thanks Lavinia. What should I call you on the film by the way? Lavinia or Reverend Lavinia? Or something else?'

'Lavinia's fine.'

'Ok. And can I just ask you again, why...why is it that you want to do this? You must know that I am not going to be entirely sympathetic.'

'No, you won't be. But you'll be reasonable and that's all I ask.' She puts her coffee mug on the floor, takes her glasses off and wipes them carefully with a hanky. She holds them to the light and squints at them before replacing them on her nose. Then she picks up her coffee again and sips it. 'I think, Adam...may I call you Adam by the way?'

'Yes of course.'

'Right. Well, Adam, I think without quite intending it, you've very suddenly become a sort of conduit here in Lantyrn Royd. A conduit for peoples' concerns and ideas. And that makes you valuable, do you see?'

'I suppose so.'

She winks.

'Much more valuable than that boring old *Globe* writer you talked about in your video.'

'You know he's my brother.'

'Of course I do. That's why I said it. Everyone in Lantyrn Royd does.'

And suddenly, I realise that I like Rev Lavinia. I realise that I like her very much indeed. And I also realise that I want to talk to her normally, about things that have nothing to do with the Rush Bearing.

'Well don't let him hear you say that I am more valuable than him.'

'Sensitive sort of chap, is he?'

'Very. And you're right by the way, it has all been very sudden.'

'I can imagine. Well anyway, that's why I wanted a chat. You're a useful conduit, Adam, a channel to people in the parish and beyond. That's useful for me. And if our conversation helps with what you're trying to do, so much the better. We both win, don't we, even if we have rather different perspectives?'

'I suppose so. Yes.'

'Great.'

I stare at Lavinia for a moment and then, to my horror, I hear myself say:

'And do you think God wants you to talk to me?'

(I honestly have no idea why I say it. There is a large old-school crucifix next to the study door which is directly in my line of sight. Perhaps that is something to do with it. But I don't think that explains it completely. Anyway, I say it and I can't take the words back.)

Lavinia looks down at her lap and then looks up slowly.

'I have really no idea. I don't claim to have a direct line. But my goodness I didn't expect you to ask that.'

'I didn't expect to ask it either. It...It just came out.'

'I see.'

'But it might come up again later, on camera.'

She nods and then says gently:

'Of course. In which case thanks for the heads up. But tell me, Adam, what do you think God wants *you* to do in this situation?'

'I've no idea either.'

Rev Lavinia bursts out laughing.

'Well, that makes us equals then doesn't it? Come on, let's get started.'

# 13

*SHAKY-CAM FOOTAGE of the proposed route of the Rush Bearing...*

When Johnny comes marching home again hurrah, tala...

*The music and the street scene fade. A white screen appears bearing the legend: 'Haxton Review: Deus Vult' in black print in a grungy typewriter front. The screen flickers in the style of an old-fashioned newsreel and then fades. It is replaced by a shot of a scuffle outside St Peter's Church gates. Three young white men are pushing a group of older Asian men as they try to leave the church grounds. A number of much younger Asians rush into shot and begin trading blows with the white men, one of whom falls to the ground. Two police officers – a man and a woman – run out of the Church and attempt to separate the fighters. They are joined by five more police officers from further down the street. The sound of the fight fades and the speed of the action is gradually reduced until the fight is unmistakably in slow motion. The Reverend Lavinia Shaw's voice is heard over the muted sound of the fighting:*

LAVINIA: At its most basic it's about getting people to speak to each other in an atmosphere of trust and mutual respect. I know that probably sounds slightly naïve, but...but if the Church isn't able to do that, then I don't think anyone else will be able to, and the consequences of that could be very dark indeed.

*The street scene fades to be replaced by a shot of Reverend Lavinia sipping her coffee in her study. She places her cup on the floor and smiles at someone behind the camera.*

LAVINIA: If you're sure it doesn't look too pretentious to be doing this in front of the books?

NARRATOR: (Off camera) I don't think so.

LAVINIA: A bit of a cliché?

NARRATOR: Not really. I think it gives you a bit of intellectual heft. A bit of gravitas. Is there anything particularly impressive that you want us to get in shot. We could shift things round.

LAVINIA: (Laughing) No thanks. As long as no one can see Lady Chatterley.

NARRATOR: (Laughing) I promise we'll edit it out. We don't want to get you in trouble. Are you ready to start?

LAVINIA: Yes, I think so.

NARRATOR: Great. Are we still ok Jason?

JASON: (Off camera) Yeah, we're still good.

NARRATOR: In which case, Lavinia, why don't you tell us your full name and your job?

LAVINIA: OK, so my name is Lavinia Shaw, and I am the Priest in Charge of St Peter's Haxton.

NARRATOR: Thanks. And for people who don't know Haxton, can you explain where St Peter's is, in relation to the local demographic geography?

LAVINIA: (Sighing) It always comes down to demographics in Haxton doesn't it. Ok, so we are halfway down East Croft, which puts us right on the edge of the white area. We're in a sort of liminal space, a border space, between the two communities in Haxton. And, without wishing to get too mystical, I suppose that is exactly where the church should be, especially in difficult times like these.

NARRATOR: Yes, I think that I can see that. And speaking of difficult times, St Peter's is significant to the Rush Bearing for more than just its location, isn't it?

LAVINIA: Well yes. Historically you would have to say that we were absolutely crucial to it. We are the church to which the rushes were delivered in the Medieval celebration, you see. So if it wasn't for us, there wouldn't even be a Rush Bearing.

NARRATOR: And in the Victorian version of the festival?

LAVINIA: Yes, that too. When the festival was reconstituted, it was still based around the Church. It was still a Christian festival, even though, by that time, there were no rushes spread on the church floor.

NARRATOR: Didn't everyone come back to the Church for evening prayer at the end of the day?

LAVINIA: Well, they were supposed to, yes, assuming they hadn't got too drunk up at the park. With the bishop in attendance, no less.

NARRATOR: But despite all that, despite all the historical baggage or context or whatever you want to call it, neither you nor the Church were responsible for the recent revival of the Rush Bearing. Isthat right?

LAVINIA: No, we weren't. Absolutely not.

NARRATOR: That sounds very emphatic.

LAVINIA: I suppose it does. And I suppose it sounds rather defensive too. Look, clearly no one at St Peters is opposed, in principle, to a revived Rush Bearing. But there are aspects of the way the thing has been managed which are insensitive to say the least, even if that wasn't the intention. And I need to be very clear that the church has nothing to do with that. It would be irresponsible of me not to be clear about that.

NARRATOR: And by insensitive, of course, you mean the crusader.

LAVINIA: Yes. I mean the crusader.

NARRATOR: Insensitive because of the Muslim community in Haxton?

LAVINIA: That's right. And also, quite unnecessary to the Rush Bearing itself. And that's the most frustrating thing. All of this could have been done so much more sensitively and inclusively, and it could still have been a fun celebration.

NARRATOR: Of course, Inclusivity and Sensitivity. The modern theological virtues.

LAVINIA: That's a bit cheap, if you don't mind me saying. Faith, hope and charity are the theological virtues, just as they always have been. But I think that charity, in particular, looks different in different contexts. And I think that here and now, in Haxton, charity probably does involve a degree of inclusivity and sensitivity. Although courtesy might be a better word from my perspective, a word with a better theological pedigree.

NARRATOR: Fair enough. I'm sorry. I wasn't trying to take the piss.

LAVINIA: I'm sure you weren't. But I'm just a little bit conscious that it's jolly easy to caricature people like me as daft and blindly 'politically correct' or 'woke' or whatever one wants to call it, and that makes it very easy to dismiss my views, or the views of people like me.

NARRATOR: 'Yes, but...'

LAVINIA: 'No hold on a sec. I was going to say that it's possibly a bit lazy, and even a bit dangerous, particularly when things are as tense as they are. I think, in these sorts of circumstances it's important to use language as precisely as possible.

NARRATOR: Of course. I think that's a very good point. There's definitely a balance to be struck on OyTube, and social media generally, between making your language engaging and smart, on the one hand, which might involve being a bit glib and silly, and, on the other hand, making it absolutely precise. I've become aware of that already, after just one video.

LAVINIA: If I were you, I would err on the side of precision.

NARRATOR: You may be right. Anyway, if we can move on, you're familiar with the phrase Deus Vult?

LAVINIA: Yes, of course. 'God wills it'. I think it was the Pope who said it first, when he preached the first Crusade, and it became a sort of slogan of the Crusaders.

NARRATOR: It was Pope Urban II. And you're right, it became the battle cry of the crusading armies in the Holy Land. It's all tied up with the Templars and their suppression as well.

LAVINIA: Fair enough. I'll take your word for it. I really don't know anything about all that. I'm afraid that my Christianity isn't that macho or that exciting. Although I've noticed that Deus Vult turns on right wing websites connected to Haxton and Islam. I don't think that it's a particularly helpful expression, I must say.

NARRATOR: I agree with you. I associate Deus Vult with the kind of people who wear MAGA hats and have pictures of beautiful Teutonic women in cornfields on their wall. Whatever is going on in Haxton, I don't think it's in any way analogous to the crusades.

LAVINIA: Thank goodness for that.

NARRATOR: But I am interested in what Deus Vult means here and now. I want to know what you think God wills in Haxton, as far as the Rush Bearing procession goes.

And, what he wills of you as a religious professional caught up in it all.

LAVINIA: Gosh, the question of God's will really has got a hold on you, hasn't it?

NARRATOR: Hasn't it got hold on you too? One would assume as a priest...

LAVINIA: Ok, ok. You're right. Of course I should be concerned with God's will. I'll try and answer your question. But please don't expect anything too neat and too packaged. As I said before we started filming, I may be a priest, but I don't claim to have a direct line. I don't think God works like that.

NARRATOR: Make it as unpackaged as you like.

LAVINIA: So, when I think about God's will I suppose that I have to start with St John, that God is love. And I think that I want to take that a stage further straight away and say that for God to be love, God also has to value and enjoy difference. Because you can't love if there isn't something or someone different from yourself to love, do you see what I mean?

NARRATOR: People can love themselves.

LAVINIA: Yes they can, in fact they should. But even then, we need other people to help us love and value ourselves properly. We only really perceive and love ourselves through other people perceiving us and loving us. If someone just adores themselves in splendid isolation we would be a bit suspicious of them.

NARRATOR: Yes, we might regard them as a narcissist.

LAVINIA: Exactly. So, for God to be love he has to make room for difference. More than that, he has to delight in difference, even play with differences. And, in fact, the Christian idea of God has difference right at its heart. We believe in the Trinity, which means, in essence, that there is variety even in God himself. God already has otherness within him in the Christian story, and he delights in it. He is not some narcissistic monad adoring himself in the sky.

NARRATOR: Ok, that's all quite impressive and stimulating, but what does it mean for Haxton and the Rush Bearing?

LAVINIA: Well...

NARRATOR: And, sorry to interrupt, but can I just check in, is this actually official Church teaching, if there is such a thing in the Church of England? Is all this stuff about difference kosher? Or are you...sort of...I don't know...making it all up as you go along? Sorry if that's indelicate.

*Lavinia frowns. She opens her mouth and closes it again. After a moment she stands up and can be seen running her finger along her bookshelves, with her back to the camera. Half a minute later, she pulls out a slim book and returns to her seat.*

LAVINIA: May I read you something?

NARRATOR: Of course, if it will help.

LAVINIA: I think it might. This was written by Fr Christopher, a French Trappist monk in Algeria. He...um...well he felt a special affinity for Islam and for Muslims, and when his monastery was threatened by Islamic extremists he wrote this letter or...or testimony...about his convictions, and about his and his brothers' situation. It's really extremely moving. It's wonderful, actually. There's been a film...Hold on just a second...Ah yes here is the bit I was after. Fr Christopher is writing about his death.

(Lavinia pushes her glasses down her nose and clears her throat)

*This is what I shall be able to do, if God wills - immerse my gaze in that of the Father, to contemplate with him his children of Islam just as he sees them, all shining with the glory of Christ, the fruit of his Passion, filled with the Gift of the Spirit, whose secret joy will always be to establish communion and to refashion the likeness, delighting in the differences.*

(Lavinia closes the book and places it on her lap)

Father Christopher is making the point that because there is difference within God, God can delight in differences among humans as well. And that's from a Roman Catholic monk and a priest, and it's firmly rooted in the Trinity. So yes, I think that what I'm saying is quite kosher, as you put it. It's quite orthodox.

NARRATOR: What happened to Fr Christopher and his brothers?

LAVINIA: They were killed, by the Islamists. And that makes it easy to laugh at them, doesn't it? For being naïve and stupid. Fr Christopher knew that people would laugh at him. But we really mustn't laugh. Those monks were the absolute opposite of crusaders. They were citizens of the former colonial power, but they were not colonists. They were not even missionaries. They weren't imposing any truth on the people they lived with. They were just being there. They understood that true love requires respect for the other precisely in their otherness.

NARRATOR: And it cost them their lives.

LAVINIA: Yes, it cost them their lives. But Christianity can cost you your life. That's almost the point of it.

NARRATOR: OK. So can we come back to God's will and the Rush Bearing.

LAVINIA: Of course. But I don't think we ever left it. To make progress here in Haxton, I think we have to begin, like Br Christopher, by uncoupling, definitively uncoupling, the will of God and the message of Jesus from any imagined idea of being Western or being English, and from any ideology of supremacy or exceptionalism.

NARRATOR: God isn't an Englishman.

LAVINIA: Exactly. Whatever it might mean to be an Englishman, God isn't one.

NARRATOR: Right, but I'm going to keep forcing the question. What about the Rush Bearing? What would you say to your parishioners who are determined to celebrate this event which centres historically on your church? And which for them, definitely is to do with Englishness?

LAVINIA: I would draw their attention to what we've been speaking about, concerning God willing and appreciating difference. And I would also point out that in the Christian story, God's word doesn't come as a heavy rule book or an ideology to impose on others, but as a living, fragile human being who is ready to talk and to be challenged. Who is ready to dialogue with the other. Who is ready to love.

NARRATOR: So, God doesn't just love and enjoy difference within himself, he loves difference in creation, among people.

LAVINIA: Exactly. That's exactly what I'm getting at. I think it's obvious just from looking around you that God enjoys diversity.

NARRATOR: And he wants us to do the same?

LAVINIA: Yes.

NARRATOR: So, what is that going to mean for the Haxton Rush Bearers?

LAVINIA: Well, I hope it means something about how we should be thinking about our Muslim neighbours here and now, how we might think about their feelings and sensitivities, and how we might manage to negotiate the difficulties we're having.

NARRATOR: Go on.

LAVINIA: I think we all have to learn not to be threatened by the otherness of neighbours, if that doesn't sound too pompous. We have to learn to accept and enjoy the fact that they are different from us. And perhaps that means reminding ourselves about respect and courtesy and listening, and the importance of dialogue.

NARRATOR: So, when it comes down to it are you pro-knight or anti-knight, Lavinia? Is God pro-knight or anti-knight?

LAVINIA: If you pushed me...

NARRATOR: Of course I'm going to push you.

LAVINIA: Well then I would have to say that I don't think that it is appropriate for a crusader knight to be included in a procession through a Muslim area. But I would also...

NARRATOR: (Interrupting) Hang on, how do you get to that from all the complex metaphysical stuff? How does God work that out?

LAVINIA: Bear with me please. I was going to say that I think that the Church's first job isn't to arbitrate in disputes like this. We're not here to be God's referees. I think our job is to create spaces where people on opposite sides can speak to each other respectfully. Gospel spaces, I would want to call them, where the good news of God's love and his delight in the other can become real. That's what we should be about. And that does touch on the metaphysical stuff as you put it, but at the same time it's very simple and very Christian.

NARRATOR: OK and it's also obviously where we get practical. Because there's a meeting arranged at St Peters tonight isn't there?

LAVINIA: Yes there is.

NARRATOR: As I understand it, you've been instrumental in putting it together. And it's got people from both sides of the

Rush Bearing dispute coming along. The first time they've met since the problems started.

LAVINIA: Yes that's right. Or at least we certainly hope people will come.

NARRATOR: And will you be making be a gospel space to celebrate difference at tonight's meeting? Will you be explaining all about God's inner otherness to the Haxton Muslims and the Lantyrn Royd whites so they respectfully dialogue things out?

LAVINIA: Look, it's always jolly easy to take the micky. And it's always a lot harder to try and do something constructive. Especially something constructive that is faithful to the gospel. But yes, I do hope that tonight's meeting will be something like that. At its most basic it's about getting people to speak to each other in an atmosphere of trust and mutual respect. And I know that probably sounds slightly naïve, but...but if the Church isn't able to do that, then I don't think anyone else will be able to, and the consequences of that could be very dark indeed.

NARRATOR: So, God wills a meeting?

LAVINIA: (laughing) Yes. I suppose God does will a meeting. That's a real vicar thing to say, isn't it? But I think he's the kind of God who enjoys the surprises that happen when people meet each other. And, actually, that would probably be my final message to the people of Lantyrn Royd. We don't have to be afraid of meeting our Muslim neighbours, and we don't have to be afraid of listening to them. We won't lose ourselves just because we engage with people who aren't quite the same as us. In fact, we might become more ourselves through meeting the stranger. If the gospel means anything in Haxton at the moment, I think it means that.

NARRATOR: Well, I hope some good comes out of tonight. I really do, Lavinia. And I'm sorry I slightly took the piss just now. For what it's worth, I think you're brave and thoughtful and...

LAVINIA: (Interrupting and laughing) And completely nuts.

NARRATOR: (Laughing) Obviously I think you're nuts. That goes without saying. But, even so, thank you for your time.

LAVINIA: Thank you for yours. It has been a pleasure.

*Lavinia vanishes to be replaced with the slowed down footage of the scuffle outside St Peter's church.*

NARRATOR: The Haxton Review was not invited to Rev Lavinia's meeting. So, we have no way of knowing how successful she was in creating her gospel space where differences can be celebrated in an atmosphere of trust and mutual respect. The fight afterwards led to one person being hospitalised and two more being arrested, however, so it seems likely that there is more work to be done in the parish around welcoming and celebrating the other.

Lavinia was right though; it is too easy to take the piss out of her ideas. Everyone laughs at a do-gooder, and the well-meaning vicar has been a figure of gentle fun in British life for generations. Lady vicars haven't escaped the ribbing either, Dawn French made certain of that. However, perhaps the urge to take the piss should be resisted in favour of a more serious critique of what Rev Lavinia had to say. Because it is serious stuff and some of it, at least, is quite mistaken and dangerous.

Lavinia is a vicar in the Church of England, which is the established church, the church that is joined to the British state. Because it enjoys that privileged position, the CofE has it in its DNA to follow the ideological commitments of the establishment, or the elite as we now call them. When Britain was about resisting Catholic powers on the continent, for instance, the CofE was a proud protestant church that was also all about resisting Catholicism. When Britain was about Empire and taking civilisation to black and brown people, the CofE became a cheerleader for Empire. When Britain was in the throes of its rapid capitalist expansion, the CofE became (with honourable exception) the religious mouthpiece of the capitalist class. The Church of England can't help it. It is tied to the elite through public schools and Oxbridge colleges, through its chaplains in Parliament and in every regiment in the British army, through the monarchy itself. In fact, it isn't quite true to say that the Church of England follows the elite. Rather it *is* the elite, albeit the elite on its knees.

Today of course, the British establishment isn't worried about anything as quaint as catholic powers or the empire, or safeguarding capitalism. Instead, it frets about keeping the lid on the tensions and discontents that arise in a nation which has enjoyed unprecedented levels of immigration simultaneously with the collapse of its moral confidence in its own history and identity. To get a handle on this problem, the elite or the establishment (call them what you will) has endorsed the ideology of multi-culturalism. We all know what this means and what it looks like in practice. No one cultural tradition is permitted to hold the commanding heights of British public life. No culture may be judged better or worse than any other. And any residual claim of Western European cultural norms to a privileged place in our public spaces is resolutely deconstructed. This idea has a complex history in education and within the media and the public sector. It has made its long march through the institutions to the point where it is now firmly established as a significant part of our national self-understanding. In this context it is difficult not to read Rev Lavinia's theology of difference as a hastily baptised version of 'diversity is our strength' and the other multi-cultural slogans. Despite what she might believe, Rev Lavinia has not separated her Christianity from ideology, she has just hitched it to the new diversity ideology of the late-capitalist ruling class.

I don't think this is just a case of the Rev Lavinia knowing on which side her bread is buttered, incidentally. I think her intentions are genuinely good. Let's face it, being the vicar of Haxton is a tough gig and I wasn't lying when I told her that she is thoughtful and brave. But that doesn't alter the fact that her strange multi-cultural gospel does nothing to help her embattled parishioners. Any more than it ultimately helped Fr Christopher and his poor butchered monks in Algeria.

*The fight scene freezes as a middle-aged white man is hustled away from St Peters Church by the police. Blood is streaming from his nose. In the background*

*Reverend Lavinia can just be seen closing the church door. The picture fades to be replaced by a montage of churches from around the United Kingdom: Cathedrals, ruined abbeys, English parish churches, Welsh non-conformist chapels, Scottish Presbyterian gospel halls. There are Christian statues, paintings and stained glass in the mix as well. As the montage plays, the narrator continues.*

If we are going to think fruitfully about the relationship between religion and the Rush Bearing dispute, we will have to begin in an entirely different place. Perhaps we could start with the root of the word religion. It probably comes from the Latin *Religare* meaning to tie fast or bind together. Religion: religious values, ideas, stories and ceremonies, are the stuff that bind a culture, that hold people in connection to one another. One consequence of that, if it's true, is that there is always an exclusionary aspect to religion. What binds my people and culture together will be different from what binds your people and culture. Religious symbols and ceremonies therefore police the boundaries and the differences between groups, which is why it has been suspect historically to have more than one major religion within the same territory.

Now it is obvious that Christian symbols, stories and ideas have lost traction in Britain and in Western Europe in the last hundred years, but does that mean that we have become less religious? I would argue not. Our story is not one of increasingly confident and straightforward secularisation. For one thing there is the bewildering mix of new age spiritualities and bastardised eastern religions on offer, which provide abbreviated answers to the deepest questions of the human heart. Most of us will have met people with bronze Buddhas on their mantlepieces or Native American Dream Catchers hanging above their beds. And some of us will know people who take things a stage further, who meditate, or who do strange stuff in the woods at the solstice. These people spend money on crystals and write that they are 'spiritual but not religious' on their dating profiles. They prove the truth of the misquote from Chesterton that when man stops believing in God, he doesn't then believe in nothing, he believes in anything.

But the cheap new age nonsense relates only to the privatised aspect of religion. It concerns the heart, the personal search for meaning, and ultimately the fear of death. It does not bind people together or police the boundaries of a society. So, a slightly different question needs to be asked: with the twilight of Christianity, have we lost any *public* sense of religiousness in this country? Again, I would argue that we have not. In fact, I would argue that a society cannot long endure without religion, understood in its broadest sense of dogmas, ceremonies and stories that are somehow sacred and binding. Bluntly, unless a society has stuff at its heart which the vast majority of its members regard with solemnity and reverence, it will not keep going. This is why the church handed heretics over to the civil magistrate for punishment. Heresy is always a crime against public order as much as it is a sin against God.

As Christianity has faded in the hearts and imaginations of the British, what dogmas and symbols have replaced it as the untouchable core of religious stuff in our common life? What are those things which command our collective attention with the peculiar power of the sacred and therefore hold us in some kind of unity? The first new dogma we should probably name is 'equality': the strange idea that people of all genders, races, classes, sexual preferences and nations are utterly equal. Equality insists that no one person is ever any better or any worse than any other. Of course, there is no evidence for this whatsoever. In fact, there is a ton of evidence that the reverse is true, that people are radically unequal in terms of virtue, intelligence, beauty and more or less any other metric you care to mention. But this evidence doesn't matter because 'equality' is a dogma and so it doesn't require evidence, just the obedience of faith.

(In passing, the newer idea of equity takes things a stage further. It is not enough merely to regard people equally, or treat them equally, says equity, rather people must specifically be treated unequally so that everyone can reach the same place in a given endeavour. Excellence is forbidden; all must have their prizes.)

The next dogma we might name is 'diversity'. This is the equally strange idea that differences between people and groups are always to be welcomed and are always both a sign and a source of strength. Once again, there is really no evidence for this and, once again, common sense would suggest the opposite, but, once again, this is not the point. The concept of diversity has the glow of the sacred about it in modern Britain. It lends its name to organisations as diverse (so to speak) as dance groups, advertising agencies and student bank accounts. We celebrate our culture in terms of its endless diversity rather than because of any positive content. We are the bare marketplace where the whole world sets out its colourful stalls. And we dare not mention that a more homogenous culture might feel more trusting and more at ease with itself. Only a heretic would challenge the diversity dogma, you see. And, as we all know, heretics do not fare well (except as firelighters).

Finally, we could mention 'individualism' as a dogma of modern Britain. This is the funny notion that each human being is a sovereign individual self, before he or she is a person in relationships or a member of society. Each individual self arrives in the world utterly self-contained, so the dogma goes, and fitted with things called 'rights'. Rights must never ever be compromised by the complexities and struggles involved in sustaining real life communities. These rights are a crucial part of the dogma of individualism. They cannot easily be enumerated because the list of them keeps growing, but there is certainly a right to sleep with who you want, a right to happiness, a right to hold and express any opinion (no matter how stupid) and therefore, ludicrously, a right to your own truth. As well as being a recipe, finally, for the most dreadful loneliness and meaninglessness, the idea of the pre-existing, rights-imbued self is complete nonsense, logically speaking. Our relationships with others pre-exist our notion of ourselves (on that at least Rev Lavinia and I agree) and our 'rights' are only granted to us as members of a pre-existing society. Man is not born free to find himself everywhere in chains. He is born dependent and vulnerable and, if he survives infancy, he finds himself a member of various communities which help him to grow into selfhood and a kind of contingent freedom.

So much for the dogmas of the modern British religion. What would its sacred symbols be? Certainly, the rainbow flag and the trans tricolour, combined now into the strange intersectional banner that flies like a conqueror's mark over our cities in high summer. (The speed at which trans rainbow has taken over public space is as remarkable as it is disturbing, implying a religious or quasi-religious force. The old, lewd, cruel and chaotic gods have apparently slid through the deep and grotty channels of our collective unconscious, straight from pre-Christian antiquity to post-Christian modernity, from Babylon to Birmingham with nowhere in between.) The red AIDS ribbon is somewhat eclipsed now, the pink triangle even more so, but they still function as religious symbols of a kind. As does - and this is more controversial - 'the minority' itself, be it ethnic, sexual or related to the bewildering number of genders available. Each of these things is afforded some degree of participation in the modern British sense of the sacred. And so, none of them may be criticised or mocked without the faint frisson of sacrilege.

The holocaust stands in a category of sacredness all of its own, of course: untouchable, unquestionable, holy and requiring near-constant obeisance. The word itself, with its strange religious connotations, puts the thing beyond normal discourse and thought.

Every religion worth its salt needs its original sin, and this is no less true of the modern British religion we are considering than of any other. There is slavery, or colonialism, or whiteness itself to fill the role. We westerners are of bad blood, and the narrow way to our redemption is at best unclear, and at worst impassible.

During my interview with Lavinia, I implicitly criticised her for becoming too metaphysical and complex, and drifting too far from the situation in Lantyrn Royd. And now I am uncomfortably aware that I seem to have done the same thing. How does any of what I have said relate to the beleaguered community of Haxton whites and their Rush Bearing procession?

The first point to note is that the new British religion has not served the people of Lantyrn Royd particularly well. Their equality with their Muslim neighbours has not spared their little festival from threat. In fact, the high priests of equality in the media and in Coxthorpe's local government seem to be dead set against it. Also, diversity is not experienced as a strength in Lantyrn Royd. The native English there have seen their community change quickly and radically, in ways that they perceive as unsettling and exclusionary, and they are left without any legitimate means to protest, because to complain about the transformation would be to sin against the sacred d-word, which one must not do. Furthermore, the individualism of the new British religion has left Lantyrn Royd residents alienated from their history and, to a degree, from each other. The revived Rush Bearing is an effort to correct that alienation, but it is a drop in the ocean, and it represents the convoluted reconstruction of history, rather than a natural and unselfconscious participation in a continuous tradition. Finally, for all that the people of Lantyrn Royd notionally have the same rights as anyone else in modern Britain, their opportunities to exercise those rights are severely restricted by the economic and social circumstances into which most of them were born. The rights and the freedoms to 'live your best life', to 'be who you want to be' or to 'explore your own truth,' mean the square root of fuck all if you're skint and poorly educated, with cultural horizons defined by a rough pub, a tanning salon, and the ever-present towering wall of the mosque.

But there is a deeper sense in which The Lantyrn Royd whites, as well as the rest of us, might do well to fear the new religion. As well as being embedded in the culture, literature and landscape of our country, Christianity has left an enormous moral footprint on the West, the loss of which, as the new faith displaces the old, is quite terrifying. We like to believe that our 'Western' values and virtues are universal and self-evident, but they are not. Rather they are the product of a very particular historical contingency, whose name is Christ. The Christian story reaches its climax, don't forget, in the dreadful, degrading execution of God himself on a cross, the punishment reserved for slaves in the Roman Imperium. The impact of this truth is historically incalculable. When it achieved earthly power, the Christian Church banned the games where slaves would routinely kill each other for the entertainment of the citizens of Rome. Later it ran monasteries where the sick and the desperate could receive help and care. It condemned chattel slavery. It speaks today in a more muted and unsure voice against abortion and euthanasia. Although Christian institutions betray the insight endlessly, the religion of Christ crucified demands care for the poor, the weak, the sick and – yes – for the foreigner. It demands love for each human soul because each is sacred and precious in the sight of God. This ethos lingers in our culture even as Christ drifts away, just as heat lingers in a room in which the fire has gone out. But the heat of Christianity will not last indefinitely. Already we speak in cold utilitarian terms about human life in its most vulnerable stages. How long before we begin to speak in the same terms about healthy lives in their prime? Good economic conditions have given us some grace and some time as Christianity's influence has ebbed away, but what happens when the good times end? Britain governed by the new religion of individualism, rights, diversity and equality, will certainly be vibrant (to use the preferred term), but it will not be gentle. For a while it may be a reasonably efficient multi-cultural mechanism, but it will be pragmatic and utilitarian rather than kind.

Back to the Rush Bearers. Unwittingly, the people of Lantyrn Royd have stumbled on a controversy which has the church at its core. I suspect that very few of them are practising Christians and only a few more would see their struggle in explicitly religious terms beyond parroting 'this is a Christian country' as a stick with which to beat their Muslim neighbours. Ironically, given what I have just said about the new religion, the Rush Bearers commonly articulate their cause as a fight to defend their rights and, beyond that, to defend their vision of their country. But - and this is the key point - if their view of England or of Britain does not include some religious element, if it does not remember the shadowy remains of the good, the true and the beautiful, if it does not lift Englishness somehow to love's high and unsure meridian, then it will not be worth having. In all the clamour of the fight, we must not forget that those over-contested rushes were originally used to keep people's knees comfy as they knelt to say their prayers.

A last thought. The Rev Lavinia has a very different perspective from mine concerning the proper relationship between Christianity and the Rush Bearing controversy. But, for all that I am sure that she is wrong, she has the obvious advantage that she actually believes what she says. At least I assume she does. She is, after all, a committed Christian and a clerk in holy orders. When she speaks about Christ and faith, she speaks with integrity and conviction. Many people who are sympathetic to my point of view, on the other hand, will, like me, find it very difficult indeed to make the same act of faith. The scientists and deconstructionists of the nineteenth and twentieth centuries – Darwin, Marx, Nietzsche, Freud – have made believing, for lots of us, exceptionally hard. We are fretting and twiddling our thumbs on Dover Beach, listening to the 'melancholy, long, withdrawing roar' of the old faith, and wondering what on earth to do with ourselves as the new faith takes hold. And this is not just a personal tragedy, of course, although it is certainly that. I am, after all, advocating a vision of England with the memory of Christ at its core. More than that, I am suggesting that without Christ and a sense of the divine, England may not be worth bothering with. And yet I am not at all sure that I believe in either Christ or in divine realities in any meaningful way.

I don't have a solution to this problem, except to suggest that there may be a dark and blurry area between proper committed believing and settled unbelief. There may be space around the crib for regretful and reverent agnostics to kneel in the rushes with the ass and the ox and the shepherds and the true believers. We may not actually pray there, in our ancient English churches, but at least we will be kneeling where prayer has been valid. At least we will be keeping faith as best we can with our ancestors, even if we are not capable of keeping faith with God.

And perhaps, not without some loss of personal integrity, we will be helping to keep the story and the ethos of Christ alive, and that may help, just a little, to preserve and strengthen what remains of our country.

*The sequence of still shots of churches and statues ends with a picture of a tiny chapel covered in snow, with an old grey slab of a gravestone in front of it. After a moment the image vanishes to be replaced with a white screen bearing the legend: 'Haxton Review: Deus Vult' in black print in a grungy typewriter front. The screen flickers in the style of an old-fashioned newsreel and then fades. As it does so 'The English Civil War' by the Clash plays softly:*

A woman's eye will shed a tear
To see his face so beaten in fear
It's just around the corner in the English civil war

# 14

When Jason and I have finished filming the interview with Lavinia we go and wait outside the church as people arrive for the meeting. We try to film the arrivals, but we are told by a police officer to put the camera away.

'We in't breakin any law,' Jason says angrily, swinging the camera to focus on the two cops who have approached us. One of them places his hand over the lens.

'I said put the camera away.'

'Stop touching it.'

'Put it away then.'

Jason steps back from the police officer but keeps filming. I say quickly:

'Can you please explain why we need to stop filming, officer?'

The policeman sighs wearily.

'Because we have people from both sides of the community turning up here tonight, in the middle of a very volatile situation, so we are expecting things to be tense. And having people shove cameras in other people's faces is one very easy way to make sure it kicks off.'

'The BBC are here,' I say. 'They're filming.'

'Yeah, but they're different.'

'How are they different?'

The cop sighs again.

'Look just put the camera away, please.'

I tell Jason to stop filming and eventually, grumpily, he agrees. We back away from the cops and watch from across the street as people arrive for the meeting: groups of Muslims, white men and women in clerical dress, a senior looking police officer, and some of the key Rush Bearers including Brenda. A few whites and a crowd of Muslims gather outside the church and there is a bit of shouting and shoving, but once the meeting is underway both groups drift off. The Muslims go back up towards Gordon Street; the whites go to The White Horse.

When it is clear that nothing is going to happen for a while, Jason and I go to The White Horse, where I buy us both a pint. The pub now has a St George's Cross flying above the door and tonight it is fuller than I have ever seen it. Everyone is talking about the meeting and, as usual, Roger Wrigglesworth has his Rush Bearing table set up opposite the bar. When Jason goes for a wee, I push my way through the drinkers to speak to him.

'Ah, Haxton's own Spielberg,' he calls as I approach. 'How was the interview with the lovely Lavinia?'

'Not bad. She is a bright woman.'

'She certainly is. What did she have to say for herself?'

'You won't be surprised to learn that she's not a fan of the Rush Bearing as it stands. She wants you all to be more inclusive. And she thinks God wants you to be inclusive too.'

'Of course she does.' Roger sips his wine and winces. 'Did she mention me at all?'

'She called you a fascist and said that she would never speak to you.'

He giggles.

'I would expect nothing less. You're the acceptable face of the Rush Bearing, aren't you, not me. Was she clear about why she actually wanted to meet you, by the way?'

'She said that I functioned as a conduit, for getting her message of peace and diversity out to the good folk of Lantyrn Royd.'

'Is that what she said?'

'Yes. Her exact words.'

'Hmmm.'

He sips his wine again.

'You're not convinced?'

'Not entirely, no. She knows you won't be very sympathetic to her, and she also knows that she'll lose control of her message when you come to put your video together. So, I'm not sure how effective a conduit you'll be, really, from her point of view.'

'I'll be fair to her though. I won't misrepresent what she is trying to say.'

Roger waves his hand dismissively. The gesture is exaggerated: slightly pissed, almost camp.

'Of course you'll be fair to her; you're a good, fair-minded chap. You can't be anything else. But you're certainly not going to present her ideas without challenge, are you? At least I bloody well hope you're not.' He sips his wine again. 'I suppose we'll find out what she's up to in time. Congratulations on the first video, by the way. We were all very pleased with it. And it was more popular than we could ever have imagined.'

'Thank you. I think I got lucky about the shares and views.'

'I think you have the Jewess to thank for your luck really.'

'Who do you mean?'

'Tanya Falk, your brother's colleague on the *Globe*.'

'I had no idea that she was Jewish.'

'Well, she is.'

'Really? Are you sure?'

He smiles.

'If you are around this sort of thing for long enough you develop a nose for the tribe.' He shrugs. 'You have to, if you're going to survive.'

'I don't see that it's relevant anyway.'

'That's true, you don't.'

Roger smiles again and then stares at the sticky carpet, cradling his unpleasant wine. He fascinates me. I still don't understand the depth of conviction that makes a man give up an academic career in order to commit himself to the most marginal and unpleasant cause in British politics. Roger left London and came to live in one of the bleakest parts of the north of England to work as a missionary for his awful ideas, with apparently no thought at all for his own welfare and prospects. I have no idea what he does for work in Coxthorpe, but I suspect it is nothing or almost nothing. And apparently he bought some of his family up here as well. I cannot grasp what motivates the man, what makes him tick, what dreams stir his imagination. Sometimes he speaks like a normal person, albeit someone with a particularly lively concern for their country. But occasionally he uses a term like 'Jewess' or 'the tribe' and then you glimpse something dark and ancient and terrifying beneath the corduroy jacket and the soft, well-mannered speech. And that thing, whatever it is, lends Roger a kind of force which causes him to be listened to and taken seriously in The White Horse. It makes him compelling, somehow, as well as repulsive.

'Did Jason tell you that we had a chat about his role as your spy?' I say eventually.

'Yes he did.'

'There was no need to keep tabs on me, you know. I would have told you exactly what I was up to if you'd asked.'

Roger raises his eyebrows and downs the last of his wine.

'Yes but, with respect, you would say that wouldn't you?' No matter if you were working in good faith or bad. I'm afraid that in my line of work, you simply have to assume the worst of people as a matter of routine. And then you have to keep on assuming it. Please don't take it personally.'

'I don't.'

'Have you encountered any gentle pressure from the opposition yet?'

'Not that I am aware of.'

'It will come I am afraid. At least it will if you keep making your videos and if they keep being reasonably successful.' He nudges me gently in the ribs with his elbow. 'Do your best to have your affairs in order so you don't leave yourself open to too much trouble.'

'I don't think there's much...'

I stop as Jason comes hurrying over, shoving his way through the crowd.

'Sup up quick,' he says. 'The meeting's over apparently. They're all coming out.'

'Over already,' Roger murmurs. 'That's rather soon. I wonder if that means good news or bad.'

'I had assumed that good news *was* bad news as far you were concerned.'

Roger giggles again.

'The worse the better and all that. You shouldn't be so cynical, Adam. Now you'd better get up there, the pair of you. You mustn't miss the story.'

'You're not coming then?'

'Good lord no. I'd just be a provocation.' He flaps his hand. 'A needless provocation.'

. . .

I down my pint and follow Jason out of the pub, together with a good crowd of Lantyrn regulars. Jason and I jog up the road ahead of the rest, so we are able to get a place on the wall opposite the church and start filming as the first big group exits the Church hall. This time the police are too busy to bother us. We film the fight outside the church and then, when it is over, we head straight back towards Jason's house to begin editing. We pass Brenda and a group of Rush Bearers on the way down Lantyrn Royd.

'Hiya Brenda,' Jason says.

'Hi Jay. Hi Adam.' She nods at the camera. 'You two doing more of your filmin, are you? I thought the first one were right good Adam. I put a comment.'

'Yeah, I saw. Thanks.'

'So, what are you up to tonight, then? Just filming the scrap?'

'Not just that. We spoke to the vicar earlier on, an all. How was the meeting?"

Brenda shakes her head angrily.

'Bullshit. Total bullshit.'

'How come?'

'Well, it wan't a discussion at all, like it were meant to be. There were loads of people there, right. Quite a lot of Muslims from up the road, of course, which is fair enough. I don't mind them coming down. But there was also a bunch of people from that Respect Haxton thing who don't live anywhere near here, and a couple of councillors and some high-up coppers as well. And a bunch of vicars from all the churches round here, like.'

'Not all the churches, Brenda,' says a gangly man in his mid-thirties who is walking with the group. His neck is covered in tattoos. I have seen him drinking in The White Horse, but I don't know his name.

Brenda sniffs, pointedly.

'Yeah, that's right, not all the churches.'

'What do you mean?' I ask.

'Well, that Nigerian Church on the other side of Albert Park, right. It's the biggest church in Haxton, easily.'

'Yeah, I know it. Or I know of it. It's the Pentecostal one.'

'Well Pentecostal or Christian or whatever it is. They weren't there tonight and when we asked why, it turned out they hadn't been invited.'

'Why not?'

'Cos they know what fucking Muslims are like,' says the gangly man.

'What?'

'Turns out they actually support us,' Brenda says. 'Nick's mum does some cleaning there and apparently they've got our leaflet up on their noticeboard.'

'Yeah they have,' says the gangly man. 'And the petition. They know what it's like to live next to Muslims from living in their own country, dun't they? So, course they weren't bleeding invited.'

'But the rest of the Church people were all against you? Even the vicar from Saint Peters?'

'Yeah. Rev Lavinia, or whatever her name is. To be fair, she tried to be nice about it all. She in't a complete bitch. She kept going on about how important it was for us to be listened to. But it din't really make any difference. In the end, she were against us all the same.'

We have reached The White Horse now. The group stops, filling the pavement and the road outside the pub. More people are coming down Lantyrn Royd from the direction of St Peters.

'So, what actually happened at the meeting?'

'We got fucked over, love,' Brenda says. 'We got fucked over hard, just like we were always gonna be.'

'What do you mean?'

'Tell him Dave.'

Dave frowns.

'Right so everyone there, everyone apart from us lot from the Rush Bearing committee, had already decided that we weren't gonna have our procession. The council and the cops had their meeting on Wednesday, apparently, and settled it all. So, there was never owt to discuss really.'

'They'd already decided it?'

'Yeah. Course they fucking had,' Brenda snorts.

'What had they decided exactly? Are they actually banning it? '

'Might as well of done,' Dave says. 'We're gonna be re-routed, just like them at Respect Haxton asked for. Tonight were all about persuading us to bend over and tek it up the arse. That's all it were. It's gonna be announced in the Argus tomorrow.'

'Shit. I didn't know they could do that. Not without consulting you.'

'Well apparently they can, love,' Brenda says. 'They can do what they want. That's why we left early and it kicked off.'

'So where can you actually have the procession?'

'We've gotta stay on Lantyrn Royd and just march up and down the street. We can't even turn onto East Croft, to get to the church. And it's meant to be about the frigging church in't it? So, what's the point of that?'

'We're in a fucking prison,' Jason mutters.

Jason, Brenda, Dave and I are now caught in a small circle in the crowd outside the pub. The atmosphere is angry and close. It's difficult to move.

'So, what are you going to do now, Brenda?' I ask.

'Get pissed, love.'

The crowd laugh.

'No. I mean what are you going to do about your procession?'

Brenda looks around and then glances up to the evening sky. It is one of the bright blustery autumn days when the year feels lively and sharp. You can feel things changing.

'We're gonna fucking have it anyway, love, just as we planned. Same route as we said, and with the knight right in the fucking middle.'

The crowd laugh again and then cheer.

'Well,' Dave says, 'We'll have to have a think about it, won't we. The committee...'

'The hell we'll have to think about it. There's nowt to think about.'

The cheer becomes a roar as Brenda turns and leads the crowd into The White Horse. A few seconds after she has disappeared through the door there is the sound of a soft explosion from the direction of St Peters. The roar dies away, and people hurry into the pub leaving Jason and I alone in the street.

. . .

'I dunno what the fuck that was,' Jason says. 'But I dun't think it's sensible to hang around. It in't a happy night. Do you want to come straight back to mine and get started, or do you fancy another drink?'

'I don't want to go back into the pub. Let's get on.'

I follow Jason back to his house again and sit next to him while he starts editing the video. I get a taxi home just after eleven and the next day I get up early and work all day on my video script, only pausing for a quick chat and a wank with Tracie, and another chat, but not a wank, with an obese 62-year-old woman named Sonja from Basingstoke. Sonja and I swap WhatsApp details but she has to go out to her cleaning job, so we agree to talk later in the week.

When I have finished my script, I go round to the off license. I buy a cheap bottle of red and a nicer bottle of gin and then go home and drink half the wine with my tea. Just as I am finishing the washing up, my phone rings. It's Rev Lavinia.

'How's the video going?' she asks, brightly.

'Not bad. We did the editing for the intro and the interview last night and I've written the script for my bit today. I'm going round to Jason's to finish it in a few minutes.'

'I hope you'll be gentle with me.'

'Do you know what, I think I've pretty much left your stuff alone in my commentary. I've just let it stand on its merits and then chucked in my own, rather different, perspective. I'm not sure if it's very joined up actually.'

'Do people who make OyTube videos worry about them being joined up? Are they that considered?'

'I don't know about other people, but I certainly worry about it. I want my channel to be serious...to mean something.'

'Of course you do. And so you should. Well anyway, as long as you haven't been too horrible.'

'I certainly haven't been horrible.'

There is a pause. And then she says quietly:

'Did you hear about the discussion? About how the meeting went?'

'I did. Um...I got the impression that there wasn't an awful lot to discuss, actually, because things had already been decided by the powers that be. It was a bit of a stitch up, by all accounts.'

'You'll have heard that from Rush Bearers. From people in The White Horse.'

'Yes, of course.'

'Bloody hell.' She sighs. 'Well, all I can say is that it wasn't meant to be like that. I feel rather used about it all actually. I didn't know what had been decided at the council. As I told you, I didn't even know for definite that their meeting had taken place. I was caught on the hop as much as anyone else was. In the end I am afraid it was just damage limitation as far as I was concerned.'

'I'm not sure how effective your damage limitation was, to be honest.'

'No, nor am I.' She pauses again and when she goes on her voice is even quieter. I have to strain to hear her. 'Did you hear about the fireworks?'

'What fireworks. Do you mean the metaphorical fireworks? At the meeting?'

'No literal fireworks. Someone threw a milk bottle full of bangers into my garden on Friday evening after everyone had gone. Apparently there was petrol in the bottom. You may have heard the explosion.'

'Yeah, of course I did, but I didn't know where it came from. I didn't know you...or...or the vicarage was the target.'

She laughs.

'It's alright to say I was the target, Adam. It seems pretty clear that I was. Although I don't think anyone actually wanted to kill me or even injure me. There would be much easier ways to do that.'

'Do you know who did it?'

'No idea at all. And the police don't have any idea either. They don't even know which side was responsible. Some extremist Muslims might want to target the church because we are central to the Rush Bearing, and...'

'And because you're a church.'

'Well, yes, I suppose that too, tragically. But, equally, some of The White Horse Royd lot might choose to target me because I set up the meeting that, from their point of view, was a complete fraud. It wasn't my fault of course, but they don't know that. Or if they do, they won't acknowledge it.'

'That's bloody awful. You weren't hurt though?'

'No. I was safely inside. Don't tell anyone about this by the way. The police are keen that it is isn't advertised at the moment. In case either side decides to take revenge, or both sides do. I am telling you in confidence, or off the record, or whatever it is they say.'

'I won't say anything. Do you...do you feel frightened?'

'Not frightened exactly. I think *exposed* is probably a better word. I don't feel particularly secure. I don't know if you realised but I live here on my own...'

'Yes. I had assumed that.'

'Oh God, that probably means that I have single vibes wafting off me. How depressing. Well anyway, being here alone obviously makes me feel a bit more...I don't know...vulnerable, I suppose.'

'Look, are you in a position to take some holiday or something? I don't know how it works with vicars. Could you get away for a few days?'

'I suppose I could, but I certainly don't intend to.'

'Why not, for God's sake?'

She laughs again, quietly.

'Yes, exactly Adam. For his sake. And for the sake of the people in Haxton he has given me to look after. It's clear to me that I have a duty to stay here and do whatever I can to help, even if that's rather uncomfortable for a while. And I'm not going to run away from that.'

'Ok. I won't waste my time arguing. But look please give me a ring if you need someone to hang around for a bit. I mean it. I'm happy to help if I can.'

'Thank you Adam that's kind. I promise I will. And I suppose now I should let you go. You will have to get your video sorted out.'

'Yeah. I should really.'

'Obviously, don't mention the fireworks, or...or perhaps what went on at the meeting, or the local reaction to it. I suspect that both would be rather incendiary, in different ways.'

'I won't. I haven't. I haven't even mentioned the council's decision. I've done something much more theoretical.'

'Ok. Interesting. I look forward to seeing it.'

'I'll send you the link.'

'Thanks. You really are kind, Adam. I mean it. Bye.'

'Bye, Lavinia.'

I shove the phone back in my pocket and collect the gin from the kitchen table. I put it in a carrier bag and then call a cab and ride round to Jason's. On the ride over, it crosses my mind that I may just have been slightly (and quite unnecessarily) manipulated by Rev Lavinia, but I choose to ignore the thought.

. . .

'I tek it, you din't walk this time,' Jason grunts as he opens the door.

'No. I think you were right about that. It doesn't feel very safe.'

I chuck my coat over the sofa and settle myself at the computer table. The books about natural history and the magazines from the Yorkshire Red Kite Society have been tidied away and there is a copy of the Coxthorpe Argus in their place. The headline reads: *Provocative Parade Re-Routed.*

'You seen that yet?' Jason asks, nodding at the paper.

'No. Not yet. What does it say?'

'That the Rush Bearing has been shifted and that the community has won a great victory, but it doesn't say owt about which fucking community that is, of course. Also, that the meeting at St Peter's was to discuss the new arrangements for next week, but that it got broken up by right wing extremists.'

'I see.'

'So, it's bollocks basically, from start to finish.'

'I don't think I expect anything better from journalists.'

'Nor do I, but it's still fucking irritating. They didn't put in anything about the shit that went on here last night."

'What happened here?'

'Muslims smashed the windows in The White Horse, as well as bunging them fireworks in the church. We've started patrolling.'

'Who has? And how come you know about the fireworks in the church?'

'Everyone knows. It's what that explosion was.'

'And it was definitely the other side that did it?'

He looks at me strangely.

'Course it were the other side. Why would anyone from our side want to throw fireworks at our own church?'

'Well, because...perhaps...perhaps...'

'Come on. I'm fascinated.'

'Perhaps because they were pissed off about the meeting. Brenda said it was a stitch up.'

'For fuck's sake Adam.'

Jason walks through into the kitchen and starts making tea. He calls through the open door:

'People talk a load of shit to try and confuse things at the moment. Not just the papers, everyone. Roger's always going on about that: false flags and fake news and whatnot.'

'If you say so.'

'People just want to muddy the waters, dun't they? It's all smoke and mirrors. You've gotta watch out for it, Adam, especially doing what you're doing.'

'I don't think I'm particularly naïve, Jason, but thanks anyway.'

'Yer welcome.'

'Who's doing the patrolling?'

'We are. We all are. It's been organised by the Rush Bearing committee. We're going right through the night, just like we did during the riots. And there's a system to offer lifts to each other, an' all. There's a website. So, no one has to walk through Haxton to get into town.'

'It's a bloody siege.'

Jason grunts, comes back into the front room and puts a mug of tea in front of me. In return, I pull the gin out of my carrier bag and hand it to him.

'What this for?'

'It's a present. To thank you for your help.'

'You din't have to do that.'

'I know I didn't.'

He stares at the bottle.

'Fucking hell. There were no need for that. You din't have to...' He shrugs. 'Do you...do you fancy a gin then?'

'Yeah alright, after the tea.'

'Ok. We'll have tea and then we'll have gin. Now give us yer camera.'

. . .

We manage to get the video finished that night, as well as working our way through the entire bottle of gin and half a dozen cans of lager. Just before midnight, I log into my OyTube account from Jason's laptop and upload the finished film to my channel. I text the link to Rev Lavinia without a message, then I phone my usual taxi company to book a cab home. The woman at the end of the phone tells me that cabs won't go to Lantyrn Royd after eight o'clock.

'Oh, that's a pity. It's...it's a bit of a shit actually. Do you happen to know of any other companies that will send a cab here?'

'Not at the moment, love. It's too risky just now, I'm afraid.'

'I got one off you last night.'

'Yeah but last night another one of our drivers ended up in hospital. So, we've stopped going there.'

'Oh. I'm sorry. It's a pity. It's awful.'

'Sorry love.'

'I just wanted a taxi home.'

'Sorry love.'

I toss my phone on the table and peer up at Jason who is swaying gently in the doorway, holding a can of lager.

'No cabs,' I say. 'Too fucking dangerous apparently. Pain in the arse. I'll have to walk after all, I suppose. Take my chances.'

'Bollocks you will,' Jason grunts. 'You'd not get to town alive. You'll have to crash here.'

'I'll be fine.'

'You won't be fine.'

'I will.'

'You fucking won't.'

'Oh God.'

He finishes the can. Beer dribbles down his chin.

'Arsehole. You can kip on the sofa. I've got a sleeping bag.'

And so the next morning I wake up on Jason's sofa, shivering with drink, with a gummy mouth and a headache, and with the whole room smelling of sweat and old farts. My phone tells me it is ten past seven. I roll onto the floor and discover that I didn't manage to get my shoes off before I fell asleep. Also, the empty gin bottle has been wedged between my back, and the sofa cushions all night. I ache all over. I get onto my hands and knees and then, slowly, up onto my feet.

I struggle into the bathroom and have a piss while I squirt toothpaste into my mouth and then go back into the kitchen. There is pad of paper and a pencil on the side. My hand is shaking so much that I can hardly write:

*Once again, Jason, thanks for everything. The video, the beer, the hospitality. I am going to stagger straight home (I'm not going to bother with a taxi – I doubt the Haxton Mujahedeen are out of bed yet). The next big video thing will be the Respect Haxton demo, next week. I will be in touch before then.*

I leave the note under the kettle and then slip out of the front door and head up the street.

. . .

The morning light is pearly grey and the air is cool as I stroll up Friendly and then turn right onto Gordon Street. Grocery shops and newsagents are already open but the road is quiet and calm, with only a few old blokes in evidence, chatting on street corners with their hands folded neatly across their chests and newspapers tucked under their arms. They smile as I approach and I make a point of smiling back and giving them a more-than necessarily wide berth, partly because I don't want to risk provoking trouble and partly because the old blokes seem decent and gentle, and there is no need to be unkind. Also, I am conscious that I stink of drink.

There was a time – I can just about remember it – when Islam signified courtesy and courage and a kind of rough chivalry, as well as astonishingly strict and impressive laws about hospitality. These latter, I am sure, included something about having to give a stranger a certain number of days shelter in your tent, extending even to defending them by force of arms if the need arose. Beyond this perception, I think there was also an outer layer of vaguer Islamic associations about the exotic and mysterious orient. This was to do with stuff like The Arabian Knights and harems and genies and sultans and jinn. I cannot now, for the life of me, remember when these old associations began to be eclipsed by the newer ones to do with bombs, stoning, and intolerance. The obvious date to locate the transition is 9/11, but I think it goes back earlier than that. The Rushdie affair perhaps, or the Islamic Revolution in Iran. The foundation of Israel is probably relevant as well. Anyway, for whatever reason, Islam has been reconstructed in Westerners' minds as the religion of conquest, burkas, bigotry and slaughter. It is all those things, of course, but I am still sad that the older associations have been lost almost completely. I read the Arabian Knights as a kid and enjoyed it. And I read about Lawrence of Arabia and loved that too. And some of the old Pakistani blokes on Gordon Street this morning have a quiet courtesy and a dignity about them, which roughly corresponds to my mental image of a Bedouin as he offers you his tent and his sword for a week or two.

Just after Gordon Street becomes Leeds Road, I pass the street where I left the woman who took the selfies outside the kebab shop. At the far end of the street there is a burnt-out car that wasn't there on Friday night. And the grocers at the top of the street has its windows smashed. A middle-aged Asian bloke is sweeping up the glass.

'Excuse me,' I say. 'Excuse me, what happened?'

The man leans on his broom.

'Trouble causers, mate. From town.'

'Oh, I'm sorry.'

'It's gonna happen in't it, mate.'

'Why is it going to happen?'

'Because some people are dickheads.'

'I suppose you're right.' I nod at the burnt-out car. 'And what happened down there, do you know?'

'I don't, mate. It's white down there int'it?'

'Do you know which happened first, the shop or the car?

'I dun't mate. Can't see it makes much difference really.'

'And did the trouble start because of the meeting at Haxton, do you know, about the Rush Bearing?'

'I dun't know, do I?'

'But what do you think?'

'I think it probably did, yeah. Like I said, people are dickheads.'

The man goes back to his sweeping. I watch him as I roll a cigarette and light it.

'It's going to get worse, you know. If Rush Bearing is finally re-routed or not. Either way, someone's going to be pissed off and it's going to get worse.'

The man shrugs but doesn't look up.

'Probably will, mate. Some people are dickheads. What can you do?'

# 15

When I get in, I have two boiled eggs and a mug of coffee and then a fag in the yard. After that, I flop on the sofa with a pint of orange juice and my laptop, and log onto *The Haxton Review* OyTube channel. The new video already has over two thousand views and two hundred and eighty comments. Once again, the comments are fairly evenly split between people who support the Rush Bearing and people who oppose it, although it is noticeable that some of the festival's supporters do not seem to be particularly enamoured with the new video. A few of them don't even seem to have watched it through to the end. *We're a Christian country. End of.* is a fairly typical contribution in this category. On the other hand, a number of the people who are opposed to the Rush Bearing are keen to engage with the content of the video seriously and respectfully, much more so than with the first one. It doesn't seem to matter that the interview with Lavinia and my subsequent commentary are not particularly connected, either. It may even help. There is apparently a constituency of philosophically sensitive progressive people out there, who are switched on to the situation in Haxton and who are keen to discuss it at length, from different perspectives. They all hate my comment about sacralising minorities, but they write thoughtfully about the risks implicit in a polity resting on rights and individualism, and some express regret (although framed rather differently from me) at the gradual loss of Christian influence in the UK. Several of the contributors seem to be religious and a few of these are genuinely kind about the stuff I included concerning the loss of faith as a personal tragedy.

Reading the positive comments from people who are opposed to the Rush Bearing makes me think again of my conversation with Jason about my own political allegiance. Roger apparently believes that I am an old-fashioned Tory and a 'cucked patriot', and I suppose he is correct, depending on your definition of the terms. But I wasn't lying when I described myself as old-fashioned Labour. I was, after all, a Labour voter until recently. I am a monarchist, a patriot (cucked or otherwise), an immigration-sceptic, an anti-multi-culturalist and a social conservative in my view of family, education, and gender. And obviously, I think the trans thing is a load of bollocks. But I also believe in strong Trades Unions, in keeping the commanding heights of the economy in social ownership, in health care that is free at the point of access, in national parks and good state schools, in progressive taxes, and in government economic intervention to build and sustain a strong manufacturing base. I know almost nothing about economics, but that's not the point. These are the things that I support instinctively. And here's the thing, I see no insurmountable contradiction between the old-fashioned Tory bit of me and the old-fashioned Labour bit of me. There are tensions between the two of course, but every political outlook has tensions if it is half-way serious. I believe in defending settled communities where the individual may grow and flourish. I believe that the state should be a moral agent to protect a generously defined account of the good, rather than claiming (falsely) to be a morally neutral arbiter which 'holds the ring' and prevents any one conception of the good from squashing the others. The morally active state that

I would like to see, would ensure that all people have access to the material and cultural resources that will enable them to thrive, but I also believe that equality of outcome and of opportunity is impossible and undesirable. I absolutely hate resentment, my own and other people's. I am sceptical about too much talk of social mobility because it disrupts communities and encourages envy, and because I think it may ultimately be cruel to the people who turn out not to be very mobile. On the other hand, I want those good state schools that I am in favour of to include plenty of selective grammars to enable the right sort of social mobility for the right sort of people. Most of all I loathe the idea that social life is all about identity, oppression, and self-assertion, with all the tasteless and narcissistic intersectional crap that goes with it. I hate the implication of this view, that common life is nothing but the play of contesting powers without any shared and binding notions of goodness and truth. (In passing, if I *had* to adopt a view of society based on antagonism and power, I would take the old Marxist account of the class conflict, in an instant, over the shitty performative oppressions of modern identity politics. At least class is objective and real, and conflict along class lines is a bit, well, *classy*. Some of the class conflict outfits were nice.) In short, I am an anti-liberal: economically, socially and culturally. I need to work out more about what that means precisely, but I know that it is my basic political commitment. It always has been, both as a lefty and then as a lefty/righty hybrid. I just wish that there was a proper, positive word for it.

. . .

The third comment under the video is from Lavinia. I skip it until I have flipped through the rest of them and then read it on my phone in the yard while I am having another fag and a second cup of coffee.

*Hi Haxton Review,*

*I am not sure if I should be writing this here, but I don't yet have your email address and what I want to write is too long for a text.*

*Thanks for sending me the link and thanks also for being so reasonable in the video. You said that you didn't think that my bit and your bit joined up, but I think they do. The viewer gets my take on the Rush Bearing and then yours, both from a - sort of - Christian perspective. The connections and, more importantly the disconnections, are obvious. They do not need to be laboured.*

*To begin I was cross at your suggestion that my understanding of religious difference may simply be the baptism of the 'politically correct diversity ideology of the late-capitalist ruling class' as you put it. (You do have a way with words, by the way!) But the fact that I was cross might mean that you are onto something, at least a little. I am going to reflect on it and when I have worked out what I think, I will get back to you.*

*I cannot agree with your horrible comment about minority groups being treated as if they're somehow sacred. It seems that in each video you have to include something that is ill judged and offensive. I don't know why - perhaps you regard it as 'edgy'. The Muslim people I know in Haxton have lives that are just as difficult as the white people in Lantyrn Royd. There is really nothing sacred going on there, except in the sense that every human life is sacred.*

*By the way, I wonder if you are familiar with Milan Kundera's idea of 'kitsch'? If you aren't, you should look it up. Kitsch, for Kundera, is purity and a kind of euphoric return to some imagined pristine state of oneness with being. But this kitsch is only purchased though the exclusion of all that is messy or difficult or compromising about human experience, and it is also the aesthetic underpinning of totalitarianism or fascism. Your religion of the guarded boundary seems to me to be very much in the service of kitsch as Kundera imagines it, but it also feels like a betrayal of the incarnation. After all, what does it mean for God to become flesh if it isn't his transgressing the ultimate boundary, between the divine and the human? And doesn't God take all the muddle and mess and of human experience to himself ('shit' is Kundera's term for anti-kitsch) when he assumes a human nature? It takes a certain sort of courage to deal with the shitiness of things. Much easier perhaps to impose order by vigorously policing the boundary between the pure and the impure.*

*Also, your point about the CofE being joined at the hip to the establishment seems slightly simplistic. I know we are the established church, but I am not sure that there is a single establishment anymore, if there ever was. My experience in this job and in my previous one is that there are actually a number of establishments, or centres of power, and they are often in tension with one another. Could it be that the idea of a single unified elite, a single power, is consoling because it makes the world appear less disorganised and frightening than it really is? A unified source of oppression is easier to look at, perhaps, than an endless sequence of cock ups and chaos? Having said that, I take your point that Britain and the West will change irrevocably when the influence of the Church finally drifts away, but from a priest's point of view, I think that I welcome the challenge. Perhaps it will feel more honest and rather bracing to have to explain myself and my role again, rather than be taken on sufferance as part of a rather tired national chaplaincy service (which is what my job feels like sometimes).*

*Finally, of course I was moved by your hope that 'There may be a space around the crib for regretful and reverent agnostics to kneel in the rushes with the ass and the ox and the shepherds and the true believers.' I don't know anything about your religious background, but it seems obvious that you are speaking personally here. If you ever want to talk about anything, please get in touch. I would be failing as a priest if I did not make myself available and quite apart from all that I would really enjoy another chat.*

*I sent the link to your video to a few friends and also posted it on couple of theology discussion groups I belong to. I hope this is ok. Everyone is up late tonight writing sermons for tomorrow so you may be getting a few comments from procrastinating vicars!*

*I hope I haven't gone on too much. I have never commented on a OyTube video before and I don't know what sort of length is appropriate.*

*Yours, L*

I have another shot of mild-revulsion at Lavinia's description of herself as a priest who is 'making herself available' to help me. Who the fuck does she think she is? She thinks that she's a priest of course, but who the fuck does she think she is, thinking that everyone else thinks that she's a priest? For fuck's sake. Anyway, despite all that, I am pleased that she has written such a long comment and I have to admit that I would enjoy talking to her again. I text her while I finish off my coffee:

*Here is my email address. Your comment was fine, but one day you may wish to contact me without the world reading what you have to say. I am really not trying to be edgy, Lavinia, just honest. I seem to be dancing right on the line between what is respectable and what is not at the moment, in my thoughts and in my videos. And that frightens me, more than it thrills me. As to my own religious background – it is a very short and very depressing story that, at some point, I would be happy to share. In the meantime, keep yourself safe and do get in touch if I can help with anything. And thanks for sharing the link with your vicar mates. I think some of them have commented – they have been really interesting. I will look up Kundera.*

When I have sent the text, I quickly send another.

*Also, please don't worry about any unpleasant comments about you, either underneath your own comment or with reference to your interview. I have learnt that OyTube attracts some very strange people, as does the politics around the Rush Bearing. Put the two together and...*

When I have sent the second text I go back inside to my bedroom and WhatsApp Sonia, the obese woman from Basingstoke:

*'How are you doing? Have you got a few minutes?'*

Sonia messages back straight away to say that she is off to church shortly, which takes me back a bit. It is clearly my day to be dealing with Christian women. We keep messaging and it turns out that she attends some sort of non-denominational charismatic church, which seems to be pretty central to her life. She is a widow, it transpires.

We message back and forth for a couple of minutes more, about Jesus and the weather, and then we message for a couple of minutes about sex, and then Sonia video calls me. She is on her bed and the subdued light in the room indicates that the curtains are drawn. She is as fat as she suggested.

'Couldn't wait any longer,' she says. 'You're cute. How's things?'

'I'm fine. You look nice too.'

'Aww, that's kind. Thanks.'

'Do you want to watch me wank?'

'Yes please,' says Sonia. She hoiks up her skirt and pulls off her pants. She shows me her vagina for a few seconds and then returns the phone to her face.

'And watching me won't make you late for church?'

'Might do a bit. But you can't be good all the time, can you?'

I can tell from the shaking phone that Sonia is already masturbating.

'No. I don't suppose you can.'

When it is over, Sonia is keen to chat, but I tell her that I have to get off to my mum's for Sunday dinner. She eventually goes when I promise to call her back that evening so we can talk 'normally'. When I have ended the call, I go downstairs for a shower but as I am pulling off my shirt, Sonia messages again:

*'Great to meet you. You cant be good all the time* 😉 *but if you say sorry Jesus always exepts you back. Thats the best thing about being a Christian.'*

I text back:

*'That does sound great. Please give Jesus my love.'*

She replies.

*'Haha. You can give him yr love yrself if you want to. Youv got a lovely cock by the way.* 😉 *Enjoy dinner with yr mum.'*

I block her, have my shower and then walk round to mum's feeling grubby and unkind.

. . .

Mum is in the dining room again. *The Globe* is folded next to her and she has a gin and tonic at her elbow. She is doing something on her phone. She looks up when I walk in.

'Adam. Hello. Do you want a drink?'

'Of course I do.'

She peers at me over the top of her specs.

'Will this one be the hair of the dog.'

'Something like that.'

Mum taps her phone and then goes to the sideboard and mixes me a drink. She never skimps on the gin, even when I look so obviously rough. Mum is never judgemental about my drinking, even implicitly.

'I was just texting Ben,' she says as she hands me the glass. 'To say thank you. He sent me the link to your new video. Actually, he sent me the link to the first one too, last week.'

'Did he? Oh right.'

'Yes he did. He was quite surprised that you hadn't sent them to me yourself.'

'I was going to. I almost did. I...I...I didn't know what you'd make of them, to be honest.'

'Hmm.' Mum sits down and unfolds the paper. 'He thought you might be embarrassed about them. He's emailed you, apparently. About the new one.'

'I haven't looked at emails yet. It was a late night.'

'Right.'

I sit down opposite mum and sip my drink.

'So, what did you think of them mum?'

'The videos?'

'Yes of course the videos.'

She pushes the paper away and frowns for a moment.

'What did I think of them? That's a jolly good question. Actually, it was Ben who said something about them, that I hadn't quite been able to put my finger on. Do you know what I mean, when someone says what you've been half thinking but haven't quite been able to articulate, even to yourself?'

'I think so. Vaguely. What did Ben say?'

'Well, he pointed out that the great thing about blogs and OyTube videos and so on, is that you don't have to reference your work as you would in an academic paper or in a piece of conventional journalism. You know, you're allowed to make fairly general, sweeping points without having to explain yourself too much.'

She glances at me, gauging my mood.

'Go on.'

'Now I can see that makes OyTube a fun medium, particularly for someone like you Adam, but it's a little bit frustrating if you're used to...if you're used to...'

'If you're used to what?'

'Well, I suppose, if you're used to serious writing.'

'I see.'

'Don't be grumpy, for goodness' sake. Apparently your videos have been very successful so you must be doing something right.'

'Can you give me an example of what you're talking about?'

'Yes I think I can.'

'Go on then.'

She places her elbows on the table, interlaces her finger and rests her chin on them.

'The stuff about the C of E for instance.'

'What about it?'

'Well, I'm not a church goer, as you know, God knows what I actually believe. I want to believe there's *something*, of course, but I don't think one can ever be sure. And I know precious little about divinity or theology or whatever you call it. But...but...are you sure that the Church of England has followed the establishment slavishly in the way you suggest? Have you got that quite right, Adam? First Protestant and then Colonial and then Capitalist and now multi-cultural or whatever? It's a neat theory; I can see that. And it made me interested and got me engaged. But I ended up wondering if it was actually true, because it seemed a bit too sweeping. A bit too black and white. The C of E is a bloody big diverse organisation as far as I can tell. From the little I know they can never agree with anything among themselves. So, I was left uncertain about what to believe.'

'Oh.'

She grins at me, and despite myself, I grin back and then sip some more gin.

'I'm quite a black and white person, I think, mum. At some level.'

'I know you are, Adam. That's part of your trouble, isn't it? There were other examples of the same sort of thing, but I can't think of them now.'

'But you didn't object to the actual content? The stuff about... about multi-culturalism and so on?'

She shakes her head slowly.

'Adam, I live in Coxthorpe. I'm not going to be offended by that sort of thing, am I? I've heard that stuff countless times, although never quite so well expressed. I know there are problems with...with things. I might not agree with you, but I'm not quite the mindless *Globe*-reading clone you think I am.'

'I know you're not that mum.'

'And beyond Ben's point, I thought the videos were really good, both of them. You're great with words and you got me thinking, at least. Which very little seems to, these days.'

'Oh well, that's something I suppose.'

'Exactly. What are you going to tackle next?'

'There's a big protest on Saturday. I'm going to film that and try and interview people.'

'Oh, that sounds interesting.'

But mum doesn't sound particularly interested. She goes into the kitchen and starts chopping spuds while I sip my gin and feel cross. Eventually, I call:

'Did Ben ring specifically then, to tell you about my channel?'

'No. He texted. Well, actually I texted him last week and then he replied with the link. And he sent the second one this morning. And after I'd watched it, we had a bit of a chat by text.'

'Oh right. So, you haven't actually spoken to him about them?'

'No.'

'Has he rung you recently at all?'

'No Adam, he hasn't.'

'He's a fucker isn't he?'

Mum appears in the door, holding a spud.

'Yes he is a bit of fucker, but luckily I have another son who isn't. A son who is generous with his time with his old mum. And who is also sparkling company, at least until he gets jealous and grumpy, and then he can out-fucker even his brother.'

'I never out-fucker Ben.'

'You do just occasionally Adam. Now get yourself another drink and get me one while you're at it.'

We have roast beef with a nice Bordeaux and then cheese with a bottle of Tim Taylors Landlord. When we have finished eating, we go outside onto the patio with our coffee. The sun is bright and warm, and the gentle rise of Weskdale is blurry with heat.

'A bit of an Indian summer,' I say.

Mum giggles.

'Christ, don't say that. You'll be wanting to send it home.'

'I didn't advocate sending anyone anywhere mum.'

'I know you didn't. I was joking. Don't be so bloody serious.' She sips her coffee and looks around. 'Do you know what, I still feel guilty occasionally about hanging on to this place when dad died.'

'Why on earth would you feel guilty?'

'Because it's so much space that I don't need. To begin with, I justified it to myself by saying that it would be useful to have a bit of room when Ben bought the family up, but obviously...obviously that hasn't quite happened.'

She sips her coffee again. For a few moments neither of us speaks and then I say:

'Please don't ever sell the house mum. It's you. It's all of us. I can't imagine you anywhere else.'

'Neither can I really.'

'And I am sorry Ben doesn't come up more often.'

'Why are you sorry? It's not your fault. Anyway, I always enjoy going down there. I get to see a bit of London, don't I? And it's more convenient in lots of ways if it's me who does the travelling. Oh, that reminds me. God, I must be going nuts...'

She puts her coffee on the garden table and pulls out her phone. She pushes her specs down her nose and scrolls through some texts.

'Yes, here we are. Are you free on Tuesday week?'

'Well, I'm certainly not working.'

'I know you're not. I checked your roster. You're nights Sunday and Monday aren't you? Then you're off for a week. And as far as you know, you're not doing anything else on Tuesday?'

'No. I don't think so. Why?'

'It was the other thing that Ben mentioned, when we texted. They're doing drinks for Miriam's fiftieth, apparently, and they're keen that you and I should both come down.'

'Are they actually? Both of us? Midweek?

'Apparently.'

'And he wasn't just pretending that he wanted us there to make you happy?'

'He certainly wasn't pretending about you. He specifically wanted to know when you'd be free.'

'That's very odd. Why would he do that?'

Mum drains her coffee and shrugs.

'Well, it is a significant birthday for Miriam, isn't it? And I suppose your success on OyTube suddenly makes you interesting as far as Ben's concerned. Maybe that's got something to do with it.'

'I doubt it.'

'Anyway, he said that he's mentioned it all in his email.'

'I'll have a look.'

I drain my coffee and put the cup down next to mum's. A breeze drifts off the moors, rustling the leaves on the apple tree at the bottom of the garden. Ben climbed that tree once and was the Saxons defending an ancient stronghold during the Normans' Harrying of the North. I was the Normans and I tried to whack his ankles over and over again with a broom while he pelted me with over-ripe apples. In the end, it was time for tea, and Saxons and Normans declared it a draw.

'Promise you won't move, mum, at least for a while.'

She sighs softly.

'I won't. Not while you're around, I won't. I promise you that.'

'Thanks mum.'

. . .

I walk home, just after three, half pissed and considerably more cheerful. When I get in, I smoke in the yard and check out the Respect Haxton website on my phone. I haven't looked at it for a while and it has been added to since I last saw it. Again, it occurs to me how well put together the site is. Respect Haxton either has some talented web designers within its ranks, or it has plenty of money, or it has both. The two big headline articles on the site concern the council's decision to change the route of the Rush Bearing (*Democracy and Common Sense in Action*) and the revised arrangements for next

Saturday's march. In response to the council's decision, Saturday has been transformed from a day of action and solidarity into a *Family Fun Diversity Day*, co-sponsored by the West Yorkshire Police Service, and the Salamanca banking group. There will be a rally and speeches in Victoria Square, and then a 'Solidarity Procession' up the Leeds Road to Haxton, with floats and bands. The day will end with a free concert in Albert Park.

I carry on scrolling down the site until I arrive at the 'Respect On-Line' section. This is new. It is a roundup of stuff that has appeared on the internet about the Rush Bearing controversy in the last week or so. There are links to a couple of videos by Resistance Media and a load more to websites that I have never heard of. There is also a short piece about me.

*Respect-on-line wants to welcome a newcomer to the Rush Bearing social media pile on: The Haxton Review OyTube channel. The cheeky fellow who runs it, or one of his friends, posted his first video in the comments box on our website. He has produced a second since then, and through a family connection, he has managed to draw comment from the mainstream media. As a result, the chap is doing very well indeed, for a beginner, with 18,000 subs and a seemingly endless stream of comments beneath his material. Sadly, the content itself is much less impressive, being boring Little-Englander racism of the nastiest, Brexitiest kind. To be fair, the stuff is delivered in rather grandiose tones with a few literary references chucked in, causing some to comment that Mr Haxton Review has aspirations to become Coxthorpe's very own B-Tec Enoch Powell. We have no doubt that OyTube will be looking at him and his work in due course and making their own decisions. In the meantime, it's probably best if we don't speak to him. The less encouragement that the Haxton Review receives, at this point, the better.*

I assume that the last bit is a reference to Lavinia. I hope I haven't got her into trouble. It is strange and more than a little disturbing to read about myself in such hostile terms, and on such a well put together website (the quality of the website shouldn't matter but it does, for some reason). It would have been stupid not to have expected criticism, of course, but I hadn't expected comments that would misrepresent me so completely and be quite so nasty. For the first time since I started the Haxton Review, I feel pressure. It's right at the back of my skull, very faint, but real. A slowly tightening cord.

I roll another fag, for comfort rather than because I feel like one, and then browse the Civitas Seminar website. There is a new article about the Rush Bearing by Roger Wrigglesworth entitled: *The Ever-Contested Commons: The Lantyrn Royd Dispute and the Struggle Against Enclosure.* The piece is densely written with dozens of footnotes on each page. I don't even attempt it. I am afraid Ben and mum are probably right, I am much happier with broad (un-referenced) brush strokes, than with detailed painstaking scholarship. I am a generalist and a bit of a dilletante. I was great at my first degree but absolutely crap when I attempted my doctorate in London.

The breeze gets cooler and so I go back inside and WhatsApp Sonia again. We message for a bit about my lunch with mum and her church service, and she tells me that she had a great time during worship and ended up full of the Holy Spirt, '*like I havnt been for ages*'. I message to say that I am glad to hear it and then slowly turn the conversation to sex. A few minutes later we video call and the Holy Spirit doesn't stop Sonia from energetically masturbating again on camera. When we have finished. I say goodbye and end the call without waiting for a reply. I block Sonia again and then have a sandwich and go to bed. I am on days tomorrow.

. . .

I am actually on days on Monday, Tuesday and Wednesday. And, in that time, I do nothing apart from work, eat, sleep, check my OyTube figures, and masturbate. To facilitate the latter, I contact Tracie on Monday and, against my better judgement, Sonia on

Tuesday. Tracie's legs are now in plaster, but that doesn't stop her masturbating cheerfully and as usual she disappears as soon as we are both done. Sonia is more demanding. She is unhappy, apparently, that I only call when I am horny and so I feel obliged to message her for a bit about her life in general. I learn that she speaks in tongues, and still works two days a week in Tesco, and that she goes on a church-run holiday for the bereaved in Lyme Regis each August. Eventually I video call and once again the room is dark.

'Hi,' she says. 'It's been nice to have a bit of a normal chat, isn't it? It's more friendly.'

'Yeah, it is. Do you want to watch me play with my dick?'

'Don't say dick,' she says. 'Say cock. It's more romantic.'

'OK. Do you want to watch me play with my cock?'

'Yes.'

So, we masturbate for each other again and, after that, I put the phone straight down and block her. I feel bad about it, but I do it anyway.

. . .

I don't open my brother's email on Monday or Tuesday and I get three missed calls from him in that time, which I do not return. The calls and the email will both presumably be about my latest video and I can't face defending myself yet. I need bags of mental energy to deal with Ben, and, when I am working, I have none to spare.

. . .

On Wednesday, just before five o'clock, I get a call from Bill Bright who manages our site. In terms of the company hierarchy, he is my boss's boss, which makes him important and not the sort of bloke you want to piss off, but not completely distant like the senior people from our head office in Birmingham. I don't see Bill much at work, partly because of my shifts and partly because my office is directly above the warehouse floor while his in the admin block at the other end of the site, but when I do see him he is always affable enough. He's tough, but he is never obviously unkind.

'It's Bill,' he says when I answer the phone. 'Are you busy, Adam?'

'I'm always busy, Bill. You know that.'

'Yeah, course you are. But is the job actually round your knackers at the moment?'

'No. It's ok today. Touch wood.'

'Right. Can you give me five minutes please?'

'Yeah of course.'

For a moment neither of us speaks and then Bill says.

'No, not on the phone. In my office.'

'Yeah ok. Sorry. Shit, that sounds ominous. Am I in trouble?'

'Dunno. Just give us the five minutes, will you?'

I jog the length of the warehouse and climb the stairs at the end, two at a time, instead of waiting for the lift. I slow down along the management corridor, but I am still out of breath when I knock on Bill's door.

'Yeah. Come in.'

I push the door open and go in. Bill is sitting behind his desk jabbing at his computer keyboard. He looks up.

'Bloody hell, you got your skates on.'

'I was worried. Do I need to be?'

'I don't think so. Not yet anyway. Look, grab a seat and we'll have a chat.'

I would guess that Bill is in his early sixties. He has been with the company since he joined as a warehouseman in his late twenties when he left the Army. He's worked his way up and now he knows the job inside out at every level, making him both a terror to bad practice and an irreplaceable asset. He is bald apart from a wild halo of greying red hair around the bottom of his scalp. He has a bushy moustache and sideburns of the same colour, and his face is unnaturally smooth, like paper. Today he looks awkward, rather than angry as he studies me.

'Are you active on social media or owt?' he asks finally.

'Depends what you mean by social media, I suppose.'

'You're not on facebook?'

'No.'

'Instagram?'

'No'

'Snapchat?'

'No. How do you know about Snapchat, Bill? Are you on it?'

'Am I chuff. It's the grandkids, in't it? I think it's a lot of nonsense.'

'Why are you asking me about it then?'

'You on OyTube?'

The strange thing is, I honestly haven't made the connection until then. Even when Bill started talking about social media. It truly hasn't occurred to me that anything to do with the Haxton Review would get back to work. I just didn't see how there could possibly be a connection. There isn't a connection.

'Yes I am,' I say carefully. 'But only recently and what I do has got nothing to do with work. Nothing at all. I don't even use my own name.'

Bill stares at his desktop. He aligns some papers neatly.

'Is it sort of *political* this stuff you do?' he asks without looking up.

'I suppose you could call it that. It's to do with Haxton and the Rush Bearing. But I don't know what it's got to do with...'

'Is it what you'd call *right wing* political?'

'Bill, can you tell me what has happened please?'

'Is it right wing stuff, Adam?'

'Well, that depends what you mean. I'm not sure right and left work as terms anymore really. I think politics has shifted.'

'Is it racist?'

'No. No, it isn't. At least I wouldn't say so. But, but it's difficult to define what that word means these days.' Bill is still staring at his desk. 'Look, can you just tell me what has happened please?'

He shrugs and then looks up.

'It's bloody strange to be honest.'

'What is?'

'I hope you han't got yerself in trouble.'

'What's happened, Bill?'

'Right. So I got a call this lunchtime. From a copper.'

'From a policeman? About me?'

'Yes.'

'But I haven't broken any laws.'

'I know you han't. He were very particular about that, was the cop. It's about a non-crime incident, apparently. He actually said that: a non-crime incident. He was a nice lad, to be honest. He was from something called the Communities Cohesion Team, no less, based in the big nick in Leeds. He sounded young, but they say younger cops is a sign your getting old, don't they?'

'Yes they do. What's the Community Cohesion Team?'

'Not community, communities. He were right particular about that when I were noting it down. And I've no idea what it is. I din't ask.'

'Ok. But why is he interested in me if I haven't broken any laws. And why was he talking to you rather than to me directly?'

'He said he were just checking in. That were the phrase he used.'

'Checking in?'

'Yeah. He said that you'd been putting some stuff online that...' Bill makes quotation marks with his stubby fingers...sailed a bit close to the wind...about racism and suchlike, and he were just checking in about your thinking.'

'Fucking hell.'

'I told you it were strange.'

'It's bloody terrifying. What did you tell him?'

Bill shrugs again.

'I told him that as far as I were concerned you were an exemplary employee and I'd never heard a thing that made me think you were some sort of Nazi nutcase, or whatever.' He leans across his desk. 'You're not are you?'

'I'm not what?'

'Some sort of Nazi.'

'Of course I'm not a bloody Nazi.'

I close my eyes for a couple of seconds and try to get to grips with what Bill has just told me. I fail. It's too ludicrous and too disturbing, I can't reach my mind around its edges. I have the strange sensation that the normal world is going on as it always does just outside Bill's door, while here, in his hot little office, everything is bonkers and wild. The cord at the back of my skull, the pressure that I had almost forgotten about, tightens perceptibly.

'How did the conversation end?'

'What do you mean?'

'How did it end? What did the cop say after you'd convinced him that I'm not a Nazi?'

Bill chuckles.

'I'm not sure I did convince him, to be fair.'

'Why? What happened?'

'He gave me his number and also the number of summat called Prevent. Have you heard of it?'

'Yeah. It's the government's anti-loony thing isn't it? I thought it was just for Muslims.'

'It in't apparently. It's for everyone who's gone off the rails and turned a bit extremist.'

'And that's me obviously. What did he say when he gave you the numbers?'

'He said that if I got wind of anything dodgy about you, I should contact him or the Prevent people, or both. And then he said summat else, summat funny.'

'What?'

'He said that his role were to be supportive of the company as we managed our DEI journey, and that would include helping us negotiate a spectrum of deliverables, going forward, regardless of what decisions we ended up making.'

'Did he really talk like that?'

'Yeah. I made a note of it, cos it were so weird.'

'What did you say to him?'

'I told him I'd have a word with you. And he said he reckoned that were a good place to start. That were actually his phrase: a good place to start. Then, as a parting shot, he told me that his team, the communities cohesion people, worked with industry at a high level and with government, providing value added across a number of departments. That's what he said...value added across a number of departments...as if it were significant somehow. I noted that down as well. Then he fucked off.'

Bill stands up and walks to the window. He peers down into the loading bays. They are the key bit of the warehouse, the heart of the operation. There have been occasions when Bill has left his office and marched down there, either to help out if things are badly backing up, or else to bollock someone publicly if he sees something dangerous. There has never been a serious accident in the fifteen years that Bill has been in charge and we have consistently outperformed our sites in Bracknell, Ashford, Solly Hull and Crewe. I'm never quite sure what 'leadership' means, but whatever it is, Bill has it. He's similar to Roger Wrigglesworth, in that respect, but less contorted.

'It's all a bit odd, in't it?' he says eventually. 'I think I preferred coppers when they used to give you a clip for being pissed up and causing bother on a weekend.'

'Well yes, I think I probably preferred that too. Not...Not the I ever got clipped. Did this bloke say how he had connected me with my OyTube channel, by the way, or with the company?'

'No. He didn't say anything about owt like that.'

'Oh.'

'I suppose they'll have their ways, won't they?'

'Yeah, I suppose they will. Look Bill, I am sorry that I've made things awkward for you, but I honestly haven't done anything illegal, or...or immoral, or anything that would bugger about with our reputation.'

'I hope not,' he says. 'I really hope not, kid.' He turns back to me, runs his hand softly over his smooth scalp and smiles. 'I know you in't some sort of fascist. But, having said that, I in't quite sure where the rules are these days. That's the trouble in't it?'

'I think that's exactly the trouble.'

'And I'm buggered if I know what that copper meant about working with industry and with government across a number of departments. He made it sound a bit threatening, even though it's innocent enough on the face of it. He were a friendly lad, like I say, but, when he said that, you got the feeling he enjoyed being just a little bit frightening.'

He shrugs.

'Anyway, I've done what I said I'd do. I've spoken to you. Now bugger off back to work and be sensible, ok?'

'Yeah.'

'We dun't want to lose you.'

'I should hope not. I don't want you to lose me either.'

'I'm serious, Adam. You're one of the better ones. We can't afford to be losing such as you.'

Which is the nicest thing that Bill has ever said to me. But it does absolutely nothing to reassure me.

. . .

I am still worried about the conversation when I leave work an hour and a half later. When I get in, I go straight round to the off license and buy a bottle of red and a couple of bottles of Stella. I go home and order a curry and then have a fag in the yard. When the curry arrives, I lie on the sofa and eat with a glass of wine on the floor next to me while I surf the internet, mostly following links from the Respect-on-Line page of the Respect Haxton website. I get another call from Ben while I am eating, which I ignore. When I have finished my food, I finally open his email from Sunday morning.

*Hi Adam,*

*Congratulations on another video. Your subs and comments are incredible for a new channel. I know that some of that will be down to Tania's piece, but not all of it will be. You are clearly striking a nerve somewhere and doing so very professionally and with a bit of style.*

*I'm guessing that you ignored my suggestion about a cooling off period, between producing a video and posting it. (Either that or you really believe that bollocks about minority groups being treated as sacred symbols in the new UK religion of political correctness gone mad?!) Oh well, I tried to tell you...*

*Can I ask a very obvious question? Do you think it's possible that you are using your videos as a kind of therapy? I am thinking particularly about the religious stuff, of course, but the rest of it as well to some extent. There is nothing wrong with therapy. We all need somewhere to let the grotty stuff surface and get sifted through, but I can't help thinking that it's best done privately, preferably with a trained professional. At the moment your grot is surfacing before the whole world. I am not sure if that will benefit you very much in the longer term.*

*I'm serious about that Adam. If you keep doing what you're doing, and particularly if you keep being successful, you will be noticed and then there could be unfortunate consequences, both for you and for other people. Please think hard before you produce more content in the same vein. Please, Adam!*

*Lecture over! More cheerfully, we are having drinks for Miriam's fiftieth from about five o'clock on Tuesday week (the 23rd). Mum said that you weren't working that day or the next, and that's partly why we chose the date. We would love to have you there. It's only going to be a few drinks and a bit of food, and I promise that it will all be over by midnight. Mum's coming and it goes without saying that you would both be very welcome to stay the night. Please make an effort to come down. Various people from work want to meet the man behind the Haxton Review (and they won't be horrible and critical like me) and I would really enjoy having you and mum here together. I know you think that I am careless about family, Adam, this is me trying not to be.*

*Right, I'm off. If I don't hear back from you, I will give you a ring to confirm about Miriam's drinks.*

*Ben*

*PS. By the way, what the fuck is 'love's high and unsure meridian'? Just asking....*

When I have finished reading the email, I pour myself another glass of wine and take a deep breath. Then I call Ben. The call goes to voicemail but just as I am about to leave a message, Ben calls me. I end the first call and answer him.

'Hi Ben.'

'Finally. I've been trying to get hold of you all bloody week.'

'I know you have. Sorry. I've been working.'

'I've been fucking working too.'

'I know. Sorry. Are you pissed?'

'Yeah, a bit. Are you?'

'Yeah.'

There is the sound of Ben sipping something. I drink some wine. If we're both drinking, we may as well drink together.

'In that case we better keep it short, or we'll end up hating on each other. Are you coming to Miriam's drinks?'

'Yes, I am.'

'Thank you. I am very grateful.'

'I think mum would be upset if I wasn't there.'

'I am sure she would be. And you don't want to miss the opportunity to be Mr Haxton Review among the metropolitan media folk, of course.'

'Fuck off Ben.'

'I'll fuck off gladly in a minute, I promise. But first, did you read my email?'

'Yes. Just now.'

He drinks again.

'Did you actually read it though?'

'Of course I did.'

'Look Adam, please take what I said seriously. Please do. Please. I don't...I don't...'

'You don't what?'

'I don't want you to be damaged,' he says quietly. 'I don't want you to be hurt. People will notice you, you know, if you keep making videos. Eventually, shitty things will happen.'

I stare at the handset for a moment, while I struggle to control myself. And then I say:

'They've already noticed me.'

'Well listen to me then. For fuck's sake listen to me.'

'I'll see you Tuesday week, Ben.'

'I'm being serious. You do have a knack for self-destruction.'

'I know you're serious. See you Tuesday.'

'I mean it.'

'I am sure you do.'

I hear him drink again

'Ok. Fuck it. See you Tuesday then.'

The line goes dead.

I take my wine outside and perch the glass on the wall at the back of the yard. I smoke two cigarettes, one straight after another, and then drink the wine while the dusk thickens around me and the hulks of piled cars in the scrap yard opposite turn blurry and vague. 'Nowt wrong with that view,' Ben said when he first visited my house. 'It's a proper Coxthorpe view, is that.' I still don't know if I was more irritated by what he actually said or by the stupid, affected West Yorkshire intonation. Finally, when I am reasonably calm, I wipe my eyes and go back to the lounge where I pour another glass of wine and WhatsApp Sonia. Sonia not Tracie because I want the challenge of her pretend reluctance to get dirty and the thrill of corrupting her stupid, infantile faith. After Bill's visit and then Ben's call, I need something resistant this evening, something that I can work against and then wank against. I need a vicious little holiday from myself, something that will loosen that horrible tightening cord. Luckily she is in. She is 'just watching telly,' apparently.

I find myself messaging Sonia, in slightly disguised terms, about Miriam's drinks do and about my relationship with my brother. She turns out to be a pretty good listener, asking sensible questions without being too intrusive. 'Aint you got any kids of your own?' she messages eventually. I answer that I haven't because I 'missed the boat', and then, gradually, I begin to turn the conversation in the usual direction. Sonia doesn't miss a trick. 'Is this just about sex for you?' she messages. And then, immediately afterwards, 'Ain't you interested in getting to know me?' It takes a long time, after that, to get to the video call. But I manage it in the end because I always do, and then, because I am pissed and mean, and frustrated that things have taken so long, I get filthy in a way that I haven't done before, with anyone. Poor, widowed Sonia who speaks in tongues and goes on church-run holidays for the bereaved in Lyme Regis, ends up on her back on her sofa with her legs in the air and her massive bum on display. She props the phone on the mantlepiece, apparently, to make sure that I get a good look. I speak to her obscenely while she plays with her vagina and her anus. I insult her. I reference her weight and her faith, in the most unpleasant terms imaginable. And then, when I have run out of cruelty, I come so hard that the semen hits my chin. Straight after that I end the call without waiting to say goodbye and then block her. I have another fag in the yard, eat a poppadum left over from my takeaway, and then stumble upstairs to collapse into bed.

I do think briefly about Sonia as I drift off to sleep. I wonder what she did when the call ended. Whether she pulled her knickers back up or just went to bed. And how she felt about what she had just done. I am not completely without empathy.

And I am sick of sin, even though I know that there is no such thing as sin.

# 16

I STAY IN bed most of Thursday, watching Netflix and snoozing, dealing with my hangover and the after-effect of the three twelve-hour shifts. I finally get up at quarter to four and go shopping for food and a couple of bottles of wine. I cook an omelette for tea and drink one of the bottles, and then I text Ben:

*Sorry we ended up rowing last time. It probably isn't best to chat when we are both pissed. To be clear, I would like very much to come to Miriam's birthday thing on Tuesday. I would also like to stay the night if the offer is still there. I can't be arsed driving round London, so I will get the train. (I've done a fair bit of overtime recently, so I'm entitled to a few treats). I will let mum know what I am thinking of doing, so she doesn't expect a lift.*

Then I text mum to tell her my plans. She replies straight away.

*Great. It will be smashing to have all three of us together, with Miriam and the kids. And don't worry about not driving, I am just as happy getting the train, and I was planning to go down the day before anyway. Also, please, Adam, make sure I don't get pissed and make a twit of myself in front of the great and the good! I think I am going to get a new dress. I will text a pic of it so you can tell me what you think.*

Ben does not reply.

. . .

I'm still tired, so I go back to bed at ten o'clock without even bothering to talk to anyone on-line. I wake up at half seven the following morning feeling refreshed. I treat myself to a leisurely breakfast of marmite toast and then call Jason while I am out in the yard, having my morning fag. He answers on the second ring.

'Hi. What do you want?'

'You're up early. I assumed you'd still be in bed and I'd be leaving you a message.'

'Well yer wrong. I've been up since six.'

'Are you working?'

'No.'

'What on earth are you up for then?'

'We're preparing stuff up here.'

'What are you preparing?'

'Have you heard owt about tomorrow's march?'

'Not really. Only what I saw on the Respect Haxton website. Did you see that we were on it, by the way?'

'Yeah, someone showed me. It's shit.'

'Well, it's worrying, but I'm not sure we can do much about it. I'm trying not to think about it too much.'

Jason laughs and I hear him light a cigarette.

'Anyway, they've toned the march down now, because they've got their way about the Rush Bearing.'

'They may have done officially, like. But there's this other lot, Coxthorpe Resist, who say they are gonna come right into Lantyrn Royd on Saturday and cause bother.'

'Have you actually heard them say that?'

'No.'

'Do you *know* anyone who's heard them say that?'

'Some lad who knows Roger heard summat, apparently. And it's on the Respect Haxton website.'

'I missed that.'

'It only went up yesterday evening.'

'What does it say about them?'

'That no one should have owt to do with them, cos Saturday is meant to be a fun day and a safe space for everyone and all that bollocks.'

I inhale deeply and then stub out my cigarette on the wall.

'Fair enough. So, what are you actually doing to prepare? Digging Trenches around St Peters? Sandbags outside The White Horse?'

'Don't take the piss Adam.'

'Sorry. But it does seem bloody odd. What are you doing?'

'Well first off, we're making sure that no one from the community has to walk or get a bus into town or back out. We've got three lads permanently in town with cars and three more up here.'

'I thought you were doing that already.'

'Yeah, but it were just a couple of them before. Now there's six. There's a rosta.'

'Blimey. What else are you up to?'

'We've increased patrols at night and we've boarded up some windows. We're making sure the old folk have a got a bit of food in and a contact number for the committee. And we're getting supplies in at The White Horse in case the trouble goes on a bit, and we have to cook for people if Tesco closes. Also, we've sorted out a couple of places along the Leeds Road where we can watch stuff tomorrow. So, we can see what's coming towards us.'

'It's all gone up a notch suddenly, hasn't it? Who's been doing all this?'

'The Rush Bearing committee mostly, and volunteers. We've got a control room upstairs in The White Horse. It's like it were during the riots, but we've got time to prepare this time. We're more organised.'

'Are you personally busy with this stuff now?'

Jason chuckles.

'Not really. Quite a lot of us got up early and met at The Horse to get it all sorted, and now we've got most of it done so everyone's just having a drink. We'll all be pissed by lunchtime.'

'Which I am sure is pretty much what they did at Mafeking.'

'What?'

'It doesn't matter. Look, if you're not busy could you help me with the next video? I was going to base it around the march tomorrow, but it sounds like tomorrow has already started.'

'Yeah, I've got nowt on.'

'Alright. I'll come up then.'

'Are you gonna drive?'

'I wasn't planning to. I was going to have a drink when I got there.'

'In which case you'll have to get one of our cars.' Jason goes quiet for a moment and I hear the sound of muffled voices. Then he says, 'Do you know the Flea and Firkin pub?'

'Yeah.'

'Can you get there in half an hour?'

'If I get a move on.'

'Right, well yer looking for a white Seat Leon. There will be a middle-aged bloke standing outside it. He'll ask you the time and you've gotta say that you dunno because your watch is broken and you've left your phone at home.'

'Are you being serious?'

'Yeah.'

'This is Coxthorpe in 2025, Jason, not Berlin in 1965. Is it really necessary?'

'Four more lads were put in hospital, last night,' he says quietly. 'That were in two fights on the Leeds Road. And a car got torched at the top of Friendly.'

'Oh. I didn't know.'

'And bring a toothbrush. I dunno when you'll get home.'

. . .

The Flea and Firkin is to east of the city centre, on the edge of what was once the town's cloth district, now one of its several red-light areas. I walk briskly down a steep cobbled street towards the low roads around the River Wesk, whose waters once powered Coxthorpe's mills. Later mills, the ones driven by steam, rise like canyon sides from both sides of the long street so that only a thin ribbon of bright Autumn sky is visible above me. The mills near the town centre have been converted into offices and flats, but the further I walk, the more of them are obviously empty and, finally, derelict. There is evidence of the area's new industry as well: condoms on the floor, a few needles and smashed bottles, and, eventually, the women themselves. They are thin and sickly-looking in leggings and t-shirts, with dark bruises on their pale skin which make them seem childlike and mischievous. Most of the prostitution in Coxthorpe is controlled by Asian gangs and, sure enough, there are Pakistani men in cars on side roads, reading newspapers or talking on their phones. There is no tension here, however. Exploiting women for sex bridges the ethnic divide in Coxthorpe. I keep my eyes on the floor and walk quickly, and the pimps and prostitutes leave me alone.

When I get to the bottom of the cobbled street, I turn left and cross William Avenue, a broader road lined with scrapyards, car dealerships, and builders' merchants. Here, there are gaps between the mills, so it is possible to look up and see the moorland to the east of the city. It hadn't occurred to me before Jason mentioned it, but he is absolutely right, there are very few places in Coxthorpe from which the moors are not visible, at least after a couple of minutes' walk. And there is no denying that the moorland looks impressive in the sunshine, dark and rough-edged against the blue. But the effect, to my mind at least, is unsettling. I love the view from mum's house, but from most places in town the prospect of the moors only serves to emphasise Coxthorpe's insularity. Despite our two railway stations and our closeness to the motorway, we are cut off from the exciting parts of the north. Coxthorpe is not a Manchester, a Liverpool or a Newcastle. It never will be. Somehow, we have missed the provincial swagger, the music, the clubs, the cheerful 'fuck you' to London. The town simmers in its isolation and sadness in its bowl of low hills, and I am fairly sure that Jason is in a small minority in making his way out regularly to walk the country around. The surrounding moors are a dark and constant limit to Coxthorpe, they are seldom, if ever, an invitation.

I walk along William Avenue for five minutes and then turn left onto Hanover Road. This winds between smaller, derelict mills and a few MOT places for three hundred yards before I arrive at The Flea and Firkin on the corner of Hamlyn Avenue. Sure enough, there is a white Seat Leon just beyond the pub. A man who is leaning against the side of the car smoking and playing on his phone. I approach him and he looks up. He stares at me and then slides his phone into his pocket.

'Excuse me, fella,' he says as I draw near.

'Yes.'

'Have you got the time?'

'I'm afraid I haven't. My watch is broken and, like an idiot, I've left my phone at home.'

The man giggles.

'Thank God for that,' he says. 'You feel a right dick asking people, especially if you've just had your phone out yerself.'

'I am sure you do. It did look a bit odd. Why do we have to meet this far out?'

'Cos the Asians will be looking for us in town. They know the registration. Now I believe you wanna lift up to Haxton. Is that right?'

'Yes please.'

'Hop in then.'

My chauffeur's name is Ryan. He is a native of Lantyrn Royd and a track worker on the railway. He has taken the day off today to help run the voluntary taxi service on behalf of the Rush Bearers.

'Not just today, neither,' Ryan says as he swings his car onto William Street. 'I'm not back on while a week on Wednesday.'

'Are you going away?'

'Course I in't going away. I've taken it for the Rush Bearing.'

'Oh, I see. Of course.'

'You know what, I weren't even gonna go on it,' he says as he we drive along the Leeds Road. 'That's the funny thing. I in't interested in some frigging church procession, or parade, or whatever it is. I dropped out of the Boys Brigade after two week, because I couldn't be arsed with that sort of thing. And some of them what are organising it are proper local busy bodies an all, do you know what I mean? Folk who you dun't want knowing your business unless you want everyone and his dog knowing it. But then, when the Muslims started campaigning against it, I had to get involved. It were just like the riots all over again.' He lights a cigarette and grins. 'You haven't got a choice then, have you?'

'Were you involved during the riots?'

'Just about everyone in Lantyrn Royd were involved during the riots,' he says quietly. 'If they hadn't of been, there wouldn't have been a Lantyrn Royd left.'

I roll a cigarette and light it. The White Horse Royd taxi company is apparently fairly relaxed in its smoking policy.

'Is that actually true, Ryan?' I ask eventually. 'I mean, is it actually, literally true?'

'Yeah, it is.' He glances at me. 'Jason said you're the video bloke.'

'Well, I suppose I've become that.'

'Right, well you gotta be clear about this then. Although some of the Rush Bearing lads are rough as owt, and some of them are basically arseholes, and a few of them are properly racist, you've gotta see beyond all that because the truth is a lot of the Asians up in Haxton want us out the way. It sort of bothers them that we're still here. I dunno quite why, but it does. And I in't saying it's true of all of them, necessarily, but it's true of a lot of them. That's what the riots were about really, just getting rid of us. And that's why this Rush Bearing thing matters as well, to show we in't going.'

'And you wouldn't describe yourself as racist?'

Ryan laughs and draws deeply on his cigarette. He looks around him. We are travelling through Haxton now, past the Asian green grocers, the sari chops and the mosques.

'Look my daughter's a teacher, right? She grew up in Lantyrn Royd. But she got out for Uni and she stayed out, and I dun't blame her. In fact, I'm happy for her. She lives out towards Sowerby Bridge now, with her partner and their kid and she teaches English out that way.'

'You must be proud of her.'

'Course I'm proud of her. She's the first one of us to go to Uni. And I'm proud of her daughter an all. I love her to bits. She's two, my only grandchild.'

'What's her name?'

'Molly.

'That's nice.'

'Yeah it is. Her surname is Bahmani.'

'What?'

'Bahmani. That's her surname. Bahmani. Her dad's Asian.'

'Oh.'

'He's not from round here. They met at uni. He's from Manchester.'

'That must feel complicated in Lantyrn Royd.'

Ryan throws his cigarette out of the window and laughs again. Then he stops laughing abruptly.

'I always say that I'm fucked off that she's got wi' a Lancastrian. To make it into a bit of a joke. But...but she won't visit me with Ayat, that's her partner, because she knows what folk in Lantyrn Royd are like. And I don't blame her really. I go and see her instead.'

'Bloody hell.'

'Yeah. So, to answer your question, I dun't think I'm too much of a racist, because I honestly don't care that my daughter's got wi' an Asian. I just care that he loves her and treats her properly, which he does. I'm happier that she's with him than I would be if she were with most of the white lads from Coxthorpe, to be honest. And I love my grandchild to bits. But at the same time...at the same time...

'Yes?'

'Look, I dun't want everything to change too much and too quick, so I dun't even recognise my own country anymore. And I definitely in't gonna let anyone tell me that I can't have a little procession on my own streets because it upsets a few Muslims. Even if the procession in question dun't particularly interest me.' Ryan shrugs and taps at his mobile phone, mounted on the dashboard. 'So, try and put all that into one of your videos.'

'I'll think about it.'

The phone rings twice and he answers.

'Yeah. Who's this?'

'It's Ryan. I'm just turning off Gordon Street.'

'Alright Ryan we'll be ready for yer.'

The line goes dead as Ryan swings the car onto East Croft. There is a van parked across the road, blocking the street about two hundred meters away, outside St Peters. As we approach the van reverses into the church's driveway. Two men step forward and wave us down. They are wearing baseball caps and jackets with collars turned up, partially concealing their faces. Both men are carrying baseball bats.

'You can't really blame her for not wanting to visit,' Ryan says. 'Can you?'

'Not really.'

'But at the same time, we've got to defend ourselves, han't we? We can't just let them walk all over us.' He rubs his eyes and then turns and grins at me. 'Like you said, it's complicated. Anyway, it were nice to meet you.'

'It was nice to meet you too. How much do I owe you for the lift?'

'Couple of quid. Just to cover the petrol.'

I give him a tenner.

'Hang on to the change. Get a pint. And I hope things work out for your daughter.'

I climb out of the car and Ryan does a three-point turn and heads off towards Gordon Street. As soon as he has gone the van moves forward to block the road again. One of the lads in a baseball cap approaches me.

'What's yer name please mate?'

'I'm Adam.'

'Adam who?'

'Why do you want to know?'

'Just gotta check who you are, mate.'

'Perhaps I don't want to tell you who I am.'

'Perhaps you han't got a choice.'

'Obviously, I've got a choice. You can't make me speak to you.'

The man smiles patiently.

'Have you ever worked on doors, Adam.'

'No.'

'Of course you han't. I wouldn't have expected you to have done. No offence like,'

'I'm not offended.'

'Right, well the trick is to control everything from the door itself. If it kicks off inside the pub or the club, in a way you've failed. You try and keep the bother outside.'

'Right. I can see that, I think.'

'Well, it's the same here in't it? We're trying to keep us all safe, so we've decided to have some control over who comes into the area. To make sure there's no trouble.'

'Seems a bit extreme.'

The man shrugs.

'If you don't like it, you can speak to the committee.'

'Would that do me any good?'

'Probably not.'

I sigh and then shrug. I'm obviously not going to win here.

'Ok then. My surname is Monkton.'

'Who are you here to see, Adam Monkton?'

'Jason Lowe.'

The man smiles.

'Fair enough. Thanks for your co-operation. You'll find Jay in The Horse.'

'Am I free to go there on my own. I don't need an escort?'

The smile fades.

'Don't be sarcastic Adam. It's a free country.'

# 17

I WALK DOWN East Croft and then turn right onto Lantyrn Royd. Many of the houses now have boards over their lower windows. Clip Lane and Kibden Street (and presumably also Wrack Street and Friendly) have cars blocking them, with men in baseball caps standing guard. St George's crosses hang from every streetlight. And the table has been erected again outside The White Horse. There is a crowd gathered round it, with Brenda in the centre, with a glass in her hand. A police car is parked just beyond.

'You all right Adam,' Brenda calls as I approach.

'Yeah I'm fine. How are you?'

'Knackered love. It's been frantic. You here to see Jay?'

'Yeah.'

'He's inside. They've got the police in the control room, talking to some of the committee.'

'I thought you were the committee, Brenda?'

'Yeah, I am. But I'm not the bit that deals with the police. Leave that to Roger and Dave and Jay and that lot. I'm happier out here with me table.'

The table has the map of the Rush Bearing procession on it, as well the petitions, and a pile of Roger's booklets. There are also some glossy pamphlets with a mosque on the front, entitled *Standing Together Against the Islamic Menace.* I pick one of them up and flick through it.

'Is this another one of Roger's?'

'Brenda shakes her head quickly and sucks air through her teeth.

'No. God, no. He didn't want us to put them out. He's right against them. Look who's published them.'

'It says here they were produced by *English Solidarity.*'

'Exactly. Them off the telly. They're meant to be coming down to protest against the Muslims tomorrow, down in town.'

'I had no idea.'

'It's on their website. There's a few round here want to go and join them, but Roger reckons that it'll kick off, so we should just stay up here and look after our own area. So, we dun't look bad.'

'I suppose that's probably sensible. They don't have the best reputation do they?'

'No, they dun't. We've not had any contact with them officially, like, but one or two of the lads know them and got hold of the booklets.' She shrugs and sips her drink. 'Like I say, Roger didn't want to put them out, but he lost the vote.'

A fat man in shades is standing next to Brenda with a pint in one hand and a cigarette in the other. He nods at the leaflets.

'We need all the help we can get. And ES know how to deal with this stuff, dun't they? They've been doing it for years. Doing it properly, I mean. They get on the news.'

The man drinks some beer and wipes his chin with his cuff. 'Roger said we shouldn't be relying on outsiders, especially not if they're likely to have a scrap. He said it were bad optics or summat.' He snorts. 'But then, he in't exactly local himself is he?'

'Leave it, Dave,' Brenda says sharply. 'Roger said his piece and he lost the vote. We dun't need to be slagging him off do we? That's just what the Muslims would want, is that.'

The third page of the English Solidarity booklet has a timeline of Islamist atrocities. It includes all the obvious ones: 9/11, 7/7, Beslan, Charlie Hebdo, Manchester, Bataclan etc. But in amongst the familiar European massacres, it also mentions Hezbollah and Hamas rocket attacks on Israel, and the October 7th assault.

'I think I know why Roger might not approve, Brenda,' I say slowly. 'It's about more than ES being outsiders I think.'

She waves her hand dismissively.

'It's all politics in't it, at the end of the day. But he said his piece and lost the vote, and that's that as far as I'm concerned. We've got to stick together.'

'Can I keep the booklet?'

'Course you can, love.'

'And you said I'd find Jason with the police?'

'Yeah, they turned up about ten minutes ago. And they weren't right happy when they got stopped on the way in. They're talking about the arrangements for tomorrow. They're in the control room.'

'And the control room's inside is it?'

'Yeah. It's basically just a shitty little storeroom, what's been cleared. It's upstairs.'

'Ok. I'll give him a ring then. See you in a bit.'

'Yeah. See you later love.'

I walk into the pub and buy a pint. Today's Argus is on the bar. It has a large picture of a stage erected in Victoria square on the front page beneath the headline: *Fun Beats Hate.* I don't bother reading the story.

The White Horse is as busy as I have ever known it, which is strange given that it is Friday morning. I wonder if a lot of Lantyrn Royd people have done the same as Ryan and taken the day off work, or if a lot of them don't actually have jobs. Either way, the atmosphere is more serious than previously. People are sitting at tables looking at their phones or at copies of the Argus and talking in low voices. There are crates of baked beans and soup stacked next to the gents and a pile of planks beside the fruit machines. I nod at a couple of people I recognise and then call Jason.

'Where've you been?' he asks when he answers. His voice is low, almost a whisper.

'I've only just got here.'

'No you han't. You went past the checkpoint twenty minutes ago.'

He sounds smug.

'Fucking checkpoint! This really isn't Berlin, Jason, no matter how much you might want it to be.'

'Well what would you call it then? The thing on East Croft?'

'I'd probably call it a couple of dickheads with baseball bats. They rang you, did they?'

'Yep. Lee said you was a bit of a knob when they stopped you.'

'I wasn't expecting to be interrogated. Where are you, anyway?'

'Upstairs. I've just come out of the meeting.'

'To speak to me?'

'Yep.'

'Can I come up, then?'

'Yeah. I've told Simon on the bar. Go and tell him you've spoken to me.'

'Ok. See you in a minute.'

'Yeah.'

The line goes dead.

I go back to the bar, cradling my beer, and catch the barman's eye.

'Is there summat wrong with yer pint?' he asks.

'Of course there is. There's always something wrong with my pint here. But that's not the point. I've just spoken to Jason. I'm going up to see him. Apparently I have to talk to you.'

'Cheeky fucker. You'd better come through then, hadn't you?'

The barman lifts the flap in the bar and I go in. He leads me passed the beer pumps, the boxes of crisps, and the big upside-down bottles of spirits. I have never been behind a bar before and it feels slightly transgressive, as if I have visited somewhere forbidden, as if I have gone through the wardrobe and entered boozy Narnia. The barman opens a narrow door with a cardboard display of peanuts pinned to it. You wouldn't know the door was there unless someone told you and you have to climb two steps to reach it, so the door appears almost suspended in the air. It just adds to the sense of mystery.

'Go on then,' the barman says. 'Off you fuck.'

(If I am in Narnia, the barman makes a shit Aslan)

Just beyond the door is a very dark staircase, without a bannister. I climb up carefully and then turn right onto a marginally less gloomy landing. There is scuffed lino on the floor and stacks of toilet roll and canned drink. Jason is standing at the end of the landing in front of a door, looking pleased with himself.

'You got here then?' he says.

'Yes. Somehow I managed to penetrate the multiple layers of security. What's going on, Jason?'

'We've got the cops here. Talking to us about tomorrow. They've actually had to come up here and talk to us, personally. It's mental.'

'How long have they been here?'

'Quarter of an hour.'

'Can we go in?'

'Yeah. Roger said we could as long as you in't recording.'

'Obviously, I'm not.'

'Alright then.'

Jason knocks softly on the door behind him, then opens it and steps inside. I follow him. The room beyond is long and narrow with the same lino on the floor as the landing, and ancient, tasteless wallpaper, covered in purple flowers, on the walls. The wallpaper is peeling above the room's only window which is partly obscured by a sheet pinned to the window frame. A white table runs the length of the room, strewn with papers. Two police officers, a man and a woman, are sitting at the table, together with Mary, the woman who couldn't stop giggling in my first video. Roger and two other men are standing at a smaller table at the far end of the room making hot drinks from an urn which is steaming on the tabletop. There is a closed door next to the table, made of unpainted chipboard. As we walk in, Roger turns from the urn and smiles.

'Excellent,' he says. 'It's the Rush Bearing media department. Nice to see you again Adam, and congratulations on the god-bothering video. I enjoyed it. A classy piece of work.'

'Thanks.'

The two cops are looking at me curiously. Roger hands them cups of coffee.

'Inspector Jones, Constable Bradley, this is Adam. He's a Oy-Tube person and a - what shall we call you, Adam? - a critical-friend of the Rush Bearers.'

'Something like that, I suppose,' I mumble. 'Fellow traveller, maybe.'

'I don't think we'd anticipated being filmed,' says the inspector.

'Of course not. And you won't be. Adam is just here to give a bit of context to his next video,' Roger glances at me. 'If it's any use, to you, of course.'

'Yeah, thanks Roger. I'm sure it will be. Thanks for letting me come.'

'No problem.'

The Inspector sighs and sips his coffee.

'Ok then,' he says. 'But I'm not going to be filmed or directly quoted, is that clear?'

'Perfectly,' I say.

'So let's go over where we've got to.'

Everyone except me sits around the table. Roger and the Inspector do most of the talking. The other Rush Bearers chip in occasionally while the constable takes notes. Roger and the Inspector are courteous to each other, but with that laboured courtesy that is only millimetres away from insolence.

The main issue (beyond the irresolvable one about the route of the Rush Bearing) is the checkpoints on the roads leading to Lantyrn Royd. The Inspector's point, made over and over again with increasing emphasis, is that it is illegal to block a public highway and that 'vigilantism' is unacceptable. Roger's counter argument, made with equal emphasis, is that the West Yorkshire Police failed to protect the people of Lantyrn Royd during the riots and again during the grooming gang scandal, and that they are co-sponsors of the diversity day celebrations. The cops are therefore not entirely trusted by the locals to keep them safe.

'With respect officer,' Roger says for the umpteenth time meaning the exact opposite, 'you are not necessarily perceived as good actors.'

The inspector meets his eye.

'Look,' he says. 'There's been mistakes in the past, right, no one's denying that. But you have my assurance that we will protect the community tomorrow and for the rest of the week. You have my absolute assurance on that. But having those vans there, it's just provocative. It's inviting trouble, frankly. And it's also against the law.'

'We've had windows smashed and a car burnt out in the last week, Inspector. And as you know numerous people have ended up in hospital. I'm afraid we don't feel very safe or very protected at the moment. Our community's security is the responsibility of all of us.'

'Well in a sense that's true, of course, but...'

'Think of us as a neighbourhood watch scheme, Inspector, but a little bit more proactive.'

And so it goes on. And the strange thing, I think to myself as I stand there with my back to the horrible, damp wallpaper, is that no one comments on the utter bizarreness of the situation. Here are the police, the representatives of the law-making function of the government of Great Britain and Northern Ireland, negotiating in a crappy pub with a rag-tag bunch of men and women about what they are permitted to do and not do in the streets outside. Surely the very fact that these negotiations are taking place means that the state's sovereignty is already compromised in Lantyrn Royd? It must mean that, at least a little. And perhaps that means that state sovereignty is not quite so solid and so effortlessly permanent as one might suppose. It's very peculiar indeed watching the inspector squirm and bluster. It's Toto dragging the curtain back to reveal the great Oz in all his crappy, panicky frailty. Of course, Lantyrn Royd is still under British government control, it would be silly to suggest otherwise. Roger has not declared UDI. No one has printed banknotes with Brenda's head on one side and a gin bottle on the other. But the fact remains that, at the moment, the state does not quite maintain a monopoly on violence here. It has to negotiate its use of force in the upstairs room of a shitty pub, and the implications of that are astonishing and rather frightening. Temporarily at least, the rules appear to have changed.

. . .

Eventually a compromise is worked out. The roadblocks will be withdrawn from Clip Lane, Kibden Street, Wrack Street and Friendly but a police car will be placed at the top of each street for the whole weekend, and 'a team' from 'the community' will be present at the end of each to keep an eye on comings and goings. The main roadblock on East Croft will remain, but it will be known formally as a 'community gateway' and there will be police stationed there, as well as locals, until the threat of trouble has passed.

'Right,' says the inspector, 'if you'd just give me a few minutes, I need to go to the car and make a couple of phone calls.'

'Of course,' says Roger pleasantly. 'Take as long as you need. We could probably do with a chat amongst ourselves anyway. Make your calls and come back.'

The inspector and the constable squeeze out of the room, grim-faced and silent. For a moment the committee members grin at each other across the table and then a round of soft cheers breaks out. Jason punches the air.

'Fucking hell,' he says. 'I weren't expecting them to give up all that. Not to let us keep the checkpoint. Not so quick anyway.'

'They didn't have any choice, Jason.' Roger says. 'Not really. We'd already acted, hadn't we? We're a community taking steps to look after ourselves because we don't trust the police to do it for us. And, anyway, the government and the cops have been negotiating with every other ethnic group for years. They're always talking to community leaders, and so on. All that's happened today is that the native community has caught up.' He drains the glass of wine he has been sipping and nods at me. 'And if the cops had messed us about, we'd got the propaganda arm on hand to hang the bastards out to dry.'

'Well, I wouldn't say...' I begin, but Roger waves me into silence.

'Oh shush, Adam. I'm joking for God's sake. Just shush.' He leans back in his chair and blows me a kiss. 'No, I suspect poor old plod was only here to keep up appearances. He just wanted to save a bit of face by squeezing some sort of concession from us. He knew he couldn't afford to start a real fight.'

With that, Roger walks to the chipboard door and opens it. Inside there is a wooden trestle table with a radio set on it and a couple of mobile phones. The room is cloudy with cigarette smoke. Dave is sitting at a table next to a woman who I don't recognise. Both of them have notepads open.

'Dave, Judy,' Roger says. 'Sorry to have kept you inside for so long. Has anything happened?'

'Yeah,' says Dave. 'Summat that's happened is that I'm bursting for a piss. Did it get sorted, Roger?'

'Yes it did.'

'Did we win.'

'Without a doubt.'

'Brilliant. You can fill me in with the details after I've had a wee. Excuse me.'

Dave squeezes past Roger and goes out into the corridor. When he has gone, the woman picks up her notepad.

'Lucy Greene from 86 Friendly, rang. Her sister's coming to visit today from Filey. She's meant to be staying the weekend. But now she dun't know how she's gonna get here.'

'Is Mrs Green elderly?'

'She's in her eighties. She's lived here for ever. She's right nice.'

'How was the sister planning to get here?'

'Train, then a bus from the station.'

'Well, she's not getting on a bloody bus. Ring Mrs Green and tell her to tell her sister to look out for our car. We won't bother with a password so if Mrs Green can send a picture, or even a description of her sister, that would be helpful. Do we know the time of the train?'

'Half three.'

'Right so one of the cars will have to be there to meet her. Tell our driver to check the train is on time and to arrive just before it gets in. We don't want him to be there too long, or he'll be a sitting duck, but we'll just have to risk a short stop. Was there anything else?'

'Yeah the lads on Friendly rang. Apparently a couple of Asian kids chucked a bottle at them?'

'Was anyone hurt?'

'No and there wan't no damage neither. They've already cleaned it up.'

'Good and you've recorded it in the contact log.'

'Yeah I have.'

'Smashing. Thanks Judy.' Roger turns back to the rest of us. 'Right, shall we go and have a drink to celebrate our negotiations, while we wait for the good inspector? I think we've all earned a glass of something.'

There is a chorus of agreement and we all troop out of the room, down the dark stairs and through the concealed door into the bar. Roger buys a round of drinks and a few minutes later I find myself standing next to him by the stacked food.

'Did you really like the last video?' I ask.

'Yes I did.' He sips his wine and looks round the bar. 'It was pretty deep stuff, though, wasn't it? I'm not sure how much traction it will have had with the locals.'

'I didn't plan it that way. I had meant it to be fairly straightforward. But I think...I think 'deep' might just be what I do.'

'I'm not complaining. It does us no harm at all to be associated with some serious thought. Anything to make it clear that we're not just a bunch of boneheads.'

'That's what Civitas Seminar's about, really, isn't it? Intellectual legitimacy for fascists?'

'For God's sake, Adam. You're better than that.'

I sip my drink.

'I'm sorry. But it is, isn't it?'

'Yes, that is part of what we try and do at the Seminar. Construct an intellectually serious tradition on the right, to challenge some stereotypes. But it's more effective coming from people like you of course. It's untainted.'

'That still makes me feel slightly uncomfortable. Did you actually agree with what I said?'

'In the video?'

'Yes.'

'Not really. Not all of it.'

'I didn't think you would. Why not?'

Roger sips his wine again and winces.

'You talked about equality, diversity and individualism as the basis of the new religion, didn't you? Now I agree with that completely. It's all good stuff and well expressed. And you nail the problem with these things, as well. You get it exactly. The deceit of them. The danger of them. The inhumanity of them, ultimately. But then, in your last gasp, you advocate for a return of Christianity, even if we can't actually believe the Christian story anymore. I don't know how that could possibly work incidentally but forget that for now. That's not my point.'

'What is your point?'

'Equality, diversity, individualism. These are specifically Christian themes Adam, as you must know perfectly well. They enter history through the life and preaching of a particular, semi-mythical, dead Jew. So, in advocating for a return to Christianity, you are advocating for a return to the source of our bloody problems. Liberalism is just Christianity without God. The relationship is as close as that.' He frowns and shakes his head quickly. 'It's painful. It's fucking painful. But it's true. And you don't have to be bloody Nietzsche to see it.'

'So, what do you want instead?'

Roger stares into his wine. Then he says slowly:

'Have you heard of Julian the Apostate? He was the Roman emperor who tried and failed to restore the Empire to paganism, after its conversion to Christianity. He said something rather famous on his death bed. I learnt it at school, and it has stayed with me, you know how some quotes do? They shape your whole outlook, somehow.'

'Yes. I think I know what you mean. And I think I know the quote. Go on.'

Roger puts his glass of wine down on top of a stack of tins of baked beans and screws up his eyes in the effort of memory.

'*Thou hast conquered, O pale Galilean; the world has grown grey from thy breath.* That was when he was actually dying and he knew that he had lost the Empire to Christ. He knew he'd lost but he still loathed the greyness, the weakness, the sadness of the new faith, do you see? He longed for the return of the old, strong, joyful gods.'

'Is that what you long for too, Roger?'

He chuckles.

'I suppose I do, really. I think that I'm probably a pagan at heart, at least some of the time. Not in the sense of dancing naked round a tree, of course. But in an intellectual sense. I want a world that is truly joyful, a world of heroes, without any grey Hebrew piety or petty resentment.' He sips his wine. 'I want everything to be colourful again, just like Julian.'

I don't know what to say to that. It is such a strange thing to hear. For a moment, I can almost see the tanks rolling down some Eastern European lane, at the bidding of another apostate Emperor, on their way to grind a village into dust. A village where a dead, semi-mythical Jew had been loved and served for a thousand years or more. '*Everything to be colourful again*'. I drink my beer in silence.

'Well, you've done an extraordinary job here,' I say eventually. 'I don't know how pagan it is, but it's impressive anyway.'

'I have only facilitated things,' Roger says. 'I have a few skills about managing these sorts of situations and I can sometimes see things on the horizon, before other people. But other leaders emerge.'

'I suppose so.'

'Of course they do. Dave of course, but also Jason, and Brenda in her way, and a few others. The plan is that I keep out of the way as much as possible. That's always the intention.'

'I think you're being rather disingenuous, if you don't mind me saying.'

'Of course I don't mind you saying. I don't particularly care what you say. But I can't do anything without the community, as you know perfectly well. You can feel them taking responsibility for themselves, can't you? You can feel them actually becoming a community, a people.'

'Yes in a way, I think I can.'

'Of course you can. It's wonderful. European people claiming themselves back from the lies and the grind of their circumstance. Becoming themselves again. Becoming strong. It's the best thing in the world.'

'So why are you opposed to English Solidarity then?'

Roger snorts and shakes his head.

'That always happens. You have to expect it.'

'What always happens?'

'Something like ES.'

'What do you mean?'

'Listen, whenever there's a bit of tension or conflict, a bit of a flashpoint, and something truly patriotic emerges organically, as it were, two things always happen. Firstly, there will always be a well-funded counter movement like Respect Haxton or Coxthorpe Resist, or whatever, who will pop up almost immediately and do all they can to shut you down. They get soft treatment from the cops and the press, of course, and pretty much everyone loves them. They are the undisputed goodies, the white hats, in whatever fight is going on.'

'Respect Haxton have just had a go at me, actually.'

'I know they have. They were bound to. It's disconcerting, but we can deal with them. They are the opposition, plain and simple. At one level, there's even a kind of honesty about them, although they are never quite straightforward about their relationship with the state, of course.'

'Ok. So, what's the other thing that always happens?'

'More complicated. Within a week or so, another so-called patriotic movement will invariably deploy to the scene of the conflict. Either deploy on the ground or else deploy online, and they will also be very well funded incidentally.'

'Ok.'

'And you can absolutely guarantee two things about this secondary movement, that comes to piggyback on the original struggle.'

'And what are they?'

Roger chuckles.

'Well piggyback might not be quite the right phase, because the first thing about them is that they will be pro-Israel. Unquestioningly pro-Israel in the *'shared struggle against Islam'.'* (Roger makes quotation marks with his fingers). 'And the second thing about them is that while they will be ferociously anti-Islamic, they will also be pro-immigration. They will be nationalists in the civic sense of the term and will talk about British values and citizenship and so on until they're blue in the bloody face. But they won't be nationalists in the true sense of caring for their own ethnic inheritance, their own kin, and worrying about their people's replacement in their own bloody country.'

'Oh. I see.'

He snorts and sips some more wine.

'I doubt that you do, to be honest. Not completely. You're too well behaved to see properly.'

'Ok, well, supposing that what you have just said is true, where's the harm in it, from your point of view? If English Solidarity can help you a bit, why not let them? I mean, I'm not a fan. I think they're awful. I think they're thugs. But...but maybe you need a few thugs at the moment. You're out-gunned up here, after all, and presumably you don't have to agree on everything to work together.'

'The harm? The harm?' Roger drains his wine glass and replaces it carefully on the beans. 'The harm with people like ES is that they mix up the message we're trying to get out and distract good people from the real crisis we face.' He wipes his mouth with his hand. 'Do you know when white Brits are due to become a minority in Britain if present demographic trends continue?'

'No, I don't.

'Of course you bloody don't. It's 2066. Ironic isn't it? One thousand years after the first conquest of Britain, the second one will be complete. We'll be replaced, or as good as. Just think about that for a moment. 2066. It's not long, Adam. So that's the harm ES and their fellow travellers do in the long term. They confuse and distract people. And in the short term they turn our folk into little bloody Zionists, which makes it easier for politicians to send our young men to go die in shitty little wars for a foreign power.'

'I suppose you mean Israel?'

'Of course I mean Israel. A power, incidentally, in whom we have no strategic interest whatsoever and whose precious, self-chosen citizens largely despise us.'

Roger is flushed and his voice had become very low indeed. It occurs to me that he is quite pissed. He was the only person in the meeting with the police who was drinking alcohol, and he bought three empty wine glasses downstairs with him.

'Oh well, thanks for the lesson, Roger. I will bear it in mind.'

Roger grins. His face slowly returns to its normal colour.

'Forgive the passion. It is something I care rather deeply about. Sometimes I say rather too much about Mr Cohen of Jerusalem. It doesn't do me any good. Anyway, here comes Jason. Just in time to rescue you from the ranting right wing nut case. Hello again, Jason, any sign of the cops yet?'

Jason shakes his head.

'Still in the car, I think.' He turns to me. 'What was it you wanted to film today then? Just people in the pub again?'

'I hadn't made any plans, but I think it might be sensible to go and get some stuff at the checkpoint. That's the most dramatic thing to look at, I think, and it relates directly to the demo tomorrow.'

Roger nods his head.

'I think that's a good idea. It lends a certain Balkan chic to the situation, doesn't it? It makes a point.' He laughs. 'Go and see the lads on East Croft, then, the pair of you. While I chase up that cop. Has Dave come back from his pee?'

'I haven't seen him. Anyway, thanks again for letting me join the meeting.'

'Don't mention it. If you can work it into your next video, it might be good for morale. To learn that the cops had to come to us.'

'I'll see what I can do.'

'Good...Good man. And again, I'm sorry I got rather excitable.'

Jason and I stroll back along Lantyrn Royd, and then turn left onto East Croft. The van is still across the street, and the two men are still there. They are standing next to the wall of the vicarage garden, talking to Lavinia who is sitting in a garden chair in her overcoat, sipping from a mug of something hot. As we draw near one of the men turns round to us. It is the one who questioned me when I arrived.

'Hi Jay. Hi Adam,' he calls. 'I hope you int planning to go wandering off into Haxton?'

'Course not, Lee' Jason replies. We've come to see you lot. Adam is the guy who does the OyTube videos and he was gonna see if we could film you. The committee know about it, like.'

'Probably ok, as long as you dunt see me face too clearly.'

'We can keep you covered up, don't worry.'

'Yeah. Sweet then. Adam and me are pretty good mates. I'd do owt to help him.'

Lee winks at me and hold out his hand. I shake it. His grip is hard.

'I was just doing me job, fella.'

'Yes, I understand that. It was just a bit unexpected.'

'Everything's unexpected at the moment. Where do you want to film me?'

'Jason's better at sorting that out than me. Give us a second Jay, please.'

'Yeah. Yeah. Ok.'

I hand Jason the bag with the camera and stroll over to the vicarage garden. Rev Lavinia waves at me. She has a couple of books by her garden chair.

'How are you doing, Haxton Review?' she calls.

'Not too bad thanks. How are you? Any more fireworks?'

'No, thank goodness, but that doesn't mean that things are calm.' She nods at the roadblock. 'I can't believe that things have deteriorated so quickly. And I feel so utterly powerless. Typical do-gooder vicar. I am reduced to sitting here telling myself that I am calming presence, while I try not to feel completely irrelevant.'

'Doing a bit of reading though?'

Lavinia glances at her books and grins.

'Oh well, yes. Just my prayer book and Pride and Prejudice. My boss in my last job was always incredibly calm in a crisis, and he attributed that to Jane Austen. He said there was nothing she couldn't defuse.'

'What was your last job? I'd just assumed you'd always been a vicar.'

'Good Lord, no. I've only been doing this for four years. A second career. I was a civil servant for years before that.'

'Really. I had no idea. Which department?'

'Oh, various ones at different times. But never mind that now. Listen Adam are you aware of just how odd things have become?'

I spin round to look at the roadblock. Lee is now peering up the street through binoculars while Jason films him from behind.

'I think so,' I say slowly as I turn back to Lavinia. 'I think I am. It's difficult to miss.'

'It's about more than a fun OyTube channel now, Adam. It's really very serious and dangerous, potentially. And you have a real opportunity to calm things down, you know. If you wanted to, you could have a considerable impact here.'

I grind my fag out on the wall and chuck it away. Just for a moment the pressure returns at the back of my skull. The cord tightens. I shake my head, and it loosens again.

'I don't think that I can do very much except say what's going on. Say what I see.'

Lavinia rolls her eyes.

'We both know that's nonsense Adam. I thought because you were so helpful about not mentioning those fireworks that got thrown at the vicarage, or that dreadful meeting at church, that you might be seeing your responsibilities slightly more in the round.'

'I'm still trying to work out what my responsibilities are, Lavinia.'

'Ok. Well, I won't push it.' Her voice drops. 'But I'll say this, I'm sure all sorts of people would be very grateful if you could pour some oil on troubled waters.' Her voice drops further. 'I got in trouble for appearing in your video, by the way.'

'Oh God, I did wonder. I'm really sorry.'

'Don't be. It was a very mild telling off from the archdeacon. And I think he only did it because he's flapping. He turns out to be rather less good in a crisis than my old boss.' She smiles. 'I don't think he reads much Austen.'

'What did he say?'

'That I'd legitimised the hard right by agreeing to take part. Goodness knows what that even means. The fact that most of the white people in my parish had watched your first video seemed to have escaped him.'

'Well, I'm sorry Lavinia. You won't get...'

Before I can finish, a young man in a tracksuit appears at the top of East Croft, shouts something indiscernible, and throws a brick towards us. It lands in the road, just short of the van.

'Has there been much of that?' I ask.

Lavinia sighs.

'A little but nothing they throw ever reaches us. That one is about the closest they've been. The barricade provokes them of course, which I suspect is what somebody, somewhere wanted.'

. . .

And that's when I should have realised that there was something not quite right about Reverend Lavinia. Something not quite as it seems. What kind of vicar reads Jane Austen in their vicarage garden, sublimely unconcerned while people lob rocks at them? What kind of *person* does that? Perhaps if Jason hadn't come over at that precise moment, I would have twigged that there was something odd going on. But he did come over and tapped me on the shoulder, distracting me and making me turn round. And so just for a moment there was perfect silence in my brain, when there should have been the sound of pennies dropping.

. . .

'I think we're ready to start. We could film them reporting that brick, which might make a good intro. Hiya Rev Lavinia, by the way.'

Lavinia smiles at Jason and picks up her copy of Pride and Prejudice.

'Hi Jason. Nice to see you. Well Adam, if it's lights, camera, action time. I will leave you to it. Go and film your brick report. Do think about what I've said, though. Anything to calm the situation down.'

'Of course I'll think about it,' I say. 'But in the meantime look after yourself, Lavinia. I assume you are still planning to stay here next week?'

'Of course I'm going to stay,' she says. 'It's my home. And I normally manage to look after myself one way or another. Don't worry about that.'

# 18

WHEN JOHNNY COMES marching home again hurrah, tala...

*A white screen appears bearing the legend: 'Haxton Review: The Revolution will be Televised and Sponsored' in black print in a grungy typewriter front. The screen flickers in the style of an old fashioned newsreel and then fades to be replaced by a shot of a man's back and, beyond that, a white van. The man is speaking into a mobile phone.*

MAN: No it were just one brick and it didn't get anywhere near us....No, no one were hurt. Like I say, it din't reach us. And the lad ran off straight away. So it were summat and nowt really...I dunno. About fifteen maybe. Fifteen or sixteen. Five foot ten, or thereabouts. Dark clothes... No he were a fucking Red Indian. Of course he were Asian...Yeah that's right. Just three or four minutes ago. Book it at quarter past...Yep. Yep. See you later.

*The man puts his phone away in his jacket pocket and turns to the camera. His jacket collar is turned up and his baseball cap is pulled down low over his eyes, obscuring his face.*

NARRATOR: I know that you don't want to give your name, but thanks anyway, for agreeing to talk to the Haxton Review.

MAN: No problem.

NARRATOR: It's just gone quarter past eleven on Friday 24th of October. Could you explain where we are and what you're doing here please?

MAN: Yeah. We're in Haxton about halfway down East Croft, just outside St Peters Church.

NARRATOR: And what are we here for?

MAN: We're here to keep an eye on who comes into the area. Into Lantyrn Royd. Most folk would say we were a roadblock or a checkpoint or summat, but I've just learnt that we've gotta be called a community gateway from now on. Go figure.

NARRATOR: Ok, that does seems rather peculiar, but we'll leave it if you don't mind. What were you doing on the phone just now please?

MAN: What it was, we just got a brick chucked at us from some lad up on Gordon Street and so I were just reporting it, to get it logged.

NARRATOR: Reporting it to the police?

MAN: (Laughing) No. What would I want to report it to the police for? I were speaking to our control, in the pub. In The White Horse.

NARRATOR: If a crime's been committed, most people would report it to the police not to a pub.

VOICE OFF: Yeah but that's if the police are gonna take you serious. It's if they in't on the side of the fella lobbing the brick.

MAN: (Laughing) I'm afraid the cops have got a bit of a credibility problem on Lantyrn Royd.

NARRATOR: Ok. So why is that then? And why do you have to be here to keep an eye on things in the first place?

*The man points over the van, up the road.*

MAN: You see up there?

*The camera moves from the man and points up the street. People can be seen walking across the top of East Croft.*

MAN: That's Gordon Street right, at the top of East Croft? It's the heart of the Muslim area. You turn left there; you come to a mosque. You turn right and three doors down you come to a Muslim bookshop. There's Halal butchers and Asian grocers and all sorts. It's also the route of the march tomorrow.

NARRATOR: This is Respect Haxton's Family Fun Diversity Day. The March protesting against the Rush Bearing.

MAN: Yeah. Yeah. Diversity Day or Hug a Muslim Day or whatever they wanna call it. It's going on just up there.

*The camera moves back to the man's obscured face.*

NARRATOR: And why is that a problem?

MAN: Right, well you can see how close we are to them can't you? And that means it dun't take much for anyone who wants to cause bother to be right down here on top of us. So, it makes sense to have people here to keep things controlled. And we've got people on the other roads into Lantyrn Royd as well, doing the same thing.

NARRATOR: But why do you think that people are likely to cause trouble?

MAN: So, since all the bother with the Rush Bearing kicked off, there's been trouble on and off on Lantyrn Royd, han't there? And that's gonna get worse tomorrow, with the march.

NARRATOR: You know that the march is being promoted as a family celebration now? With music in Albert Park and so on. So why should anyone cause trouble?

VOICE OFF: Bollocks.

MAN: (laughing) Shut up Mick. Look, what it is, there'll be a peaceful march with Asian food and music and brass bands all that, and that's what will get on the telly, right? Fair enough, we han't really got a problem with that. But there's other people coming down as well. People who definitely want a fight and it's them we're worried about.

NARRATOR: Are you talking about Coxthorpe Resist?

MAN: Yeah, that's them. Anarchists or communists or summat. As well as some of our Asian neighbours, of course. They're gonna get excited tomorrow as well, aren't they? With the whole bleeding world on their side.

NARRATOR: I suppose so. But look, assuming this Coxthorpe Resist group turn up, they're not the only outside group coming to town tomorrow are they? What about English Solidarity?

VOICE OFF: Southern puffs.

MAN: (laughing) Mick, stop being a dick will yer? Listen, if ES want to come down and have a row in town with the marchers and that, that's up to them. I in't gonna say anything against them, cos they're on our side at the end of the day. But we in't joining them. We're just gonna stay up here and look after our own streets. Nice and quiet. That's our job.

NARRATOR: Defending your territory?

MAN: Yeah, defending Lantyrn Royd. Looking after our own.

NARRATOR: Well, thank you very much indeed for talking to us. I hope that tomorrow stays relatively quiet.

MAN: I doubt it will, but cheers.

*The man turns away from the camera and looks up the street. For a few seconds the camera remains focussed on his back and then the shot fades. It is replaced with a shot of Victoria Square in Coxthorpe town centre. The square is full of people, many of whom are carrying hand painted signs: Say No to Racism, Haxton Against Crusaders, Good Knight Islamophobia, Rush to Fight Bigotry. The signs are written on identical boards, bearing the logo of the Salamanca Banking Group in the bottom left hand corner and the badge of the West Yorkshire Police in the bottom right. There are also a number of rainbow flags in the crowd. The camera pans from left to right before focussing on a stage at the opposite side of the square. Here, a man is making a speech, but his words are mostly indistinguishable above the noise of the crowd. A large banner to the right of the stage displays the Salamanca Banking Group logo with the legend: Salamanca: Spanish Bank, English Town, Global People, while on the left of the stage there is a banner bearing the badge of the West Yorkshire Police and the legend: Working with Communities. Promoting Diversity. A third banner above the stage simply reads Respect Haxton. The camera pans to the left, to focus on the south side of the square. Here there is a line of police officers in riot gear, three deep. Behind them a number of St George's Crosses, Israeli flags and more rainbow flags are on display. Most of the noise is coming from here, with protesters in the body of the square making obscene gestures at the smaller group behind the police line. Despite this, the demonstration feels broadly good natured. The atmosphere is more of a carnival than a political rally. As the camera pans around, the narrator speaks:*

NARRATOR: On the face of it, it seems a preposterous comparison, but on the day of the Respect Haxton demonstration, or Family Fun Diversity Day as it has been re-branded, it is the Spanish Civil War that springs to mind. Thank God there aren't guns in Haxton yet, and no one is executing priests or socialist painters, but nevertheless the comparison stands. Spain was a dispute which belonged to the discontents and hatreds of a particular place, and yet it attracted people from all over the world. Barcelona, Andalusia, the Aragon Front all became proxy battlefields for ideologies that were, to varying extents, external to the Spanish situation. The same has become true to a degree in Haxton. The dispute between local Muslims and local whites about a young man dressed up as a knight has attracted anarchists, communists, liberals, members of the gay community, and the strange LGBTQI nationalists of English Solidarity, to name but a few. It is hardly surprising, therefore, that there should be tensions *within* each side in the dispute as well as between then, just as there were in Spain.

The Haxton Review has not previously reported straightforward news, but today's demo was too good an opportunity to miss. Just so that everyone is clear about what's actually going on: the main gathering here in Victoria Square in Coxthorpe town centre was called by Respect Haxton, the anti-Rush Bearing organisation. It was originally planned as a demonstration to lobby the council into changing the planned route of the procession so that it didn't pass through a Muslim area with its offending knight. Following the council's decision to re-route the Rush Bearing, however, today has been re-designated as a Family Fun Diversity Day, co-sponsored by the Salamanca banking group and the West Yorkshire Police. The whites from Lantyrn Royd are noticeable by their absence and the only counter protesters in evidence are from English Solidarity, most of whom we believe are from out of town. There is no sign yet of the mysterious Coxthorpe Resist, the anti-racist group who have threatened to take the fight right into Lantyrn Royd. As of now, eleven am, everything is peaceful and friendly, as far as we can tell.

As you can see, the police are keeping the English Solidarity lot well away from the crowd of protesters and the cops themselves seem to be pretty well received by everyone. There have been speeches from local councillors, senior police officers and the regional director of the Salamanca Banking Group. All of which have been filmed by the local telly. And, as you might expect, all the speakers said pretty much the same thing: that Coxthorpe is proud of its diversity, that diversity is its greatest strength and that intolerance and hate will not be tolerated. On another day, it will be worth making a video about the use of the word 'hate' in diversity discourse. Hate is anything which challenges the fundamental assumptions of the multi-cultural experiment. Hate is heresy. Hate, therefore, must be hated, just as intolerance must not be tolerated. Everyone in dissident politics quotes Orwell much too often, but there is something in his idea about corrupting language in order to restrict the opportunity for dissent. 'Hate' has been weaponised within the working lexicon of woke politics to make it problematic to challenge, or even to think about challenging, woke ideas.

So, as I said, things are quiet so far, but that doesn't mean that they will stay that way. We have to assume that the situation will become more tense when the march actually moves off and reaches Haxton. Yesterday we were in the meeting where West Yorkshire police effectively ceded control of the streets of Lantyrn Royd to members of the local community, and the locals' roadblocks, such as the one we saw yesterday, are still in place, albeit in a reduced form. Presumably the police don't make compromises like these unless they are nervous, and with English Solidarity and Coxthorpe Resist in the mix today, as well as the ever-vigilant Muslim community and the stubborn foot soldiers of Lantyrn Royd, you have to say that they are probably right to be.

Right now, we are standing at the west of the square on the steps of the Royal Bank of Scotland. Our plan is to have a bit of a wander in the crowd and see if we can chat to people from the various sides. Later on, we're going to follow the march and see what we can see up at Haxton. That's the Haxton Review for you, dear viewer, engaging the woke and the wanky so that you don't have to!

*The shot of the square fades to be replaced with close-up footage of the crowd. The cameraman is pushing his way through people, and the atmosphere remains cheerful. Eventually, the camera arrives at the bottom of the stage. Here there is a local television team filming the speaker and also three younger men with a smaller camera and a microphone. The mic is marked 'Resistance Media'. The cameraman swings his camera towards the Haxton Review team, creating the impression of a camera standoff.*

NARRATOR: (loudly, above the noise of the crowd) Excuse me, would you be prepared to speak to us for a moment please.

RM PERSON: Can you get that camera out of my face?

NARRATOR: Your colleague's pointing a camera at us too.

RM PERSON: We're here to make a film. It's what we do. Now stop fucking filming us.

NARRATOR: We're here to make a film too.

RM PERSON: Stop filming us.

NARRATOR: We'll film who we want.

*The Haxton Review camera seems suddenly to tip forward as if the person holding it has stumbled. There is more shouting and a punch is thrown.*

NARRATOR: Hang on Jason. No! Jason!

RM PERSON: Don't. Jez. Fuck's sake. Don't. You'll have the cops.

*The camera swings round to reveal three men in black trousers and tops, and baseball caps. They melt into the crowd.*

VOICE: Fucking cunts.

NARRATOR: Jason, calm down. Please. Are you alright?

VOICE: Course I'm alright. Fucking little cunts.

NARRATOR: Go back to filming the camera team, please Jason. Please.

VOICE: I'm not going to get fucking pushed over again.

NARRATOR: I don't think they'll do it again. They didn't like being filmed. I think they've gone.

*The camera swings back slowly to the Resistance Media team.*

RM PERSON: Sorry about that, fellas. It all got a bit excitable there, didn't it?

NARRATOR: Yes it fucking did. Although I am not sure if excitable is quite the right word for assault.

RM PERSON: I'm not saying it was our comrades who shoved you, right. It could have been anyone. But we have to think about our security.

NARRATOR: Why?

RM PERSON: We're Resistance Media. We challenge fascism and, ultimately, the state. We lock horns with some serious people.

NARRATOR: Yeah, I've seen your work. Is that what you're doing here in Coxthorpe?

RM PERSON: What?

NARRATOR: Challenging fascism and the state?

RM PERSON: Yeah. It's what we do everywhere. Who are you anyway?

NARRATOR: Are you anarchists then?

RM PERSON: We're diverse politically. But yeah, basically we're libertarian communists. We're anti-capitalists. Anyway, that's enough about us. I still want to know who you are, mate?

NARRATOR: That's fucking nuts.

RM PERSON: What's fucking nuts? And who the fuck are you?

NARRATOR: Do you think the people up at Lantyrn Royd are fascists, or capitalists, or agents of the state, or all three?

RM PERSON: Fuck off mate.

NARRATOR: Another scoop for the Haxton Review. Resistance Media: the anti-capitalist, anarchist media company that makes common cause with The Salamanca Banking Group and West Yorkshire Police. Brave street-fighting revolutionaries to a man. Sorry, not to a man, to a person.

RM PERSON: Did you just say you were the Haxton Review?

NARRATOR: I thought you weren't talking to us anymore.

RM PERSON: Fucking fascists. Quick get their faces. They're Haxton Review. They're the ones who film up at Lantyrn Royd, who that bitch wrote about in *The Globe*. They're fucking viral.

*The camera standoff continues for a half minute while the Resistance Media person texts hurriedly on his phone. Then the picture fades. It is replaced by a shot of a narrow street. The person holding the camera is walking along the street quickly.*

NARRATOR: So, we've left Victoria square now and we're making our way up Needle Street to try and reach the English Solidarity counter demonstration. As you probably saw, there was no way to get at the ES lot from the square because the police have them very effectively sealed it off. You can probably hear the cheering in the background. It is now ten to twelve and the atmosphere is still pretty relaxed. So far the only violence we've witnessed was directed against the Haxton Review itself, when our cameraman got shoved by some people who we assume are associated with the Resistance Media. But that seems to be the exception so far today, rather than the rule.

VOICE OFF: Fucking arseholes.

NARRATOR: Well, yes. They were arseholes and they didn't like being filmed did they? Which seems a bit hypocritical.

VOICE: Too fucking right.

NARRATOR: So, we're now turning right onto St Michael's street. We've got the town hall on our left and other council buildings on our right. And I'm hoping that we might be able to join the ES lot at the end of the street here.

VOICE: Police van, down the bottom.

NARRATOR: Yeah, I can see it, but there's no kettle or anything is there? Just the van? So let's just walk down the road and see what happens. You might want to be a bit discreet with the camera, though, until we're past.

*The camera drops to focus on the pavement.*

NARRATOR: (quietly) Just walking past the police line now. There are actually four vans here. And also a number of cops who seem to be independent of them. Some of the police are in riot gear, some not. And they all seem pretty relaxed. No one has challenged us so far. And we're almost there, just turning onto Tinder Lane now and, yes...yes, there is the back of the ES demonstration. That was astonishingly easy. I guess we could film again now, but let's be careful, ok.

*The camera lifts to focus on the back of a crowd of approximately seventy, mostly young men who make up the ES demonstration. Their Pride flags, Israeli flags, St George's Crosses and English Solidarity pennants (St George killing a dragon with 'English Solidarity' in gothic script beneath) are snapping in the breeze. As the camera approaches, the crowd begins to chant 'Muhammed is a Paedo' to the tune of 'Come on and Join the Conga.' A number of men at the rear of the crowd are wearing high visibility vests with the George and the Dragon symbol on the back above the word 'Steward'. One of these approaches the camera.*

STEWARD: Can I help you mate?

NARRATOR: I hope so. We're from a OyTube channel called the Haxton Review and we would like to have a word with someone about what's going on today, if that's possible.

STEWARD: Depends really. You gonna be fair?

NARRATOR: Yes. We are definitely going to be fair.

STEWARD: What did you say your channel was called?

NARRATOR: The Haxton Review.

STEWARD: Ok. And what's your actual name?

NARRATOR: *(garbled audio)*

STEWARD: You got any ID on you?

*From out of shot the steward is handed what appears to be a driving licence. He studies it briefly and then hands it back.*

STEWARD: Cheers fella. Obviously we've gotta be careful who we speak to.

NARRATOR: I understand.

STEWARD: Just wait here for a sec please. I'll go and see what I can sort out for you.

*The steward walks back towards the crowd, where he can be seen speaking to a colleague. The second man pulls out his phone and taps at it. The pair of them study the screen.*

NARRATOR: So, I can only assume that we are now having our credentials checked. Not that there is an awful lot to check. At the first meeting, English Solidarity seem pleasant enough, even if their songs are a bit ropey. They're certainly a lot pleasanter than Resistance Media, although that isn't saying much. I'm assuming that everyone can see the Israeli flags and the Pride flags amongst the ES crowd. They're obviously quite a complicated movement, ideologically speaking, which is one reason why it will be good to speak to them if we get the...Oh, hang on...it looks like we're in luck... They're coming back.

*The Steward is walking back towards the camera with two men. Both are well built, and both are wearing black balaclavas embroidered on the forehead with the George and the Dragon symbol. One of the men is carrying an Israeli flag and the other is carrying an English Solidarity pennant.*

STEWARD: So, you two are actually from Lantyrn Royd, then, yeah?

NARRATOR: Well, I'm not personally, but I am from Coxthorpe. And my colleague is from Lantyrn Royd, yes. We're both well-known up there. And we've made content about the situation with Lantyrn Royd people involved.

STEWARD: Yeah a couple of our boys have seen your stuff. Apparently you're kosher. Shame none of the Lantyrn Royd lads came down today to join us.

NARRATOR: Yeah. Well, I suppose you'd have to ask Lantyrn Royd people about that. I think most of them are committed to keeping their own streets safe today. That's the priority up there.

STEWARD: I guess it must be. Still a shame though. Anyway, this is Dave and this is Phil. They've got clearance to talk to you, but only on the condition that you don't ask about their identities and you don't try and find out anything confidential about ES operations. Do you understand?

NARRATOR: (Laughing) Operations? Do you actually have operations? I thought you just got pissed and sang rude songs about Muhammad.

STEWARD: (Definitely not laughing) Yeah mate, we have operations. Now, listen, we're talking to you bec-ause apparently you treat people reasonably, but if you're gonna take the piss you can fuck off.

NARRATOR: Sorry. I don't want to take the piss.

STEWARD: That's better mate. Off you go then. Fill your boots.

*The Steward folds his arms and steps back, unsmiling.*

NARRATOR: Thank you. Now, I'm not sure which of you is Dave and which is Phil and I don't suppose it really matters because I doubt they're your real names. I wonder if either of you could start by stating the obvious and telling me what you're doing here in Coxthorpe today. Let's start with you, please, Israel flag man.

ISRAEL FLAG: Yeah, so we're here to counter protest the Muslims and the socialists and all that lot. To stand up for the people of Coxthorpe. To show solidarity. (The man laughs) The clue's in the name, really, mate.

NARRATOR: Of course it is. English Solidarity. And why do the people of Coxthorpe need standing up for? Why do they need solidarity? And perhaps you could answer that, please, ES pennant man.

ES PENNANT: Because they're not being allowed to have their St George procession, are they? Because the Muslims are kicking off about it and all politically correct people on the council have banned it.

VOICE OFF: It in't a St George's procession, mate. It's got nowt to do with St George.

ES PENNANT: Well, what is it then?

VOICE OFF: It's s Rush Bearing procession with a knight. Just a normal knight, from the crusades. It in't St George. It were a tradition round here for centuries.

ES PENNANT: What's a Rush Bearing?

NARRATOR: (Quickly) It doesn't really matter. It takes too long to explain. The point is you've come to Coxthorpe to defend the locals against the Muslim community and against the politically correct council. That's right isn't it, as you see it? You're showing solidarity for your fellow English?

ISRAEL FLAG: Yeah. And we don't have to know all them details about crusades and knights and what-have-you to show solidarity, do we? We've just got to know that English people are being attacked. That's enough for us.

NARRATOR: I suppose it is. But may I ask an obvious question? If you're all about English solidarity, why the Israeli flags?

ISRAEL FLAG: What?

NARRATOR: Why the Israeli flags? Coxthorpe's a long way from Tel Aviv.

ISRAEL FLAG: It's obvious mate. It's cos they stand up to Muslims too.

NARRATOR: Ok. So, it's a sort of 'my enemy's enemy' situation is it? Israel is anti-Muslim and so they are automatically your friend?

ISRAEL FLAG: Something like that, yeah.

NARRATOR: I suppose that makes a kind of sense. But it still seems a bit strange to fly the flag of another country on the streets of an English town, if you're all about English solidarity. Do you know what I mean?

ES PENNANT: It's global, though, isn't it?

NARRATOR: What is?

ES PENNANT: The struggle. If anyone's standing up to Muslims and Jihadis and all that, anywhere in the world, we've gotta show solidarity.

NARRATOR: So, you could be called Global Solidarity, not English Solidarity.

ES PENNANT: No, cos we're English, mate. But we're part of a global fight.

NARRATOR: Fair enough. Now can I also ask you about those Pride flags that some of your members are flying.

ES PENNANT: Yeah, what about them?

NARRATOR: Well, they're interesting to me as well, because there are people on the main demonstration, the Respect Haxton demonstration, who are flying the same flag. And that feels odd.

ISRAEL FLAG: Why does it feel odd?

NARRATOR: Because you're on opposite sides, but you're flying the same flag. That just feels confused or mixed up, somehow. To me anyway.

ES PENNANT: Listen mate, English Solidarity is open to everyone. Doesn't matter what colour you are, or what religion you are. Or if you're gay or bi or trans or whatever. We're all English together aren't we? And we've all gotta stand up to radical Muslims or else we're all in trouble mate. We're all fucked.

NARRATOR: I see, so Englishness, and English Solidarity, are open to just about everyone from your point of view, are they? Anyone can join as long as they're not a Muslim.

ES PENNANT: A *radical* Muslim, mate. As long as they ain't a *radical* Muslim.

NARRATOR: Oh right, so moderate Muslims are welcome. Sufis are ok but Salafis are not?

ISRAEL FLAG: Yeah. Yeah. And them gays and lesbians and whatnot on the other side with rainbow flags are fucking ignorant. Cos if Muslims got power in this country they'd all be getting chucked off buildings, wouldn't they? Like in Gaza.

ES PENNANT: Exactly. You know the only place in the middle east where it's safe to be gay?

NARRATOR: I'm sure you're going to tell me.

ES PENNANT: The state of Israel.

ISRAEL FLAG: It's true, fella.

ES PENNANT: So, the gay people on the other side, they're like turkeys voting for Christmas. Even if they don't know it.

ISRAEL FLAG: (laughing) Except that Christmas will probably be banned as well, soon. Like your Russian thing.

VOICE OFF: It's a *Rush Bearing*. It's got nowt to do wi' Russia. Or St George.

ISRAEL FLAG: Well, whatever.

NARRATOR: (Laughing) Oh God, not that again. Listen lads, I think we're more or less done. Thanks for your time.

ISRAEL FLAG: You're welcome.

ES PENNANT: No problem.

NARRATOR: One last question, what are you going to do with the rest of the day? Any plans when the march heads up to Haxton?

STEWARD: (Stepping forward) We said you ain't allowed to ask about ES operations.

NARRATOR: Oh sorry. I didn't know that was what I was doing. I was just being friendly. Apologies.

ISRAEL FLAG: (Laughing) Probably just get pissed anyway.

NARRATOR: (Laughing) Well that sounds like a very sensible operation. Enjoy your day lads.

*The shot fades to be replaced by an image of a town centre street in Coxthorpe. Imposing Victorian civic buildings line the street on either side. The cameraman is walking up the street quickly. There are very few members of the public in evidence, but a number of police wagons are visible on side roads.*

NARRATOR: Ok, so we are back on St Michael's Street now, heading away from the English Solidarity demo, or 'operation' as they would no doubt prefer to call it. The plan is to head up the Leeds Road to the point where it turns into Gordon Street, at the beginning of Haxton. We're hoping to set up shop there ahead of the march and maybe speak to some of the Respect Haxton marchers as they pass us. We're slightly nervous about filming any further inside Haxton, in case we get identified.

Just as we make our way up, though, some thoughts about English Solidarity. It was obvious from their accents that none of the three members we spoke to were from Coxthorpe or even from the north of England. And that seems oddly appropriate, as ES turns out to be quite a cosmopolitan movement, at least theoretically. Their reputation has them as a bunch of lads who like getting pissed and having a fight, and I'm pretty sure that's accurate, but the members we spoke to were not straightforwardly ignorant. They had digested a basic ideology which they seemed committed to. English Solidarity, it seems, are first and foremost anti-Islam, or anti-radical Islam. Beyond that they are Zionists, multi-culturalists, and violent defenders of sexual and gender diversity. You'd expect there to be tensions within a movement which employs the symbols and language of nationalism while simultaneously articulating the standard platitudes of multi-culturalism, but apparently not. In the same breath ES can celebrate St George slaying his Dragon, speak of an Englishness which is diverse and inclusive to the point of meaninglessness, and point to Tel Aviv as a model of gay liberation. It's a weird mix but apparently it works to get the ES stormtroopers out of bed on a Saturday morning for their street protest, even if they don't quite understand what the protest is about.

Apart from the sheer oddness of seeing multiple Stars of David flying over the streets of a West Yorkshire town, the strangest thing about ES, for me, is how similar they are to the people they are protesting against. And, I suppose, the image of the rainbow flags on both sides of today's police lines is the most obvious expression of that. At some level, the clash between English Solidarity and Respect Haxton looks very much like a civil war within the diversity cult. Diverse brother has taken up arms (or banners) against diverse brother. The result is quite shouty and sweary and, from the outside, rather baffling.

I'll stop there because I've only ever spoken to three members of English Solidarity so it might be a bit premature to develop a thorough ideological analysis of them. I suppose my last thought about ES for the time being is this, that you have to ask the old detectives' question about them: Cui Bono? Who benefits? Who are English Solidarity really helping, in the long term? I don't have an answer to that question, but I'm certain that it is worth asking.

Anyway, that will do for now. See you up at Haxton.

*The image of the street fades to be replaced by another street scene, this time taken from a stationary vantage point. The street is lined on both sides with a small crowd and a flatbed truck is passing by, decked out in the red and yellow colours of the Salamanca Banking Group. Red and yellow bunting loops around the top of the truck and helium balloons in the same colours float upwards from each end. A large inflatable globe floats just above the truck's centre. Young people in red and yellow polo shirts and baseball caps are dancing around the globe to music that is blaring from speakers behind the cab. A banner mounted on a frame above the truck, also in red and yellow, reads: Salamanca: Spanish Bank, English Town, Global People. Another banner, this one attached to the base of the truck, reads: No to Hate: You've Got this Coxthorpe. More young people march by the side of the truck distributing baseball caps, key fobs and mobile phone cases to the crowd. The camera focuses on one of the baseball caps as it is handed over to an enthusiastic teenage girl. It is also in red and yellow, and it is branded with the Salamanca Banking Group logo and the slogan No to Hate: You've Got this Coxthorpe. As the truck passes down the street the music fades. A crowd of marchers follows it, many of them carrying the hand painted signs that are branded by West Yorkshire Police and the Salamanca Banking Group.*

NARRATOR: So, it's now ten past one and we're standing on Gordon Street at the very edge of Haxton. And to prove it, here is the Welcome to Haxton sign and the suburb's coat of arms. No muezzin or Quran on the coat of arms yet, I am happy to say, just the familiar Haxton helmet and lamb.

*The Camera swings round to focus on a road sign. Welcome to Haxton is in large white letters beneath a coat of arms depicting a lamb dangling in a sling flanked by a goat and a lion and topped with a medieval helmet. There is white rose to the left of the dangling lamb, and beneath it the tag: DACTER ET SINCERE.*

NARRATOR: God knows how long the coat of arms will survive in its current form. I've never really thought about the helmet before, but I suppose it's possible that it is another reference to Haxton's crusading past. If that is the case, I assume it will be on someone's to-do list, or, more accurately, on their to-cancel list. The motto means Boldly and Frankly, incidentally, which doesn't seem like a bad match for Haxton people. And I suppose that it's a pretty good fit for the Haxton Review as well.

Anyway, what you just saw going past was the float belonging to the Salamanca Banking Group which is leading the demonstration or procession or carnival (I'm not sure what you'd call it, really) from Victoria Square in the centre of Coxthorpe to Albert Park up in Haxton. There are going to be bands and games and food in the park, apparently, and things are slated to go on until early evening. That's slightly ironic, given that one of the Muslim community's complaints about next week's proposed Rush Bearing procession was the noise it would cause. But let that pass. We've been told that there's a West Yorkshire Police float making its way to us as well, with coppers dancing all over it. Obviously if it gets to us while we're filming here we'll have a good look and a bit of a giggle. Right now, though, we're hoping to speak to some of the marchers. As you can see, the atmosphere is still pretty relaxed, and the police presence is fairly low key so it should be easy enough to have a chat. Let's see if anyone will talk to us.

*The camera moves out towards the marchers.*

NARRATOR: Excuse me

*A friendly-looking young couple stop and turn to the camera. They are white and in their early thirties. The man is pushing a pram while the woman is carrying one of the hand painted signs on the branded boards. The sign reads: Knights of the Living Dead - Not Welcome*

MAN: Hiya.

NARRATOR: Hi, have you got a couple of minutes for a chat please?

MAN: I suppose that depends a bit on who wants to chat with us.

NARRATOR: We're a local OyTube channel called the Haxton Review, we're trying to document some of the stuff around the Rush Bearing controversy.

MAN: Kind of a social history thing?

NARRATOR: Yeah. Something like that.

MAN: Fair enough. We've got a minute or two, haven't we?

WOMAN: Yeah. I don't see why not (she puts her sign down). Gives me a chance to rest my arms.

NARRATOR: It's a funny sign. Very original.

WOMAN: Thanks. I'm not sure it's as funny now as it was when I thought of it. And it's bloody heavy after a while.

NARRATOR: I'm assuming it's a reference to the knight from the Rush Bearing procession?

WOMAN: Well yeah, obviously.

NARRATOR: He's the knight of the living dead.

WOMAN: (Laughing) Well yeah, not literally, of course. But yeah.

NARRATOR: And you obviously feel quite strongly about the knight and the Rush Bearing procession, given that you've turned up today?

MAN: Yeah. We're both from Coxthorpe and we care about the town, and what it's gonna be like round here when our kids grow up. So...So, we want to do our bit, I suppose.

NARRATOR: And doing your bit today means protesting against the Rush Bearing procession? And the living dead people who organised it.

MAN: Well yes. Protesting against racism.

NARRATOR: Protesting against racism. Ok. And that's what the Rush Bearing knight represents as far as you're concerned? Racism?

MAN: Of course. In a way it does. Yes.

WOMAN: Look we're not saying that everyone in Lantyrn Royd is a card-carrying Nazi or a member of the Ku Klux Klan or whatever. But it's insensitive to march a crusader through a Muslim area. I think everyone can see that. It's not going to help the town is it? Not in the long run. It's just silly.

MAN: Yeah and it's not about attacking the community in Lantyrn Royd either. Not at all. But if you know Coxthorpe, you'll know that the people up there aren't going to be the most...well...the most *considered* or...or the best *informed,* are they? Perhaps they were genuinely trying to do something decent and well intentioned to begin with, but things certainly haven't worked out that way. And so...

WOMAN: Which isn't their fault necessarily.

MAN: God, no. Not at all. Like I said, it's not about attacking them.

WOMAN: There's been a failure of leadership up there. From the council, community leaders, schools, the police, everyone involved. There must have been, for things to have gone so wrong.

NARRATOR: And so now, because of that failure of leadership, ordinary people like you have got to step in and sort it out.

WOMAN: Well, *help* sort it out, maybe.

NARRATOR: Ok, *help* sort it out. And you're pleased, presumably, with the Council's decision to re-route the procession.

WOMAN: Yes, of course. For this year, that's the best we can hope for. But next year let's have an inclusive Rush Bearing with people involved from across the whole community. Let's make it something that brings people together, rather than dividing them. Let's make it something really worth celebrating. There was a thing in the paper...

NARRATOR: Yes there was a thing in *The Globe*. I saw it. May I just ask what you do?

WOMAN: We're teachers.

NARRATOR: Both of you?

WOMAN: Yep. Different secondary schools in Coxthorpe.

NARRATOR: Ok. So that's maybe why you mentioned schools just now. Let me ask you this, then. If this sort of thing had cropped up in a school where you were teaching - not the Rush Bearing perhaps but something similar - how would you have wanted to see it addressed?

WOMAN: Well, there's not exactly a blueprint is there? But I think it's about having very clear and established boundaries about what's acceptable and what's not. So that inappropriate behaviour or speech can be challenged right from the start. And I think we'd want to involve the families in that as well. So, we would be challenging and teaching the unacceptable element within the whole community. Not just the kids.

MAN: Mostly the kids are just a symptom

WOMAN: Exactly. They're just a symptom of something deeper.

MAN: And I guess we'd want to be working with the police and community groups as well.

WOMAN: Of course we would. We'd want to involve the whole community. Responsibility for tackling this sort of thing isn't just for schools. That'd be ridiculous. It's for everyone. And it's not just for issues around ethnicity and religion either. It's around gender, sexuality, trans issues, disability. Everything really.

NARRATOR: Thanks. That seems really clear. And now a last question if you don't mind. What do you think of Respect Haxton bringing in Salamanca Bank to sponsor today? Does it strike you as odd at all?

WOMAN: (shrugging) Not really. I guess a day like this costs a fair bit of money, doesn't it? Everything is going to be free up at the park apparently, so I suppose they've got to get the cash from somewhere.

NARRATOR: I suppose they do. But what do you think Salamanca are getting out of it?

MAN: Dunno really. I guess they don't like racism either. Most people don't, I find.

NARRATOR: (Laughing) Yeah. I guess you're right. Most people don't. Well listen, I won't keep you any longer. Thanks very much for your time. As I said, we are Haxton Review on OyTube.

WOMAN: (Lifting her sign back up) We'll look you up.

NARRATOR: Ok. Bye. Thanks again.

*The couple re-join the marchers and move off up the street. The camera remains focussed on them until they disappear and then returns to focus on the stream of demonstrators.*

NARRATOR: And so there they go. Decent Coxthorpe people who are proud of their town and worried about what it will be like round here when their kids grow up. They've come here today to do their bit, they said. And I couldn't help liking both of them for that. They want to help build a tolerant, fair and diverse Coxthorpe. And they don't want that in a silly or a sentimental way, or because they hate England or the English. They want that kind of Coxthorpe because they genuinely believe in it, for whatever reason. And, given that they teach in Coxthorpe schools, you have to assume that they are aware of the significant difficulties that stand in the way of getting the sort of city they want. The tragedy may be that those difficulties are now insurmountable. In fact, they've probably always been insurmountable, although that's almost impossible for decent people like our friends to admit. Tolerant, fair and diverse Coxthorpe may only exist in their kind and well-intentioned imaginations, I'm afraid.

And as we're watching all these signs go by, with their branding from West Yorkshire Police and Salamanca, I can't help thinking again about the significant level of sponsorship that Respect Haxton have enjoyed today. As our friend said, they had to get their money from somewhere. And don't forget it's not just the people who have turned out who have seen the signs and the floats, the whole thing has been televised as well. So the cops and the bank have got into peoples' homes all across the region, possibly across the country, promoting themselves as guardians of multi-culturalism and diversity. Now I guess it's fairly obvious what the police get out of the arrangement. They gain kudos from the council and from what remains of the political left here in Coxthorpe and, more importantly, from the minority communities themselves. Relations between cops and Muslims are always fairly fraught in West Yorkshire, so I suppose sponsoring today's event is an easy win from the police's point of view.

The involvement of the Salamanca Banking Group is more puzzling, at least superficially. I'm not sure that I quite buy our friend's explanation for their sponsorship, that the bank just *doesn't like racism.* If Salamanca was suddenly to develop a social conscience they could start by disinvesting in Saudi oil, Bangladeshi clothing, and US ordinance, all of which presently sit in their portfolio. Closer to home they could re-instate the Trades Unions which were booted out of their Coxthorpe headquarters last year following a dispute about overtime pay. Half an hour online is all that I needed, last night, to reveal that Salamanca are bastards, even by the standards of banking multi-nationals: slave driving, arms dealing, union-breaking bastards. So it seems a little strange, not to say inconsistent, that the bank should suddenly pin its red and yellow colours to the cause of anti-racism and diversity.

Unless of course it isn't strange at all. Tellingly the sign above the Salamanca float said that Salamanca is a bank for 'global people'. I don't know if that means that global people work at Salamanca or that global people bank there. Possibly both. Whatever the bank thinks it means, though, the phrase might be true as more than just a crappy corporate slogan. To unpack this, let's go back to basics. Capital is completely unconcerned with nations. In fact, it's completely unconcerned with everything apart from its own increase. It doesn't care about peoples, or belonging, or home, or beauty, or goodness, or meaning. And it certainly doesn't give a toss about impending environmental catastrophe, despite the eco-consumerism bollocks that is pushed at us from time to time. These things simply don't register in capitalist logic because they relate to the *ends* or *purpose* of human life, and in capitalism, ends constantly get trumped be means. There *is* no end to the human being under capitalism. The person is simply a factor of production and a consumer, a means of profit and an object of manipulative marketing. And the natural world is just the same. It is not a gift, a joy, or a sacred charge. It is just stuff to make money out of. With this in mind, maybe – and we can say this without being silly or conspiratorial – maybe it is exactly in Salamanca's interest to promote anti-racism and diversity. Maybe the bank, and international capital generally, want people to be rootless, secular and interchangeable, without earthly loyalties or metaphysical commitments which would impede their final commodification, and the commodification of the world around them.

One of Salamanca's recent commercials featured a mixed-race guy getting money out of a cashpoint at a gay pride event. The ad became fairly well known - I think it even won awards - and I watched it again last night on OyTube. It is understood from the ad's narrative that the bloke needs the money quickly in order to pursue some other bloke into a club. You see the mixed-race guy getting his cash and then propositioning the guy he fancies. He buys him an expensive bottled beer, using his crisp Salamanca cash, and the final scene has the pair of them dancing together, drinks in hand. Everybody, it has to be said, is extremely beautiful, especially the mixed-race guy, and everything in the ad is very cool indeed. It looks like it might be set in Brighton or somewhere similar, but that's incidental. The place, wherever it is, is monied and warm and relaxed. (It's definitely a long way from Coxthorpe, incidentally, despite the town hosting the bank's northern headquarters. The gay scene here is one tatty night club and a handful of aging rent boys behind the bus station.) Anyway, the point of the advert, as far as one can work it out, is that Salamanca's customers, its global people, are as cool, as beautiful and as cheeky as the gay mixed-race bloke. And implicit, of course, is the message that we should all aspire to be like him, not least in our choice of bank.

Now think about that for a second. Just think about the imagery involved. The guy's mixed-race ancestry, I assume, is a signifier for his having transcended the normal condition of rootedness which comes from belonging to one specific nation and people. And his homosexuality functions as a signifier for his having transcended the more intimate rootedness that comes from belonging to a traditional biological family. Salamanca's beautiful man floats above everything that is given and connected and homely about the human condition. He is the perfect global person, the ideal citizen of the late capitalist world where everything that was once solid and meaningful about human relations, such as families and nations, is finally melting away into air.

And, of course, when his weekend is over the poor bloke will turn up dutifully to work at Salamanca on Monday morning, hung over and shagged out. And he will spend forty hours a week inputting data for shit pay in shit conditions, so that he can go out again and have his fun at the weekend. And, don't forget, there is no Trades Union he can appeal to at Salamanca if he is treated unfairly. Because, and here's the rub, you are only allowed to enjoy the brief and questionable thrills provided on the deck of the good ship global capitalism if you are prepared to shut up and spend most of your life slaving in the filthy engine room, alienated, skint and humanly pointless.

And with that crunching metaphor, I'll leave you. It's been a strange day in Coxthorpe and I'm still not quite sure what to make of it all. But as you can see the crowds of Respect Haxton demonstrators are still coming. Hundreds of them, apparently.

*The camera pulls back and focuses down the street to show an unbroken line of protesters reaching back towards Coxthorpe town centre, as far as the eye can see.*

NARRATOR: There you have it. Respect Haxton's anti-racist demo, bought to you, courtesy of the Salamanca Banking Group. The revolution, it seems, will be televised and sponsored.

*The street scene fades to be replaced with another. The camera is focussed across a street along which a few Respect Haxton marchers are trailing. A small group of men in balaclavas and track suits are visible opposite, throwing stones down a side street. Pop music is faintly audible.*

NARRATOR: Ok, so it's twenty-five to three and we're filming the corner of Gordon Street and East Croft, in the heart of Haxton. We're trying to be reasonably discreet, so we are in the doorway of a grocers shop that is closed. We had planned to pack up after the last bit, but we were contacted by people inside Lantyrn Royd who reported that the area is being attacked by stone throwers and, as you can see, they're quite right. There are six, or maybe seven, blokes across the street, that will be on the west side of Gordon Street, chucking stones down into East Croft. The white van you can just see across the road halfway down East Croft is the roadblock where we filmed yesterday. That seems to be stone throwers' target. There are apparently no police around the march anymore. And that's not really surprising because, as you can probably see, it's practically over. There's traffic on the road again and the diversity festival, or whatever it's called, has already begun in Albert Park. You may be able to hear the music in the background. Now we know that there are police at the community's roadblock on East Croft, but so far they have made no effort to stop the stone throwing. And as far as we can tell there has been no response from the community in Lantyrn Royd either.

*The shot drops to the floor.*

VOICE: Better get back quick.

NARRATOR: Oh shit, yeah.

*Shot of pavement and the sound of heavy breathing.*

VOICE: Quick, down here.

NARRATOR: Ok.

*More footage of pavement. Finally, the camera stops moving, still focussed on the floor.*

NARRATOR: (quietly) Have they gone past?

VOICE: Dunno, do I? Just stay here for a bit and keep quiet.

NARRATOR: Ok. I'd better explain. We just spotted a gang of Asian lads coming down the Gordon Street towards us. This was a separate group from the stone throwers, and we've got no indication whatsoever that they wanted to cause trouble. But, clearly, tensions are high here at the moment, so it seemed sensible to get out the way. We're now hiding behind some bins down a back alley that's roughly opposite East Croft, on the other side of Gordon Street.

VOICE: What d'you mean we had no indication they wanted to cause trouble? Two of them had fucking cricket bats.

NARRATOR: Really? I didn't see that.

VOICE: Yeah. Well, they did.

NARRATOR: We knew that filming in Haxton was going to be risky. Anyway, just to be clear about what's going on, we still don't know if the stone throwers are locals or if they're outsiders, perhaps from the Coxthorpe Resist group that was meant to be coming down for a fight. Our contact in Lantyrn Royd told us that stones had been chucked into the area from the roof of a local mosque, as well as from Gordon Street. So that would imply that locals are involved.

VOICE: We're getting a proper kicking today, in't we?

NARRATOR: Yes, I'm afraid you are. Do you think it's safe to go back up now and have another quick look?

VOICE: Might be. Just be ready to run.

*There is footage of a back alley filled with bins, and then of Gordon Street. There are still a few stragglers marching up the street and the stone throwers are still there, their numbers swelled by seven or eight spectators. The spectators are young Asian men, and two of them are carrying cricket bats.*

NARRATOR: So, as you can see, the stone throwers are still in business, now with an audience, and as far as I can tell there is still no police presence. Also, none of the marchers are challenging the stone throwers. As far as possible the two groups seem to be ignoring each other...fucking hell...

*A blue van has arrived, while the narrator has been talking, and has parked across the street from the camera, next to the stone throwers. A cardboard box has been unloaded from the van, which has then driven off along Gordon Street. Three of the stone throwers have gathered around the box and one of them has thrown a petrol bomb down East Croft towards the Hanging Royd roadblock.*

*The petrol bomb lands in the centre of the street, several meters short of the roadblock and flares briefly.*

NARRATOR: (Breathlessly) So the Haxton stone throwers have just switched to petrol bombs. And this is in the middle of the afternoon, in broad daylight. We just saw a van arrive which apparently bought the stuff. We may even have the registration and then...Fucking hell, there goes another...and another...Haxton in flames! Coxthorpe in flames! You can see what's happening. Beneath the woke politics and the trendy music and the cute Salamanca merchandise...shit there goes another, that one was close...beneath all that you can't ignore the fact that...that you have two communities fighting each other here simply because they can't live together, they can't be together. It's just war, really. That's all it is. Low key and just starting, but still...

VOICE: Shit. Trouble.

NARRATOR: Oh shit.

*One of the lads with a cricket bat has apparently spotted the camera. He points it out to his friends and after a moment's discussion four of them set off across the street.*

NARRATOR: Shit. Fuck. What do we do?

VOICE: Quick follow me. Quick.

NARRATOR: Have you stopped...

*The picture goes black to be replaced with footage of the first petrol bomb exploding repeatedly in slow motion. After thirty seconds this picture also vanishes to be replaced by a shot of the Respect Haxton demonstration in Victoria Square. The camera is pointing south towards the English Solidarity demonstration, and rainbow flags can be clearly seen flying in both demonstrations, on either side of the police line. The shot is also in slow motion and in sepia effect. In the background, 'The English Civil War' by the Clash plays softly:*

A woman's eye will shed a tear
To see his face so beaten in fear
It's just around the corner in the English civil war

# 19

Jason and I run down Gordon Street into Haxton, away from the lads with the cricket bats. Turning back, I see them jog across the road, towards us. Jason sees it too. He grabs my arm and, without pausing, pulls me into the traffic, and into the few remaining Respect Haxton marchers. We zig zag across the street as a van crawls past us slowly, concealing us for a few precious moments from the lads with the bats. We continue to run down the other side of the street, until Jason stops abruptly.

'Quick,' he mutters. 'Down the ginnel.'

'Ok. Ok. You still got the camera?'

He waves it at me.

'Course I have. And the mic. Now get a fucking move on, will yer?'

The alley is between a news agents and a solicitor's office, and it is only wide enough for one person. I sprint down it and Jason follows. I can hear his breath behind me, coming in sharp gasps. Both of us are middle aged and both of us smoke. Neither of us is very fit. The stone throwers, on the other hand, were young and looked very fit indeed. Jason and I are in trouble if they saw us go down the passage unless we can get to somewhere safe quickly.

The passage ends in a yard that functions as a mini car park. It is cramped, with three cars in it as well as four wheelie bins and a pile of foul-smelling cardboard boxes rotting in the corner. By car, the yard is accessed down a narrow lane, not much wider than our ginnel, which runs away to the left towards East Croft. In front of us is a high fence, made of creosoted wooden panels and concrete pillars. There is a gate in the fence. Jason pushes it. It doesn't budge.

'Shit. Worth a try.'

'What are we going to do now?'

Jason looks up at the fence and rests his hand on one of the panels.

'Well, if you can't...go through it...'

He can hardly speak for shortness of breath.

'What? What Jason?'

'Gotta...Gotta go over it.'

'But it's massive.'

There is a burst of shouting from the top of the alley. Jason shrugs and inhales deeply.

'You got any better ideas? Wanna take yer chances down onto East Croft?'

'Not really.'

He cups his hands into a stirrup and bends down.

'Put yer foot in here then. I'll give you a shove. And, here, take the mic.'

I take the microphone and step into Jason's hands and then find myself hoisted surprisingly quickly upwards. I grab the top of the fence with my free hand and yank myself over and then tumble down helplessly to the other side. I land on my back in a rose bush. I roll over slowly and then crawl forward, unhooking my clothes from thorns as I go. After half a minute there is a crash behind me and Jason's voice mutters 'Fucking hell.' Turning round, I see that he has landed on his side, also in the bush. He has the camera cradled to his chest, like a rugby player clinging to the ball in a ruck.

I struggle to my feet and turn back to help him. He gives me his hand, and I pull him out of the thorns. He brushes himself down.

'You alright?' he whispers.

Yeah I think so.'

'Nowt broken or sprained?'

Not that I'm aware of. You?'

'Nah. I'm good.'

'Where are we, Jason?'

He wipes his hands on his jeans and turns round. We have fallen into an unkempt garden. On our left there is a long-abandoned vegetable patch. On our right there is a greenhouse, its windows smeared with green slime and, beyond that, a collapsing polytunnel. A path made from a strip of weed-infested carpet runs between them and, further on, there are raised beds made of what look like rotting railway sleepers. Approximately 200 meters beyond these, the garden apparently comes to an end in a scruffy and overgrown hedge.

'Where are we?' I say again.

'Dun't you know?'

'Obviously not.

'We're in Rev Lavinia's garden. I think it's a bit much for her to manage on her own, like.' He points down the garden. 'It turns left down at the leylandii where it looks like it ends and runs towards that library room where we interviewed her.'

'Bloody hell, I had no idea it came this far up towards Gordon Street.'

He shrugs.

'Why would you?'

'It's a bit of a weak spot, though, in fortress Lantyrn Royd. Isn't it? Anyone could climb over here and you'd know nothing about it until they were right on top of you.'

'Fuck me. We never thought of that. I wish we'd had someone as clever as you to help us plan things up here, Adam.'

'What do you mean?'

'Over there.'

He smirks and nods towards the greenhouse. In front of it there is an unkempt rhododendron bush. A figure emerges from the bush slowly. He is in a balaclava and camouflage fatigues and is carrying an air rifle. He waves at us and puts his finger to his lips.

'Over there an' all.'

Another figure emerges up from behind the boxed compost heaps next to the vegetable patch. He is also in camouflage and armed with an air rifle.

'Fucking hell,' I say. 'Does Lavinia know about this?'

'Course she dun't. Like I say, the garden's way too big for her. I doubt she even knows what she's got up here.'

'It's bonkers.'

'It's necessary.'

'It's like the bloody army.'

'Yeah, well. It should be with these two. They've both got a bit of a past. Come on, let's say hello.'

I follow Jason down the carpet path and into the polytunnel. The man from the rhododendron bush follows us. When we are inside he pulls off his balaclava. It is Nick, the man with the neck tattoos who I met after the meeting at St Peters. He shakes hands with both of us.

'Owt happening up here?' Jason asks quietly.

'Is there chuff. It's a waste of time us being here. All the action's on East Croft in't it? Or at the mosque.'

'Has there really been bother at the mosque then?'

'Yeah. Stones and bottles chucked off the roof. Still going on as far as I know.'

'Fucking hell.'

'What've you bin doing?'

Jason holds up the camera.

'Been filmin all day.' He jerks his thumb at me. 'For his OyTube. Roger and the committee know about it, like.'

'So how come you ended up down here, fence hopping?'

'We were filming the stone throwers on Gordon Street but they spotted us so we had to leg it. The bastards had cricket bats. This was the only place we could get to.'

Nick turns to me.

'You alright?'

'Yeah. I'm fine thanks.'

'Cos you both looked like a sack of shit coming over that fence.'

'I'm sure we did. I'm too old for this sort of thing. Are there no police around?'

'There's a couple on East Croft with the van. And there's a car at the top of Clip Lane, Kibden Street, Wrack Street and Friendly. At least I assume there is. There were this morning.'

'But they haven't done anything about the stone throwers?'

Nick shrugs.

'Not yet they han't.' He turns to Jason. 'Where you off to now then?'

'Down to the White Horse. See what's happening.'

'Fair enough. I'll let the lads know yer coming. Keep away from the backs next to the mosque.'

'Will do'. Jason turns away and I follow him.

'Oh yeah, and another thing.'

We stop and turn back. Nick has pulled his balaclava back on. He is holding his air rifle across his chest.

'What?' Jason says.

'Try not to let the vicar woman see you leaving her garden. We dun't want to upset her do we? Not unnecessarily, like.'

. . .

Jason and I make our way down the garden and skirt the darkened vicarage. There is a layer of vague, smudgy cloud in the sky and it is raining with the sort of fine spiteful rain that you hardly notice until it has soaked you to the skin. I don't know when it started. Jason holds his hand into the drizzle and grunts with satisfaction.

'Should fuck things up a bit for them in the park.'

'Yeah. I suppose it will. Might dissuade the stone throwers as well.'

Jason snorts and shakes his head.

'Will it fuck.'

'How do you know?'

He grins.

'They're tough lads, int they? Them Muslim kids. You gotta give 'em that. A bit of rain won't stop them.'

We climb over the vicarage wall next to the white van. There is a police car parked a little way back from the van with two police officers inside, and there are four Lantyrn Royd men at the roadblock itself. Three of these are sitting on camping stools behind the white van, covered by a grey tarpaulin that extends from the van's roof. Baseball bats lean against the vehicle's side. The fourth is leaning over the bonnet, peering up the street through binoculars. One of the seated men waves at us as we clamber over the wall.

'Hiya Jay.'

'Hi lads.'

'You two ok? We heard you got chased.'

'Yeah we did but we're too nippy for them. It's what comes of keeping meself fit.'

The men jeer.

'We got away from them didn't we? Anyway, you lot alright?'

'Yeah. Except we're wet and bored. Nothing's come close to us so far. And it looks like they've fucked off since those petrol bombs.'

'Might change when it gets dark.'

'Yeah, probably.' The man nods at the bats. 'We're ready for them.'

'Good to know. Anyway, we'd better get off.'

'Yeah, fair enough. They know yer coming at The Horse.'

'Thanks. Take care lads.'

'Yeah, you take care too.'

'We'll do our best.'

We turn right down East Croft and then right again onto Lantyrn Royd. More widows have been boarded up since this morning. There are a few people standing in their doorways, chatting quietly. They nod at Jason and murmur hello as we walk past. Other than that, Lantyrn Royd is silent. The only noises are the muffled thump of the music from Albert Park and the occasional burst of shouting from Gordon Street. The little enclave feels more cut off than ever. And the rain has got heavier. The St George's crosses dangle limply from their lampposts.

. . .

The White Horse, in contrast, is crowded and cheerful, as if all the life of Lantyrn Royd is concentrated in the pub's single grotty room. People chat loudly and check their phones, pointing things out to one another on the little glowing screens. There is a game of dominoes being played at the centre table and a chaotic-looking game of Monopoly involving a large group of kids going on in the corner, on the floor. People are eating stew and jacket potatoes off paper plates, served from a food station next to the fruit machines. The grub is being dished up by a couple of teenagers, supervised by Brenda who is wearing a large chef's hat and a pinny with a picture of a naked women on it. The pinny woman's breasts and vagina are obscured by fig leaves. The large-screen television at the far end of the pub is switched on to News 24, although it is muted.

As we stand inside the door looking for somewhere to sit, Jason nudges me in the ribs.

'What?'

He points to the display table, opposite the bar. Roger is sitting at one end, as usual, next to a glass of wine and an empty wine bottle. His face is red, and he is peering at his phone and frowning, with his glasses pushed up onto his forehead.

'Oh dear,' I say. 'Do you reckon he's alright?'

'Yeah. Yeah, I should think so. He likes a drink though, does Roger.'

'I know he does. I suppose he's got a lot on his plate. Especially today.'

'Yeah he has, but he can't be getting too pissed. We need him.' Jason frowns and nudges me again. 'Go and have a chat with him while I get us some drinks.'

'Ok. A pint please. Stella.'

It takes me several minutes to reach Roger because people want to speak to me about what has been going on in town. When I finally squeeze through to him, he looks up and smiles glassily, then hauls himself to his feet.

'Ah, Adam, good to see you. Very, very good indeed to see you. I trust you've had a prod...prod...productive day.'

Roger annunciates carefully. When he has finished speaking he nods in satisfaction.

'Not bad thanks.'

'You managed to film the leftists in full flood? In full spate?'

'Yes we got an interview. They were nice people, the ones we spoke to.'

He picks up his drink and sips from it.

'Of course they were nice. They're always nice. We are nice people and that's the problem, isn't it? We're too bloody nice. We are path...path...pathologically altruistic. And it may well be the death of us.' He grins wolfishly. 'And you can bloody well look that up if you don't know what it means.'

'I know what it means.'

'Of course you do. You're a bright lad. Much brighter than your traitor fucking brother, let me tell you, despite the rather obvious differences in achievement.' He stares at me for a moment, struggling to focus. 'I wonder what your background really is, young Adam. I wonder what your game really is.'

'You know what my background is. And I don't have a game.'

'So, you say. But then you would, wouldn't you? Of course, you fucking would.' He sips his drink again and giggles. 'And did you manage to meet the brave philosemitic pat...patriots of English Solidarity?'

'Yes. We spoke to them too.'

'Israel uber alles and so on.'

'Yeah. Something like that. Although that's extraordinarily offensive, even for you.'

'How did you find them?'

'Strange. Complicated. Not unpleasant, but very, very odd.'

'Yes they are that. Definitely. Very odd indeed. Amongst other things.' He drains his wine and wipes his mouth with the back of his hand. 'I am afraid traitors are everywhere, in this business, Adam. Absolutely everywhere. And if you dare to dip your toe in the water and put...put your head above the parapet you get lied about and leant on and eventually slapped down. As sure as eggs is eggs.'

'Yes. You said something similar to me before.'

'It's damn well true.'

'It hasn't happened to me yet, apart from the Respect Haxton business, and a...and a...thing at work. I'll let you know if it does.'

Roger isn't listening to me. He grabs my elbow. His grip is surprisingly hard.

'You could be a traitor. I could be a traitor.'

'Well, I know I'm not.'

Roger grins and releases my arm.

'Well stat...stat...statistically one of us probably is, so I guess it must be me. What a shame. What a bloody shame, after all the effort.' He giggles then nods towards the bar. 'Ah look here comes master Jason, with ale. How goes it Jason? How goes the day?'

Jason hands me a pint.

'Not bad, how are you?'

'I'm fine thanks.' Roger grins broadly. 'I have temporarily rel... relinquished command to David upstairs, for the sake of a bit of a break amongst the people I care for. Amongst the folk.' He giggles again. 'Folk with an 'f' of course. Always with a fucking 'f'.'

Jason nods at the wine bottle.

'I can see yer on a break, like.'

'I'm sure you can. You're a bright boy too.'

'I put me head round the door of the control room. Dave says that there's been stones thrown for an hour or so and about a dozen petrol bombs on East Croft, and some stones and bottles chucked off the mosque, but that's it. No incursions or owt yet. And no one hurt.'

Roger nods.

'Yes. Yes. I believe that's about the size of it.'

I sip my beer. It's delicious even though it is awful. I hadn't realised how much I had wanted a pint.

'Did they say anything about the police?' I ask. 'What have they been doing?'

'Ignoring us, pretty much. They turned up after the petrol bombs, but that's it. As long as we keep things sensible they're kind of pretending we don't exist. We're being contained, Dave reckons. He's in touch with the inspector, like we agreed.' Jason drinks half his pint in one go. 'Oh yeah, the cops escorted the ES lads to the station and put them on their train. There was a bit of a scrap outside The Eagle, apparently.'

'And are they definitely chucking stuff off the mosque roof?'

'Yeah. Only stones and a couple of bottles though. No petrol bombs.'

'Is it worth us trying to film them? It would be good if we could catch it.'

Jason shakes his head.

'I asked that. Our lads have been trying to film it already, but they only chuck summat every five minutes or so, and you never get to see them cos they stay back. So you'd be lucky to catch owt on film.'

'That's a shame.'

Jason shrugs.

'We've got enough as it is. We've got more from today than anyone else, I reckon. We just need to get it out. Quicker the better.'

'Yeah. Yeah. I know. I'm happy to get started, after the drink. We could get some cans or something on the way to yours.'

'I'm happy to get cracking.' Jason drinks the rest of his pint. 'We may as well get some food here though. I've got nowt in and it's all free, courtesy of the committee.

'Fair enough. Smells nice.'

'Oh yeah, and Rev Lavinia wanted to have a chat with you too. She asked if you'd come over when you were done.'

'Rev Lavinia. What? Is she here?'

Jason points across the pub with his empty glass. Lavinia is standing next to the ladies' toilets with three men who I don't recognise. Two of the men are black and one of them is wearing a clerical collar.

'Ah yes, our very own little amen corner over there.' Roger lifts his glass to his lips, frowns at it when he realises it is empty, and replaces it on the table. 'She's made damn all effort to speak to me, I must say.'

'I don't think she approves of you Roger.'

'Of course, she bloody doesn't approve of me. Why would she? But you'd think out of courtesy if nothing else, wouldn't you?' He waves his arm around the pub. 'I am res...res...responsible for all this, after all. Or most of it. You'd think she'd at least say hello. Just to be polite.'

'Who are the black people she's with?'

'Nigerians,' says Jason. 'From that church that dun't like Muslims. Over the park. They turned up here this morning for some reason.'

Roger bursts out laughing. Jason raises his eyebrows at me.

'What's so funny?'

'Sometimes all you can do is laugh.'

'What do you mean?'

'Nigerian Christians, in the heart of all this.' He shrugs and waves his arm round the pub again. 'A couple of Nigerian Christians show up for some bloody reason and everybody scrambles to buy them a drink. Black...black as the ace of spades as well. Just turn up out of the blue. It is very, very strange.'

He giggles again and then slumps back into his chair. Jason glances at him and shakes his head.

'Do you want to go and say hello to Rev Lavinia, then?' he says quietly.

'Yes. Let's go and have a word.'

Jason taps Roger on the shoulder.

'You look after yourself, Roger. Get someone to help you home when you've had enough.'

'Can't really desert the ship, Jason, I'm afraid.'

'Dave's ok upstairs. He's got people with him.'

'Yes. Yes. Of course he has. Don't worry about me.'

'I mean it though. Get someone to help you home if you need it.'

Roger flaps his hand, vaguely.

'Yes. Yes.'

. . .

We squeeze across the pub to Lavinia. She grins at me as we approach.

'Look at you,' she says. 'The brave war correspondent, back from the front line.'

'Well, sort of.'

'Was it all ever so dramatic?'

'It had its moments. A lot of shouting.'

'But no violence.'

'Not on the march. Some stone throwers at the top of East Croft. And then a couple of petrol bombs.'

'Petrol bombs! Anywhere near the vicarage?'

'No just at the top of the street and apparently they've gone now. The police turned up finally. We managed to film them.'

She raises her eyebrows and then sips her drink.

'Gosh. That's going to be rather different from your normal style, isn't it? Marchers and petrol bombs instead of rural churches and homespun wisdom.'

'It'll be a bit different. But I stayed at Jason's last night and we did some research. So it's not just going to be shots of shouty people with banners. There's going to be a bit of wisdom in there as well.'

'Excellent. Just please don't make it too offensive. I don't want any more guilt by association.' She peers at me for a moment over the top of her specs and then steps back. 'Anyway, let me introduce you to my friends. This is Reverend Lazarus Babalola from Lock Lane Apostolic Church of Christ, and this is his associate Deacon Charles Adebayo. Gents, this is Adam, the man behind The Haxton Review that we were talking about, and this is his colleague Jason.'

The black man in the dog collar takes my hand and holds onto it tightly.

'It is good to meet you, Adam. Very good indeed to meet you.'

'Thank you. It's good to meet you too.'

'It is important work, you're doing.'

'Thanks.'

'Exposing the lies of the beast. It is important work. And courageous also. God will bless you for it.'

'Thanks. I mean...I mean that's not all I've been trying to do, to be honest...' I catch sight of Lavinia shaking her head quickly and grimacing. '...but...but it's certainly part of it, so thanks. Can I just ask you something?'

'Anything my dear brother.'

'Um...what are you doing here please? If it's not too rude. I don't think I've seen you in here before. And it's not an obvious haunt for someone like you, is it?'

Rev Lazarus is suddenly very serious. He drops my hand and steps back. He stares at me hard.

'Why not? Why is it not an obvious haunt?'

'Um...um...'

'And what do you mean, someone like me?'

'Um...'

'Do you mean because I am a minister of God or because my skin is black?'

'Um...um...Well, I suppose...um...'

Suddenly, he throws his head back and laughs. Not just his mouth, but his whole body laughs. It begins somewhere in the depths of his stomach, twitching behind the straining buttons of his black shirt, and then rolls upwards through his shaking chest and throat. Finally, it bursts through his quivering lips.

'You mean both, I think,' he gasps. 'Am I right, dear fellow? Am I right?'

'Yes. Yes, I suppose you probably are.'

Rev Lazarus pulls a white hanky from his pocket and dabs at his face as his laughter subsides.

'Well let me tell you then. I am here to show solidarity with my brothers in Lantyrn Royd. I am here to bear witness to Christ. Of course, people said: "Rev Lazarus, they will be disrespectful to you. They will be racist to you. The people of Lantyrn Royd are racist people." That is what they said, Adam. And I said: "We shall see. But still, I must show solidarity to my brothers who take a stand against the Anti-Christ of Islam." Do you understand?'

'I...I think so.'

Rev Lazarus drinks deeply and then puts the glass down and raises his finger.

'But look around you, Adam. There is no racism here. Just good fellowship and resistance to the menace of the beast.' He sighs and his voice drops. 'We are here to help you carry your cross. We are here to be Simon of Cyrene for you, Adam. We are here to be part of your band of brothers.'

'Right,' I say. 'Well, that's nice.'

Rev Lavinia clears her throat.

'Yes it is, isn't it? It's very nice. We're all brothers, except for those of us who aren't, because we are sisters. Anyway, Adam, this is Fr Mike Shaw from the Immaculate Conception.'

The other man smiles and we shake hands. He is in his late fifties and dressed in an open neck shirt and jeans.

'How you doing.'

He has the faintest trace of a scouse accent. Father is a long way from home. There will be a story there.

'Fine thanks, father. Nice to meet you.'

'You too.'

'Mike came over this morning to keep me company,' Lavinia says, 'because we knew it was going to be a rotten day. And then, when we decided to pop down here for a lunchtime drink, who should we find but Rev Lazarus and Deacon Charles, already established. And now, with all the bother, it looks as if it might be rather difficult for any of them to leave. It's begun to feel like a clergy quiet day. It's very odd indeed.'

'It must be.'

Rev Lazarus roars with laughter again.

'Very odd. Very odd. Have you seen the film Zulu, Adam?'

'Um, yeah. Yeah, I have.'

'With the great actor Michael Caine?'

'Yeah, I know the one.'

'It is just like that, I am afraid. We are stranded together in the great siege of Lantyrn Royd, gathered from our different confessions and races.'

'Right.'

'We are thrown together here in the pot. While the barbarians batter at our gates.'

For a moment no one says anything while the Rev Lazarus beams round at us. Then Fr Mark mutters:

'Well, there are worse places to get stuck, I guess. Do any of you want another drink?'

There is a chorus of yes's from the group and Fr Mark nudges me.

'Come and give us a hand, will you?'

'Yes of course.'

We elbow are way to the bar and the priest gets served. While the barman is getting the drinks, he turns to me.

'It's a funny business isn't it?'

'What is?'

'All of it.' He looks round the pub. 'All of this.'

'Yes. Yes, it is. It was funny enough already. But Rev Lazarus has made it positively surreal.'

Fr Mark chuckles.

'Yeah. He's a strange guy. I think maybe he tries a bit too hard to be the big Nigerian pastor, do you know what I mean?'

'I think so.'

'But there's no doubt that he loves his people. And I think he's serious in what he says about Islam. He dreads it. He's terrified of it. And he really does want to show solidarity, as he puts it.'

'I'm sure.'

'It's brave of him to come down, actually, even if all he's doing is swigging rum and coke.'

'I suppose there may be good reasons for his feelings about Islam, coming from Nigeria.'

'Yeah. Suppose so.' Fr Mark frowns. 'More complicated for us though, isn't it, kid?'

'What do you mean?'

'Well, it wasn't that long ago that we were the big threat, was it?

'What? Who was the big threat?'

'Us. Catholics. Breeding too quick. Disloyal to king and country. A bit violent, maybe. And sympathetic to dangerous foreign powers, if you go back far enough. With bombs as well.'

'What? What do you mean?'

'The gunpowder plot was basically the Jacobean 9/11 wasn't it?' He shrugs. 'Perhaps it gives us a slightly different take on it all.'

The barman loads the pints and the rum and cokes onto a tray, and Fr Mark hands him the cash.

'Um, maybe...But I don't...I don't think it's an exact comparison.'

'Nothing's ever exact, is it? But it's close enough.'

The priest takes his change and hands me two of the pints.

'Cop for them, will you?'

'Yes, of course. Um...by the way, how did you know that I was a Catholic?'

'Well, I've watched your videos for one thing and there are some hefty clues there.' He grins. 'But you just get a nose for it, in my job. I'd guess you're a convert.'

'Yes.'

'And now lapsed, judging from your last video.'

'Yes, I'm afraid so.'

'Like I said, you get a nose for it. Please don't be offended.'

I don't think that I'm offended, but it's odd to hear that someone has a nose for you. After a moment I say:

'That's pretty much exactly what Roger said about Jews. You get a nose for them.'

'Did he indeed?'

'Yes. He calls them the tribe.'

The priest picks up the tray and turns to face me.

'Listen,' he says, his scouse accent suddenly more pronounced. 'Listen, Lavinia isn't gonna tell you this, because polite women vicars don't say this sort of thing. So, I'll have to. You keep away from Roger Wrigglesworth. You don't have to stop making your little videos, although if you want my opinion you should stop them as well. But, whatever you do kid, keep well away from Wrigglesworth. Keep away from him or...or...'

'Or what?'

Hi voice drops so that I can hardly hear it above the chatter.

'Or you'll damage your soul.'

I stare into the pints of beer.

'I think I damaged my soul a long time ago, father.'

The priest chuckles, softly and not particularly kindly.

'Yeah. Well with all due respect, that's the kind of self-indulgent crap a certain sort of Catholic convert comes out with when they're trying to sound like a Graham Green character.'

'I think it's how I feel though.'

'Ok. I'll take your word for it.' The priest nods at Roger who is now practically slumped over the table. 'Bloody hell, look at him.'

'Yeah. I'm afraid he's pretty pissed.'

'He's more than pissed. He's damaged. And he's damaged badly enough to make him want to pass some of the damage on to other people. That's the shame of it. You keep your distance.'

'I don't spend too much time with him, to be honest. He's not been directly involved in either of the videos.'

'I'm glad to hear it. Now, come on, let's take them their drinks. I'm sure Reverend Lazarus is ready for another glass of solidarity.'

As we are threading our way back to the others I say:

'How do you know about Roger, father? I didn't think he been in Coxthorpe very long.'

'Just under a year.'

'So how do you know he's damaged, or whatever you said?'

The priest shrugs

'He's a parishioner.'

'Bloody hell, really?'

'Yeah. I mean, he doesn't help out with the old folks' lunch club, or the St Vincent de Paul, or whatever, but he's a regular communicant and a penitent. For months now.'

'But I thought...I mean...I got the impression...I thought he didn't care much for the Church. He pretty much said that explicitly. I certainly didn't expect him to be any kind of Christian.'

'He doesn't know what the hell he is, kid. That's the tragedy.'

. . .

When Fr Mike and I have delivered the drinks, Jason and I go to get some stew. We are met at the food counter by Brenda who greets us with smothery, ginny kisses.

'You boys all right? You kept yerself safe out there, have you?'

'Yeah we're fine, love. Just hungry.'

Brenda taps Janson's paunch.

'You in't gonna fade away, Jase.'

'True but I need to keep me strength up so I can get hold of you later. That pinny's got me right excited.'

Jason makes to grab Brenda's leafy vagina. She giggles and whacks his hand with her ladle before slopping stew onto his paper plate, and then onto mine.

As we are turning away she grips my arm, unexpectedly hard. She nods in the direction of the door.

'Bloody hell, look who it is.'

A woman in her early thirties with long brown hair, smart specs, and a dark overcoat with the collar turned up, has just walked into the pub. She stands in the doorway looking round the crowded room. She looks displeased, even wary.

'Who's that?'

'It's Rosalind. Roger's daughter. I expect she'll be here to collect her dad. Someone must have rung her.'

'She doesn't look very happy.'

'Of course she dun't. She's a right snobby bitch. She never comes down here, if she can help it.'

Rosalind spots Roger who is now slumped against the wall, and his glasses stuck at an angle, halfway up his forehead. She shakes her head quickly and begins to pick her way through the crowd towards him. Brenda snorts and turns back to the pot of stew.

'Oh well,' she mutters. 'Probably best he's going home. Poor Roger, though. He's gonna get a proper bollocking from the looks.'

Jason shrugs.

'He han't really helped himself, Brenda.'

'I know he han't. Still shitty for him though. With that cow coming for him.'

. . .

Jason and I rejoin the clergy and then, when we have finished out stew and our drinks, we make our excuses. Lavinia hugs briefly me before we go.

'Try and do something positive this time,' she whispers. 'Something completely positive and helpful. Don't forget what I said. I'm sure all sorts of people will be grateful if you do. In fact, I know they will be.'

'And you don't want any guilt by association.'

She releases me and smiles.

'Exactly. That too.'

'I always try and do something positive.'

'Good.'

I shake hands with Rev Lazarus, deacon Charles and Fr Mark, and then Jason and I leave the pub and walk quickly to his house through the rain, picking up a bottle of red wine and some cans at the off license on the way. We haven't done much clearing up since last night when I stayed over, so we spend twenty minutes washing pots and tidying the kitchen. Then I open the wine as Jason kneels by the stove and fills it with kindling.

'May as well get it lit,' he says. 'It'll be the first time this year.'

'Well, it is Autumn.'

'Yeah, I know it's Autumn. Mists and mellow fucking fruitfulness.... I'm the Coxthorpe Dalesman, remember.' He strikes a match and holds it against the paper. 'Not that I've been out and about much recently. It's four weeks since I made a video.'

'Is that because of the Rush Bearing?'

'Yeah, mostly. It's about priorities in't it?' He frowns and closes the stove door, then heaves himself to his feet and plugs the camera into his computer. 'You've gotta make choices. Now come on let's have a look at it.'

I slip into the chair next to him as the computer boots up and hand him a glass of wine. We both light cigarettes and for a while neither of us speaks. There were moments like this last night as well, when we were researching the talking points for today. Suddenly we were silent and slightly awkward, but also (I think) pleased to be in each other's company. Jason and I are friends now. There is an intimacy between us, based on our shared work, and on the complex solidarity that comes from us both being single men in our forties, and on the sheer amount of time that we have spent together recently. Jason has worked incredibly hard on the Haxton Review videos, for no reward apart from a few drinks. And he seems genuinely pleased when circumstances have meant that I have to stay over at his house. I have grown to like him more than I care to admit.

'I do appreciate everything you've done,' I say quietly. 'With the videos and letting me stay and giving up your time and all that. I really do appreciate it all.'

Jason inhales his cigarette and scratches the red kite tattoo on his forearm.

'It's alright,' he mutters. 'It's been worth something.'

'I think so too.'

He inhales again and taps at the keyboard. The picture of the demonstration in Victoria square appears on the screen, in silence.

'Yeah it has. And we've got to win now, Adam.'

'It would be a massive shame if we didn't.'

'It would be more than a shame.'

'Well yeah, it would, but...'

Jason grips my arm and nods at the screen. It is now filled with a picture of the stage in Victoria Square, with the television crew in front of it.

'We've been on television,' he says quietly. 'We've been in the papers. And we've been all over the internet. It in't just about us anymore. If we lose, it shows everyone that there's no point organising anything. It shows that yer country's not yer own, no matter...no matter what it says on your passport.'

'I...I hadn't really thought of it like that. Not quite so broadly.'

'Nor had I until today. Not until I saw all them marchers and realised how much all them people hate us. But it's right. It in't just about us anymore.' He releases my arm. 'Hang on, let me show you something.'

Jason gets up and walks to the bookshelves nearest the window. He leans down and pulls a book from the bottom shelf, the shelf that he told me was reserved for politics.

'This is a book Roger give me,' he mutters. 'It's about Europe basically, the history of Europe, and this is a quote from a fella who was fighting against the French revolution. He were French himself, like, but he were fighting against it.'

'Ok.'

Jason clears his throat and holds the book up high, like a town crier with a scroll.

'Ready?'

'Yeah. Course I'm ready.'

'Sure?'

'Course I'm sure. Just read the bloody thing.'

He clears his throat again.

'Ok then. Here goes. "Our homeland - for us - is our villages, our altars, our tombs, everything that our fathers loved before us. For them, homeland seems to be only an idea; for us it is a land. Their homeland is in the brain, for us it's under our feet, it's more solid."'

'That's a nice idea,' I say after a moment.

He shuts the book and replaces it.

'Yeah, it is. I made a note of it when I read it, and I thought about it again today with them marchers. I agree exactly with what this fella's saying'

'Why's that?'

He sits down next to me again and puts the book on the desk.

'My country in't just a nice idea, like it were for that couple with the kid, or for them from English Solidarity. It in't a thing called 'democracy', or 'solidarity against Islam', or 'British values', or 'land of hope and glory', or whatever else. It in't an idea at all. It in't in me head. My country is these shitty little streets, and the people who live here, and the shops and pubs down in town, and the hills and moors around, and...and my mum's grave up in Highcliffe. And... and if we lose this...if we lose here with this fucking stupid knight and this Rush Bearing business...if we lose...then it tells me...it tells everyone...that country's been taken away from us. That we've lost everything that's solid and real, and all that's left is a nice idea about values, or tolerance, or summat else that most people dun't give a shit about or even understand.'

He picks up his fag from the saucer, re-lights it, and inhales.

'I see,' I say after a moment.

'Yeah I think you probably do see, Adam. I really think you do.' He jabs at the keyboard. His neck has turned bright red and he won't look at me. 'Look, I din't know what to think of you when I met you. In fact, I thought you were probably a stuck-up wanker and...and a liar. But now I reckon I know you well enough to know that yer honest and decent, and committed to the right sort of things. So you don't have to thank me for me time. Or for me help. I'm proud to be helping you. I'm proud to do my bit for...for...well for all this stuff.' He shrugs. 'For the things that are real. D'you know what I mean?'

'I know exactly what you mean. The things that are real.'

'Good so let's get on with it.'

And so we get on with making our video while outside in the dark, the siege of Lantyrn Royd is fought out sporadically and ludicrously with rocks and bottles. And Jason, my extraordinary friend, will never know how proud I am too, that we are working together, or how touched I am that he called me honest and decent.

. . .

Not everyone is involved in the Rush Bearing thing, and comparable struggles, out of hate, you see. Some people are, but some people get involved out of a bitter, blurry, unbearable, kind of love. That is what has happened to Jason, and it is a frightening, complicated truth that no one will ever, ever, ever acknowledge. But it is a truth. I've touched on the idea of love before, in the very first video I made. And I will return to is again, right at the end, when the Rush Bearing has collapsed, and Jason wants to kill me.

As I said before, in one sense love is the most important thing about all this.

# 20

We get the video done by midnight and upload it straight away. By then we are both pretty pissed and the room is thick with cigarette smoke. Jason staggers to his feet, fetches the spare duvet from upstairs and chucks it on the sofa.

'Night then,' he says.

'Night Jason. Thanks again.'

He grins.

'Oh, fuck off with yer thanks. I'll see you in the morning.'

'I doubt it. I've got to go to my mum's. I'll be gone before you're even awake.'

'Oh well fuck you then.'

He sways out of the door leaving me alone. I have a piss and do my teeth, then slide under the duvet and message Sonia on WhatsApp. I apologise for being so rude the last time we chatted. Sonia reads my message immediately but takes nearly ten minutes to respond.

*We both got carried away but you werent respectful. And you blocked me. You were a bit evil. I spoke to my pastor and he sed you might have a demon. I got filled with the spirit again to get rid of you*

I reply.

*No demon. Just a hard dick.*

Sonia answers immediately.

*You need Jesus*

I reply

*Do you want to watch me wank?*

Sonia answers.

*Only normal this time. And I'm watching you. And its the last time.*

So, I call Sonia and masturbate for her by the soft light of Jason's desk lamp and the softer light of his flickering fire. And then I block her and go to sleep, my demon's appetites apparently being sated. Neither of us says a word during the call.

. . .

I wake up at seven the next morning feeling rough. I do my teeth and then slip out of the house and walk down to the White Horse. Dave is standing outside the pub, munching a sausage sandwich in the morning sunshine.

'How was the rest of the evening?' I ask.

'Quiet. There were a bit more stone throwing and some bottles and then a couple of crossbow bolts off the mosque, but that were about it.'

'Crossbow bolts?'

'Yeah, at about seven o'clock. They didn't hit anyone, like. And the cops went round and sealed the mosque off, to be fair.'

But no one tried to get into Lantyrn Royd?'

'No. The cops stayed up all night and so did our lads. They're still there, matter of fact.'

'No sign of Brindley Resist?'

'None at all. Not a squeak. Makes you wonder...'

'What does it make you wonder?'

Dave swallows the last part of his sandwich and brushes the crumbs off his hands.

'Nowt,' he says after a moment. 'It dun't matter. I've not been to bed yet. I in't thinking too clearly.'

'Have you been up all night?'

'Yeah. In the control room. Not that there were much to control after midnight, so I got a bit of kip. And I'm finished now. Alan's taken over.' He nods his head back at the pub. 'And they're doing breakfast inside for the lads who've been up with me.'

'Is Roger still around?'

Dave grimaces.

'Nah. He went off with his daughter, and no one's seen him since. Someone must've called her.'

'Yeah I saw her. She didn't seem very happy. Brenda didn't seem to think much of her.'

'She keeps herself to herself. And the son in law an all. It's a right funny set up. They all live together at the bottom of Kibden in two houses knocked together. They don't mix a right lot.'

'All three together? That is a bit odd.'

'Yeah, it is. But Roger in't really one of us, is he? Never mind what he says.' Dave shrugs. 'Anyway, what are you up to today? More filming?'

'No. We finished last night. It's already uploaded. I need to get back into town. I'm on nights tonight.'

Dave pulls his phone out of the back pocket of his jeans.

'Hang on a sec then. I'll call you a car before I go.'

The Lantyrn Royd car takes me home, and I jump straight in shower. When I get out, I have a coffee and a fag out in the yard and check the new video. It already has 893 views and 77 comments. The majority of the comments are opposed to the marchers and in support of the Lantyrn Royd whites. The comments on the other side are much more hostile to me personally than previously. A lot of the criticism centres on my analysis of the Salamanca ad.

*'Racist. Homophobic. Ignorant. Bullshit. Thank fuck for Salamanca (and I say that as a socialist).*

*'You protest too much about the mixed-race guy, you repressed, fucked up little arsehole. Did you go home and watch the ad again and have a big wank?'*

*'Will someone just dox this cunt quick so he fucks off.'*

This last comment is interesting as well as frightening, given I have already been doxed (or at least half doxed) by Tanya Faulk. OyTube Commentators apparently have short memories.

There is no text or email from my brother, but I do have an email from Lavinia:

*Adam,*

*It is half past one as I write this and I have only just got rid of Lazarus and Charles and Fr Mike. Someone in the pub gave us a number we could call to make use of the unofficial taxi service that is operating (you probably know all about it) and in the end we took advantage. Apparently the stone throwing has eased off sufficiently for cars to get through. I must say I am rather relieved that they have gone, I wasn't looking forward to waking up in a house full of clergymen and cooking them all breakfast. Anyway, when they had left I had a quick look on line, and I had a notification that you had produced a new video so I watched it before bed...*

*The great tragedy here, Adam, is that you have real talent. You have the knack of asking important questions about the situation in Haxton and the bigger issues that it raises, and you also have the sort of mind which can arrange information logically and simply so that people can digest it. It's obvious that you could have used your life differently in writing or in journalism or something, and it's also obvious that you could have used your OyTube channel differently, so that it actually helped the situation here. So that it helped the people here.*

*Instead, we have this! I really don't understand what you mean when you say that the mixed-race ancestry of the man in the Salamanca ad is a signifier for his having 'transcended the normal condition of rootedness'. And nor do I understand what you think his homosexuality is meant to signify. I am not sure that you really understand these things either, Adam. Forgive me, but I am not sure that you have read and understood enough of the literature about semiotics and the signifier and the signified and whatnot, to grasp what your own ideas mean. I will be blunt and say that you may not be quite as clever as you think you are. Please don't be too offended by that, very few of us are. I will be blunt again and say that I suspect that the truth about your attitude to the mixed-race man may be much more simple: that you just don't like black people or gay people very much. Whatever the reason for that section of your video, it was revolting to listen to. People are never just signifiers. They are human souls, meaning that they have value and worth regardless of their parentage or who they choose to love.*

*As I said, the tragedy is that you actually raise some good points. What are Salamanca doing sponsoring the anti-racism day? What are they really about as an organisation? You could have put something really good together.*

*And of course, I am personally fed up because I am tangentially involved in all this due to giving you that blasted interview. I still think it was the right thing to do, knowing what I knew at the time, but I regret it now. The archdeacon was basically correct. I seem to have lent credibility to a racist.*

*Look, I am not suggesting that our friendship (if that's what we have) is over. But I am not going to give you any more help with your OyTube stuff, so please don't ask me to. It goes without saying that my door is always open if you want to discuss anything personal, or if you find yourself in difficulty. Above all else I am a priest.*

*I'm rambling. It's late and I am cross so I will stop.*

*Yours,*

*Lavinia.*

I finish my cigarette and then email back.

*Dear Lavinia,*

*I can't stop long because I have to go round to my mum's for Sunday dinner. I am sorry you didn't like my video, and I am more sorry that you feel personally compromised by your association with the racist who made it. I know what I was trying to say in my commentary on the Salamanca ad. If it didn't come across correctly, that's a shame.*

*I am quite certain, however, that I do not dislike black people or mixed-race people. Personal likes and dislikes really do not come into it. But since I have become involved in the Rush Bearing business it has become increasingly clear to me that we do need to talk about the demographic change that is happening in the UK. We at least need to acknowledge that it is happening, that it is not nothing. And in this context, the disproportionate prevalence of mixed-race people and mixed couples in popular culture is at least odd and possibly even slightly sinister. It definitely signifies something. You won't agree of course. Or if you do agree, you won't dare to say so.*

*Finally, I know that you think of yourself above all else as a priest. I have known since we met that your 'priesthood' is the core element around which you have built your identity. I am afraid that I do not think of you as a priest, however, so I will not be coming round for spiritual guidance.*

*Having said that, if you ever want a chat, do get in touch. My door is always open too.*

*Adam.*

As soon as I have sent the email I feel mean and uncomfortable, so I go back inside and log on to the chat sites to distract myself. I get talking to Siobhan from Seattle. She is 54, skinny and much more articulate than the women I normally chat with online.

'Are you looking for some kind of fun?' she writes. 'Because that is not something I would rule out.'

That's a surprise because we had been messaging about the weather. But I message back quickly.

'Yes I am. Shall we go to WhatsApp?'

We go to WhatsApp where Siobhan calls almost immediately, and after a couple of minutes small talk we both masturbate. I lie on my sofa while Siobhan sits on a little fold-down seat thing in her shower. She is completely naked and works a purple vibrator over her vagina. At one point she even holds her labia open for my viewing pleasure which is something no one has ever done before. When it is clear that I am about to come she says:

'Can you hold the phone right up close to your dick? I love watching men shoot.'

I do my best, but apparently I judder too much.

'All I saw at the crucial moment were your pants,' she says, laughing, when it is all over.

'Oh gosh, sorry.'

'Don't worry. We can work at it.'

We talk for a bit about work. It turns out that Siobahn is a therapist, so we chat about CBT and Jung and so on, while I hold my shirt up so that it doesn't fall into the fast-cooling semen on my stomach. Finally, Siobahn says goodbye and I waddle into the bathroom to clean myself up. As I am tucking my shirt back in, I get a WhatsApp message from her:

*That was fun. Hope we can do it again. How are you feeling? No negative feelings I hope?*

I message back:

*None yet. Why did you think that there would be?*

To which she replies.

*I'm a therapist!*

I block her and drive round to mum's.

. . .

Mum is doing roast pork for lunch and so the house smells deliciously warm and savoury again. She is in the front room, today, with her gin and tonic. *The Globe* is spread out on the floor, and the wood burner is roaring away. I join her and she makes me a drink. I sip it twice and the next thing I know, mum is gently pushing my shoulder.

'Adam. Adam.'

'What?'

'It's time for lunch.'

I wipe my face.

'Oh gosh, right. Sorry.'

Mum looks worried.

'You're exhausted, aren't you?'

'I'm a bit tired, yes.'

'Have you been burning the candle at both ends?'

'I suppose I have a bit.'

'Is it to do with this OyTube business?'

'Yeah, mostly.'

'Ben said you'd made another video.'

I lever myself out of the chair and stand up.

'Did he indeed?'

'Yes this morning. He actually called.'

'Fucking hell. Wonders will never cease.'

'He wanted to make sure we were both still alright for Tuesday. He mentioned your video in passing. He said that you had some footage of Asian lads throwing petrol bombs. A sort of scoop, he said, although he thought it might have been more sensible not to have used it. People might not appreciate it.'

'Is that what he said?'

'Yes. He also said the video was quite nasty in places.'

'Well, he's wrong. Have you seen it?'

Mum leads the way into the dining room.

'No,' she says quietly. 'I didn't want to watch anything nasty. Not if you'd done it.'

Mum does most of the talking over lunch. I am too tired to say much, and mum is excited about our trip south. She whitters about the boys and their girlfriends, and Ben's piece in today's paper, and about Miriam's new book.

'Is she writing another one?'

'Yes. I just said she was.'

'What's this one about?'

'A Welsh woman who pioneered vaccinations in the 1830s, in the Astro-Hungarian Empire.'

'Gosh. That's pretty niche.'

'Well yes, I know. It is a bit. But listen Adam, Ben's very proud about it all, so please don't say anything silly about it when we're down there.'

'Of course I won't say anything silly.'

'Miriam gave up the paper for the kids so...'

'I know she did mum. She deserves her writing. I hope her book is the best-selling thing ever published about Welsh women involved in Austro-Hungarian vaccinations. I won't say a word.'

Mum grins.

'Great. Apparently the woman from Bloomsbury is going to be there on Tuesday, as well as Miriam's agent.'

'That'll be exciting.'

'Yes it will. The agent represents Margaret Atwood in the UK, so she's obviously pretty high powered.'

'She must be.'

'And all Ben's friends from the paper will be there of course. Ben said again that they're interested to meet you.'

'That's nice.'

Mum peers at me over the top of her specs.

'Are you being grumpy, Adam, or simply exhausted?'

'I'm just tired, mum. I'm sorry.'

'And you're working tonight aren't you?'

'Yeah. Tonight and tomorrow. Then I'm done for a week.'

'Do you need to go home before work.'

'Only to make food.'

Mum puts her knife and fork down on her plate.

'Right, well sod that. Eat up and then you're going to bed. You can get four hours here, before you have to go in. And I'll make you some tea.'

And so, when we have finished eating, I clamber upstairs and climb into bed in my old room, untouched since I left home a quarter of a century ago. I snuggle into a foetal position and pull my duvet up to me ears. And I fall immediately into a deep and untroubled sleep while mum potters around downstairs, caring and worrying.

# 21

WORK IS RELATIVELY quiet on both Sunday and Monday night, so I spend a lot of time in the office, doing paperwork and watching the numbers of views and comments creep up on the Haxton Review's new video. For the first time this year, I have to switch on my headlamps when I drive home from work, and there is a pleasing chill in the morning air. Also, now that the Rush Bearing is only five days away, the local radio carries reports about it almost constantly. I catch the bulletins as I drive to and from work, and all of them emphasise that Haxton is calm *at the moment*. The sporadic violence has dried up, apparently, and no one was charged following the disturbances at the diversity day. In fact, the celebration is judged a great success by cops, councillors and locals alike, with the stone throwing and petrol bombs hardly mentioned (the two crossbow bolts are lost completely). Haxton's imams are regularly interviewed and they all say pretty much the same thing: that last Saturday shows what Coxthorpe can do when the town's citizens come together in unity and peace, and that next Saturday must demonstrate the same Coxthorpe qualities of hope, common sense and respect. Everyone talks about respect, almost constantly. But as usual the Lantyrn Royd Rush Bearers remain grimly silent.

. . .

Bill visits me, on Monday evening, shortly after I have arrived at work. He is wearing his coat and is clearly on this way home. He knocks on my office door and then walks in without waiting for a reply.

'You ok?' he grunts.

'Yeah fine thanks. How are you?'

'Not so bad. Did you see that email about the forklift servicing?'

'Yeah. I sorted it out last night.'

'Good.'

He runs his hand quickly over his smooth scalp.

'Did you want anything else, Bill?'

'Yeah.' He nods and runs his hand over his scalp again. 'Yeah, I did. That copper called again.'

'The one who was asking about me?' I manage to say. My voice sounds astonishingly calm.

'Yeah. That's the one. He called after lunch today.'

'What did he want this time?'

'He just said he was checking in.'

'What does that mean?'

'I dun't know, do I? You han't been doing owt else on yer internet have you?'

I clench my hands under the desk.

'Nothing illegal. Nothing that has anything to do with work.'

Bill nods quickly.

'Good.'

'What did you tell him?'

'The copper?'

'Yes. Of course, the copper.'

'I told him that we'd had a chat. And that you'd said you weren't doing owt wrong.'

'What did he say to that?'

'He said that he hoped I'd managed some focussed messaging. And that I should give him a ring if you were giving me cause for concern.'

'By doing what, invading fucking Poland?'

Bill shrugs.

'Fuck knows. I just thought I'd better tell you.'

'Thanks.'

'Alright. I'll get me sen off. Have a good shift.'

'I'll try.'

Bill turns and walks out. When he has gone, I get up and pace up and down for five minutes and then go down to the loading bay for a fag. I have the overwhelming urge to phone Jason and tell him about what's just happened, but I don't. For one thing, it doesn't seem fair to worry him, for another, talking about it will only make the conversation more real and more difficult to disregard. I more or less forgot about my last chat with Bill after a couple of days, by consciously not thinking about it. I intend to try and do the same thing again. The implications of what he has to say are too dreadful to deal with in any other way.

Because I haven't done anything wrong. Nothing wrong enough to involve the police anyway. Nothing which could possibly justify them phoning my boss, at work.

It's absolutely awful to think about, so I don't.

But the pressure is there all the same. The cord has come back, tightening slowly.

. . .

I leave work on Tuesday morning at half six and I am home in bed for seven. I go to sleep immediately and am woken by my alarm at half eleven. I have a text from mum.

*I know I'm probably being silly, but I am just checking that you are up and about and that everything is still ok for tonight. I went into town with Miriam yesterday and we had a lovely time pootling round Chelsea. I had a coffee and a sandwich for lunch, and it cost £18. Miriam paid which was lovely. Everyone is really looking forward to seeing you, so do please get here on time. And don't forget a card for Miriam. I have said that the painting I got her was from both of us, so you don't have to worry about a present. I know I'm being silly but do send me a text to let me know that you're on your way. Then I will stop worrying.*

I text back.

*I'm up mum. You can relax. Will get going straight after breakfast.*

I get out of bed and have a shower. Before I get dressed, I unblock Siobhan the Seattle therapist and send her a message saying simply 'Hi'. She messages back:

*Do you know that it is 3.30 am here? I'm only up because I'm working on a paper.*

Before I can answer she sends me a picture of her on all fours, taken from behind. Her vagina is just visible and so, of course, is her slightly open arse crack.

*Like what you see?* She messages. To which I reply:

*Yes. Obviously.*

She messages.

*Tell me, where do you most like to put your dick? Pussy, ass, mouth or tits?*

I message back.

*Pussy, but I prefer the word cunt.*

She replies immediately.

*Interesting. So why don't you call me and tell me about putting your dick in my cunt and come for me?*

So, I call and, curiously, we chat for ten minutes about her paper, which is about the role of virtual communities in gender identity formation. It all sounds quite interesting but it's difficult to take in all she says because I have to keep wanking discreetly so that I don't lose my hard on. Finally, Siobhan says:

'Go on then, come for me. But hold the phone right close to your dick this time so I can see you shoot.

'Do you like that bit especially?' I ask.

'Yeah I do. Very much. And all men do it differently.'

'I had no idea.'

'It's true. It's fascinating. Come on, come for me baby.'

When I am finished, I end the call immediately and block Siobhan, then wipe my tummy and get dressed. I have a cup of coffee and a fag for breakfast and then pack my overnight bag. I leave the house at ten past twelve and walk to the corner shop to pick up a card for Miriam, before getting the bus to the station and climbing on board the Kings Cross train with five minutes to spare. Once I am settled, I get a four pack of lager and a sandwich from the buffet, then write Miriam's card and drink the beer straight from the can. I peer out of the smudgy window as the train trundles out of the platform, quietly saying goodbye to my little world of mills and moorland and sadness. I keep looking out of the window for a long time, longer than is comfortable, with my forehead resting on the glass, avoiding facing forwards towards London, and my extraordinary brother, and all that achievement and glamour.

. . .

*Bright and fierce and fickle is the South, And dark and true and tender is the North.* I don't have a clue what Tennyson means. But when I am a bit pissed and riding on the train from Coxthorpe to King Cross I get melancholy and thoughtful, and then the words seem true, even without my understanding them.

. . .

My brother and his family own a small, terraced house in Aldborough which they let out through Air B&B for most of the year. They also have an apartment in Budapest which is empty much of the time, but which they will visit for odd weekend breaks throughout Spring and Summer and for a week after Christmas. Their main residence, however, is a six-bedroom terraced villa, spread over four floors, in Victoria Park.

One Christmas when we were both drunk, Ben and I had a vicious little conversation about the value of the house and he had the grace, briefly, to look slightly embarrassed. I remember him waving his hand dismissively.

'I know it's worth a fucking mint,' he said. 'And I know it's outrageous. I do get it. But listen, Adam, everybody in London is a property millionaire, pretty much. If you own property, you can't help it.'

I just stared at him.

'Well not everybody,' he said after a moment. 'Obviously not everybody here is a millionaire. But you know what I mean.'

'I haven't got a fucking clue what you mean, Ben.'

'Oh, fuck off Adam. You're happy enough to stay here.'

'I'm also very happy to leave.'

'Be my fucking guest.'

Ben on his own is hard work. Ben as lord of the six-bedroom manor is pretty much unbearable.

Happily, today it is Miriam who opens the door. She has a glass of wine in her hand, and she is grinning madly. Mum is bobbing about behind her.

'Adam,' Miriam says. 'You got here. Smashing. Come on in. Thanks so much for coming.'

'It's nice to see you, Miriam.'

As I step over the threshold we have a quick hug.

'We've sorted you a room,' she says as she releases me. Let's get your bag up there shall we and then we can get you a drink and start showing you off.' She winks. 'I think you're going to be rather in demand.'

'I told him that he would be,' mum says. 'Thanks so much for getting down so quickly after the shift, darling.'

Then she leans forward and kisses me on the mouth. Her lips are warm and sticky with drink. She has had her hair done and is wearing a dress that I have never seen before, swirling green and slightly low cut, so that it reveals a bit of tit.

'It's fine, mum.'

'Did you get enough sleep?'

'Of course. I'm fine, honestly. And I'm off all week now, anyway.'

Mum pats me on the cheek while Miriam winks and sips her wine. Then George shambles into the hall. He is wearing an outsize hoody and jeans that end half up his groin, and he is carrying a can of lager. He grins amiably.

'Oh cool,' he says, 'Uncle Adam's here. The OyTube guy!?'

He holds his hand up and we have a limp high five that somehow turns into a handshake and while that is going on, and while our two mothers are grinning their benedictions at us, the thought slips into my mind unbidden: *there will be bad behaviour here tonight.* And another thought follows it immediately: *and some of it will be mine.*

It's the house. It's the size of the fucking house, I'm afraid, together with the unspoken view of the whole family (absorbed by osmosis from Ben) that to live somewhere like this is somehow normal. I try not to let it trigger me, but it does, especially if Ben gets opinionated and preachy. People who live in Victorian multi-million-pound houses should not lob stones of progressive virtue everywhere. Anything more than three bedrooms in London and you should settle down in your tasteful fucking kitchen at your fucking kitchen island, and shut the fuck up about climate change, or poverty, or pay gaps, or anything else remotely left wing. The alternative, if you *do* talk about these things, is that you look like a posturing cunt.

Perhaps, the fact that I'm under pressure at the moment doesn't help things. But, if I'm honest, that only makes me less resilient and easier to trigger. It's the fucking house that actually does the triggering. I know that's resentful and stupid, but I can't help myself.

# 22

George is instructed to take me to my room. I am at the top of the house, and my room has the kind of satisfyingly angular ceiling that you only get in a proper old fashioned attic. It also has a double bed and an *en suite* loo. There is a tastefully framed black and white photo of Coxthorpe town hall on the wall, and a view of Victoria park from the dormer window.

'Do you want to be left on your own for a bit?' George asks when I have chucked my bag on the bed.

'What for?'

'I dunno. Freshen up or something?'

'Are you trying to tell me that I smell?'

He grins.

'Nah. Well not that I can tell anyway. I was just being polite.'

'God. Please don't start being polite. I don't think it will suit you.'

'You're happy to come straight back downstairs then?

'Yes, I think I'd better get stuck into it.'

George nods and turns for the door. Then he turns back.

'Are you actually alright, Uncle Adam?'

'I think so. I'm a bit tired but I'm ok.'

'I meant about your OyTube channel and all that.'

'What about it?'

He frowns and drinks his beer.

'It's not exactly conventional stuff is it? It's all slightly...I don't know...heavy. I was worried in case you were going a bit nuts...or... or...if you were unhappy somehow.'

When the boys were little I lived in London, and I used to visit more often than I do now. Whenever I called, I told them stories about Ethelred the Unwell who helped defend Coxthorpe from the Normans during the Harrying of the North. I can't remember how the stories started but I know that Ethelred always had a cold, or toothache or haemorrhoids when the Normans attacked, causing him to nearly fuck everything up. Luckily he also had battalions of Eskimos and Cyborgs to help him fight, as well as a small air force of hot air balloons. And so, in the end, the Normans always got walloped. For some reason, Ethelred lived in a canal boat and drank whisky and smoked cigars. Anyway, when the Ethelred stories got going Josh was already old enough to understand the conventions of fiction and realise that I was basically talking bullshit against the backdrop of a real historical event. He grasped that truth and fiction were woven together, sometimes quite finely, in the nonsense I was spouting. But George was younger and struggled constantly to work out what was true and false in the Ethelred cycle. It worried him immensely. I can still remember him begging to know exactly what was going on:

'But there weren't *really* polar bears fighting the Normans were there, Uncle Adam?' he would ask, with his little face screwed up in anxiety. (The Eskimos rode polar bears into battle). 'And there weren't *really* balloons flown by mice, were there?'

'There were in the story, Josh.'

'But were there *really* polar bears and mice, Uncle Adam?'

George is a sensitive, anxious lad beneath all the drugs stuff and the baggy clothes and the silly teenage cool. And now, apparently, his anxiety has been directed towards me. It is extraordinarily touching, suddenly, to be loved and worried about by my chaotic nephew.

'I don't think I'm any more unhappy than anyone else, Josh,' I say after a moment.

'And do you really mean the stuff you say in your content? Do you mean all the racist stuff?

'I do mean it, I think. Although the word racist is a very difficult one to pin down. I'm trying to work out exactly what I mean as I go along, I suppose.'

'I never knew you were into that sort of thing, that's all.'

'Nor did I, really. I'm still not sure that I am, in fact.'

He nods.

'As long as you're ok. Come on then. I'll get you a beer.'

The party is happening on the two lower floors of the house. The first floor has the living room and a room which used to be called the playroom but is now known as the library. The two rooms have people sitting around on sofas, drinking and chatting, and eating classy nibbles from the bowls arranged on coffee tables and mantlepieces. Downstairs there is a kitchen-cum-dining room running the length of the house. There is more substantial food laid out here, on the dining room table, with a pile of paper plates and cutlery, and a bunch of wine and spirit bottles on the marble kitchen island. A plastic dustbin contains iced water and bottles of continental and Japanese lagers. Three steps down from the kitchen is the dayroom, which Ben and Miriam added to the house a few years ago. It is large and airy with wooden floorboards and ethnic rugs, and three substantial skylights. The crowd in the kitchen and the dayroom seem livelier than the lot upstairs. More people are standing up, and a few are even swaying slightly to the jazz that is playing. I would guess that there are about seventy guests altogether. They are smart and bright and fun looking. There are bangles and pendants in evidence, as well as designer specs and endless untucked, open-necked shirts and tasteful tattoos. If there is such a thing as the London media elite, and if you had to describe them, you would come up with a group very similar to the bunch that my sister-in-law has gathered for her fiftieth drinks do.

'Are you sure you're ok, Uncle Adam?'

I am standing next to the dining room table and Ben is offering me a bottle of beer.

'Yes, I'm fine.'

'You looked like you were miles away.'

'I was just thinking about the pub I go to sometimes, in Lantyrn Royd.'

'Really. Why?'

'Just the contrast, I suppose. It's difficult to work out how there and here can possibly connect or...or relate. In any sense at all. Or even be in the same world. It's a bit...dizzying.'

'Have a drink.'

I take the beer and sip from it. As I do so, Josh appears through the crowd, with a young woman in tow.

'Uncle Adam.'

'Hi Josh. Good to see you.'

'You too.'

We shake hands and then Josh steps back.

'This is Julia, my partner. I don't think you've met.'

'We haven't. Nice to meet you, Julia.'

'Nice to meet you too.'

She holds her hand out unenthusiastically and we shake.

'So where do you two know each other from?'

'I'm at Jesus as well.'

'Ah. I see.'

For a moment no one speaks, and then Julia says:

'And you're the OyTube uncle, right?'

'I am. In fact, I'm the only uncle.'

She frowns and peers into her glass of wine and then looks up again, straight at me.

'Look, it's probably not the right place to say this. But I think sometimes you have to say things even if it's not quite appropriate. The stuff you've made for OyTube is pretty bloody horrible and damaging, to be honest. Are you aware of that? Are you aware of how much harm you might actually be doing?'

'Julia...don't...' Josh mumbles.

'No. It's ok Josh. Julia's entitled to her say.'

I meet her gaze. She is, it has to be said, extraordinarily beautiful, with bobbed dark hair and unsettlingly blue eyes. Her tits, under her spotless white blouse, are magnificent. And, my God, how proud of herself she is. How proud for challenging the nasty uncle. How proud of her own courage and conviction. She has the native certainty of youth combined with the endless self-assurance of the beautiful and the unshakeable conviction of the modern liberal. What a shitty combination. It is unbecoming for a man in his late forties to hate a woman of (I suppose) twenty, but for a moment I can't help myself. I also want to fuck her, of course.

'Thanks for that at least,' she mutters.

'You're entitled to your say, just like anyone else is. But you have to recognise that your say will be formed by your own, experience, won't it? It can't not be.'

'Of course not.'

I know I should stop there. Obviously, I should stop there. But I really do seem to hate the silly bitch.

'So, let's think about that experience, just for a minute. A nice family. A private school, somewhere in the south I'm guessing. And then Cambridge. There's nothing wrong with any of that. Honestly, there isn't. I don't have any problem with elite education. I think it's great. But, let's be honest, it's a very different experience, a much more privileged experience, than that of the people in Lantyrn Royd who I've been talking to. And it's those people's lives and experiences that has informed what I've tried to do on OyTube. So that might be something to bear in mind.'

Her cheeks flush pink, making her even more lovely.

'So, because I'm at Cambridge that invalidates what I have to say, does it?'

'No, of course not. But it might mean that you should check your privilege - I believe that's the phrase - before you say it.'

'That's fucking ridiculous,' she mutters. 'That's not what that means. And you know it.'

We all stare into our drinks for a moment and then Josh says:

'Anyway, how's work, Uncle Adam. Your real work, I mean.'

'It's ok, thanks. It's a warehouse, Josh. It doesn't change much to be honest.'

'No. I suppose not. Glad it's still good, though.

'It's fine. And, talking of work, your dad said that you'd been a bit of a hit on the paper over the summer.'

Now it is Josh's turn to blush.

'Oh, I wouldn't say that I'd been a hit exactly.'

'You say it all the fucking time,' George says.

I grin at George and then turn back to Josh.

'I looked your stuff up online. It was great. You've certainly inherited Ben's way with words, for your sins.'

Josh pushes his big-frame specs up his nose and leans forward, very much the earnest writer all of a sudden. He looks like a self-important owl.

'I was hoping we could talk about that, actually. You'll have seen that I wrote some stuff which relates to your own material, about politics on campuses and diversity and stuff. It's what I'm interested in. It's the area I want to work in. Anyway, I was wondering if I could maybe write a piece about you. If I could interview you. If you feel comfortable with that, of course.'

Of course I don't feel fucking comfortable with it. 'My uncle the Nazi.' I don't feel comfortable with it at all. But now doesn't seem the time to say so. I don't want to piss off Josh as well as his girlfriend.

'Yeah...Yeah...I suppose so. Not immediately, and I'd have to think about how we'd do it. But, yeah, certainly it's possible.'

'There's no guarantee I'd be able to sell it anywhere. And...And I'd have a different take on things from you obviously.'

'Of course you would.'

'Because you're not a fucking fascist,' Julia mutters.

Those dreadful blue eyes glare at me, and I hate her again, as well as desiring her with the horrible, haunting desire of the aging for the young. Julia's beautiful body and her pure mind are no county for old men, or middle-aged men. I hold her gaze for a moment and then, without intending to, I remember all the time I spend wanking over lonely old women online, and suddenly I feel mortal and sad, more than angry.

'I'm not a fascist by any reasonable definition of the term, Julia,' I say quietly. 'You must know that if you've seen my videos.'

She snorts and Josh winces. Mercifully, at that moment, Ben arrives.

'Adam! Hanging out with the cool kids of course. Great to see you.'

We shake hands.

'Good to see you too.'

'Thanks so much for coming down.'

'I never turn down free booze, Ben. You know that.'

'But you look like you could do with a refill. And, actually, if you can bear to be dragged away from the yoof, there's someone I'd like you to meet.'

'Yes of course. I wouldn't mind nipping for a fag first, though.'

'Perfect. The bloke I'm thinking of is doing exactly the same thing. Come on. I'll get you a drink on the way.'

'Excellent. See you around, you lot. We'll talk about the writing thing later, Josh. If that's ok.'

'Yeah. Great.'

George grins and winks at me while Julia stares into her wine. I turn and follow Ben through the crowd.

'You going to stay with the beer?' he asks, when we reach the kitchen island stacked with drink.

'No. I'm in the mood for wine now I think. Anything red.'

Ben pours a very large glass of merlot, hands it to me and then leads me down the steps into the dayroom. We edge through the crowd to the glass sliding doors in the opposite wall and slip outside on to the patio.

The air is cool and refreshing. There is a man standing at the edge of the patio smoking and staring into the garden. As we come through the doors he turns and smiles. He is short and rather skinny, and his suit is baggy. His hair is thinning, and he wears round wire-rimmed specs like John Lennon's. When he smiles his face is extraordinarily kind.

'Now then Simon,' Ben says. 'Here's my brother Adam, as promised. He's the genuinely Coxthorpe part of the family.'

'Ah,' he says. 'Smashing. Nice to meet you Adam. I'm Simon.'

He steps forward and we shake hands.

'So, I'll leave you too to get cancer together while I go and be the perfect host. See you later.'

Ben slips back through the sliding doors, while I roll a fag. As I am lighting it, a gale of hooting laughter sounds from the day room. Simon rolls his eyes.

'It's hard to explain how a laugh can sound smug isn't it? But they manage it somehow.'

'Yeah. Yeah, they really do.'

'I suppose if you put several dozen rather pleased-with-themselves media people in one place, you have to expect that.'

I glance at him as I inhale.

'You don't work for *The Globe* then?'

'Do I heck. I'm a civil servant, more or less.'

'Oh right. Which department?'

'I work across a number of departments. I'm sort of semi-detached these days.'

We smoke quietly for a moment. Then I say:

'So why did you want to meet me? If you don't mind me asking.'

'I don't mind you asking in the least. It's you're OyTube stuff, of course. I've been fascinated with it.' He nods at the house. 'You're the man of the hour here I think.'

'If that means that I'm popular, I'm afraid you're mistaken. I've already pissed off my nephew's girlfriend, I think permanently. And I'm not sure that *The Globe* crowd are going to be any more enthusiastic.'

Simon grinds out his cigarette in the ash tray provided on the edge of the fire pit and lights another.

'Find it's best to double-up at parties like these,' he says. He exhales happily. 'And I'm sure you're right. *The Globe* lot will be polite to you to your face, no doubt. And some of them are probably genuinely interested in what you've done, but they're never going to be fans of the Haxton Review, are they?

'No, they're not.'

'It's just too brutal and too honest. Perhaps a bit too nasty as well.' He inhales again, deeply. 'And it deviates from the acceptable line, doesn't it? *The Globe* lot have a rigid rule to follow. All of them, even your brother. It has the feel of a puritan cult these days, the *Globe*, which is sad when you consider its history.'

'Yes, I've thought pretty much the same thing myself.'

'They don't think of themselves like that of course, as far as they're concerned, they're the same progressive, lefty force they've always been, but something has changed profoundly there.'

'I've stopped buying it.'

'Interesting.' He smiles again. 'And, of course, the cult's dogmas conflict absolutely with what you've been saying.'

'Of course. Are you sympathetic to what I've been saying?'

'No. Not really. Or not entirely. But I've appreciated it for its candour.'

'Thank you.'

He shrugs.

'No need to thank me. If we're ever going to sort out the kind of mess you've got up in Haxton, we need candour above all.'

I grind my cigarette out and roll another. If Simon is going to smoke two at a time I may as well do the same.

'So, was there anything in particular you wanted to know?'

'About the Haxton Review?'

'Yes.'

'Well I suppose I was keen to know how you put it together so well, for one thing. You apparently started from absolutely nothing, but right from the beginning you've had pretty high production values. The quality of these channels normally evolves as they go along, but you looked pretty smart, right out of the gate.'

'I've had help. A bloke I know has his own channel and he's taken care of all that side of things. Left me free to get on with the scripts and so on.'

'And do you work on the scripts a lot? Do you think precisely about the content beforehand?'

'I work on them for quite a long time. I check references and so on, as far as possible.'

'And is it conviction, or performance mostly, would you say?'

'A few people have asked me that. I suppose it's a bit of both really. I want to tell the truth as I see it, and I think that I mean what I say when I say it. But I also want to make videos that are, I don't know, *compelling*, I suppose. I want clicks.' I shrug. 'Maybe the two things conflict occasionally.'

'Interesting.'

Simon smokes quietly for a minute. Then he says:

'Your brother doesn't know what on earth to make of you, of course.'

'I know. He hates it.'

'I suspect he's jealous as much as he's appalled.'

'I hadn't even considered that. Do you know Ben well?'

'Not very well. We met though work.'

'How come?'

'Well, one of the things I'm involved in is helping to manage narratives around community cohesion and so on. Especially when there are difficulties.' (He makes quotation marks with his fingers around 'difficulties'.) 'As I said, I'm a civil servant, but I work with newspapers and PR-type agencies of various stripes. There's a very loose kind of network; we try and give things a nudge in the right direction when things get sticky. And that's how we met. Ben's been very obliging, as one would expect from a good *Globe* man.'

'Interesting job.'

'It can be. That was why I was so fascinated by what you've been doing. It was partly in a professional capacity.'

'I had no idea that anyone would be interested in me like that.'

'Of course they are. You grew very quickly after the Tanya Faulk piece, didn't you? These things get noticed. And talked about.'

'I suppose so. It had just never occurred to me.'

He smiles.

'Don't undersell yourself, for Christ's sake. There are plenty of people who will do that for you. Look, just out of interest, have you ever thought about using your skills in a more official, more lucrative, sort of way?'

'I'm not sure quite what you mean.'

He takes his glasses off and wipes them with a hanky then squints through them and replaces them.

'Nor am I really. I'm certainly not offering you a job, I'm in no position to do that. But I'm fairly sure that some of the agencies I work with would be very grateful indeed to find someone with your particular skills.'

'Really? Are you sure? Off the back of three videos?'

'Absolutely. You've managed to touch a collective nerve very quickly and very astutely. That makes you interesting.'

'And would this...this work...would it be in London?'

He shrugs.

'You can work where you want, doing the sort of stuff you'd be doing. But, actually, I suspect people would value you more in the north. You have a kind of kudos up there. An authenticity.'

(My hand is shaking, now, as I smoke. It's awful when your most hidden and unacknowledged dreams come true, but in completely the wrong context. It's disorientating.)

'I mean...I mean...what would this sort of thing involve exactly?'

'Measuring moods. Working with people who know people who do the sort of thing you're doing at the moment. And doing more of the same yourself. Nudging people a bit. Influencing, is what they call it, isn't it?'

'Doing exactly the same sort of thing as I do at the moment?'

Simon turns and looks straight at me. He flicks ash off his cigarette.

'Well, no, not quite. You'd have to have a broader editorial view, if that doesn't sound too pompous to describe a OyTube channel with three videos. We're not all *Globe* puritans but there is still a rough sort of line that needs to be followed.'

'I see.'

'Hmm.'

We smoke again, in silence for a while and then Simon pats his pockets, absent-mindedly. Finally, he reaches into the inside pocket of his jacket.

'Look, here's my card. Have a think about it. Like I said, I'm not offering you a job, but I can introduce you to people who might. There is work, Adam, fascinating, well-paid work, if you're interested.'

I take the card and put it in the top pocket of my shirt.

'Thank you. I don't know what to say.'

'You don't have to say anything now.' He frowns and picks up a glass of wine from the edge of the fire pit and sips it. 'But you might have to think about it rather quickly. A change of tone about the situation in Haxton would probably be a precondition for coming on board with the sorts of people I'm talking about. And, as you know better than most, time is of the essence up there. Give me a ring over the next couple of days if you're interested.'

'Of course.'

'Good. You do understand what I've just said, don't you?'

'Yes...Yes, I think so. I think that I understand perfectly.'

'Excellent.'

Just then my mum slips through the sliding door.

'Ben said I'd find you out here, Adam. You can't stay outside hiding all evening, you know. Come on inside and get another drink.'

Simon smiles his lovely smile at mum, who smiles back at him.

'Apologies. It's me who's kept him talking I'm afraid.' He lifts his cigarette. It's always nice to find another pariah.'

'Oh, I'm sure it is. I'm Ben's mum. And Adam's of course. And I don't think we've met yet. Do you work for the paper?'

'No. I'm afraid that I'm just a civil servant. I'm Simon.'

'Ah. Ok.' Mum's smile fades a fraction. 'Well, it's nice to meet you Simon. But if you don't mind I will capture Adam back off you now. If you're finished with him.'

'Of course. Be my guest. It was good to meet you, Adam.'

'You too.'

'Do think about what I've said.'

'I will.'

'And don't forget the time constraint.'

'I won't.'

Simon nods and turns away, and I put my fag out and then follow mum back through the day room and into the kitchen. She takes my empty glass and refills it with merlot.

'There we are. Now for God's sake circulate with some of *The Globe* people. They're the ones who want to meet you.'

# 23

THE REST OF the party becomes increasingly blurred. I speak to various colleagues of Ben's and, just as mum said, most of them seem pretty interested in the Haxton Review and the situation in Lantyrn Royd. No one is directly challenging or disapproving, as Julia was. No one else calls me a fascist. I suppose this is partly because people don't want to cause a scene, but I sense that their restraint also stems from the professional journalists' reluctance to punch down to the lucky amateur. And I think they are nervous, as well, about challenging the authenticity of the Lantyrn Royd residents too forcefully ('authentic' is a word that gets used a lot). There is still something slightly untouchable about genuinely working-class people as far as the *Globe* writers are concerned, I realise, even working-class people who are hopelessly lost in racist false consciousness. They ask about the individuals I've interviewed and the Lantyrn Royd community generally. They want to know more details about the Diversity Day celebration, especially my meeting with English Solidarity. They probe me about the comments I have received under the videos, and about people's attitudes to the Rush Bearing in Coxthorpe and in West Yorkshire more broadly. Without ever stating as much, the *Globe* writers seem to recognise that they are cut off from the stream of English opinion that is represented in the Rush Bearing dispute, and they perceive me as a rare and articulate visitor from that other ideological shore. They seem genuinely to want to get a handle on things. I am unfailingly friendly in my replies to their questions, and I try my best to be honest. They are, it has to be said, really friendly and attractive people. Increasingly so, as I get pissed.

. . .

I speak to George briefly when I nip outside for another fag and find him perched on the edge of the fire pit, smoking. He gives me a light for my roll up, which he has never done before. It feels like minor rite of passage, an acknowledgement that he isn't quite a boy anymore.

'Any idea what you're planning to do after GCSEs?' I ask as I inhale.

'Yeah...yeah actually. I kind of want to leave school and go to a sixth form college, for A levels.'

'That's interesting. Why?'

He shrugs.

'I'm sick of the uniforms and the all the bollocks at our place. Being treated like we're seven. And I'm sick of feeling that the only thing that counts is exams. It's just a fucking sausage factory, Uncle Adam.' He inhales, then goes on more quietly. 'And I'm sick of being Josh's brother as well.'

'Yeah. I can see that must get a bit wearing. Head boy and all that.'

'And captain of the debating team,' George counts on his fingers. 'And editor of the school magazine. And winner of the national sixth form political essay competition. And then straight into fucking Cambridge.'

'Fucking hell, I see what you mean. I'd get as far away from the bloody place as you can if I were you. Do you know what A levels you fancy?'

'English, History and Politics.' He grins sheepishly. 'Same as Josh.'

'Ah.'

Miriam comes out onto the patio. George looks at me appealingly and shakes his head. Apparently his mum and dad still don't know about his plans.

'The smoker's corner! I should have known I'd find you two out here. I hope you're both having fun.'

'I'm having a great time, thanks,' I say.

'Met some nice people?'

'Loads of them.'

'Wonderful. I do wish you'd come down more often. We should do more family stuff.' She sips her wine. 'I know Ben worries that you two don't see enough of each other.'

'Yeah, I should make more of an effort. You're always welcome to come up north of course.'

'I know. I know. We should do. We really should. It's just so bloody busy. Now more than ever with the blasted book.'

'Oh yes. I meant to ask, how is it going?'

'Deadline in March. It's fucking terrifying.'

'I bet. It's vaccinations in the Austro-Hungarian empire or something, isn't it?'

'God no. That would be much too broad. Impossible to cover. It's vaccinations in the Austro-Hungarian Empire between 1825 and 1850. There was a Welsh woman involved. A Quaker. That's what makes it so interesting, from a feminist perspective as much as anything.'

'I see.' I put my cigarette out. 'I'm sorry, but I'm not sure that I can ask you a single intelligent question about any of that.

I'm afraid that I don't know very much about vaccinations in the Austro-Hungarian Empire between 1825 and 1850. Or Quakers. Or Welsh people, come to that.'

'Oh Adam.' She giggles and kisses me on the cheek. 'You must damn well buy the book then and find out all about them. If I ever get the bloody thing finished, that is. Now come on, let's go and get another drink.'

. . .

Shortly after that I find myself queueing for the toilet behind Julia. She turns round as I approach.

'Oh, it's you.'

'I'm afraid it is. Can you cope with weeing in the same toilet as a fascist?'

For the briefest moment, a grin plays round her lips.

'I suppose I probably can, given that I think that most of what you produce is a load of shit anyway.'

I can't help laughing.

'Nicely put.'

'Thank you.' She bites her lip. 'And look, I'm sorry I called you a fascist or a Nazi or whatever it was. Josh has explained that your background is quite weird and you live alone, and that you're a bit of a...well of a *free thinker* or a *free spirit*, or something. But I do think that a lot of your stuff is pretty unacceptable and...and it's caused no end of bother for Josh. He won't tell you of course. But he was really upset by it all. He thinks quite highly of you, you see, and...'

'Does he really? I had no idea.'

'Yes he does. You used to tell him stories about knights and stuff apparently. He still talks about them. He credits them with making him want to write.'

'Blimey. That was quite a long time ago. I had no idea they had such an impact.'

'Well, they did. Perhaps you should have stuck to them.'

'Ouch.'

'I'm sorry. That was rude.'

'It's ok. Look, I meant what I said earlier. You're perfectly entitled to tell me that my opinions are horrible and wicked. Lots of people have done the same. I just don't want to be misrepresented, I suppose. And I don't want people to be lazy in their language about it all.'

'I can understand that. And I agree completely that language matters.' She flicks her hair out of her lovely eyes. 'I'm not going to back down completely, because I think I'm right about what you've done, and I think it's important. But perhaps we can talk about it all again. When everything has calmed down. At Christmas or something.'

'Excellent. We'll declare a Christmas truce and meet in no man's land for football and debate and mince pies.'

'Sounds divine.'

'Well, we'll see. And, if we're doing humility and apologies, I'm sorry that I said what I did about your background. That was mean.'

'It's alright.'

'It's not alright. I don't know you from Adam.'

She grins properly.

'The irritating fucking thing is that you got most of it right.' Her voice drops. 'Look, I don't know if it matters, but I only went to a private school because I won a scholarship. Mum and dad are teachers. They couldn't have afforded to send me otherwise. I know I've been lucky but...'

'Oh God, please don't justify yourself. I feel enough of a prick for saying what I did in the first place.'

'No but you had a point. Sort of. I should...'

Just then the toilet flushes and a woman walks out and squeezes passed us down the landing. Julia goes inside and a few minutes later the toilet flushes again. Then Julia reappears.

'I'd leave it a few minutes, if I were you,' she says, laughing. 'Take that fascist!'

On reflection, I can't help thinking that Julia makes a very suitable girlfriend for my owlish nephew.

. . .

And all the time, throughout all the conversation and the drink, I am acutely aware of the card that Simon gave me, lying softly in the breast pocket of my shirt. It seems to flutter there, lightly, like a bee's wing, against my heart. I want to talk more to Simon, to hear him say again the things he said while we were smoking. I want to hear about jobs and nudging and public relations. I want to feel the warm rushing pleasure of it again. But it is not to be, because lovely Simon has apparently vanished and taken his glad tidings and his lovely smile with him. The little, lively card in my pocket is the only evidence that he was ever here.

. . .

Just after eight o'clock I wander into the living room and come across Ben slumped on a sofa. Most people have drifted downstairs by now, and the only other people in the room are a couple in their mid-thirties chatting quietly on the sofa opposite. I sit down next to Ben. He turns to me and smiles, glassily.

'You alright?'

'Yeah.'

'Glad you came?'

'I am actually. Your colleagues are nice people.'

'For a bunch of media elite liberal cunts.'

'Exactly.'

'I knew you were thinking it.' He takes a large swig of wine. 'You're the famous Haxton Review, for Christ's sake, what else are you going to think? Still, I'm glad they were gentle with you. Did you have a good chat with Simon?'

'Yeah...yeah, I did.'

'Are you going to think about what he said?'

'Did he tell you?'

'Yes of course he did, that's why I introduced you. That's kind of why you're here, Adam.'

'Oh. I see.'

Ben frowns and peers into his wine glass.

'Sorry. Probably shouldn't have said that.'

'It's ok. I don't...I don't suppose it matters.'

'Are you then?'

'Am I what?'

'Going to think about what he said.'

'Yes, I am going to think about it.'

'Make sure you do.'

(Which is when I should have got up and walked away, of course. I should have got up and walked straight out of the room and chatted to my mum about the nice people we'd both met, or to George about sixth form colleges and A levels, or to Julia about fascism, or even to Miriam about vaccinations in the Austro-Hungarian empire between 1825 and 1850. But I simply can't. I can never walk away from Ben, and it's worse than usual today because I am so pissed and so close to him. More than ever today, I can sense his rage and his need to control and to win. My own rage, the rage that always answers his, has me planted here, next to him on the sofa in the living room of his six bedroom, multi-million-pound house and I just can't budge. It's not a question of lacking the will, *I literally can't budge*. I couldn't stand up and leave now, even in exchange for a weekend city break in Nuremburg with Julia, where I got to bang her repeatedly in an SS outfit.)

'What the fuck is that supposed to mean?'

Ben rolls his eyes.

'Oh Christ, don't get fucking precious and defensive. I just mean that, if there is some kind of opportunity for you, you should give it your careful con...consideration.'

'And you assume that I need you to tell me that?'

He is about to sip his wine again, but he snorts into it.

'Well, it can't hurt to hear a bit of advice.'

'From you?'

'In the absence of anyone better. Oh Christ, Adam, I don't want a row. Honestly I don't. Not today. But you've been lucky enough, somehow, to stumble into a real opportunity. Something serious for once. Instead of just fucking around with religion, or in that bloody warehouse, or whatever. It's sen...sensible to think hard about it. That's all I'm saying.'

'Well don't fucking say it,' I say quietly. 'I don't want you to say it. I don't want to be like you.'

Ben leans over to the wine bottle on the coffee table and refills his glass. He raises it at the couple opposite who are staring at us and grins at them, and then he drinks.

'Of course you don't want to be like me,' he says after a minute. 'Of course you don't.'

'Let me qualify that. I would like the money and the houses and the prestige and so on. I would like the whole life, I suppose. But I cer...certainly don't want the...the...the shitty narrowness of it all. I'd rather stay fucked up and a bit skint, and hang onto some of the things that matter, thank you very much.'

He throws his head back and laughs.

'What's so amusing?'

'Who says "thank you very much" these days?' He's still giggling.

'I dunno. I do, apparently. When I'm fucked off. I don't see why it's funny.'

'Yeah. Yeah. You're right. I shouldn't laugh. It's just such a weird thing to hear.' He wipes his lips. 'By the way, what are those creatures called that have their skeletons on the outside?'

'What?'

'Those insects that have skeletons on the outside instead of inside? What are they called? What are the skeletons called?'

'Dunno. Exoskeletons?'

'Yeah. Exoskeletons. Something like that. Carapace perhaps. Little bugs and things.'

'What about them?'

'It's what you remind me of, I'm afraid, Adam. With your 'things that matter'. I've thought it for ages, but I've never said it to anyone, apart from mum. That's what you are, I'm afraid. A fucking little exoskeleton man.'

'Can you explain exactly what you mean?'

I hear my voice say the words but I'm not actually aware of speaking them. I am cold, suddenly. Cold and immobile and terrified.

Ben shrugs.

'Well, most people have a proper backbone on the inside, don't they, which means they can stand up straight and face the world. We take some knocks of course. We all do. But most of us have a bit of strength and sp...spine to deal with them. But you're...you're.... you're different. You can't face fucking anything without something hard and protective around you to keep you safe. Like your own personal scaffolding. It's either mum and dad, or it's the bloody church, or it's this weird fucking thing about the Haxton Third Reich. You can't just grow a backbone and be yourself and deal with shit, because you're too fucking scared of everything.'

'I see.'

'Just fucking sc...scared. You always have been.'

'I see.'

'And you always dress it up as if it's something noble, that's the really irritating thing. You pretend that you're caring for mum, instead of leeching off her, or that you're following the Church out of sanctity or whatever, rather than dread, and now that you're doing your bit to save the native fucking English out of a sense of civic responsibility or something. But it's not that at all, is it? It never is. Not at root. It's just fear.' He gulps more wine and goes on. 'Mostly, of course, it's only you who gets hurt, apart from mum. But this time it's different. This time you're hurting me, and by ex... extension my family. And God knows how many other deluded, frightened people who watch your shitty little videos. And all this because you haven't got the bollocks or the back...backbone just to live fucking nor...normally.'

He drains his glass and puts it on the coffee table with a sharp click. Then he swallows twice and buries his face in his hands.

'I shouldn't have said that,' he says quietly.

'No, it's good to be clear.'

'Fucking hell.'

'But just tell me, Ben. What does living normally mean, exactly?'

'What?'

'What does living normally involve?'

'I shouldn't have said any of it. I'm sorry. I'm drunk.'

'What does living normally involve Ben?'

He takes his hands away from his face and looks round the room. The couple opposite are absolutely still. They hardly seem to be breathing.

'It means this. Friends. Family. Kids. Work. Just normal stuff. Oh, for Christ's sake sit down Adam.'

I hadn't realised that I had stood up. I am standing right over Ben now, staring down at him. Vaguely, I notice that my fists are clenched.

'To what end?'

'What?'

'What's the point of it all? Of the houses and the kids and the great job etc? The normal stuff?'

'Oh, fuck off. I'm too drunk to get metaphysical.'

'Try. Indulge me.'

He shrugs.

'Just to be free and enjoy your life, I suppose.'

'Ok. Ok. I see. To be free and enjoy life. I see.' I unclench my fists and grip my hands behind my back. I feel bizarre, like an aging grammar school teacher lecturing a cocky sixth former. And when I speak again my voice doesn't sound like my own. It is higher pitched than normal, and the intonation has become laboured and pompous. 'You've been as clear and as honest as you're able, I believe, so I will be too. I think you are a vacuous, vain, selfish cunt, Ben. If you ever had the capacity for independent thought, it left you long ago. You pretend to be a serious thinker and a great humanitarian, but that's all self-indulgent wank and, at some level, you know it. You've no commitment to anything apart from yourself and your fragile, fucking self-image.'

'Adam, please....'

'No, you can fuck off. I had to listen to you. Now you can listen to me. That's what being free and enjoying life means as far as you're concerned, burnishing your fucking ego. And to that end, you write whatever you think will make you look good, often without even understanding what you're saying. You certainly don't give a fuck about home or mum or me, and I'm pretty sure you don't care about your own wife and kids either, except as ad...ad...adornments to the great Ben Monkton project.'

'That's just not true.'

'It is true. It's all fucking empty.'

'No, it's not.'

'I think it is. And if I'm a exo...exo...exoskeleton, you're a...a....

'What am I, Adam?' he says. 'Tell me.'

'A fucking husk. A little, fragile, vacuous husk. Fucking empty. Nothing inside at all.'

We stare at each other. For a moment, the image of Ben in mum's apple tree during the harrying of the north floats across my mind's eye and I want to hug him and say sorry. But I also want to punch him, hard, over and over again. He opens his mouth and then closes it. After a minute, I turn around and walk quickly out the room.

'Adam. For Christ's sake, Adam,' Ben calls after me.

. . .

Luckily there is no one in the hall. I go upstairs to my room and grab my bag, then run back downstairs again. George is standing in the hall, with a bottle of lager.

'You alright, Uncle Adam?'

'Yes. Well, no. Not really. I've just had a row with your dad.'

'Oh shit.' He nods at the bag. 'What've you got that for? Are you going home?'

'Yeah, I think I'd better. We're both too pissed to sort it out tonight.'

'Oh.'

'Look I'm really sorry. Please give my apologies to your mum and tell her that I hope she has a great birthday.'

'What about nan?'

'Oh yeah, her too. Tell her I'll ring.'

'Ok. If you're sure.'

'I'm absolutely sure. And look...'

'What?'

'Look, it was great to talk to you. And I hope it all works out with sixth form and what have you.'

George shrugs unhappily.

'Thanks.'

'And, for what it's worth, I think the trick about dealing with Josh is just to forget that he exists, as far as possible. Just make up your mind to do what you want to do and ignore him, if that makes sense.'

'I'll try to do that.'

'Good lad.'

I step forward and hug him tightly. He is slighter than he looks under the baggy clothes. I can feel his heart beating quickly.

'Fucking hell, you haven't done that for a while,' he says as I release him.

'I know. I'm obviously more pissed than I thought. No wonder Ben and I had a fight. I'd better go. Look after yourself, George.'

'You too, Uncle Adam.'

I turn and let myself out, then jog down the steps and on down the path. I am just closing the gate behind me and reaching for a fag when the front door opens and closes again. I turn round and there, standing on the top step, is the woman who was sitting opposite Ben and me when we had our row. Now she is wearing a tight-fitting grey overcoat and as I watch she takes a woolly beret out of her pocket and pulls it onto her head.

She waves and walks down the steps.

'Well, that was exciting,' she says as she steps through the gate. She has long black curly hair spilling from under the beret. It frames a face that is pale and sharp and pretty, and apparently genuinely amused.

'I'm glad you thought so.'

'I did. I really did. And at that point I was ready for some excitement, to be honest. Ben and Miriam try ever so hard with their parties, but there's always something that doesn't quite fit, isn't there? Something that doesn't quite work. I think, in the end, they're just a teensy bit too respectable, despite all the drink and the flirting and gossip. Let's face it, no one's going to get arse-fucked in the utility room tonight are they?'

'Wouldn't...wouldn't have thought so.'

'Probably just as well, it could play hell with Miriam's whites.' She grins and nods back at the house. 'Don't worry, by the way, no one's going to chase after you. Ben's telling everyone that we should give you some space. He's doing his best to be calm and emollient, but that's just so you'll look like the pissed up, emotional one, of course.'

'Sounds about right.'

'Yes, it does for Ben, I'm afraid. I think he's actually quite shaken underneath it all.' The woman holds out her hand. 'Anyway, it's good to meet you finally, Adam, even if the circumstances are a bit weird.'

'It's good to meet you too.' I take her hand. She has a surprisingly firm grip. 'Um, who are you, by the way.'

'Oh my God, how rude of me. I thought you knew. I thought someone would have pointed me out.'

'No. No they haven't.'

'Obviously not. I'm Tanya Faulk.'

# 24

'I JUST ASSUMED someone would have pointed me out,' she says again.

'I'm afraid not.'

'Well, that's a boot in the arse of my vanity, isn't it? I'm obviously not quite as central to everyone's world as I think I am.' She grins. 'Anyway, like I said, it's good to meet you. Can I offer you a lift anywhere, assuming you're not going back inside to make peace?'

'I'm certainly not going to do that. I'm going home.'

'I don't blame you. Let me give you a lift to the station. Silly to waste money on a taxi. And my car's just round the corner.'

'Um...'

'Come on, I won't eat you.' She giggles. 'Or write about you. I promise. I'm just trying to be nice.'

'Ok then. Thanks. That would be great. As long as you don't write anything.'

'Oh, you needn't worry about that. I don't need to go back there. Come on.'

We walk down the street together, Tanya clip-clops smartly, a little ahead, while I lollop along unsteadily and smoke. After two minutes, she stops at a red Fiat 500 and clicks it open.

'Tanya, you're not...you're not pissed are you?'

She laughs.

'No, I'm absolutely not. On the contrary I am sober for 428 days and 23 hours, give or take. Thanks for asking, though. Hop in.'

I chuck my cigarette away half smoked and slide into the passenger seat. Tanya starts the car.

'Are you alright?'

'Yeah. Yeah, I think so. It's just...It's just...I don't think we've ever had such a vicious, shitty row before. Certainly not publicly.' I rub my eyes and peer out the window into the darkness. 'Oh Christ, and on Miriam's fucking birthday as well. Fucking hell.'

'It was certainly a bit intense.'

'Did I look like an absolute prick?'

She turns the engine off again.

'No. You definitely didn't. Look at me for a second. Look at me.'

I turn to face her.

'Okay. I'm looking.'

'Good. Now listen. Your arsehole of a brother was patronising, boorish and stupid. And when you challenged him, quite correctly, he compared you to a fucking insect without a backbone. And he did it all with an audience, of which he was well aware. I think calling him a cunt was remarkably restrained, all things considered.'

'I can't stop myself from biting, every single time.'

'And he knows it. He's a bully and a narcissist. I don't doubt that he enjoys the power he has to make you react. It's part of his game.'

'And...and obviously I'm jealous of the house and the family and the job and everything. And he knows that too, of course, and... and...' I rub my eyes again. 'Oh God, I'm sorry. I don't know you at all. It's not fair to dump all this shit on you.'

'On the contrary. I think it's often best to dump on people you don't know. It's easier, isn't it?'

'I suppose so.'

She pats my leg and says quietly.

'And, for what it's worth, you needn't resent Ben as much as you say you do. Not everything in the garden is quite as rosy as he is determined to make it appear. Certainly not the family.' She pulls her beret off and stuffs it in her pocket. 'Well, not the marriage anyway.'

'How do you know?'

'Believe me, I know.' She frowns and turns the engine on again. 'Anyway, enough of all that. Where can I take you, King Cross?'

'Yeah, Kings Cross. Yeah, I suppose so.'

'You suppose so? That is the station for the Yorkshire bit of the north isn't it?' She grins. 'Not that I've ever been there of course.'

'Yeah. Kings Cross is the one for Yorkshire. Yeah. Um, how much time have you got?'

She shrugs.

'I've been to my meeting, and I've not got to do any work until tomorrow afternoon. I'm free all night, within reason.'

'Would you take me to Kensington, then? Before the station. If it's not too much bother.'

'Kensington?'

'Yes please, if that's alright.'

'Why Kensington? You don't strike me as a particularly Kensington person. No offence.'

'I'm not a Kensington person. Not at all. And I'm certainly not offended. But I would like to go there please. I'll tell you why on the way, when I've got my head together.'

'And now, of course, I'm fascinated.' She pats my leg again. 'Ok then. Let's go to Kensington.'

She flicks the indicator and drives off down the empty street.

. . .

We do not speak for the first ten minutes of the journey. Tanya hums breathily as she drives, sometimes swearing quietly at other drivers, while I stare straight ahead and replay the scene with Ben in my mind, feeling alternately hateful and ridiculous. The row has knocked me off kilter, somehow, setting me adrift from the neon city that flits by in the darkness, and from the world beyond. I am without moorings temporarily, almost selfless, drifting through the vagueness of the streets and through a tide of emotions that I cannot even begin to control. 'Lost' is probably the best word for my condition, but I will not entertain it. It is much too close to what Ben had to say about me, and, let's be honest, in Christian terms, it is also too close to 'damned'.

I am still drunk, don't forget. I don't think about damnation when I am sober.

A phone beeps.

'Is that you or me?' Tanya asks.

'Me.'

'Aren't you going to look at it?'

'No. It'll be my mum. I don't want to think about her yet.'

'Will she be pissed off?'

'Yes, but she won't say that. She'll say that she's wo...worried about me, which is worse.'

Tanya shrugs.

'Fair enough. All families are fucking death traps, as far as I'm concerned. To a greater or lesser extent. Where are we going precisely?'

I peer out of the window. We have passed through Islington and are now skirting the south side of Regent's Park. Even at half eight the streets are busy with late shoppers and office workers who haven't made it home yet. London's crowds, and its business, and its nonchalant disregard for the conventions of day and night, light and dark, disorientated me when I lived here. London almost dissolved me. And the effect tonight is worse. I shiver and look away.

'Left at Edgeware Road Tube,' I say after ten minutes driving. 'Then right at Hyde Park Corner and onto Kensington High Street.'

'Righto. Do you know London well?'

'A little bit. I lived here for eight years, after university.'

'Really? What were you doing?'

'Training to be a priest with the Laurentian Fathers.'

Tanya turns and looks at me.

'Seriously?'

'Yes. I never made it though, not even to be a deacon. I left just before ordination. I ran away and hid.'

She throws back her head and laughs.

'My God, you Monktons. You really are the gift that keeps on giving, aren't you?'

'It doesn't feel like that, particularly.'

'I'm sure it doesn't.' Her laughter dies away. 'But even so, you do retain a capacity to surprise. Is that where we're going then, The Laurentians? Next to the V and A?'

'Yes please. If it's not too much bother.'

'It's no bother at all.'

Five minutes later, Tanya pulls into a side road in the maze of narrow streets behind South Kensington station and parks.

'The Laurentians are the ultra-posh ones aren't they?' she asks as we set off back towards Kensington High Street. 'Public School and Oxbridge and all that?'

'Yeah, that's them.'

'So why on earth did you choose them?'

'Because...' I lick the roll up I have made and stick it together. 'Because I was young and keen. And the Laurentians have a reputation for being conservative, for actually believing things, as well as being posh. And I wanted all that.'

'A bit Brideshead Revisited?'

'Yes, exactly that.' I light my fag. 'Evelyn Waugh went to Mass with the Laurentians, when he fell out with the Jesuits in Farm Street. And Chesterton and Gerard Manley Hopkins too. So yeah, Brideshead and all that stuff was exactly what I was after.'

. . .

After five minutes' walk, we arrive at the Laurentian church, more properly the Church of Our Lady of the Immaculate Conception, the parish served by the Priestly Fraternity of Saint Laurence Dupont ever since Cardinal Manning introduced the community to London in 1872. Manning had hoped that the conservative Laurentians would bolster his own hard-line views against Cardinal Newman's more liberal Oratory in Birmingham. And he also wanted the fraternity priests to minister to the working class, particularly the Irish working class, whose slums surrounded their church, full of the awful vices and sufferings of the Victorian urban poor. Unfortunately, the demographics around the Laurentian church changed rather quickly so that, within 100 years of its foundation, the community found itself serving one of the richest parishes in the country. The Laurentian Fathers' commitment to the poor inevitably slipped, but the conservative tradition had remained. Now it is bankers, ambassadors, judges and their families who fill the vast Italianate church on Sundays, to hear Mass celebrated in Latin. The community has a reputation for ministering to continental moneymen, exiled in London, as well as those members of the British establishment who find themselves, either by ancestry or by conviction, inconveniently Catholic.

There is nice wine, as well as tea and freshly ground coffee, after mass at the Laurentians. The church offers the thrill of an elite belonging combined with the glamour of an ancient and easily borne exclusion. And, crucially, the Laurentian Mass is as far as you can get, aesthetically and theologically, from the stern non-conformist chapels which are the commonest expressions of Christian faith in Coxthorpe. No wonder, then, that the place bewitched me when I stumbled into it as a student, on one of my rare trips to visit Ben. No wonder that I joined the smart congregation for drinks after mass, despite having witnessed only the last twenty minutes of a service that was unintelligible to me. No wonder that I went home and read first Waugh, then Chesterton, then Hopkins, then Manning and Newman with an eager, receptive mind.

I entered the Catholic Church at Easter of my second year of my degree, at Coxthorpe University's concrete and unlovely ecumenical chaplaincy. A group of students danced around the sanctuary barefoot, trailing red ribbons as I received Christ for the first time: body and blood, soul and divinity. And after the service there were sandwiches and crisps in the chaplaincy lounge, and cheap Tescos wine served from cardboard boxes to celebrate my entry into the one true ark of the redeemer. The Chaplaincy sister, a middle-aged nun who drifted around campus in a blue trouser suit wearing a tangled silver pendant that might have been a cross, or a dove, or a broomstick, approached me as I was helping to wash up. She was carrying a package wrapped in blue paper.

'A little present for you Adam.'

I dried my hands, took the gift and unwrapped it. It was a book entitled *Christ at the Margins: Living and Praying Beyond the Hierarchical Church, an Ignatian Introduction.*

'Thank you, Sister Theresa.'

She hugged me.

'Welcome aboard. Just don't get all funny now you've joined us.'

'I won't Sister Theresa.'

'Don't get all silly.'

'I won't. I promise.'

'Good lad. I'll be praying for you.' She winked. 'And watching you.'

My vocation to join the Laurentians followed my reception into the Church with indecent haste. I entered the noviciate just ten months after I graduated. Sr Theresa never spoke to me again.

. . .

'It's huge isn't it? I've driven passed it loads of times, and it's registered that it's pretty big, but you don't get a real sense of the scale of it from the car.'

'It's even bigger than it looks. The Church joins up with the community house and the parish rooms, so there's a network of passages and stairs inside that goes on for ages. You lose track of where you are and even which floor you're on. It's a fucking Tardis.' I drop my cigarette end and stamp on it. 'It's got two postcodes.'

Tanya whistles quietly.

'Bloody hell. It must be worth millions. What happened to that business about the camel and the eye of the needle?'

'The fathers don't tend to emphasise that side of things. It doesn't play well with the punters.'

'I bet it fucking doesn't.'

We are standing in a little courtyard, surrounded by iron railings, in front of the Laurentian church. Soft, golden light spills onto marble steps from the glass revolving doors on the left and right of the frontage. Between these doors, are much larger ones, made of brass. These are bolted shut, only being opened to mark the visit of a Pope or of a Catholic Monarch. The Mother of God and St Laurence Dupont peer down at us severely, in marble, from their plinths on either side.

'Are you actually planning to go inside,' Tanya says after a moment, 'Or are we just going to admire the place from out here?'

'No. I...I want to go in.'

'And what are you hoping to achieve, exactly? If it's not impertinent to ask.'

'Why would it be impertinent?'

'Well, you know, speaking as an atheist and a Jew, I might not be expected to appreciate the nuances of...of...' she waves vaguely at the church '...of all this stuff.'

'I don't know what I want to achieve, really.' I shrug. 'I just wanted to come here. I still get the urge sometimes.'

She glances at me and frowns.

'Fair enough. So, your religious status is '*it's complicated*', or something similar, is it?'

'Yeah I suppose so. Something like that.' I take a deep breath. 'Come on, let's go in.'

We climb the low marble steps and slip through the left-hand revolving door. Inside, the air is full of that candle-lit, incense-sweetened, twilight that only Roman Catholic churches can really manage, so different from the sombre dust-and-stone stillness of the Church of England. The building fades, on either side, into the tangled darkness of the side chapels, while in front of us the shiny dark-wood pews stretch away to the blaze of gold and flame that marks the high alter. Reflexively, I dip my hand in the holy water stoop and bless myself.

'Should I do that too?' Tanya whispers.

'Do what?'

'Make the sign of the cross with that water?'

'You can if you want, I suppose.'

She stifles a giggle.

'Nah, I'd better not. It might sizzle. What's going on down the front?'

'I'll show you.'

We pad down the central isle, passed the great oak pulpit and the bronze of St Peter, his toe worn smooth and golden by years of pious touch. There are perhaps twenty people kneeling in the front three pews, mostly women, mostly Latin or Pilipino (the maids, I assume, of the judges and moneymen). Eyes are fixed in wonder.

Jewelled rosaries are worked silently through well-manicured fingers. Lace mantillas lie decorously on heads. I slide into a pew three rows back from the worshippers and sit down. Tanya joins me.

'Go on then,' she whispers, nodding towards the sanctuary. 'Tell me what's going on. What's that thing?'

The altar is decorated with a gorgeous green and gold frontal and is filled by banks of candles reaching twelve feet or more into the air. More candles spill from the altar on either side, their flickering reflected in the marble of the sanctuary floor. At the centre of the candles, at the heart of the whole display, there is what appears to be a golden candlestick without a flame. It is perhaps two feet high, its base inset with jewels while at its top, shards of gold and silver form a circle of brightness like the rays of the sun. At the centre of the rays there is a smudge of white, easy to overlook against the lavish backdrop.

'What's that thing?' Tanya whispers again.

'It's the blessed sacrament. And the gold stand is called a monstrance.'

'I'm none the wiser. Look, if you want to pray or meditate or whatever you do, that's fine. I'll just sit here and soak up the vibe. You can explain it all to me outside.'

I nod and then surprise myself by sinking to my knees and closing my eyes. I am drunk and faithless and if there was such a thing as grace, I would be a very long way from it, but apparently I still want to pray. For a second the image of Sonia from Basingstoke, on her back with her arse in the air, drifts unbidden though my mind and I manage to feel genuinely revolted at myself. The image fades slowly but the revulsion remains. The urge to pray become acute. Softly, I begin the act of contrition:

*Oh my God, I am heartily sorry for having offended Thee, and I detest all my sins because of thy just punishments, but most of all because they have offended Thee my God, who art...*

I realise that my face is sweaty. I stop speaking and wipe it with the cuff of my jacket and then close my eyes and try and start praying again but discover that I have lost my place. I decide to start from the beginning, but I can't remember, now, how the prayer starts. And I'm struggling even to make the effort. Sonia from Basingstoke doesn't make me feel penitent now. On the contrary she makes me feel mildly horny. I hawl myself back into the pew and rest my chin in my cupped hands. Tanya glances at me.

'You ok?'

'Yeah. I'm fine. But...but it turns out that I'm not in the mood.'

'No God today?'

'No. No God. Just me watching myself trying to think about God. And then watching myself watching.' I shrug. 'It's ridiculous really.'

'That does sound a bit awkward.'

'Yeah. Sorry to have dragged you here.'

'Don't be daft. I'm absolutely enthralled.' She nods towards the altar. 'Tell me about the monstrance.'

'It's designed to display the blessed sacrament, which is the little white thing in the middle. That's...That's what it's all about really.'

'And what is the blessed sacrament when it's at home?'

'Good question. Depending on your point of view, it's either a little piece of bread or it's Jesus, hidden under the appearance of a little piece of bread.'

'Is that what they call transubstantiation?'

'Yep. That's exactly what it is.'

'In that what we're seeing then? Transubstantiation in action?'

'Well yes, I suppose so, if you believe that sort of thing. That's certainly what this lot would believe.'

'Do *you* believe that sort of thing, Adam?'

I peer at the monstrance. The little blur of whiteness at its heart is as inscrutable and as demanding as ever.

'Sorry, is that too personal?'

'No, not at all. Not at all. You know the really difficult thing about being a Catholic?'

'Oddly enough, no I don't.'

'It's that you actually have to believe it. It's not like being a Methodist or an Anglican or something, where the faith happens at a respectable distance and things can stay nice and vague. If you're a Catholic, it's different. The faith is shoved right in your face, literally in your face, every time you go for communion, in that little wafer. It's physical and real and right in front of you, and you have to decide each time if you actually believe it, if you believe that you're about to ingest God. And if you don't believe... if you don't believe it's God...well then you have no choice but to leave, ultimately, because to receive communion without believing would be...would be...well, it would be blasphemous. A Judas kiss.'

'Is that what happened to you?'

'Yes, of course it was. And the sad thing about it - or one of lots of sad things about it - is that the blessed sacrament, that little bit of whiteness, built a whole civilisation, once upon a time. It built my civilisation, or at least the one I identify with. I'm not exaggerating. They held processions to honour it. They built cathedrals and abbeys to house it. They fought wars for it. They painted and sculpted and embroidered to exhibit it worthily. They carved out whole kingdoms for it and for the mystery it's supposed to represent.' I nod at the altar. 'That wafer held everything together, Tanya. It enchanted the whole world. It was the still point at the centre of it all: the crusader armies and the artists and the kings and builders. If...if you believe it of course.'

'Mm.'

'What?'

'I wonder.'

'What?'

'Did they kill Jews for it as well?'

I turn sharply to look at Tanya. She is staring straight at the altar and frowning slightly. Her face is very pale in the flickering light of the dozens of candles. She is chewing her lip.

'I don't know.'

'I think they did, you know,' she says lightly. 'I think I remember learning about it at school. Not content with actually killing God, we were also supposed to have desecrated him in his transubstantiation bread, or whatever it's called. I think we paid Christians to steal it, which we could afford, of course, because we were all such rich, usurious bastards, and then we stabbed it and pissed on it and did all kinds of other horrible stuff. Pretty grotesque really.' She smiles faintly. 'No wonder people killed us.'

'I don't know anything about that.'

'No. Of course not. It's not nice.' She shrugs and turns to look at me. 'Look, if it's all the same with you, I'd quite like to go now. This place is beginning, ever so slightly, to give me the creeps. I can kind of see the attraction, I think, but still...'

'Oh. Oh. Ok. Yeah.'

'And it doesn't seem that you're going to find much inspiration here, anyway.'

'No. No, it doesn't.'

'I hope that's not my fault. And I'm sorry that I interrupted your meditation on Christian civilisation.' She stands and shuffles out of the pew. 'I suppose that's just what we do. Come on, I'll take you to the station.'

Tanya turns and walks quickly up the aisle, her footsteps making sharp, disapproving little clicks on the floor of the knave. I genuflect and shamble after her. Outside she waits for me in the courtyard as I make a cigarette.

'Do you still go to church at all?'

'Not really. Only weddings and funerals and stuff.'

'You spoke about that in one of your videos, about going to church even if you don't quite believe it anymore. To keep hold of the tradition and the goodness of it and all that jazz.' She nods at the church. 'Couldn't you take your own advice?'

'I was thinking more of the Church of England really. You can do all that doubting agnostic stuff there. In some places, it's positively encouraged, it's regarded as a mark of intellectual integrity. But if you're a Catholic you actually have to believe it, at least if you're playing by the rules.'

'Because of the transubstantiation bread?'

'Yeah. Most immediately because of that. But there's other stuff as well. Catholicism's difficult. It's sharp-edged and demanding. That's the beauty of it.' I light my fag and inhale. 'And the awfulness of it, of course.'

'So go to the Church of England.'

'I can't do that. I'm a Catholic. The Church of England's bullshit.'

'Oh, for fuck's sake. I give up.'

. . .

Twenty minutes later Tanya pulls up at Kings Cross.

'How long until your train,' she asks as she kills the engine.

'Quarter of an hour.'

'And what time will you get home?'

'The train gets in at twenty to twelve. I'll get a cab and be home just before midnight.'

'Are you going to speak to your mum?'

'Tomorrow. When things have calmed down.'

'Fair enough.'

For a moment neither of us speak and then Tanya leans across and kisses me on the cheek.

'Thank you for a fascinating evening. And look, I'm sorry if I dragged you away from the Church sooner than you wanted.'

'It's fine. It's just nice to see it sometimes, to remember that it's there. I think that's all it amounts to, really. Comfort.'

She peers through the windscreen.

'It's a funny thing, being Jewish, at least for me. I don't think about it for fucking ages, I eat bacon sandwiches and stay out on Friday night and what have you, and then it all comes rushing back at me like a tide, just like it did back there in church. And it turns out that it has a hold of me somewhere deep, where I can't quite prise it loose. It's weird.'

'Do you want to prise it loose?'

'No, not really. Maybe sometimes. I don't know. And actually, I don't think it matters what I want, because I don't think it's possible. It's not my perception of myself that makes me a Jew, you see, it's other peoples' perception of me. That's...that's mostly where the tide comes from. That's the hold. If that makes sense.'

'Ah. I see.'

'Do you fuck, see.' She rolls her eyes. 'I don't mean to be rude. But, honestly, you don't see at all.'

'Ok. Ok. Sorry.'

'It's alright. It's fine. I'm not pissed off; I'm just being clear. You couldn't begin to understand so you mustn't try. Thanks again for an interesting evening. Now go on, you'd better get going or you'll miss your train.'

I undo my seatbelt and open the door and then I turn back to her.

'Look, Tanya, I should have said it earlier. Thank you for the piece you wrote. I know it was a piss-take, but it wasn't unkind, and it got me thousands of views. I think...I think...I think The Haxton Review would probably have disappeared after its first video if it hadn't been for you.' I grin. 'Basically, you created me.'

'You know I wrote it mostly to piss off your brother, don't you?'

'Yes. I know it was all about Ben. But I'm grateful, even so.'

'I said 'mostly'. Ben wasn't the only motivation. He was the main reason, perhaps, but he wasn't the only one.'

'Oh. What else was there?'

She switches the engine on and peers in the rear-view mirror. She tucks a lock of hair up into her beret then says quietly. 'My mum and dad's synagogue was attacked last month. They had every window smashed. Every single one. Whoever it was climbed right over the gate. They had bricks and airguns, apparently. It was organised; it wasn't a spur of the moment thing.'

'That's awful. Do they know who did it?'

'There was CCTV footage but apparently it was just three blokes in balaclavas. Nazis or Muslims are the usual suspects, aren't they? It doesn't matter much as far as I'm concerned.'

'It would matter to me. I'd want to know who hates me.'

'I know perfectly well who hates me. Lots of people hate me.'

'Fair enough, I suppose. But...but what's that got to do with me and OyTube?'

'The point is, whenever anything like that happens, and this sort of thing is happening more and more, as I'm sure you're aware. Whenever it happens, do you know what I always think?'

'No. I don't. And I don't quite see...'

'Just shut up for a moment please.'

'Okay.'

She frowns. Her eyes are almost black now, in the dark of the car.

'There are three things actually, the same sequence every time. First I just think *Bastards! Cunts! How dare they?* Which I think everyone would agree is a reasonable reaction.'

'Yeah. I would say so.'

'Exactly. Anyone would. It's natural. It's healthy. But the second thought I have is a bit less so. It's an impulse to get as far away from it all as possible. As far away as possible from my own Jewishness. Just to avoid the fucking squalor and shitiness of everything that comes with it.' She bites her lip again and wipes her cheek quickly with her hand. 'And that's less acceptable, isn't it? That's self-hating, blame-the-victim stuff, at least in part. I'm ashamed of it. I'm ashamed of thinking like that. But I do.'

'I think...'

'But listen, my third thought is the interesting one. It's this...I...I always think this: *if things get really bad you can always go to Israel.*' She turns to face away from me and inhales sharply. '*You can always go to Israel. You can always go home.*' That's what I think. Every single time. And that's fucking me saying that *You can always go home.* And I'm the most assimilated, sold-out, bacon-loving Jew you could imagine.'

'That doesn't seem completely illogical.'

'No, but it's not consistent either. It's not truthful. It's not me. I'm as British as Balti. I've only been to Israel once and I hated it. It wasn't home at all. It's small and smug and nasty. It's built on a fucking crime scene, for God's sake. It's awful.'

'Maybe. But...But...I still don't understand what all that has to do with your piece.'

'Yes you do,' she says softly. 'At least, I think you do. And if you don't, I'm afraid that I'm not going to spell it out. I'm too...I'm too ashamed.' She shrugs and then turns, leans forward and kisses me again, and this time her lips are wet and warm with tears. 'You really are one of the most fucked up men I have ever met, by the way. But you are also rather lovely.'

'Thanks.'

'It can't have been easy for you. None of it. Look, if you are ever in London, get in touch. It would be fun to see you again, I think. You can always call me at the paper.'

'Thanks. Thanks, I will. And if you're ever in Coxthorpe, the same applies.'

She giggles and sniffs, then dabs her eyes with a tissue.

'Why the fuck would I ever be in Coxthorpe? And, just to be clear, the invitation to meet up, doesn't include an invitation to fuck. We certainly won't be doing that; I need to manage your expectations.'

'My expectations are suitably managed.'

'Good. Now fuck off and get on your train back to Eretz Yorkshire.'

# 25

I SLEEP FOR most of the train journey and get the last cab at Coxthorpe station. I am home by five to twelve, by which time I have three missed calls from mum. There is also a text from her, which I don't open.

I go straight to bed but I'm much too stimulated to sleep, so after twenty minutes I stop trying. I make a cup of tea and WhatsApp Sonia:

*Are you up?*

She responds almost immediately:

*Yes. Just gone to bed. Bad hip so can't sleep. How are you?*

To which I reply:

*Sorry about hip. Can't sleep either. Big family row.*

We message for a while, and I describe in general terms what happened in London. Once again Sonia turns out to be a pretty good counsellor. Surprisingly, after five minutes, she is the one who brings up the subject of sex:

*If your fed up I dont mind going on cam for a bit.*

I message back:

*Ok. Only if you want to*

She replies.

*I don't mind. I'm lonely too. And I'll say sorry to jesus tomorrow.*

So, I video call and Sonia holds her phone alternately at her face and vagina as she masturbates. She cums loudly and then holds her fingers close to the camera so I can see that they are wet. She is even bigger than I remember her.

'Do you want me to watch you now?' she asks.

'Not really.'

'Why not? Ain't you excited.'

'Yes I am, but not...not physically. I'm sorry. It's been a long day.'

I end the call, quickly, before she can reply. But straight away I receive another WhatsApp message:

*We don't have to do naughty stuff. I am happy to chat normal too. Your a nice man I think underneath it all. But don't ever say anything about me being big again like you did before. Or about Jesus cos he is the most important thing to me. I know youll block me but message me if you wont anytime. I'll always listen.*

I block her and lie on my back in the dark with my hands behind my head, thinking about Ben and my mum and Sonia and exoskeletons. The edges of the curtains are turning grey when I finally fall asleep.

. . .

I wake up just after eleven and get out of bed straightaway. I had chucked my clothes on the floor last night, and as I pick them up to put them in the washing basket the little card that Simon gave me drops out of my shirt pocket. It is thick and cream coloured. It reads: *Simon Sinclair Consulting: New Media and Community Relations.* There are two phone numbers and an email address.

For a moment Ben's face floats through my mind. He is confident and drunk as he was last night, and he is telling me again to think about Simon's proposal. I close my eyes and shake my head quickly so that the image dissolves. But when I open them again the card feels grubby and tainted with Ben. I place it face down on my chest of drawers and then get dressed and go downstairs for a coffee. While the kettle is boiling, I check my phone. There are another two missed calls from mum and a further message. Yesterday's message from her reads:

*Adam, I desperately hope you are alright and not too upset. Ben is dreadfully distracted by your row. The party has fallen a bit flat, which is rotten for Miriam. Knowing you two, it will be six of one and half a dozen of another. I know you love each other, but something is broken between you, and it needs mending. Please just let me know that you have got home safely. Love, Mum. xxx*

The one from today reads:

*Adam, I've called you five times now, so I have to assume that you are deliberately not answering my calls, rather than just missing them. Fair enough. You probably need a bit of space. Just call when you are ready. Everything here is a lot calmer in the cool light of day. Miriam is pleased with her party, despite the row and even Ben says that he doesn't blame you for 'flipping out'. He knows that he sometimes speaks rather thoughtlessly. Some of the people from the paper were telling me that he is known for being a bit sharp at work. I don't suppose you get to the sort of level he has reached without being quite a big personality. Anyway, everyone is still really glad that you came down yesterday and we're all worried that you are alright. Please just send me a text to let me know you're alright and, above all, please, please, please don't run away again. I can't do all that again. Love, mum xxx*

I text back:

*I'm fine mum and I'm not going to run anywhere. I will give you a ring later. Please say sorry to Miriam for me.*

As soon as I have sent the message, another one appears in my inbox, this time from Jason. It contains a link to the *Resistance Media* website. Below the link Jason has texted *You seen this?*

The link is to a short piece advertising a forthcoming video which will *expose the fascist OyTube team at the Haxton Review*. There is a picture of me with my face pixilated out, taken during the altercation in Victoria Square, and beneath it some bullet points:

- Who are the men behind the Haxton Review?
- Who is really backing them?
- How did their mainstream media connections enable their channel to grow so quickly?
- How dangerous are they? And how violent?
- What do Lantyrn Royd locals really think of them?

I put my phone down on the side and walk carefully to the toilet. I stand in front of the pan; arms drooping and wait to be sick. I gag a bit and spit down the loo and then, when I realise that my body is refusing to puke, I straighten up and walk unsteadily back through the kitchen and into the lounge. I sit on the sofa, staring straight ahead and then stand up again and walk back into the kitchen and re-read the Resistance Media thing. Finally, I call Jason. While the phone is ringing, I put it on loudspeaker and place it back on the side. My hands are shaking too much for me to hold it to my ear.

'Had you seen it, already?' he asks without bothering to say hello.

'No. But I have now. Who sent it to you?'

'Dave.'

'Dave the chairman?'

'Yes.'

'When did he send it to you?'

'Yesterday evening. He got it from mate of his who's a copper. I didn't want to fuck up yer party so I din't send it straightaway.'

'It was pretty fucked up anyway, but thanks for the thought. Have you spoken to Roger? What does he have to say about it?'

Jason snorts.

'I've texted him and called and emailed but he in't answering owt. He han't been around.'

'What do you mean?'

'No bugger's seen him since Saturday.'

'Oh.'

I look at the picture of me on the website again. I seem ridiculously cool and self-assured, in my leather jacket and jeans, poking my microphone towards the Resistance Media people. I hardly recognise myself, and not just because of the pixilated face.

'What do you reckon then?' Jason says eventually. 'What d'you think we should do?'

'I don't know. I'm not sure that we can stop them. Unless we contact them and retract everything we've done and claim that we've had a massive change of heart. There's more joy in heaven over a sinner who repents and all that. They might...they might go easy on us then, I suppose.'

'I in't doing that.'

'What will happen to you at work if they find out that you're involved with this?'

'I dunno. Probably be ok. People already know I'm mixed up with the Rush Bearing. And I've just been the tech guy, han't I? Apart from that first interview, I han't been on camera or owt.'

'Good. That's something anyway.'

'What about you?'

'Might be a bit more complicated.'

'Why do you say that?'

'The police have been in touch with work already, asking about me and the channel. Twice. My boss has spoken to me.'

'Fucking hell. Why didn't you tell me?'

'Head in the sand,' I say quietly. 'Couldn't bear to think about it.'

Jason is silent for a moment. I roll a cigarette. It is uneven because my hands are still shaking. I take the fag and the phone out into the yard and after four attempts manage to light up.

'You'll have to think about it now,' Jason says.

'I know I will. Look...Look...There's something else as well.'

'What?'

'Last night at my brother's house, I met a bloke from the government who offered me a job. At least I think that's what he did, even though he said he wasn't doing that. But it was on the condition that I changed my tune about the Rush Bearing.'

'Bloody hell. What sort of job?'

'I don't know exactly. It was vague. Everything about him was vague. He wasn't even directly employed by the government. It was some sort of social media thing but working with community relations and so on. Similar to the stuff we've been doing but with... well, with a slightly different take.'

'I hope you told him to fuck off.'

'I couldn't do that.'

'Don't fucking tell me you...'

'Please don't be angry, Jason. Please. I did nothing at all except chat to him and take his card.' I inhale and flick ash off my fag. 'The point is, we've been noticed. There are big, grownup people out there who've noticed us and they're gathering. I suppose it's because the Rush Bearing's coming to a head. Perhaps we've been a bit naïve, thinking we would be able to stay under the radar. It's... It's not just a hobby anymore.'

'It never were a hobby for me,' Jason says softly. 'It might have been for you, it never were for me.'

'And...and my brother knows something about it as well, although I'm not sure quite what exactly. The smug prick tried to tell me to take the job offer.'

'And what are you gonna do?'

'There's a sort of pressure building up everywhere, Jason. It's like a string or a cord or something tightening around my head. It's horrible. It's absolutely horrible. It's been there for ages, but it's tightening now.'

'What are you gonna do, Adam?'

Jason's voice is even softer now. I don't know if the softness if menacing, or sad, or both.

'I'm going to make a video, Jason.'

'What sort of video?'

I don't answer straight away. My brother's face drifts into my mind, and then my mum's, and then Brenda's, and then Jason's, and finally Simon's. Each face, except one, is marked with a very specific emotion: rage for my brother, worry for my mum, joy for Brenda and, for Jason, that strange, vulnerable anger which makes him so unsettling. Only Simon's face is smooth and emotionless, and haloed in soft cigarette smoke. That makes sense. Simon Sinclair (if that's his real name) wasn't a real human being at all. He was just a function, a cypher, a device. He doesn't deserve a face. I inhale again and notice that my hands have stopped shaking.

And suddenly, just like that, the cord around my head snaps. I feel free, and excited. I feel light and giddy and brave.

'What sort of video?' Jason says again.

'About emptiness and finding our way back home.'

'What the fuck are you talking about? What emptiness? What home? What's this got to do with the Rush Bearing?'

'It's got everything to do with it. We've got to do our bit to defend the Rush Bearing, haven't we? To the last ditch, Jason. Fuck the pressure. Just like you said, if we don't win in Lantyrn Royd, the whole world will see that everything really is ruined and we'll be homeless forever.'

'I still han't got a clue what you're talking about. Are you alright?'

Another face drifts into view: that of Tanya Faulk. She is sitting is the shadows of her car, outside Kings Cross and I can just make out the unexpected, unwise tears glistening on her cheeks.

'Because we haven't got an Israel, have we?' I whisper. 'None of us have. No Galilee shining in the sun for us, no Negev, no snowy Horeb. No milk or honey or redemption. We've just got Lantyrn Royd with the White Horse and its shitty beer, and the tanning place, and Tesco Express. And your mum's grave up in Highcliffe.' I chuck my fag on the floor and stamp on it. 'Sorry, I'm not making much sense, am I?'

'No, you in't. You're talking bollocks.'

'Apologies. To answer your question, I'm absolutely fine. Honestly I am. Are you free today by any chance?'

'Yeah, I'm not back at work while Monday. Dave's called a meeting of the committee for tomorrow evening, to sort out what we're gonna do on Saturday, but apart from that I've got nowt on.'

'Oh, that's interesting. That might be good to talk about. Can you text me his number please? I'll ring him and see if he'll be in our video. It would be good to have the chairman, now things are getting close.'

'Yeah, I can do that.'

'Great. And put the kettle on. I'll buy some cans and crisps on the way over.'

. . .

Before I leave the house, I go back upstairs and collect Simon's card. I set fire to it in the yard and watch the ashes float away in the bright Autumn breeze.

# 26

WHEN JOHNNY COMES marching home again hurrah, tala...

*The music and the street scene fade. A white screen appears bearing the legend: 'Haxton Review: The Way Home' in black print in a grungy typewriter front. The screen flickers in the style of an old-fashioned newsreel and then fades to be replaced by a picture of a man in partial silhouette. He is wearing a peaked cap and shades and is sitting in front of a window.*

NARRATOR: So, welcome to the video. I'm here in the heart of Lantyrn Royd with Dave. Dave, as we agreed we won't mention your surname, but I wonder if you can explain where we are exactly and also what your role is in the Rush Bearing celebration?

DAVE: (laughing) It's hardly a celebration at the moment, is it?

NARRATOR: That's true. But all the same...

DAVE: Yeah, I know what you mean. Right, so I'm Dave and I'm the chairman of the Rush Bearing committee. I have been since a couple of weeks after it all got going. And we're in the upstairs room of the White Horse which is a pub on Lantyrn Royd. We've been using it as our control room.

NARRATOR: Who's been using it as a control room?

DAVE: We have. The committee.

NARRATOR: And what does the committee do?

DAVE: Well, we're the people who arranged the Rush Bearing in the first place. We've sorted the costumes and the permissions, and the food and music and all that kinda stuff...

NARRATOR: Which all sounds a bit tame and boring compared to what it's turned into.

DAVE: I wouldn't say boring exactly, but I know what yer saying. Because of all the politics what's happened, people forget that the Rush Bearing were just meant to be like a street party or summat. In the beginning, that is. So yeah, we was the ones organising all that.

NARRATOR: And since what you call 'the politics' has kicked in?

DAVE: Okay, so since then it's been a bit different. We've been the ones taking a lead in trying to defend the Rush Bearing, by appealing to the Council and talking to the police and whatnot.

NARRATOR: And how about defending Lantyrn Royd itself? It's been obvious for the last couple of weeks that things have changed round here.

DAVE: Yeah. That too of course.

NARRATOR: Can you say a bit about that please?

DAVE: I dunno what there is to say really. Anyone who knows Haxton knows that the community here at Lantyrn Royd is cut off from the rest of Coxthorpe, and that means we're a bit exposed, like. A bit vulnerable...

NARRATOR: Vulnerable from whom?

DAVE: I guess from the people who don't like us and who might want to come in here and cause bother.

NARRATOR: I'm going to push you. Who would those people be?

DAVE: Well, there's bin tension with the local Muslim community for years...Actually, that in't quite right, there's bin tension with *some of the local Muslim community* for years. Not all of them, like. In all the bother we forget that, but a lot of the Muslims are decent normal people. They just want to earn a living and raise their kids and be left in peace. Most of the time we only have problems with a few of them.

NARRATOR: But that's enough to make you feel threatened?

DAVE: Yeah. Cos although it's only a few of them who cause bother, like I said, when it kicks off people tend to pick a side pretty quick, don't they?

NARRATOR: I suppose they do.

DAVE: Or I should say, they go back quick to the side that life picked for them. People harden when stuff goes bad. They look to their own to keep them safe.

NARRATOR: You sound like you're speaking from experience.

DAVE: Well yeah...yeah I am. The Rush Bearing is an example in't it? Ordinary Muslims and ordinary whites have all started feeling more Muslim and more white since it all started. That's always gonna happen int'it?

NARRATOR: I suppose so.'

DAVE: And, before that, there was the riots.

NARRATOR: So, would it be fair to say that people in Lantyrn Royd perceive themselves as a community under siege?

DAVE: Different people perceive things differently. But some people certainly do. And at times, it's pretty undeniable.

NARRATOR: And I think this may be a leading question, but I'm going to ask it anyway, do you feel under siege exclusively from local Muslims? Is it just Muslims you're worried about?

DAVE: Not just them, no. All sorts of people want to have a pop at us at the moment. Either in the papers, or down here in real life. You saw all them on the march last week.

NARRATOR: I did. But there wasn't actually any trouble inside Lantyrn Royd on Saturday was there?

DAVE: No. We got a few bits of things chucked at us, and there was a couple of crossbow bolts what no one talks about, but we made sure that we kept ourselves safe. No one got in.

NARRATOR: And by 'we' you mean the committee?

DAVE: Yeah, we took a lead in organising it all. The patrols and the community gateways and whatnot. And we sorted out transport for people, and food in case things got really bad, and so on. But obviously it weren't just the committee doing all the work.

NARRATOR: Yeah, from what I saw it was a pretty big operation, with lots of people involved.

DAVE: It were, yes.

NARRATOR: Got it. And now, where are you up to with the Rush Bearing itself, please? What's the state of play?

DAVE: Well, as it stands, we've had our original permission from the council to march the route we wanted withdrawn. So, all we can officially do is parade up and down Lantyrn Royd itself.

NARRATOR: And that means that you won't be going into the Muslim area?

DAVE: Well, yeah. Yeah, it does. Nowhere near it. At least by what the council's said we can do.

NARRATOR: And so, I suppose the big question is: do you intend to stick to the council's ruling?

DAVE: Well...yer right that is the big question?

NARRATOR: And what' the big answer?

DAVE: Look, it's still summat we're talking about, amongst ourselves. The committee's having a meeting tomorrow night to work out what we're gonna do. People have got different views, like.

NARRATOR: So, you're not ruling out trying to parade up on Gordon Street, as you planned in the first place.

DAVE: Um...Um...Look, if you dun't mind I'd rather not answer that at the moment. Like I say, folk have got different ideas about it. We need to wait for the meeting.

NARRATOR: Fair enough. I certainly don't want to compromise you or anyone else. Can I ask you another question then? What do you think it will mean if you end up *not* marching up on Gordon Street?

DAVE: (laughing) That's another big question.

NARRATOR: I understand that, but still...

DAVE: Well first off, it will obviously mean that we've lost, won't it?

NARRATOR: Who will have lost, exactly?

DAVE: Us. Lantyrn Royd people. English people.

NARRATOR: And what will it mean to have lost?

DAVE: It'll mean that we han't got the right to celebrate something that's ours, in our own way, on our own streets. It'll mean saying clearly that Gordon Street and the rest of Haxton in't really English anymore.

NARRATOR: Because you can't have your Rush Bearing parade up there, with your own symbols? With the knight?

DAVE: Exactly. But...but...like we were talking about before. It's...It's about summat more than that an all. Summat bigger.

NARRATOR: Go on.

DAVE: It's difficult to say on camera. It were difficult enough when we were talking before, without the camera.

NARRATOR: (laughing) Well forget the camera then. Just have a go and if it goes wrong, we can cut it out and start again.

DAVE: Look, you can live yer life, if you want, going to work and then spending yer pay on crap that mostly you dun't even need or want, and watching telly, and going to football or rugby or whatever. Then going on holiday for a couple of weeks a year. And most them things are good enough in their way. But there's a question still, in't there, about what it's all for. What's the point of all them things? If that's all yer doing, what's the point of anything, really?

NARRATOR: I agree, I think. But those are very, very big questions indeed, aren't they? They're existential questions. What's the connection between them and a kid dressed up as a knight in the Rush Bearing procession?

DAVE: Like I said, it's right hard to explain. I think it's mostly something you *feel* more than it's something you *think*. But I can tell you this, being involved in the Rush Bearing has meant that I've felt involved in summat that's bigger than me. Bigger because it's to do with all of us who live round here, and also because it's all linked up with history, with our history. And...and... and even though I in't religious, that means that I've felt like my life's about something, if that dun't sound too stupid. I feel like I mean something for once, even if that something has turned into a big bloody fight about a kid in fancy dress. (Dave sighs and scratches the back his head). I don't know if I've said that right. Like I say, it's more summat that you feel, than what you think.

NARRATOR: I think you've said it perfectly, Dave. Thank you very much for your time. I hope that the meeting goes well tomorrow.

*The picture fades to be replaced by a shot of a brightly lit supermarket. This fades to be replaced by a picture of a shopping centre, crammed with shoppers. This fades to be replaced by a picture of a crowd at a football match. This fades to be replaced by a picture of a beach full of sunbathers. There follows a montage of shots of contemporary life: shops, nightclubs, amusement parks, television talent shows, sporting fixtures. While the shots come and go, the narrator speaks.*

NARRATOR: If someone were to ask us what the Rush Bearing dispute was all about, we would have to say that it concerns primarily the right of one bunch of Brits to hold a celebration which another bunch of Brits - from a different ethnic and religious background - finds offensive. The basic question in Haxton, therefore, is about how to manage the conflicts that will occasionally arise in a multi-cultural society. This seems uncontroversial. Even the most committed advocates of multi-culturalism will admit that placing different groups of people with radically different beliefs, value systems and historical sensibilities on the same small island will not come without its tensions.

Beyond that, however, things do become slightly controversial. If we were pushed to articulate what issues are at stake in Haxton, beyond the presenting one of the offending knight, we would probably have to say that the Rush Bearing raises questions, in microcosm, about the very viability of the multi-cultural experiment. However the Rush Bearing dispute is resolved on Saturday, it is clear, at the very least, that there *has been a dispute* in Haxton, and that this dispute has cost money and effort to manage, as well as further damaging the already frayed social fabric in Coxthorpe. When one group erects barricades in order to protect itself from another group, only a couple of hundred yards down the road, it is self-evident that there is something profoundly dysfunctional going on.

Of course, the supporters of the Muslim community in local politics and the media, will locate the source of this dysfunction in the unenlightened, unsympathetic and finally racist attitudes of the Rush Bearers. But even if we grant this argument (which the Haxton Review definitely does not) we are still left with the point that multi-culturalism persistently brings tensions which require careful and expensive management. In the scheme of things, the problems in Haxton are relatively minor but there will be (in fact there are) larger and more damaging tensions at play in our diverse society, as radically different communities rub up against each other. It is true that for lots of us living in a diverse nation is exciting and stimulating in terms of arts, culture and (of course) food, but that diversity comes at a cost. At present, in good times, the cost is relatively low, and it is mostly paid by the white working class, but what will the cost become when there is an economic crisis, or a war, or even a serious public health emergency? In times of crisis, cohesion, solidarity and trust are prized above excitement, stimulation and readily available sushi. But it is precisely in these difficult times that people retreat into their most immediate solidarity groups. As Dave said *People harden, don't they, when stuff goes bad? They look to their own to keep them safe.*

I don't think that this is fearmongering. The former Yugoslavia is one obvious example of what I am talking about. There was far less difference, culturally and religiously, between Yugoslav Serbs and Croats, than there is between Haxton's Muslims and whites, and yet, after years of living peacefully together as neighbours, Serbs and Croats set about butchering each other, in the early nineties, when their shared society began to wobble.

So, the Rush Bearing dispute raises questions both about how to manage the tensions that arise in a multi-cultural society and also about the ultimate viability of the multi-cultural experiment. And we should acknowledge, of course, that these questions will probably become more acute as the demographic balance in the United Kingdom shifts away from the white population.

But is there a still deeper question implied in the Rush Bearing controversy? I would argue that there is. It's a question that Dave and I discussed before we started filming and which we touched on again at the end of the interview. This is complicated, so bear with me. I promise to get back to the Rush Bearing at the end. Think again about the differences between the Lantyrn Royd whites and their Muslim neighbours.

They are obviously different in terms of background, ethnicity, outlook. But they are also fundamentally different because the Muslims in Haxton have a religious narrative and religious institutions which are powerful enough to confirm their sense of who they are and of what their lives are finally for. I do not claim to be an expert on Islam, but I understand enough to recognise that it provides a comprehensive framework through which to connect the ordinary stuff of living: work, family, food, sex, death, to something mysterious and transcendent. And it doesn't really matter how much individual Haxton Muslims believe of what their Imams tell them. The faith of their community is embodied in laws and prohibitions, in feasts, fasts and ceremonies, and this is enough to sustain their sense of meaning, both individually and collectively. Personal, intellectual assent to a set of dogmas is secondary.

The Lantyrn Royd whites do not have an equivalent framework to provide identity, meaning and solidarity, at least not to the same extent as their Muslim neighbours, and this lack has a lengthy pedigree. Arguably since the late Middle Ages, the trajectory of Western thought has been away from the idea that there is a sacredness and a givenness about what it means to be human. We have gradually abandoned the idea that there is an inherent truth about us which means that our lives can be lived purposefully and can touch something divine and beautiful. As the Chrisitan narrative has faded from our collective understanding, the bonds between western people have also weakened. Little by little, we have turned away from our common life and sunk inwards into our own selfhood and subjectivity.

Now all that we are left with in our common ethical space is the overbearing ideology of *choice* understood as a kind of rootless and unaccountable individual freedom, *identity* understood as the semi-sacred expression of the self which we construct through our choosing, and an anaemic conception of *happiness*, understood as the intended result of our choosing. Fundamentally, then, choice is what we have in common, and it is also what drives us apart. And, ironically, it doesn't ultimately make us happy.

Of course, choice is a good thing. Freedom is a good thing. It is great to be free to choose what to have for tea, or where to live, or who to marry. But choice-as-the-fundamental-value, choice without any reference to what is good or true or beautiful, means that choosing becomes the core of who we think we are, and this is inevitably corrupting. If we are single, we may choose to be married and then, when we are married, we may choose to be single again. And both choices, without any authoritative standard by which to evaluate them, are equally valid. If we are male, we may choose to be female. If we are female, we may choose to be male, and the simple act of choosing makes it so. If we are fat, we may choose that our fatness is beautiful. If we watch porn and masturbate ourselves to hollow-eyed, penis-aching numbness each day, we may choose that this is normal and healthy. If we chose to believe, even, that the hand in front of us has six fingers and a thumb, well that belief is our choice, and no one may ultimately contradict us. (It is not The Party which finally destroys human dignity at the arse-end of modernity, but the tyranny of our own unhinged freedom.) For us late moderns there is nothing but choice after choice after choice, made in pursuit of a happiness which recedes and recedes and recedes with each empty exercise of our will.

(We have spoken before on this channel about how this ideology of choice-as-the-fundamental-value is the perfect cultural expression of late capitalism. We will not revisit the theme now.)

Several things follow. Firstly, as we are discovering, the dreadful commanding power of the choice-as-the-fundamental-value does not only not make us happy, it also does not ultimately make us free. For one thing, the experience of being abandoned to our own basest and most demanding passions does not feel particularly liberating. For another, in the absence of a commonly held (even if vaguely apprehended) account of the good, the government and its proxies end up having to police our behaviour more comprehensively than ever before. If you don't believe me, try announcing at work that you are not sure that gay marriage really counts as marriage in any meaningful sense, or that the transgender woman in accounts is really a bloke in a dress, and see how long it takes for HR, and possibly the police, to be on your case. Gone are the days when, in A.J.P Taylor's memorable phrase, 'a sensible, law-abiding Englishman could pass through life and hardly notice the existence of the state, beyond the existence of post office and the postman.' A society without a shared view of the good needs a state that is very noticeable indeed. It needs cops and then censorship and then prisons to keep the show on the road, especially in relation to the tensions between the different communities that compose it.

Secondly, choice-as-the-fundamental-value lends itself to dreadful banality in public life, specifically in public cultural life. Writers still write, painters still paint, sculptors still sculpt, and architects still design buildings, but the results of their efforts are often self-indulgent and vile in the case of contemporary art and brutally utilitarian, or else ironic and trivial, in the case of architecture. If the lack of a given notion of goodness leaves us floundering in our relationships with our neighbours, the absence of a shared account of beauty leaves us struggling in relation to our public and cultural spaces. We watch tedious crap on telly, buy ugly crap on-line and consume both, more often than not, in ugly dehumanising buildings. Our culture could no more build a Chartres Cathedral than it could raise the dead. And even if we could still build a Chartres, most of us would find the heart-breaking loveliness of the Cathedral's stained-glass rather boring. Certainly, it would not be worth missing the Jungle or Strictly for. Similarly, most of us can't be arsed to read Dostoevsky or watch Shakespeare. We have lost the taste for complexity and beauty (the two so often being connected).

Historically, it is the job of a (rather ill-defined) cultural elite to preserve and disseminate, as best they can, the greatest stuff of our literary and artistic canon, and it is the job of the rest of us to assimilate this to the limit of our ability. But if the very idea of 'the best', of beauty itself, has drifted away, this work becomes impossible. And so, all we are left with in our cultural life is distraction, vulgarity and, finally, conflict. The very notion of 'the classic' becomes oppressive and exclusive. The notion of an established canon even more so. And the idea that there may be a group of thoughtful, educated people who have a special responsibility to curate the cultural inheritance we share is literally unbearable. Who do you think you are, telling me what to read or watch? I'll make my own judgements and choices, thank you very much! Get this fucking syllabus decolonised! Get your dead white males out of my fucking face! Etc. Etc. Etc.

Thirdly and most terribly, choice-as-the-fundamental-value inevitably builds an absolute nothingness into the heart of our life together. If all we have in common is a vague consensus that unconstrained choice is the most important thing about being human, then all we really have to connect us is an agreement to disagree about what is most fundamental in our lives. Not only is this unsustainable in the long run, it also means that we have no sacred and meaningful stories to pass on authoritatively to our kids, or to share authoritatively amongst ourselves. The key word here is *authoritatively*. If we each cobble together our own stories to give us meaning and identity (and perhaps mark them with tasteless tattoos), then there is nothing *given* about the narratives we live by and they remain flimsy by their very nature, just as their individual choosers are flimsy. Self-constructed meanings remain trivial and subordinate, they cannot enchant or transform. Even worse, in the absence of any external authority, the sovereign choosing individual not only *controls* its own life narrative, eventually it - the individual - *becomes* the narrative. The great operatic (and Oprah-atic) self of late modernity finally mutates into its own attempt at meaning. All that matters is that ***I*** find fulfilment, or realisation, or authenticity. Eventually, nihilism meets narcissism as the empty, meaningless world becomes a vast mirror to reflect the self-seeking self, back upon itself. Everything - sexual preference, gender, mental illness (sorry neuro-divergence), physical disability, fatness - becomes a chosen (or at least an 'embraced') identity to be paraded before an endlessly adoring community. And when the real, brutal world intrudes in, for instance, the death of a loved one, we have no sacred ceremonies or shared stories to help us confront the dreadful mystery of their passing. We have nothing at all. We gather around a shiny sealed coffin to 'celebrate the life' of the deceased with pop music, balloons and sentimental anecdotes.

Of course, we tell ourselves lies and distract ourselves endlessly to avoid confronting the terrible emptiness of our life together. The internet, in particular, provides ample opportunity for joyless encounters and infantilising distractions.

Please continue to bear with me. I am nearly back in Haxton. If I had to sum up in a single word the lack that the Rush Bearers experience, that represents all the frightening symptoms of our late modern, hyper-free society, I would describe it as a lack of *home*. It is home, in the sense that I am speaking of it, that roots us, holds us, and properly limits our choosing. It is home which gives us a sense of self which is not our own laboured and fragile construction. And it is the absence of home that sends us spiralling off in our great modern flights of narcissism and despair. The Rush Bearers all have houses of course - gritstone terraces, small, cosy, and for the most part formidably clean and tidy – but, like most indigenous western Europeans, they do not have a proper home anymore, understood as the common space where shared meanings and values are encoded in flesh, stone and custom, and where culture is diffused in stories and ceremonies. Churches, memorials, scout groups, friendly societies, Working Men's Clubs, local shops, local pubs, families (nuclear and extended), and familiar neighbours are the stuff of home in this sense. As are, in a different way, school nativity plays, Harvest Festivals, Easter Egg Hunts, Remembrance Sunday. All these things make connections between people and their neighbours, between people and their history, and, ultimately, between people and inherited, transcendent meaning. All of them call the individual bit by bit beyond their solipsism and narcissism into a common world of belonging and shared purpose.

Yes, obviously I am aware of how silly and pompous all this sounds in relation to the situation in Haxton. But it is true, nonetheless. Virtue and meaning are not ultimately discovered in complex philosophical tomes, or at least they are not discovered there by most people. Instead, they are acquired in the little platoons of our most immediate circumstances: in honest work, in the hard slog of belonging to a family and a community, in our relationships with our neighbours, in the stories that we tell ourselves about the lives and sacrifices of earlier generations. And they are acquired also in the residual ceremonies that still mark the passing of the seasons, thereby imbuing them with some vague sense of the sacred. In short, we learn goodness and gratitude and meaning in the middle of our most ordinary circumstances. We learn them at home, if we have a home worthy of the name.

Back to the Rush Bearers. Is it possible to read their bloody-minded determination to hold their little procession, not primarily as an expression of their racism, but as a full-throated revolt against the homelessness which is the salient characteristic of modern life? Their proposed celebration represents a renewed connection between the citizens of Lantyrn Royd themselves, but it is also a connection between them and their common history, between them and the geography of their neighbourhood, and (at a stretch) between them and the Christian tradition that has shaped their culture and country. Their fight has become grubby, and their cause is often ill-expressed but perhaps the Lantyrn Royd residents are fundamentally asserting their determination to be at home in their dark little streets, rather than be isolated, rootless, endlessly consuming vagabonds. As Dave put it: *I feel like I mean something, even if that something has turned into a big bloody fight about a kid in fancy dress.*

And this is the main reason why the Rush Bearers must have their procession on their original route, with the original cast, and why all of us who care about real human flourishing must support them. The Rush Bearers are not really fighting about a kid in fancy dress, still less are they primarily trying to piss off their Muslim neighbours. They are fighting to find their way home, and that fight is undertaken for everyone, whether they know it or not. At the deepest level, the issue in the Lantyrn Royd dispute is this: is our country a meaningless space where money is made and where the diversity dogma rules supreme to oil the wheels of commerce (picture an out of town shopping centre running round the clock from coast to coast, stuffed to the gills with diverse, disconnected, atomised shoppers,) or is it a real home, a land encoded with connections to the past, with subtle representations of the sacred, with shared truth and meaning.

A final thought: the complex business of homecoming is one of the foundational narratives of the West, both pagan and Christian. Odysseus aches for home in the Odyssey. The Prodigal Son longs for his father's house in the gospel. And, at the other end of the western cannon, we have Tolkien's Shire, the homely home par excellence. Perhaps these stories tell us something fundamental: that no matter how sophisticated or successful we may become as adults, we all have a need and a responsibility to come home (intellectually if not geographically) to the places and people that formed us. And this may be as true of whole cultures as it is of individuals. Once the great, false certainties of adolescence have drifted away, we need to return to the basic, foundational things of our lives and we need to know them with new tenderness and humility. We need to see them with the eyes of Odysseus viewing Ithaca from the deck of his galley, or of the prodigal son catching sight of his father on the desert road. Because, unless we learn to be at peace with the old things of home that live inside us, we will be vagabonds forever: wealthy, clever, and adequately distracted vagabonds perhaps, but vagabonds nonetheless, never quite at home again, even in our own skins. And, as I said, this may be as true of whole cultures as it is of individuals.

The Rush Bearers, in all their tattooed, tatty, angry glory are obviously not Odysseus. Their scrappy little procession is not the Odyssey. But, like Odysseus, they are seeking a way back home. And that matters overwhelmingly because homecoming is both a foundational narrative of the West and the most pressing moral task in the great homeless spaces of modernity. For this reason, the Rush Bearers must march and they must, must, must pass. No matter what the cost in terms of prosecutions or injury or deterioration in community relations. We can sort out how to placate angry Muslims later. For now, the Rush Bearers simply must win their fight. There is no alternative. The stakes are too high for them to fail.

*The sequence of shots of contemporary life fades and is replaced by a picture of a tiny chapel covered in snow, with an old grey slab of a gravestone in front of it. After a moment the picture of the chapel also fades to be replaced with a white screen bearing the legend: 'Haxton Review: The Way Home' in black print in a grungy typewriter front. The screen flickers in the style of an old-fashioned newsreel and then fades. As it does so 'Run for Home' by Lindisfarne plays softly:*

Run for home
Run as fast as I can
Oh-oh running man
Running for home

# 27

JASON AND I get the video done by half ten on Wednesday evening and we upload it straight away. By then we have had four cans of lager each and munched our way through a couple of big bags of crisps and several rounds of cheese and pickle sandwiches. Jason nods with satisfaction when the video appears on the channel

'There she is. Job done. Fancy a gin?'

'Yeah, suppose so. We've earned it.'

Jason gets a bottle from the kitchen and we get drunk. It is an unspoken rule now that if neither of us is working we will spend time drinking together. Neither of us mentions what this implies about the state of our relationships outside the Haxton Review. We never ask each other anything personal about family, friends, sex, or partners. We never trespass onto the difficulties and the loneliness that are implicit in both our lives. I think it's healthier that way. Anyway, I get drunk and crawl into the sleeping bag on Jason's sofa sometime after two. I get a Lantyrn Royd car back home after breakfast.

When I get in, I have a fag in the yard and check my video. It has had twelve thousand views and there are 265 comments. There are the usual cluster of insulting or threatening posts, some of which refer to the upcoming Resistance Media documentary. Of the rest, some people comment only to say that the Rush Bearing must happen. There is a lot of 'Stay Strong Lantyrn Royd' and 'No Surrender'. Other commenters make more effort to engage intellectually with the content of the video, analysing my use of 'home' and quoting conservative philosophers to elaborate my points. Roger Scruton and Russel Kirk get mentioned a lot (which is reasonable because I had both of them in mind – Scruton particularly – when I wrote the script). Some of these comments are at a higher intellectual level than I can follow and when people start commenting on each other's comments the threads often move away from the video entirely. But it is flattering, nonetheless. I recognise a number of the commenters as contacts of Lavinia's, who commented on my *Deus Vult* video.

Some of the serious commenters also make the point that my thoughts about home, virtue, beauty and meaning don't add up to a solid argument for the Rush Bearers marching with their knight through the Muslim part of Haxton. These comments irritate me the most, largely because I accept that they are true. I *felt* that I had made the connection between the Rush Bearing and the ideas bit of the video, but on playing it back, I realise that I didn't quite manage it. I got carried away. The basic structure of what I do with my videos, of relating the situation in Lantyrn Royd to the big themes, has broken down.

When I have finished checking the comments, I go back inside, make a cup of tea and ring my mum. She answers almost immediately.

'Adam, thank goodness. Are you ok?'

'Yeah. I'm fine thanks. How are you?'

'I'm fine. Of course I'm fine. I've been worried about you though. Obviously.'

'You really didn't have to be worried mum. All that happened is that Ben and I had a row. It's not the first time is it?'

'No, it's not the first time,' she says. 'But you left without saying goodbye. I thought...I thought you might have gone again.'

I sip my tea.

'I won't ever do that again mum. I've promised you that.'

'Yes. I know. I know. But I do worry and if you were so upset...'

'I was pissed off. I was angry. But I wasn't in pieces. Anyway, I don't know if you heard, but Tanya Faulk took me under her wing, so I was fine. *The* Tanya Faulk, from the paper.'

'Yes, Ben told me. I didn't get the chance to speak to her at the party. What's she like?'

'Friendly. Kind of tough. Complicated. And very, very bright.'

'I don't think Ben's too keen. She wrote that mean little piece about him, didn't she?'

'Yeah but it was about me too. And she got me loads of views. For my channel.'

'I know. But it was Ben's work she was being spiteful about. And it is his actual job, Adam. Not just your hobby channel thing.'

I sip my tea again and count to five.

'Adam?'

'Yeah mum?'

'Have I said the wrong thing?'

'No. No. Not at all. You're fine. But I suspect Tanya may have had her reasons for writing what she did about Ben. How is he, anyway? Did he say anything about our bust up?'

'He was ashamed Adam. And worried about you. He was flat for the rest of the evening and the next day.'

'Hmm.'

'Ben just blows up sometimes. He's always been like that, but he knows when he's overdone it. And...and he always says sorry, eventually.'

'Did he say what he called me?'

'No. And I don't want to know, Adam. I really don't. I just want you two to find a way to make peace. That's all.'

I drain my mug and put it in the sink.

'I think he hates me, mum,' I say quietly.

And then, because I am just as vicious and stupid as the rest of my family, I take pleasure in the pain and the silence at the other end of the phone.

'Well, I hope...I hope that's not true,' mum says eventually.

'Of course you do.'

'Oh Adam, please...'

The doorbell rings.

'Look, I'd better go, mum, that's the door.'

'Ok. Ok. Are you coming round for dinner on Sunday?'

'Course I am. And I promise I will have cheered up a bit by then.'

'Good. I can't bear to think of the pair of you not getting on. Not liking each other. It's terrible.'

'I know it is. I know. And I'm sorry it upsets you so much. At some point I'll phone him, I promise.'

'Please do, Adam. Please do.'

The doorbell rings again.

'I'd better go mum.'

'Yes of course. Love you.'

'Love you too.'

'Bye.'

'Bye mum.'

I put the phone down on the kitchen work top and walk through the lounge to open the front door. Rev Lavinia is on my doorstep. She is dressed in jeans and a green roll neck jumper, and she has a briefcase in her hand. It's the first time I've seen her out of her clericals.

'Bloody hell. Hello. What on earth are you doing here?'

'Can I come in Adam?' she says. 'There's something we have to talk about.'

And from her tone, and from the way she looks me directly in the eye as she speaks, and from the way her hand tightens on the handle of her briefcase, I know without absolute certainty that this thing that we need to talk about will not be good.

. . .

'Yeah, of course,' I say as I lead her back through the lounge and into the kitchen. 'You're lucky to have caught me. I was about to nip out to the shops.'

'I wasn't lucky.'

'Oh. How's that?'

'Doesn't matter. Look Adam, I'm sorry to have dropped in on you unexpectedly like this, but I didn't really have any choice.' She puts the briefcase on the worktop next to my phone and smiles thinly. 'I know it's cheeky to ask, but may I have a cup of tea please?'

'Yeah. Yeah. Of course. How do you like it?'

'Just milk.'

'Ok.'

I make a cup of tea and hand it to her. She sips it and smiles.

'Oh, thank you so much. That's lovely.'

'It's a pleasure. Now what do we have to talk about? What are you doing here, Lavinia?'

'I'm here about this.'

She undoes the briefcase, reaches inside, and pulls out a copy of today's Coxthorpe Argus. She places it flat in the worktop. The headline reads. *Three Hospitalised as Parade Tensions Rise.*

'That was last night,' she says. 'One of them is in a coma.'

'Were they Lantyrn Royd people or Muslims?'

'As it happens, they were neither. They were white lads from Leeds who came up to Haxton looking for trouble and got more than they bargained for. But it's extremely sad that that should be your first question, Adam.'

'Well...'

'No, just be quiet for a minute please. You mentioned in your video that there is a meeting of the Rush Bearing committee this evening.'

'Yes.'

'And, as you said, they're going to be deciding whether to follow the council's revised plans for the Rush Bearing on Saturday, or whether they are going to try and march on the original route.'

'Yes. It's crunch time, isn't it?'

'Yes it is. It's definitely crunch time.' She sips her tea and looks straight at me. 'The point is, they absolutely must decide to follow the route prescribed by the council. They absolutely must.'

'Why must they?'

'Because of the potential consequences if they don't.'

I roll my eyes.

'You know that we disagree about this Lavinia.'

'Well, I'm afraid that we're going to have to start agreeing about it.'

'So, the Rush Bearers should just consent to be bullied should they? By the council, the papers and everyone else? They should just give up? Is that what you're saying?'

'It's time to leave all that silliness behind, Adam, and look at the situation in Lantyrn Royd like an adult. Like a responsible, serious adult.'

'What does that mean?'

'I think you know what it means, somewhere deep down.'

'I really don't.'

She sighs and nods at the newspaper.

'If the Rush Bearers try and march down Gordon Street on Saturday, and if word gets out that's what they're planning, every bored racist in the north of England will turn up to support them. The English Solidarity nut jobs, for one thing, but anyone else who has access to the internet and fancies a fight. And there will be Muslims coming as well, of course, on the other side, and anarchists of various stripes. Haxton will be a war zone.'

'There will probably be some trouble, yes.'

'Which is a ludicrous understatement as you know jolly well.'

Since I opened the door to Lavinia, I have been off balance. It is due to her unannounced arrival, and to her directness of speech, and her steady gaze, and that sinister bloody briefcase. I have been almost submissive. But now I begin to feel resentful. I don't like being bossed around. Especially not in my own home. Especially not by a woman. Especially not by a woman who thinks she is a fucking priest.

I shrug.

'It may be an understatement. I suppose we'll find out on Saturday. I assume you watched my last video?'

'Yes, of course I did.'

'What did you think?'

'You tried to say too much in too short a time. And I'm afraid it didn't quite work. There was something about nominalism in there, I think, and, again, I wasn't quite sure that you completely knew what you were talking about. You're not an academic, Adam, and I'm afraid that you look ever so slightly ridiculous when you try to be. It's absurd to try and join such significant ideas to a racist bloody march. Not that what you were saying had much to do with the Rush Bearing, in the end. If you want my opinion, you're much better when you do more straightforward local stuff. Then you are reasonably good.'

'Thank you for the feedback, I'll take it on board.'

She rolls her eyes.

'Please try not to be quite so defensive. It's not going to make this any easier.'

'I don't really care if *this* is easy or not. If you watched my video to the end, you'll know that I said quite emphatically that the Rush Bearers should march along its original route, complete with the knight. That's what I believe, Lavinia. I said it because I genuinely believe it. I'm not going to back down.'

'Even if it means people getting hurt and arrested.'

'Yes. Even if it means that.'

'Even if it means Lantyrn Royd getting trashed?'

'Yes.'

'Even if it means people getting killed?'

'I think you're ridiculously overstating things. But, yes, even then. It's become too important an issue to surrender, I'm afraid. For all sorts of reasons. You know I think that.'

Lavinia swirls her tea around in her mug and sips it. She raises her eyebrows.

'Sorry,' I say, 'I'm afraid that you've had a wasted trip.'

'No, Adam, I haven't.'

'What do you mean?'

She reaches into her briefcase again and pulls out three old sepia photographs. That's not quite true. They are photocopies of old photographs; all the creases and frayed edges are faithfully reproduced on the shiny new paper.

'Do you know what these are?'

'They look like pictures of the Rush Bearing.'

'That's exactly right. Second iteration, obviously.'

'Obviously.'

'Have a good look at them and tell me what you see. Or, more specifically, tell me what you *don't* see.'

I study the photographs. They are all shot outside St Peters, presumably taken in different years as each has a different Rush

Maiden perched on a makeshift throne mounted on a cart. There are bunches of flowers arranged around the cart and greenery fixed to the throne itself. The Rush Maidens have more flowers garlanded in their hair. There are crowds around the cart in each of the pictures, facing the camera with that dreadful solemnity that always seems to accompany early photography.

'So, what do you see, Adam?'

'Three rather beautiful, rather self-conscious young women.'

'Anything else?'

'A crowd of Haxton locals looking forward to a piss up, rather cheerlessly it has to be said.'

'Anything else?'

I peer at the pictures again.

'Oh yes. Look, there is lad who is supposed to be the Cavalier, you can tell by the hat. And there is the shepherd, I assume, in the fleece thing, and the monk at the back, and...oh...'

'What?'

'Who is the lad with the oar? There's...There's a lad with an oar in each of the pictures.'

'Meant to be a bargeman,' Lavinia says slowly. 'To represent Coxthorpe's industrial growth with the coming of the canal. Thomas Sedgewick was heavily invested in the Coxthorpe Navigation apparently.'

'I didn't think canal boats used oars.'

'I'm sure they didn't. It's symbolic. Whatever else he was, Sedgewick wasn't a literalist, was he?'

'No. I suppose not.'

'What *can't* you see in the pictures, Adam?'

I pick up my rolling tobacco and go to the back door. I stand there looking out into the yard while I roll and light a cigarette.

'Had you seen any of the pictures before?' Lavinia asks quietly from the behind me.

'Only in the pub, where the lighting is awful. And I only glanced at them. I never actually studied them before.'

'I don't suppose many people did.'

I inhale and blow cigarette smoke up into the sky.

'Are we sure about this?'

'About what?'

'About the absence of a fucking knight, Lavinia. What do you think?'

'There is no mention of a Rush Bearing knight in any document earlier than last year. Nothing at all.'

'So how the fuck did that happen?'

'Roger Wrigglesworth made it up, I'm afraid. As simple as that. I imagine that was his plan from the start. He came up here with the specific intention of reinventing the Rush Bearing to cause trouble, and to make sure he got the trouble he wanted, he came up with the knight. And the rest is history.'

'But why wasn't it challenged? Why didn't anyone fucking check?'

'Who was there to challenge him? He wrote the book on the subject, didn't he? Literally. And he's a ballsy bloke, you have to give him that. And he's an academic of sorts. Certainly, the Lantyrn Royd lot didn't have the intellectual resources to challenge him. And it obviously didn't occur to you too.'

'I just accepted what I was told.'

'I wouldn't feel too stupid about it. I did the same. So did everyone else.'

I stub my cigarette out on the wall and put it in the wheelie bin at the end of the yard. Then I push passed Lavinia and go back into the kitchen.

'Except you didn't accept it permanently, did you, Lavinia? You got suspicious. How did you find out?'

'We'll talk about me in a moment, if we get that far.'

'I'm interested to know about you now, actually.'

'No,' she says firmly. 'In a moment. First, I hope you can see that the situation has changed quite significantly.'

'How has it changed?'

She rolls her eyes and then speaks slowly, as if she is explaining something to a child.

'Well, the whole thing is a fraud, isn't it? The whole procession has only been reinvented to provoke Muslims, and the knight is completely made up. The most contentious bit of the whole thing is an invention. It was all designed to make trouble. It's race baiting, pure and simple. That is literally all that is going on here.'

I stare out of the kitchen window for a moment, looking across the scrap yard and the abandoned mill beyond to the grey-green line of the distant moorland. Again, it occurs to me that Jason was right, there are not many places in Coxthorpe from which you can't see the moors. There's always that rough horizon of heather and rocks hemming you in and overseeing you, outlasting you and your vague plans to get away. And it works as well. No one ever really leaves Coxthorpe. Not permanently. Not on the inside. Not even Ben.

'I don't see that makes much difference really,' I say quietly. 'Not at the point we've reached now.'

'What do you mean?'

I go to the fridge and get a beer. I open it and drink.

'Well, look, the Rush Bearing was a hodgepodge of pagan and Christian elements from the beginning, wasn't it? It was a muddle right from the start. Then it got banned by Cromwell. Then it got reinvented by Sedgwick, very much in his own image. Then it got dumped. So, I don't see why it can't be reinvented again now, albeit under rather murky circumstances.'

'Oh, for goodness' sake.'

'No hear me out, Lavinia. There is no pure Rush Bearing tradition to get back to. There really isn't. You could even argue that the crusader figure reflects genuine contemporary concern about the community being Islamicised to some degree. And, as such, it's a legitimate development.'

'But that's not what the poor Rush Bearers think. For them it's all about authenticity. That's why they insisted on the bloody knight in the first place. They've been duped.'

'Maybe they have. But they've allowed themselves to be duped, just like I have. And at the point we've got too, the Rush Bearing *is* the knight. That's the focus of it all now. It would be fantastically demoralising at this stage for the Rush Bearers to learn they've been conned.'

'But if they *have* been conned...'

'In one sense it doesn't matter. They've been planning the Rush Bearing for months. They've discussed it non-stop, they've been slandered because of it, some of them have been physically assaulted because it. They'll never fucking recover if they learn the truth before Saturday.'

'But...'

'And it goes further than Lantyrn Royd. I assume that there are groups of Brits in similar situations watching to see what happens here. In fact, I know that there are. Can you imagine how demoralising it would be for them if the whole thing fell apart? It would be Black Lives Matter all over again with cops and footballers kneeling down fucking everywhere. It would just be another humiliation.'

Lavinia looks straight at me again. Unblinking. She didn't like what I said about Black Lives Matter, but I am past caring.

'So, just to be clear. You are saying that you feel no responsibility at all to tell the people of Lantyrn Royd the truth about the situation they're in. Despite the fact that they've been duped. Despite the fact that not telling them could lead to some of them being injured or arrested on Saturday. Or worse'

'Yes, that is exactly what I am saying. You tell people if you want, but I won't. In fact, I'll make a video rebutting you if you try.'

She shrugs.

'There's no point in me telling anyone anything. I'm just the bloody vicar, no one will believe me. It's you they trust.'

'Exactly. And that's why I'm not going to let them down.'

'Right,' says Lavinia. 'I see. We're probably at the point where we need briefly to talk about me and my former job.'

'What? What's that got to do with anything? You were a civil servant, weren't you?'

'Yes I was. I worked for the government. And, as I told you, I worked across a number of departments.'

'Yes, yes I remember. But what...'

'Now please listen carefully, Adam. Part of my work was to do with social cohesion, and sometimes that involved me working with people who were in the various branches of the domestic security services.' She swallows the last of her tea and puts the mug down next to her. The click it makes on the worktop is unnaturally loud. 'Obviously I now work for the Church of England, but the thing about my old career is that one never quite completely leaves it. The term that my former colleagues would use is simply that I remain '*useful*'. It's all very understated.'

'What? What are you saying?'

'I think you probably understand what I am saying. You're not stupid.'

'So, are you a spy, Lavinia? Is that what you're telling me?'

'No of course not. Do I look like a spy?'

'I've no idea what a spy looks like.'

'Well, I'm not one. Although if I was, I assume that I wouldn't tell you.' She smiles briefly and goes on. 'I worked adjacent to the security services, but I was never part of them. Anyway, friends of mine from my old line of work, are keen that you should see something. So today, I suppose I'm not so much a spy as a courier.'

With that, she reaches into her briefcase again and pulls out an iPad. She enters her password then lays it down on the worktop, on top of the old pictures of the Rush Bearing.

'You do understand how serious this is, don't you Adam?'

'Yes. Yes, I think so.'

My voice sounds like it is coming from far away. I feel completely disconnected from the sound of it, and from my own body, and from the kitchen with the autumn sunlight streaming through the window which makes the grease show up on my oven. I am miles and miles away, high on the moors that overlook Coxthorpe from every side, walking in the sunshine. I am miles and miles away from everything, especially from the strange woman standing opposite me with the sunlight illuminating half of her face, who wants me to understand how serious everything is.

'It's really very serious indeed,' she says. 'This sort of thing is very rare indeed and it's never, ever undertaken lightly. Now look, I'm going to go and wait in the yard and while I'm gone, I want you to press play and watch the video. It only takes a few minutes.'

'Ok,' I say.'

'Can you do that?'

'Yes.'

'Good.'

Lavinia slips past me and goes out into the yard. When she has gone, I walk over to the iPad and look at the screen. The front is dark, official looking blue. It has this written across the centre:

rushb.25.stock/sibling.4323

I press play.

. . .

It's me masturbating. It's the video call to Sonia on the night that I was unspeakably horrible to her, when I ejaculated so hard that I hit my chin. It's exactly the image from my phone. Sonia is the main picture, but I am in the top right-hand corner, just as was at the time. I insult her for her weight, and for her stupidity, and for other things, while I wank ferociously. Then I describe exactly what I wish to do to her, and it is horrible and violent and obscene. My face is contorted and cruel. Sonia's voice is included in the recording. She is making soft wet moaning noises, which I didn't notice before. I can't tell if she is moaning with pleasure or crying. I think she's probably crying.

. . .

After a minute I press pause. I sip my beer and scratch my cheek. Then I sip my beer again. I feel extraordinarily calm. I walk quietly to the back door and join Lavinia in the yard. She is standing dead still next to the bins with her head tilted to the sun.

'You chose the worst one,' I say. 'I am not normally quite such a piece of shit.'

'I know.'

'Have you seen them all?'

'I haven't seen any of them. I didn't want to. But...but there are transcripts.'

'I see.'

'I'm really very, very sorry, Adam. I was hoping very much indeed that we wouldn't get here.'

'But we did.'

'Yes. You weren't going to change your mind, were you? About the Rush Bearing and your video. I did tell them that you wouldn't. There is a kind of purity about you, I'm afraid. It's quite a nice characteristic in a way.' She shrugs. 'In most circumstances anyway.'

'What makes you think I'll change my mind now?'

She sighs and looks straight at me again. She pushes her specs onto her forehead.

'This is the offer, Adam. If you make a video disavowing the Rush Bearing and explaining about the fake knight, no one will ever see any of the material that has been gathered about you. It will be secured very safely indeed. But if you don't do what they want, if you don't make the video, the material will be sent to your friends and family. That includes your mum, your brother, your nephews and your employer.'

'Oh.'

'Do you understand?'

'Yes.'

'There's more, I am afraid. If you do what my friends want, the Resistance Media presentation about you will never see the light of day. No one will ever contact your employer again to talk about you, and the short piece about you on the Respect Haxton website will come down. Also, the job offer that Simon spoke about still stands.' She pats my arm, gently. 'That's the positive bit in all this.'

'You know about that?'

'Of course.'

'I burnt his card,' I mumble. 'So, I don't know his number.'

'Well, that's neither here nor there. But listen, I have to say this, if you don't do what's asked, the Resistance Media piece will come out tomorrow, and it will contain footage of you that you really don't want to be made public. You will also lose your job as a matter of course, as will Jason, incidentally. And it goes without saying, that the possibility of the work you discussed with Simon will be gone forever.'

For a moment I can't speak. Then I mutter:

'You're thorough, aren't you? I'll give you that.'

'The people I'm talking about have to be thorough, Adam. The work they do is simply too important for them to be otherwise. Now I'm afraid that we don't have time to mess around. What is it going to be?'

'You say that as if I have a choice?'

'Well, I suppose in one sense you do.'

'Hardly.'

I roll another cigarette and inhale. I have to put my beer down on the ground as I make the fag, but when it is lit, I pick it up again and drink.

'I understand that your position is absolutely horrible,' Lavinia says gently. 'But it really will all go away today, after the video's done. You have my word on that.'

'Why should I believe you?'

'Well for one thing, because I am not given to telling lies, and for another, after today you will have served your purpose, so there is no need for anyone to put pressure on you anymore. You've stumbled into a complicated, sensitive situation, Adam. And so, for the moment have become quite important, but that ends today. You're not...you're not particularly significant in the long term.'

Despite everything, I can't help laughing.

'Is that supposed to be reassuring?'

Lavinia laughs too.

'Well, it didn't come out quite as I intended, but actually, yes, it should be very reassuring indeed.'

I chuck my fag end away in the wheelie bin.

'The thing is, I can't just produce a video out of nothing. Not just like that. Even if I wanted to. It takes time to sort out the script and the graphics and everything. And I need Jason, of course, for the tech stuff. And he would never agree....'

'You don't have to worry about any of that. Come inside for a sec.'

I follow Lavinia back into the kitchen. She goes to the briefcase and lifts out a slim folder. 'It's written already, with directions about the graphics and inserts and everything. And if we get into a muddle, Simon is waiting to help out.'

'I bet he fucking is.'

She pulls out her phone and glances at it.

'Several people are waiting actually. In case we get stuck.'

'I see.'

'We need to get on with it though, if you agree to do it.'

'It has to be done now, does it?'

'Yes, Adam, it has to be done immediately.'

# 28

When Johnny comes marching home again hurrah, tala...

*The music and the street scene fade. A white screen appears bearing the legend: 'Haxton Review: Bad Knight in Lantyrn Royd' in black print in a grungy typewriter front. The screen flickers in the style of an old-fashioned newsreel and then fades to be replaced by the digital picture of the Highcliffe angel, the cover image for the Haxton Review channel. The image fills the whole screen.*

NARRATOR: A different kind of video today to reflect different circumstances. First of all, I am sorry that the graphics are so much less interesting than normal. For various reasons, I am without my technical team for this video. More importantly, I don't suppose that what I have to say today will make people very happy, but it still needs to be said. From the start, I have tried to be honest with The Haxton Review and it is in the spirit of honesty, real painful honesty, that I am making this video. It is the last one that I will ever post and on this occasion the comments will be switched off.

I became involved with the Rush Bearing because, like many people in Coxthorpe and beyond, I was angry about British people being forbidden from celebrating an authentic native tradition, due to what I regarded as silly and unjust sensitivities concerning the Muslim community in Haxton. Quite soon after I met the Rush Bearers, I began making my videos, in part because I was worried that the Lantyrn Royd Brits were not making their case particularly effectively and were being caricatured in the mainstream media and in popular opinion. Quite deliberately, I have never said that the Muslim community does not have the right to be offended by a crusader knight being paraded through their streets as part of the Rush Bearing celebration. Of course they have the right to be offended, I am sure I would be offended if I was a Muslim. My point has been that the Muslim community's offence should take second place to the right of the Rush Bearers to have their procession. After all, none of us have the right not to be offended in a free society, rather we have a responsibility to deal with offence as we encounter it.

In the four videos I have made, I have tried to stay true to my original impulse, to represent the Rush Bearers' point of view, not uncritically of course, but fairly. I have also tried to relate broader questions about nationality, identity and culture to the Rush Bearing debate. How well I have succeeded is not for me to say. But my channel has grown very quickly so I must have done something right, or at least irritated people sufficiently for them to want to keep watching. Through the process of making my videos, I have become good friends with many Lantyrn Royd people. I have shared their hopes and frustrations about the Rush Bearing, and I have come to respect them greatly as a resilient, generous and intelligent community. My last video was about coming home, and I suppose that partly reflects my experience in Lantyrn Royd. I really have felt at home there. I am very grateful for the welcome that I have received from the Rush Bearers, and for the tolerance they have extended to the funny man with the camera and the awkward questions.

In that last video I said in quite robust terms that the Rush Bearing procession should run on its original route, on Saturday, complete with the offending knight. I said that the possible consequences in terms of arrests, injury, damage to property etc. did not outweigh the right of the Lantyrn Royd whites to have their celebration. At the time I meant what I said. However, since I made the video, I have received new information (I am not going to say from where) which has made me revise my opinion. I am making this video to explain my change of mind. The saddest thing about all this is that the people of Lantyrn Royd who have been so kind to me will be offended and outraged by what I have to say, and a lot of that outrage will probably be directed at me. Nevertheless, I wouldn't be true to my friends among the Rush Bearers, if I didn't share what I have learnt. In particular, the people within the community who have responsibility for deciding what the Rush Bearers should do on Saturday, need to hear what I have to say.

In my introductory video '*Somewhere Called England*' I asked some Lantyrn Royd locals whether the impetus to reinstate the Rush Bearing was properly home grown within their community, or whether it came from outsiders or newcomers to the area. I asked this because the rumour around Coxthorpe at the time, particularly among those people who were opposed to the Rush Bearing, was that the celebration's reinvention was not truly indigenous to Lantyrn Royd. On the contrary, the common view was that people from outside Haxton had whipped up excitement about the Rush Bearing with the specific intention of stirring up trouble with the Muslim community. It is worth replaying the moment that I asked the question in my first video. I am speaking to Brenda, Jason and Mary in the clip, three Lantyrn Royd people and Rush Bearing activists.

*The angel picture disappears. It is replaced by footage of Brenda, Jason and Mary in the White Horse, taken from the Haxton Review's first video:*

NARRATOR: Ok. Ok. So, what we have here is this traditional procession that you're trying to revive in Lantyrn Royd, and one part of that involves a knight. And even though it's not a real knight, or even a real pretend knight, it's this knight that has caused the problem with the Muslim community. Is that correct?

JASON: Yeah. Pretty much.

NARRATOR: Can I ask who decided to revive the procession? Who came up with the idea originally?

*Brenda, Jason and Mary look at each other nervously and, apparently, at someone off camera. Brenda and Mary both sip their drinks.*

JASON: I don't see what that's got to do with owt.

NARRATOR: Well, some of the papers have reported that the idea came from people who weren't really local. Who might have come here to cause trouble.

BRENDA: No one on our side's after starting trouble, love. It doesn't really matter whose idea it was to begin with. The thing is, we all got on board with it, din't we? That's the main thing.

NARRATOR: Ok. I'll leave that for now. Tell me about the bad knight. Why is it that the muslim community are objecting to him?

*The picture freezes and then disappears to be replaced again by the angel.*

NARRATOR: As you can see, when I asked the question, all three of the interviewees hesitated and looked off shot for support, the implication being that they felt uncomfortable answering. I didn't press the point at the time, because I was keen to get onto what seemed like the more important stuff, but the fact that Jason, Brenda and Mary didn't immediately answer the question is significant. They are all honest people. They could not easily lie on camera, but nor were they prepared to compromise the integrity of their celebration by admitting that it was not truly home grown. In the end Brenda thinks on her feet and settles on the formula that 'we all got on board with it' as a way of dodging the question.

The truth is that the revival of the Rush Bearing was instigated by one man who is not a native of Lantyrn Royd, or of Haxton, or even of Coxthorpe. His name is Roger Wrigglesworth, and he is the bloke that my three interviewees were looking at out of shot in the clip I've just played. Roger moved to Lantyrn Royd last year with his daughter and he does not own property there. As far as I am aware he does not work anywhere in Coxthorpe or West Yorkshire. He is an academic by profession, and he has spent the last six years of his life in London and Belgium. This is not the new information that I received this week, incidentally. On the contrary, it was clear from the very beginning of my involvement with the Rush Bearers that Roger was the force behind the revived festival, and it was equally clear that he was determined to remain in the background as much as possible. The question, of course, is does this matter? Does it make any difference that an outsider should have been the driving force behind the revived celebration? To begin with, I was clear in my own mind that it did not matter at all. If Roger had managed to reconnect the Lantyrn Royders with one of their own traditions, I reasoned, well, he had done a good thing. Who cared where he came from? The important thing was that, as Brenda said: 'we all got on board with it.'

My attitude to Roger Wrigglesworth changed significantly when I learnt that he was a member of a London-based group called the Civitas Forum. This is an anti-Semitic, neo-fascist think tank whose members publish papers, run conferences, and agitate for various unsavoury right-wing causes. The group were mentioned in the recent *Globe* article about the Rush Bearing and I will paste the link below. An important distinction needs to be made here, and very clearly.

Anyone who has watched my videos will know that I have been concerned to address key conservative talking points: national identity, patriotism, tradition, and what I suppose we must call 'the woke agenda'. Most of the people I have met in Lantyrn Royd are interested in these issues as well. Living where they do, they could scarcely help being interested in them. But, and this is the key distinction, neither I nor the people of Lantyrn Royd have ever expressed fascist or white nationalist views, such as those promoted by Roger Wrigglesworth and the Civitas Forum. Here's a picture of Wrigglesworth, by the way, attending a Civitas Forum conference in London last year.

*The picture of the angel fades again to be replaced by a still taken from the Resistance Media exposé of the Civitas Forum. Roger is in shot at the back of the room next to a table that is stacked with books.*

NARRATOR: Roger Wrigglesworth is the man with the beard standing at the back next to the book stall. He's the one with the glass of wine in his hand. If the Civitas Forum's on-line book shop is anything to go by, the books on the table will include stuff about Race and IQ, Jewish influence in the banking and media industries, the plight of white South African farmers and other white supremacist concerns. The conference was hosted in an exclusive drinking club in Covent Garden, and its theme was 'Jewish Evolutionary Strategy and the Frankfurt School.' It should be obvious that this is a long way - geographically, culturally, ideologically - from the Lantyrn Royd Rush Bearers and their little procession.

I have got to know Roger Wrigglesworth reasonably well over the last few weeks and it has become apparent not only that he is a hard-core anti-Semite, given to vile descriptions of Jewish people and Jewish culture, but also that he views the Rush Bearing not primarily as a jolly revival of fun custom, but as an opportunity to stir up trouble with local Muslims, thereby gaining exposure for his repugnant views. It has also become obvious that Roger has a drink problem. His anti-Semitism is particularly vile when he is drunk, which is most of the time.

*The picture disappears to be replaced by the angel again.*

NARRATOR: Even when I had discovered Roger's repulsive politics and the degree to which he was responsible for the revived Rush Bearing, however, I did not walk away from the Rush Bearers or speak about Roger on my channel. There are a few reasons for this. Firstly, The Haxton Review was meant to be about the Rush Bearers themselves, and how their campaign related to broader questions of politics and philosophy, so Roger Wrigglesworth's horrid ideas and his entryism did not seem like a natural fit. Secondly, I persuaded myself that it didn't matter much that the original promoter of the revived Rush Bearing was a fascist who had involved himself in the celebration for disingenuous and grubby motives. What mattered, I believed, was that the Rush Bearing dispute was actually happening, now, in real time. In the heat of the ideological battle, it seemed more important to support the Rush Bearers than to expose Roger. Finally, despite myself, I grew to like Roger Wrigglesworth. I know that is shocking, but it should not be. We deceive ourselves if we believe that every fascist is a cartoon baddy. On the contrary, these people are dangerous precisely because they are not obviously horrible. When he is sober and not talking about his Jew-baiting politics, Roger can be fun and charming company. He made it possible for me to make my videos and offered me feedback on them. Had it not been for him I would not have been able to speak directly to Lantyrn Royd people, and it was this, I think, more than anything that made my channel successful. Perhaps I was worried that if I criticised or exposed Roger, my privileged access to the community would be withdrawn.

I recognise now that that's not good enough. In retrospect, I wish I had pressed Brenda, Jason and Mary further in my first video, concerning the inspiration for the Rush Bearing's revival. And I also wish that I had spoken about Roger's role in the celebrations and about his grotty political background. Let's be clear, Roger has used the people of Lantyrn Royd for his own ideological purposes, and in remaining quiet about his background, I have facilitated his dishonesty. Today, however, I have chosen to tell the truth about Wrigglesworth. So why the change of heart? To answer that question let me show you some pictures, that I received this week. They are of the Rush Bearing festival at it looked in the Victorian period when it was under the control of Thomas Sedgewick, the Coxthorpe industrialist.

*The picture of the angel fades again to be replaced by a black and white image of the Rush Bearing procession outside St Peter's Church. The Rush Maiden is centre shot, mounted on her cart. She is surrounded by a crowd.*

NARRATOR: This picture is from 1886. You can see the Rush Maiden, on the cart, and all around her are locals from Haxton, looking forward, no doubt, to their fun. You can clearly see a Shepherd and a Cavalier to the right of the cart. These are two of the four characters added to the Rush Bearing by Sedgewick when he reinvented the celebration, as symbols of Coxthorpe's history. They represent the city's involvement in the wool trade and its Royalist sympathies during the civil war. On the left side of the cart, you can see the other two characters Sedgewick introduced: a monk representing the Cistercian Abbey which once owned most of the land around what it now Coxthorpe and also an oarsman, representing the city's more recent involvement with the canal network. (The fact that canal boats are not normally powered by oars is neither here nor there. Sedgewick was rather free flowing with his reinvention of folk traditions). The crucial point is that there is no knight in the photograph. And nor is there one is these two photographs taken from 1888 and 1890.

*The picture is replaced by a second one with a different Rush Maiden, and then by a third.*

NARRATOR: As you can see, no knight. And, in fact, if you spend some time researching Sedgewick's revived Rush Bearing, as I have done this week, you will not find a single reference to the knight anywhere. Let's be clear, there was an historical figure called Sir William de'Curzon, who held lands near to Coxthorpe, who joined the third crusade and died at the battle of Arsuf. But there is no record of Thomas Sedgewick having any interest in him whatsoever, and he certainly did not include him in his version of the Rush Bearing procession. In fact, and this is the really crucial point, the first text that I can find which refers to the Rush Bearing knight is Haxton's Rush Bearing: An Ancient Tradition, by Roger Wrigglesworth. This is a pamphlet outlining the supposed history of Rush Bearing celebration, published last June by Civitas Seminar. Following its publication, however, the Rush Bearing knight crops up everywhere: on websites and news reports, in campaigning leaflets opposed to the procession, and over and over again in the Coxthorpe Argus. In all of the noise, no one (including me) bothered to check the historical veracity of the figure. The knight became an established fact overnight and then very quickly turned into the centre of the Rush Bearing dispute. A lot of people (again including me) are guilty of dereliction of duty.

*The picture disappears to be replaced by the angel.*

So what conclusion are we supposed to draw from all this? I am afraid the answer to that is obvious and rather shocking: there never was a crusader knight in the Haxton Rush Bearing procession. Let's say that again: *there never was a knight in the Haxton Rush Bearing procession.* The figure was deliberately created by Roger Wrigglesworth with the intention of weaponizing the revived Rush Bearing to make it as offensive as possible to local Muslims. Of course, even without the offending knight, the Rush Bearing would have caused tensions in Haxton. Community relations are strained at the best of times up here, and a procession of Lantyrn Royd whites through the Haxton's Muslim area would certainly have turned heads. But Roger wasn't content with that, he wanted to create maximum aggro with his Rush Bearing celebration (that was, after all, the whole point of him coming to Coxthorpe) and the pretend knight was the best way of achieving this. The insertion of William de'Curzon into the parade was ingenious as well as dishonest and manipulative.

Incidentally, there is a fascinating question about how Roger got away with his lie. It is, after all, a pretty big deception, especially when you consider that so many of the Rush Bearers decided that the knight was a hill they were prepared to die on, in the name of the authenticity of their revived festival. The irony is awful. I don't really have an answer to the question, except to say that if you tell a lie confidently and consistently enough, and if you present yourself as the expert on the subject you're lying about, you apparently have a reasonable chance of getting away with it. Until now, Roger Wrigglesworth certainly did.

The more pressing question is what should happen next, in light of what we now know about Roger Wrigglesworth and his untruths. What are the Lantyrn Royd community supposed to do with their Rush Bearing now? I think the only sensible answer to that question, the answer that I am recommending, is what might be best described as a 'tactical retreat' on the part of the Rush Bearers. I know that is shocking coming from this OyTube channel, so let me explain myself. The plain truth is that the decent, patriotic people of Lantyrn Royd have been manipulated by an outsider into campaigning for a lie, for the sake of unpleasant political ends which they do not share. Things obviously need to be reassessed.

Think about the context for a moment: everyone in Lantyrn Royd has been determined to resurrect the Rush Bearing authentically (that has been the key word throughout) and, when the Rush Bearers ran into conflict, they mobilised to protect what they perceived as the legitimate interests of their community. But we now know that the authenticity of the Rush Bearing is a sham, and the interests that the Rush Bearers have ultimately been serving have not been those of decent patriotic Brits, but of an extremist group which none of them are personally associated with. As it stands, therefore, the Rush Bearing is a lie, wrapped within a con, tied up with knots of manipulation. None of this is the fault of the people of Lantyrn Royd of course, but it is true, nonetheless.

In this situation, it is pretty much indefensible as well counterproductive to continue to lobby for the revived Rush Bearing in its current form. Frankly, it is bonkers to try and defend the thing. And this year, we are too close to the date of the celebration to try and sort out exactly what other form the Rush Bearing should take. It seems sensible, therefore, to call the thing off this time, or at least have a very, very small celebration without the knight and without any intrusion into the Muslim part of Haxton. The people of Lantyrn Royd can then spend some time thinking calmly about how the celebration might be re-modelled in the future, in a way that is true to its history, and which will not cause them to end up injured, isolated or arrested. Crucially, Roger Wrigglesworth should be excluded from the Rush Bearing planning, going forward. He should be shown the road out. He is not really part of the Lantyrn Royd community, and he has an agenda which in inimical to the interests of the Lantyrn Royd whites.

I know this is deeply disappointing advice (some will even regard it as treacherous) but to recommend anything else would be an invitation for the Lantyrn Royd community to appear morally bankrupt and utterly stupid in the eyes of the media and the country, and also to risk injury or imprisonment for the sake of a total fiction. We have to hope that there is sufficiently strong leadership amongst the Rush Bearers for the right decisions to be made, even in the midst of the high emotions and confusion that Roger Wrigglesworth has succeeded in stirring up.

I'm nearly done. Let me end by referring again to the article in *The Globe* newspaper which I have linked below. I was quite critical of the article in my first video. I didn't like the fact that the journalist suggested that national identity was not real and, of course, I resisted his view that the inclusion of the knight within the Rush Bearing procession was unacceptably offensive and should be abandoned. I stand by a lot of my criticism of the piece, but, in retrospect and in light of what we now know about the history of the Rush Bearing, I accept that the final passage of the article is worth considering. Here, the journalist argues that the Rush Bearing should not be abandoned completely but re-imagined in such a way as to involve the local Muslim community. The knight would have to go, of course, but, beyond that, the procession could survive and remain true to its roots while changing to reflect the changing nature of Haxton. At one level, that will seem to the people of Lantyrn Royd like a surrender of 'their' celebration to the forces of inclusion and diversity, but maybe it doesn't have to be. Perhaps we can think of a diversified Rush Bearing as symbolic of a broadening or a deepening of English identity, rather than its dissolution in a sea of politically correct multi-culturalism. After all, as Brenda pointed out so effectively in my first video, Englishness does not stand still. Maybe, therefore, we can talk about our nation changing and even co-operate with the process of change without turning into classic (and classically stupid) multi-culturalists. The risk of sticking to a rigid and narrow definition of Englishness, as we have learnt at Lantyrn Royd, is that we become prey to extremists and charlatans, whose view of what England means is miles apart from the simple homeliness, dignity and patriotism of the Rush Bearers.

In conclusion, there must be a middle way between Roger Wrigglesworth's lies and fascism on the one hand, and the madness of extreme multi-culturalism on the other. If they make the correct decisions over the next twenty-four hours, the Lantyrn Royd Rush Bearers will set a great example of how to negotiate that tricky path. They may become a model that others can follow. If they make the wrong decisions, on the other hand, the consequences are almost too awful to contemplate.

*The picture of the angel vanishes to be replaced with a white screen bearing the legend: 'Haxton Review: Bad Knight in Lantyrn Royd' in black print in a grungy typewriter front. The screen flickers in the style of an old fashioned newsreel and then fades. As it does so 'The English Civil War' by the Clash plays softly:*

Your face was blue in the light of the screen
As we watched the speech of an animal scream
The new party army was marching right over our heads

# 29

'I DIDN'T THINK you'd come.'

'I almost didn't. Budge up.'

Lavinia shuffles along the tomb stone she is sitting on. I plonk myself down next to her and roll a cigarette.

'I didn't even think you'd answer my text.'

'I nearly didn't do that either, to be honest. But...' I light my fag and nod to Coxthorpe spread out beneath us. 'But I didn't want to be on my own today, during the last act. I don't know why.'

She smiles.

'Still, I'm surprised you agreed to meet me of all people.'

'Who else is there? None of the Lantyrn Royd lot will ever speak to me again, unless it's to tell me to fuck off. My mum isn't interested. She's slightly embarrassed by it all, I think.' I shrug. 'And, anyway, after yesterday, I feel like I'm stuck with you as far as the Rush Bearing concerned. We're connected even though I don't particularly want us to be. It's a bit Stockholm Syndrome.'

She laughs.

'And that makes me the terrorist and you Patty Hearst, does it?'

'I guess so. Something like that.'

'Well, I don't suppose that I've got any right to complain. And I'm very glad you answered my text. I didn't particularly want to be stuck on my own today either. I certainly didn't want to be at home.'

'I don't think you've got the right to complain about anything at all.'

That comes out angrier than I intend. Lavinia turns and looks straight at me.

'How are you anyway?'

I smoke for a minute without answering.

'Adam?'

'I heard you. How am I? I don't know, Lavinia. I honestly don't. I'm absolutely nothing at all, at the moment. I'm numb. I'm not pissed off, or ashamed, or embarrassed, or anything. I'm just numb for now. It's quite calming actually.'

'Hmm.'

'What?'

'I think that might change eventually.'

'Probably.'

She pulls a thermos from her rucksack and unscrews it.

'I do love Highcliffe,' she says as she pours a cup of coffee. 'It's definitely the best view of Coxthorpe. I drive up here sometimes to calm down when the parish is getting difficult. It's not a bad place to get things in perspective. Now then, do you fancy a coffee? I've bought two cups. It's milked but not sugared.'

'Yeah. That'd be nice. And you're right, it's a great view. I've loved it since I was a kid. Me and Ben used to come blackberrying up here in Autumn. It's beautiful.'

She pours a second cup of coffee and hands it to me. I chuck my fag away half smoked and take it.

'Thanks.'

'You're welcome.'

I sip my coffee and nod towards Haxton. The green dome of the Lantyrn Royd mosque is clearly visible, rising above the dark little streets. It hovers there in the Yorkshire sunshine, as strange and commanding as a spaceship.

'Has anything happened?'

'Not much yet. But do you see the helicopter?'

'Yeah.'

'That's the police. They're right above Haxton apparently.'

'How do you know?'

She puts her coffee down on the tombstone, pulls her mobile phone out of the pocket of her coat and jabs at it.

'It's in The Argus. They're running a live commentary from Lantyrn Royd.'

'Oh right.'

'Did you see their piece on Thursday?'

'Of course I did.'

'The Haxton Review was front and centre.'

'I know. I got thousands of views off the back of it, not that it matters anymore.'

She glances at me sideways.

'Still nice though, surely.'

'I'd rather no one saw it at all.'

'Ok.'

'It's almost as if The Argus were waiting for it to drop. Almost as if they knew it was coming.'

'Mmm. Maybe.'

'Yeah, maybe. Let's change the subject. What's the paper saying?'

She peers at her phone.

'Not much. There was a scuffle twenty minutes ago, outside the White Horse. But that's about it.'

'Right down at The Horse? Between Asians and Brits?'

'No. Between Brits and Brits, apparently. One person got arrested.'

'Oh, so the police are back inside Lantyrn Royd?'

She sips her coffee and nods.

'Yes. They reappeared on Thursday night, straight after the committee meeting. They voted to end the community patrolling, which made sense after they'd decided to abide by the council's ruling about the Rush Bearing. There was nothing left to protect at that point was there? All the flags came down, and the boards came off the windows, and the police came straight back in. They haven't left since. There's a van outside the Church and another on the corner of East Croft and at least one car driving around Lantyrn Royd all the time.'

'I see.'

'The official line is that they are calming tensions, which they are in a way.'

'But they're also making a point, aren't they?'

'Of course they're making a point. I suspect there's going to be more of that sort of thing before too long.'

Lavinia's phone buzzes. She picks it up and looks at it, scrolling down with her thumb.

'Ok,' she says after a moment. 'So there has a been a little protest, apparently. Right when the Rush Bearing was meant to start. Ten o'clock.'

I stare at her.

'What? A protest, as in a Rush Bearing protest? Has there actually been a Rush Bearing then, after all?'

'No. Not, as such. Don't get excited. It's a protest at the *absence* of a Rush Bearing. It's the ultras. The die-hards. There are only eleven of them apparently, and no knight.'

'Oh, I see.'

'Here, look at the picture.'

She hands me the phone. Under the Coxthorpe Argus banner there is photograph showing three people in front of the White Horse. On the right is a man who I recognise, but whose name I don't know, in the centre is Reverend Lazarus, dressed in an overcoat and a trilby, and on the right, is Brenda. All three of them look angry and Brenda is carrying a handmade sign reading: *No Sell Out. No Justice. No Peace.*

'Oh dear,' I say as I hand the phone back to Lavinia. 'Her sign doesn't even make sense.'

Lavinia shakes her head and scrolls down further on her phone.

'I don't suppose she cares. Brenda was never going to compromise easily, was she? Never in a million years.'

'Not really. But I wouldn't worry. They won't be able to do much with eleven people.'

'I was thinking about afterwards. Picking up the pieces.'

I shrug and swallow the last of my coffee.

'Good luck with that. Anyway, speaking of leaders, I wonder if Roger has turned up this morning, finally crawled out from under his hangover.'

'He won't have done. I would be very surprised if he's still in Coxthorpe.'

'Why's that?'

She takes my mug, knocks out the drips and puts it away in her bag. Then she screws her own mug back onto her thermos.

'Hmm.'

'Oh, for goodness sake, Lavinia. Whatever it is that you know, I doubt it's a state secret, or else you wouldn't have hinted at it.'

'No, no. It's nothing like that. It's not a secret at all really. It's just a bit odd. Did I ever mention that I met his daughter?'

'Whose? Roger's?'

'Yes.'

'No. No, you didn't. I saw her at the pub on Diversity Day, but I didn't speak to her.'

'No one spoke to her that day. She just grabbed her dad and left. But I met her well before all the trouble. She was with Roger up on Gordon Street, outside the florists. I was in clericals and Roger spotted me and was keen to chat. I suppose he wanted to sound out what my view of the Rush Bearing was likely to be.'

'Seems reasonable.'

'Yes. And he was perfectly pleasant.'

'He can be very pleasant indeed.'

'I know he can. Anyway, at one point I asked the Rosalind - that's the daughter - what she did, and she told me that she was a civil servant.'

'Okay.'

'It was very odd.'

'What's odd about that?

'I just don't think it's true.'

'Why not?'

Lavinia frowns and kicks her feet against the tomb stone. She looks uncomfortable.

'Well what sort of civil servant in her mid-thirties moves out of London to come and live in Coxthorpe?'

'I suppose it might depend on which department she worked in.'

'That's just what I thought. Benefit of the doubt and all that. So, I asked her.'

'What did she say?'

Her frown deepens.

'That she worked across a number of departments.'

'Ah.'

Just then her phone buzzes again. She picks it up and taps it.

'The protestors have tried to access Gordon Street at the top of Friendly but have been turned back by the police. There have been two more arrests. But it's business as usual up on Gordon Street, apparently. There's not even a counter protest.'

'Oh.'

She scrolls down.

'Hang on, it says that the rest of the protestors have returned to the White Horse without further comment. It really does look like it's over, Adam. Properly over. I'm sorry.'

'No, you're not. Tell me about Rosalind Wrigglesworth.'

'Ok.' She puts the phone down again. 'Well look, it might mean absolutely nothing, but I happen to know that that phrase - working across a number of departments - is one that people tend to use if they want to avoid being too specific about what they actually do. If they work for the government.'

'Right. Fair enough.'

'Now I was never in the security service, despite the impression I may have given you yesterday, but, as I said, I was close to it occasionally and I've heard that phrase more than once. *I work across a number of departments.* For people in the know, it serves to dissuade them from asking any more questions. For outsiders, it's just waffle to bore them and shut them up.'

'In which sense do you think Rosalind was using the phrase?'

'Neither. That's the point. She almost seemed to be boasting or certainly communicating something. The silly woman was practically winking as she said it. It was very odd indeed.'

She raises her eyebrows and shrugs.

'Lavinia, please tell me.'

'Tell you what?'

'Whatever it is that you're not telling me.'

'Well...'

'Go on...'

'Look, I'm not breaking any rule telling you this, but, even so, you had better keep it to yourself. At one level, it is nothing but speculation.'

'Cross my heart, hope to die, stick a picture of me wanking in my mum's inbox. I won't tell anyone, I promise.'

She giggles.

'There will never be any pictures in your mum's inbox, Adam. You don't have to worry about that. Not now.'

'So, you said. Just tell me what it is that you think you know.'

'Let's rewind a bit. What do you think, honestly, are the final consequences of the whole Rush Bearing drama? As it stands today, right now. What's been the upshot of it all?'

'Well, it has failed hasn't it? In the most basic terms, it been a complete failure. And specifically, I suppose, it's been pretty disastrous for the people in Lantyrn Royd.'

'Anything else?'

'A few people have put their heads above the parapet and got themselves identified as trouble causers.'

'Yes. That's true. But what about the impression that will be left in peoples' minds beyond Lantyrn Royd? What do you think the impact has been there? What message has gone out from Coxthorpe?'

'Well...I think...I think that the Rush Bearers probably didn't look like a very attractive group, in most peoples' minds from the start. Even before the revelation about the knight. They looked pretty grim to most people. Pretty ignorant and strident. White working-class people always look grim if they start talking about things to do with identity, don't they? That was partly why I got going with my videos.'

'Yes, I know. And that's true. But how about since the knight revelation?'

I think of my last video, and of Jason and the rest of them down in the cramped little streets beneath the mosque. And I can't stop myself from shivering.

'Sorry,' Lavinia says gently. 'I know it must be unpleasant to think about.'

'Now they are associated with stupidity and deceit. All of them. And...And with hateful bigotry, of course.'

'Yes, I would say that is pretty much correct. And there will be more in that line before it's all over. At the very least I would expect today's events to be in the Sundays.'

'But that doesn't reflect the truth of things down there. It's just the way that the thing has played out. Or...Or been made to play out.'

'Of course, but if I'm right, that's the point.'

'What is the point then?'

'Well...'

She shrugs again.

'For God's sake Lavinia, you can't stop there. You can't just leave me hanging.'

'I know. I know I can't. And I do want to tell you. I think that's probably why I texted, as a matter of fact. I think that's why I wanted to meet you to explain my hunch. I almost feel that you deserve to know.'

'Well go on then.'

'It called spotlighting,' she says quietly.

'What is?'

'Oh goodness,' she frowns and scratches her cheek. 'Where to start? Look, you must be aware that there are considerable government resources expended on what one might call *preserving the narrative* in the area of community relations and multiculturalism and what-have-you.'

'Yes, I suppose so. I'd never thought about it in any depth, but I suppose so.'

'It's a useful term, *narrative,* isn't it? It implies a kind of accepted gap between the truth of a given situation and what a particular set of people are saying about it. One doesn't lie or dissemble anymore; one simply maintains a narrative. It's quite a new thing. Since the internet.'

'Ok.'

'Now, take my word for it, lots of agencies are involved in this area, without always acknowledging that is what they are doing. The police, of course, whose work will range from the community coppers who turn up at mosques for Friday prayers and run meetings at temples and whatnot, right up to the guys who kick in Islamicists' front doors before they blow something up.'

'Obviously.'

'Or kick in fascists' front doors before they stick a knife in an MP.'

'I think I probably knew that already.'

'Yes, of course, it's not a secret. But it's not just the police. There are also people like our mutual friend Simon. They're in the same line of work as the cops, but they're a looser network of PR folk and influencers and journalists and so on. Their thing is to control the narrative in the media, as far as possible. They're nudgers. They work with the government, but most of them will not be employed directly by it.'

'Is Simon employed by the government?'

'It doesn't matter. Sort of, but it doesn't matter. Now it may surprise you to learn that the army is involved in this stuff as well. There's the 63rd Brigade down in Didcot who you probably haven't heard of, although they're not really a secret either. They do something called Information Interrogation and Outreach, which is similar to what Simon and his people are engaged in, but they work in a more directed way and, theoretically at least, they can function in a proper theatre of conflict. They're for when things go bad.'

'You're right, I haven't heard of them.'

'They're basically the infantry but with X accounts. They spend a lot of time worrying about Russian bots as well as the community relations stuff.'

'They sound fascinating.'

'They are. And a bit nuts. You may get to meet them one day, if you decide to give Simon a call. And, of course, it goes without saying that the domestic security service is involved in this business as well. Their job is rather less defined, but they also have responsibility for keeping the narrative on track.'

'I get it, there are loads of people promoting diversity and what have you. But I still don't see what it's got to do with Roger Wrigglesworth. And what is Spotlighting?'

'I'm coming to that. What you've just said is true. You have a range of stakeholders within government, and just beyond it, who are involved in community relations and narrative building. So, you can see, can't you, that there is a considerable amount of soft-power at play?'

'Yes, I suppose so.'

'Good'.

'Actually, Lavinia, I don't see at all. I'm getting muddled. Please can we get to the bit about Roger and Lantyrn Royd?'

Suddenly she stands up and shoulders her rucksack.

'Come on,' she says. 'Let's walk. We're not going to see anything more from here. A quick trot round the cemetery and then I'll buy you a sandwich and a pint.'

I stand up and follow her along the footpath that runs between the graves and the low wall marking the end of the cemetery and beginning of the steep, rubble-strewn slope down into Coxthorpe. Nettles and ferns brush against our ankles as we walk.

'The thing is,' Lavinia says without turning around. 'This network of agencies does not always work reactively. From time to time its people want to take the initiative, as it were. That's where the spotlighting comes in.'

'Right.'

'And the network is loose enough for spotlighting projects to be almost entirely unaccountable, and powerful enough for them to be pretty much guaranteed to succeed.'

'Go on.'

She still doesn't turn around. She won't face me. She marches along the cemetery path with her hands shoved in her pockets. Thomas Fairfax sited his parliamentary cannon on this ridge and battered royalist Coxthorpe into submission. And then, when the civil war ended, the commonwealth came, and the Rush Bearing was banned until Queen Victoria's time. And then it got going again until another, more terrible, war ended it forever. Even the deepest hatreds wear out eventually. Death finally folds old enemies into a single party.

'Right,' says Lavinia, 'so supposing your work was to do with preserving the narrative that we've been speaking of, concerning how we deal with difference and community relations and what sort of country we are and so on, do you think you might be tempted, just occasionally, to coordinate something that would challenge the very narrative that you were supposed to be guarding?'

'Why?

'So that potentially awkward people would stick their heads above the parapet and get noted for one thing. Just as you said. But more importantly, so that the thing you had co-ordinated could eventually collapse pathetically, thereby reinforcing the official line. Do you think that might be something you would countenance, even though it might seem a bit sneaky or counterintuitive? Well, that's spotlighting.'

'What sort of thing are you talking about?'

'It could be anything, couldn't it? A protest. A parade. A petition. Even a small political party or pressure group. It doesn't matter what it is, as long as it can be controlled. And as long as it ends up undermining the sorts of ideas that it seems to want to promote.'

'Lavinia,' I say slowly. 'Can you be really clear about what this means about Roger and Lantyrn Royd and the Rush Bearing please? Can you just be really, really clear?'

'Well, I'll start by saying that I'm not party to anything like this in relation to Haxton. It only occurred to me what might be going on, after I had met Roger and Rosalind. I was wondering, you see, why Rosalind had gone out of her way to signal to me that she was involved in security work at some level.'

'And what conclusion did you come to?'

'That she was a silly girl who was out of her depth. But that only raised another question.'

'Which was?'

'Why would such an inappropriate person be used in domestic security work at all?'

'And what conclusion did you come to?'

'That Rosalind had something that made her useful, despite not being able to keep her mouth shut.'

I've been rolling another cigarette as we have been talking. Now I stop to light it.

'Hang on a sec, Lavinia.'

'Yes?'

'Are you saying that Rosalind was able to corrupt her dad, or blackmail him or something? That's what got her recruited as a spook? That she was able to control him somehow?'

Lavinia peers over Coxthorpe. She shields her eyes against the sun.

'Oh look, the police helicopter is going home.'

'Not enough going on to keep them entertained at Lantyrn Royd.'

'Apparently not. Good. And no, I am not suggesting that Rosalind will have compromised her dad. Family doesn't normally reach family. And I've no doubt that a man like Roger will have been reachable in all sorts of ways, without his daughter's help. What Rosalind will have bought to the table is the ability to support her Roger when he was working. To *run* him, although no one will have used the term to her face.'

'What does that actually mean?'

Lavinia shoves her hands back in her pockets.

'It means my best guess about what's happened here is that Roger and Rosalind came to Haxton with the specific purpose of promoting the Rush Bearing in order that it would finally collapse. It means that Rosalind is a conventional civil servant whose job bought her somewhere close to security work, but who got seconded into the thing to keep her pathetic, alcoholic dad on track while he did his spotlighting. To stop him falling apart.' She shrugs again. 'That's what I think it means.'

Then she turns round and walks off again, quickly, along the path. I follow her without speaking. Her pace and the hunch of her shoulders suggest that she is furious and, ridiculously, I feel that she may be cross with me. Slowly, I feel myself get cross with her in return.

'Is that what you are doing in Haxton, Lavinia?'

'What?'

'Maintaining the narrative, or whatever you call it? Placed here to keep an eye on things? Are you here to spy on people?'

'No, I am not.'

'Really?'

'Yes, really. I am here to be a priest. I am a priest, Adam, whatever you may think about me. I am here to celebrate the sacraments and care for the people in my parish.' She shakes her head quickly. 'And that's it. I am most certainly not equivalent to those grubby

Orthodox clerics who snitched to the KGB whenever someone asked for their child to be baptised.'

'But you were conveniently on hand to threaten me when the need arose.'

Lavinia stops again and turns around.

'Adam, people like you inevitably crop up in these sorts of scenarios, amateur people who involve themselves in things without quite realising what they are doing. You, or someone like you stumbles into shot and you are always, absolutely always, reachable. You're accounted for before the thing even begins. There's always some stupid, squalid secret, you see. To do with sex or gambling or money. Mostly sex. There absolutely always is.'

'Oh.'

'I'm sorry, but it's true. And assuming I'm right about what happened here, neither of us made the slightest difference to things, in the long run. You were a minor liability who became an asset, and I was just a low-grade asset from the start. I was on site, and I was on the books. I was useful. And for what it's worth, I asked to be the one who came to see you because I thought I could make it less humiliating for you.'

'Well thanks for that.'

'Don't be sarcastic, Adam.'

'I'm sorry but you weren't the one who was fucking blackmailed.'

'No, I wasn't, she snaps. 'I was the fucking blackmailer, wasn't I? I'm a priest and I'm also a fucking blackmailer. Even if I only blackmail part time and in a good cause, that's still what I am.'

She turns again and walks quickly down the path. We are near the cemetery gates now. There is less vegetation so her boots crunch on the gravel.

'To what end?' I call after a moment.

She spins round again.

'What now?'

'What is the point of it all? What is the good cause, which justifies the spotlighting and blackmailing and everything? You're a vicar, after all. You are meant to believe in things. So please tell me, Lavinia? To what end are you doing this?'

She walks slowly back down the path towards me and stops when she is just a few inches away. She shoves her hands deep into her pockets. Her cheeks are red now, and she is out of breath. She is no happier than I am, I realise suddenly. She is single and middle-aged and childless, and her religion is perhaps a kind of comfort. She is no more settled than me, no more adult. She's just better at pretending.

'Don't be ridiculous,' she whispers. 'Don't be so bloody ridiculous and naïve.'

She holds my eye for a moment and then pats me on the arm.

'If I were you, Adam, I'd try not to think about ends very much. In my experience it doesn't do one much good. It gets rather uncomfortable. Now, come on, I'll buy you that sandwich.'

# 30

*Dear Jason,*

*I suppose I should begin by thanking you for your text. I notice that you sent it the day before you were sentenced, which might explain its tone. It was blunt even by your standards (as well as rhyming with 'blunt'). But, even so, I was glad to receive it. It would have been far worse not to have heard from you at all.*

*As I understand it, you were arrested at the top of Friendly for shoving a policeman, on the day of the Rush Bearing. And I learnt from the Argus that you got three years for violent disorder, two days later. I don't know what to say, except that I am dreadfully sorry, and shocked, and furious about it all. Somebody somewhere is making a very vindictive point, I think. Apart from anything else, the whole thing happened with such indecent haste. (I know you won't care what I think, incidentally, and that's up to you. You can't stop me thinking it.) I don't know what prison means for you in terms of work, money, house etc. I hope that some things, at least, are salvageable. I also can't imagine what it is doing to your mental and physical health to be locked up, but I imagine that it must be absolute hell for the Coxthorpe Dalesman to be shut away somewhere without a view of the moors. Look, this will be cold comfort, but those hills have been there for thousands of years. They will still be there when you come out, complete with the harebells, the skylarks and the rocks, complete with the rain and the sunshine. I hope that you can see all those things in your head in prison, even if you cannot see them literally.*

*Anyway, enough of all this. I'm writing because I think you are entitled to an explanation for my final video. God knows whether you will even get this far through the letter, but at least by writing to you I have done all I can to explain myself. I'm going to write it quickly, like taking off a plaster. I was got at (I'm not going to tell you by whom) and pressured into changing my public point of view about the Rush Bearing. Basically, I was blackmailed into making that last video. There are things in my life which are not illegal, but which are awful and humiliating, to say the least. The people who got at me had evidence of this stuff and they were very clear that they would make it public if I didn't do exactly as they told me. They also showed me their pictures proving the absence of a knight in the Victorian Rush Bearing. I can't be completely sure if the pictures were genuine, of course, (I remember you quoting Roger about false flags and fake news, and I understand that absolutely everybody lies in this sort of situation), but they looked pretty realistic. You can judge for yourself. Assuming for a moment that the pictures were real, and that Roger invented the knight to stir up tension, that would still not have been enough on its own to make me produce the final video. It made me feel slightly less awful about having to do it, but that's all. I made the video because I was frightened of my secrets being revealed. It's that simple.*

*And, yes, of course the thing that gave the anti-Rush Bearing people leverage over me is to do with sex. You can probably hazard a pretty good guess at what it is. Just to re-iterate though, it does not touch on anything illegal. I may be lots of things, but I am not a sex offender.*

*I really wish, Jason, that I was stronger and braver than I am. I wish that I had the courage to tell the people who blackmailed me to go and fuck themselves. But I am not very strong or brave. That's not quite true. Apparently, I have the kind of rough and ready courage that can put its voice to controversial videos or confront a hostile film crew at a demonstration, but that's not what I mean by courage in this context. What I am talking about is a lack of courage that is old and ingrained, to do with wrong decisions and weakness from years ago. It's difficult to explain, so I won't even try.*

*I am not writing this because I want your sympathy, I have no right to that. I am just trying to offer you as full an explanation as I can for what I did.*

*I had a pub lunch with an acquaintance on the day of the Rush Bearing. I agreed to meet them because I couldn't bear to be in the house on my own, but I couldn't bear to be away from Coxthorpe either. Anyway, this person had seen all the Haxton Review videos (I guess you could describe them as a very critical fan) and they made the point that the arguments we made, to do with belonging, culture, the loss of a sense of home, were basically valid and healthy, but were coloured and distorted by a thread of fear running through everything. They thought that fear was the genesis of all we had done with the Haxton Review, and they thought that it was a false genesis, which corrupted all that came after. I haven't had time, yet, to work out quite what I think about what they said but I suppose that they could be onto something. Perhaps we were much too afraid of everything from the start (or rather I was) and it somehow skewed our view of the Rush Bearing and the related issues. Whatever else, however, I don't think that our videos were pointless, and I hope that you don't think that they were pointless either.*

*This is not at all the letter that I had planned to write. There is something about putting literal words down on literal paper that apparently makes me much too confessional and intimate. Apologies. The main thing I had meant to write was just this: that my time involved with the Rush Bearing, and with the Haxton Review in particular, has been one of the most fulfilling and happy periods in my life. I have absolutely loved the last weeks, which makes it almost unbearably painful that I should have ended up alienated from all of you and effectively on the opposite side of the dispute up there. In particular, Jason, I have valued getting to know you. You have been incredibly generous with your time, your hospitality and your friendship. And the hours that we have spent together working on our videos or just talking and getting drunk have been a real joy to me. I can't ever repay all that, but it is right that you know it, even if it only makes you angry.*

*Another thing, you once described what the Rush Bearing row meant to you by quoting something a Frenchman had written about the being part of a nation. I can't remember the quote, and I can't remember exactly what you said about it either, but it was something to do with valuing the streets of Lantyrn Royd and the moors around and being aware of your mum's grave up at Highcliffe. Your point was that these things best represented the stuff that you wanted to protect by defending the Rush Bearing. These things somehow moved you and held you, much more than abstract ideas about Britain, or British values, or whatever. As I say, I can't remember exactly what you said now, but I remember thinking that your words were the best summary I had heard of what was at stake in the Rush Bearing dispute. They were words marked not by fear, but by love. Genuine love. You will cringe reading that, but I am convinced that I am right. More than anything, I hope that you and the other Rush Bearers will hang on to some of that love even though everything has fallen apart. I also hope (although I am not sure that I have the right to) that our videos may have helped some people to reflect on that kind of love in a systematic way, and to think through the implications of loving a place deeply, intimately, and fiercely, and knowing it as home.*

*Back to the Rush Bearing and Roger. As I said, I suppose it's just possible that the people who blackmailed me had faked the evidence that there was no knight in the Victorian procession, but it seems pretty unlikely. It seems more plausible that Roger invented the bloody thing to stir up trouble. In all our conversations, you and I didn't speak much about Roger, did we? I know that you felt he had educated you to some extent about politics, and I know that he sent you to keep tabs on me in the first place, and that you disapproved of his drinking. But that is about it. We never discussed his character or his motivation. I think it's clear, though, that he had a political agenda from the start that went well beyond the Rush Bearing dispute, and in a certain sense he was using the people of Lantyrn Royd for his own ends. He was a very effective local campaigner (when he was sober) but he was also pretty unscrupulous. Just one example of his lack of scruple: did anyone ever see any evidence of Coxthorpe Resist, that lefty group who were supposed to be turning up at Lantyrn Royd to cause trouble on the Family Fun Diversity Day? I'm pretty sure no one did, and I'm pretty sure that's because they were another one of Roger's inventions, as a way of making everyone feel even more threatened than they already did. Quite what his true agenda was, I don't suppose we will ever know. I had conversations with him that implied that he was more complex than he let on and that his motives were more tangled than any of us supposed. The long and the short of it is that I don't know what to make of him. He is a kind of absence in my mind now, a darkness, and I am afraid that he will stay that way. At any rate, I am clear that issues such as the Rush Bearing, which involve endless controversy and multiple conflicting actors, need honesty and openness from the start. Whatever else he supplied in terms of experience and direction, Roger did not supply these.*

*That's all I have to say, Jason. I am sorry it has been such a rambling letter. If you ever feel like writing, I will always write back. I believe I can also visit you, but you have to send a visiting order.*

*I am sorry about everything, not just the rambling letter.*

*Best wishes,*

*Adam.*

*PS. I have printed off a copy of your Highcliffe Angel from the channel cover. It's framed now in clip frame, and I've hung it above my fire. It's such an odd picture, Jason, but I love it. I can't bear to look at any of our videos anymore, but the angel still makes me happy, somehow.*